The Trickies
Demolition

Julie Anne

Copyright © 2020 Julie Anne

All rights reserved.

ISBN: 9798665784991

DEDICATION

For my family.

The Trickies

CONTENTS

Acknowledgments vi

The Prologue

1. Gone
2. Trip to Somewhere
3. Zilch
4. Mr. Wace
5. Mr. Larry
6. The Nicky and the Ema
7. Strange
8. Evening
9. Moto
10. School
11. Miss Cherry
12. Imitations
13. New place, New people
14. Tricky Trials
15. Mission Almost Impossible
16. Early

The Trickies

17 Mrs. Slendersan and Her Class
18 The Twig
19 The Little Troublemakers
20 Miss Idadosi
21 Halloween
22 Hairy Questions
23 Robotic Arachnid
24 Dan and the Letter
25 The Scheme
26 Heights
27 Mission Getting Closer
28 Two Days Till the Mission
29 The Start of Long Day
30 Barriers
31 Found you!
32 Real Mission Begins
33 The Sea Trip
34 Battle
35 Decision

The Trickies

36 Funny Ends of Surprises

37 Landing

38 Ema's Curiosity

39 Mystery Hatching

40 Celebration

41 Ring of Death

42 New Day

43 The Dectectives

44 Unsettle

45 Trial

46 Departure

47 Home

48 Joyous

49 Encounters and Answers

ACKNOWLEDGMENTS

I would like to acknowledge the people who have helped and supported me while writing this book: my mother, my father, Debra Atwood, and lastly, my brother, who has helped me so much. I am extremely grateful for all of you.

The Prologue

The house, far in the distance.
The family, hidden from society.
The secrets, no one needed to know.

The mother's hands squeezed the polished staircase railings. Fear and anxiety sat on her face in plain sight, too conspicuous amid the clamber and cacophony upstairs.

"Come down." Her voice trailed a bit. The quaver took a high leap and a strong step. "Come down, you two. Your father is in an important call. Come down." She was in a battle with herself to abstain from charging up to the second floor and dragging down her two children.

"I'm just listening!" Came her son's reply.

That was it for the mother.

"Do not listen to that call. Come down here—right now!" The mother hollered from below. It was still silent, except for the murmuring behind the door on the phone.

"Piden?" The mother called. "Pulie? Where are you?" Her heart thumped and thumped, burning the insides of her chest.

A pause. The mother heard footsteps approaching the father's office.

Then came an erratic and boisterous shout. "Spider!" hollered a voice.

The mother froze midway on her first step. "What?"

"Spider!"

In a flash, the mother bolted upstairs and burst through the hallway and found the two children lying on the ground with their ears on the door.

"Get away—from that door," the mother pulled the children back with fury. "What do you mean, Spider?"

"Spider." The boy, named Piden, whispered in his mother's ear with great excitement. The mother was grabbing the girl, Pulie, by the hands and telling her to stop shouting.

By now, the father had finished his call and joined the commotion. "Spider? What do you mean by this?"

Curiosity pervaded the girl's face.

Piden answered promptly, "Underneath the door. A large spider, big—big legs. White string nest—"

"That's a spider web," The girl corrected the boy.

"Yeah! Web. Spider. Scary."

The fear melted away from their parent's faces. The father adjusted his tie. "Well—" The father cleared his throat. "Nevermind. Piden, you know better than that. They are just arachnids. Next time, don't scream and shout like it's a big deal. Scared the lights out of me at first…"

"Why, Pap?" Piden chirped.

"Nothing," he answered quickly, "Just don't act like six-year-olds —"

"I am *six* years old, father—"

"And hurry to get dressed. We are going out to dinner at Primprose Diner, so please wear your *neat clothes*. Not whatever you're wearing—" The father looked down at his children's clothes, muttering something about raising *ragamuffins*.

"Come on." Pulie dragged her little brother down the glass stairs. "We need to *talk*."

"Come on, Pulie," Piden squeaked. "I'm sorry I screamed too loud—"

Pulie shut the bathroom door. "It's not about that. It's about Mother and Father." Pulie bit her lip. "Didn't you notice what happened?"

"For the first time, I called him *Pap*, and he didn't care. My strategic plan worked!"

"No!" Pulie smacked her forehead. "They were scared when we said *Spider.*"

"*Arachnophobia*: fear of spiders," Piden said, matter-of-factly. "You're scared of spiders too."

Pulie shook her head. "That's not it. They said, *what do you mean.*" Pulie pulled out her brush. "*I* would've said *where.*"

***

"What are their jobs?" Pulie asked.

"Who?" Piden made air sounds with his lips as he plunged his toy plane into the mound of paper.

"Our parents, that's who." She could see the long picture frame in the corner of her eyes, with the silver aesthetic leafy and ivy-like swirls on the border. And in the middle was the picture. About thirty people all in the same photograph, standing in the blurred out background. Twenty-eight of those people's faces were blurred out as well. That left their parents. Pulie and Piden's parents. Who were the rest?

"Maybe they work at the bakery shop they always go to and never let us go." Piden crashed his plane into the table. "Or maybe they're scuba divers!" He raised both hands and cheered. "That would be cool!"

Pulie shook her head and glanced at the photograph again. There was a secret that had been kept from them. Maybe it would answer all her questions. Where was she from? Where was the rest of her family? What did her parents do? And what was her future?

And despite these questions, there was something else they didn't know. That some many years later—their parents would receive a phone call that would change their lives.

GONE

Pulie glanced at all the tightly packed luggage lying on the floor, wondering what her parents had packed for. One moment they were all reading books in the living room to escape the summer heat, and the next moment, her parents stood by the door, clutching their luggage, about to leave.

"Come here now." The mother's hand firm on the door handle. "It's time we leave."

"To where?" Pulie asked, approaching her father and mother by the front of the house. "Why, all of a sudden?"

"So many questions as always." Her father smiled a little. "I know it's quite strange that our business trip is going to be longer than ever before. Two years is a long time. Do what fits you while we're away, and just *follow* the directions given to you."

"Yes. Don't worry. We have a surprise waiting for you. When it comes, just say no word and just go with the flow." The mother winked as well. The father bent down at eye level with his children.

"Piden, just *focus* on what you need to do. Follow orders and follow directions. You will succeed if you do so. And Pulie—"

He smiled. "Keep you and your brother are safe—always. Oh, keep your necklace with you at all times. It'll do you well later on."

Pulie felt the necklace with her hand. It was cold against her sweaty palm. It had been given to her at birth.

"And both of you—try to decrease the trickery," Her mother whispered.

Odd.

Suddenly, a car engine sound echoed throughout the fields around their house. A vehicle was driving straight towards their home.

"Remember, take the pizza out of the oven the moment we leave the house. Look for clues and differences. Okay? And lock all the entrances at night until our relative comes. Alright?" Mother said quickly. "Be safe. Stay together—"

The door creaked open, and the fresh sweet chilly air swept into the warm house. There was a black car far at the front gate. The parents dragged their suitcases outside and the door shut behind them.

A few seconds later, Pulie and Piden tried to look outside between window blinds, but there was nothing and no one now. Their house felt empty. Empty was a weird feeling.

Their parents were gone.

And they would not be back for a long time.

***

They were the Jark Family. Samuel, Natalie, Pulie, and Piden, to be exact. No one knew why their great grandmother had given them such names as Pulie and Piden. It was a mystery to even their parents.

Although living in complete solitude, Pulie and Piden still received ordinary lifestyles. Their history was what made them unusual. One specialty was the guile. It ran through the family's blood.

Their parents worked in a mysterious hidden group. As essential members, they stressed that *what* job was not significant. When Pulie and Piden asked *why*—the answer was that there had been a dangerous incident involving their ancestors. That was it. All the children could conclude was that their parents liked to keep everything a secret.

Their parents taught them everything from the alphabet and numbers to how to exercise in their built-in gym, but the children's need to break free grew stronger and stronger every day.

However, forbidden to exit their homes, Pulie and Piden were mistaken by their parents. They were not to be kept inside. They were not to be hidden from the world. Ringing bells inside their souls sent them galloping away to do the things they do best.

TRIP TO SOMEWHERE

It was the day after the leave-taking of their parents. Ever since then, they had feasted on only peanut butter and jelly sandwiches and ice cream and pretzels, never touching the stove or oven, not once.

Staring up at the blank empty ceiling, rolling around aimlessly on their wide beds that sat parallel on either end of the bedroom, Pulie and Piden noticed that the morning was almost coming to its end.

"No work at least—no chores either. Do you think that's a good thing?" Pulie asked all of a sudden, breaking the odd quivering morning silence.

"Yeah." was the dry reply. "No tutoring work."

Pulie folded her arms underneath her head, staring straight up. "I don't get it. I mean, why?"

"At least we can eat ice cream," Piden chuckled, "for *breakfast!* Should we go get some right now?" He rolled out of bed and slid his feet into his slippers.

Pulie wasn't listening. "Isn't it so weird how they left all of a sudden?"

"What flavor?" hollered a voice from down the stairs.

She didn't respond. Instead, she sprang out of bed, pulled on a new shirt, and rushed down the glass stairs.

"I didn't know what flavor you wanted, so I gave you strawberry." Ice cream sloshed all over Piden's tan face when Pulie entered the kitchen. He looked like a painting gone wrong.

"Thanks," she said, scooping hers with a spoon. "What I was trying to say," she drew a deep breath. "Isn't it weird how Mom and Dad all of a sudden left us to go because of some *important business?*"

"Well, yeah, I just thought of it as like a happy business trip. You know, last year they left in the middle of Christmas week."

"Yeah, but they told us a month before that time. And it was only for three days then. Father got this call a week before he left today," she retorted.

"They're probably coming back. They can't possibly just leave—for two years." He took a bite of a green apple. "*Right?*" His tooth sunk in too deep, and he let out a yelp.

She shrugged. "Mother said that one of our relatives is coming on Thursday anyway. We can probably ask whoever's coming then. But what if they tell our parents..."

Piden furiously attempted to pull the apple from his mouth. He sighed and spoke with the fruit attached to his teeth. "Pulie, calm down. A day hasn't even passed, and you're stressed about nothing. Besides, someone is coming in two days. Also, they promised to send a good surprise while they're gone. So *enjoy* your time right now."

"No." Pulie shook her head. "This is weird." Pulie rummaged through her backpack. "Our parents would tell us about this and would have told us ahead of time. They don't just leave us here as if their trip is a day or two. It's for *two years*. Are you kidding me? Don't you see something is weird?"

Piden didn't respond, continuing to try to pull his tooth out of his apple.

Pulie continued. "It's so— well, *obvious*. And besides, when did our parents ever tell us about their job? Not even the name? Or a little summary?" Pulie stopped. "Oh my gosh! What if they were kidnapped?"

"Jesus, something's gotten into you." Piden licked his spoon. "Look, I know you miss Father and Mother. But I'm over it now. There's nothing we can do about it. And it doesn't matter right now, does it? You really have to control yourself. It's not like someone kidnapped them. It was their will to leave."

Her brother did not know what was wrong right now. She didn't quite know yet either. But she knew *something* was not right. But maybe this was the chance. To figure out why her parents *always* left on Sunday mornings for five hours. Perhaps even figure out *what* her parents' jobs were once and for all. There had to be some way to figure everything out at once.

Pulie slapped her hand on the glass table as she stood up. The vase with the five fresh roses shook and almost fell. "We need to find out where they are and what they are doing."

"Mom said that we're going to get us a surprise." Piden excitedly shimmied in his seat. "I mean, she can't possibly mean another set of dino blocks, right? I mean, I have ten of those, but it'd be nice if I could get another one. *Or* maybe even a new play shelf."

"I don't think she meant *that* kind of surprise—"

"—or maybe tickets to the movie theatre. I've always wanted to go to one of those."

"We have a TV at home. Besides, Father said that you could get murdered at the theaters."

"Yeah, but it'd be nice. Either way, they told us to just go with the flow."

"What if they're wrong." Pulie caught sight of the papery leather-covered book on the table next to the vase with the roses. There was a diagram of a floor plan and the title of House Modeling at the top. Pulie had never seen it before.

"Well, what are you going to do about it?" Piden threw his hands up. "What are you going to do?"

There was a deafening silence in the house the moment he said those words.

Pulie frowned and frowned harder until a smile lit up on her face. She whispered, "I know just the plan."

***

"Father is going to kill you." Piden stood by his older sister, who was bent over a box, searching for the keys.

"It's not going to be there," Piden sang, impatiently fidgeting and glancing at the closed room at the end of the hallway. Father's office. Always locked.

"Just me?" Pulie huffed, blowing the black strands of hair out of her face. She put the box away with empty hands. "Father's going to kill you too if he finds out."

"It's useless, just give up. Why don't we just watch some TV? And act like it's a movie theatre. Popcorn and moldy seats." Piden tapped Pulie's shoulder. "Like normal people. Just relaxing on a couch watching Moose Boost—"

"No!" Pulie snapped. "No."

She paced around the hallway, eyeing the keyhole of her father's office. The ivory doorknob. The gray wooden door. The ghostly silence and secrets that lay behind it. She had to get in.

"You know what?" Piden began, "I don't think you need me. So I'll just make my way down—"

Pulie grabbed her brother by the shirt and dragged him to the door.

"Where was that paper clip set you used like two years ago?"

"In the twelfth drawer?" Piden squeaked.

"Go get it."

When he returned with the set, Pulie immediately set off to work with the paper clips. She pushed and squeezed and turned the clips until she heard the click behind the door.

"Yes." She whispered, slowly standing up.

She reached out to unlock the door she had been waiting to enter for years. But when her fingers crumpled and her hand tilted, the door did not budge. She had not unlocked it.

"What?" Pulie cried in disbelief. "I—I just opened it—"

"Let me see." Piden pushed her to the side. He, too, failed in opening the door. "Maybe there are more locks behind the door."

Pulie's eyes grew wide. "Exactly. I knew it. They're hiding something from us."

They made their way downstairs to the glass table again and collapsed in their chairs.

***

"We need to go to the village," Pulie finally declared, drumming her fingers on the table. She had finished four bowls of ice cream. "Right now."

"What?"

"The village."

"The village?"

"Yeah. Our parents might be down there. They never let us go to the village."

"We can't leave the house!"

"What do you think?" Pulie threw his hands up, "They left us here. We have to fend for ourselves. Do they expect us to do nothing?"

"They have *cameras* in the dining hall."

Pulie raised an eyebrow.

Piden opened his mouth. "*Which* Father taught me at age *six* how to shut those off... I guess you're right."

Pulie glanced at the picture of her parents that hung on the wall of their dining hall.

They were not here anymore. At least, not for two more years.

ZILCH

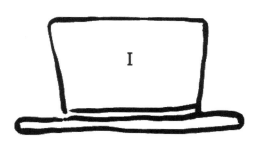

"Piden? You have no concept of time."

"What is that supposed to mean?"

"Hurry up!"

The door creaked open, letting in a gust of air. Pulie stood at her doorsteps, scanning the world around her. The crickets chirped, and the souls of the mountains and the garden were fast asleep. It was deserted almost.

"I had to shut down the camera system," Piden hollered as he pointed to his shoes. "And I tripped on the stairs because you tied my shoelaces together." Piden tumbled out the door, his shirt on backward. "I don't think you understood that when Mother said to *decrease* the trickery, she meant to—"

"I know," Pulie said flatly. She didn't want to care about that too.

They pulled their long cloak over their heads that cast a shadow on their faces, so their face wouldn't reveal their identity. A lengthy stroll took the two of them down to the village. It was a small village, and it had been a while since they had last visited. It did not go so well. And after that, they were forbidden to go again.

Crowded streets, dirty dirt pavements, the ringing of bells, and the sound of doors shutting, families in coats, officers in vests, cooks in aprons, dashing across every inch of the road. There were shouting, bicycle screeches, and doorbells were ringing from every side of the narrow streets.

As they quietly strolled through the busy streets, nobody took much notice of them. It was easy to blend in. They passed a large hat shop, and the vendor offered them a hat.

"For free?" Piden asked, trying not to look up from the hood that covered his face.

"No." The man's smile disappeared. "If you don't have any money, then go along your way, you filthy beggars." He turned around and put the hat back on the rack.

"Beggars?" Piden gritted under his teeth, about to pull his disguise down. Pulie elbowed him and dragged him down the street.

"Do you know *anything*?" Pulie shook her head, pulling him away from the shop.

"You're a filthy beggar yourself!" Piden shouted, but the man had already gone inside.

"Piden, shut up and listen," Pulie ordered. They past the curb and to the alley.

Pulie pulled off her cloak and pointed at his chest. "Revenge a man behind their back, not in their face. Remember what Father said." She pointed to the hat on the stand. "Now, go."

Piden tugged the cloak back over his head and slipped back down the street to the hat shop while Pulie, disguised again, made her way past the second block. From the corner of her eye, she caught a stranger eyeing her from the other side of the street. It was as if he had recognized her, even though the black cloth hung silently over her head. The stranger had big shiny boots that shone like midnight underneath the roof of the shop behind him.

He wore gray pants and had silver strands in his brown hair, but that was all Pulie could see. She tugged on her hood some more.

Her brother appeared behind her in a few minutes with the velvet hat in his hands. Pulie could see the revelry in his grin.

"Satisfaction," he murmured.

They spent the rest of the hour scanning for familiar faces. They split up and circled the village, searching and searching for anyone who knew their parents. But no one could help them.

***

They both collapsed on the sidewalk at the far end of the village, hopeless and deprived of a motivation to keep going. Pulie and Piden were— completely— despondent.

The sandy burning air whipped at their faces every time they tried to take off their cloaks.

"My throat." Piden clutched his neck. "I'm thirsty. I want to go home."

Pulie sighed, nearly falling over herself. But she was not thirsty nor hungry. She was tired. Tired of not knowing. Tired of having to stay at home all her life. Coming to the village was— refreshing, but it wasn't enough. Pulie wondered why all these villagers were free to go wherever they liked, but she—she had to stay at home… because she wasn't allowed anywhere else.

There must be a better way. But until then, she wanted some rest.

"Let's go home." Pulie finally stood up. To her right was a quiet dirt pathway from the alley leading straight to the hills where their house was—a short cut.

Piden grabbed the nearest ledge of the dumpster to help himself up but instead, a load of filthy waste drowned him in his spot.

"Ahh!" He cried, wiping the muck off his cloak. Something hit his head with a thunk—a glue bottle.

Pulie helped her little brother up and wiped off the rest of the garbage stuck to his clothes.

They took the dirt trail, which was a short cut back home so no one would see what a mess they were.

"Piden, you're still carrying that bottle of glue?" Pulie asked.

"Yeah. I like glue." His voice said quietly. He held up his hat as well. "At least this hat didn't get ruined."

The trail grew quieter when the sun hiked up the sky until its peak. So soft, they could hear the silent footsteps behind them.

Pulie glanced over her shoulder. There was a figure behind them, wobbling up the same path.

"Someone's following us." Pulie froze.

Piden dropped the glue bottle, and it cracked on the ground. The liquid oozed all over the dirt. The stranger began to walk faster and faster.

"Quick, hide over there!"

They dove for the nearest bushes and crouched in between the shrubs with a clear view of a man walking along the dirt trail between the prickly leaves and the twigs' entanglements.

"Oh, no." Piden gasped. "My hat."

And there it was—the velvet hat sitting on the dusty ground right beside a bubbling puddle of fresh glue. But Piden had no time to retrieve his new attire, for the stranger behind them was too close now.

And it was no stranger. It was a man, with gray pants and black boots, clunking along the trail with his cane.

Shoot. Pulie realized. It was the man that had been looking at her in the village. From underneath the shrubs, she could see the boots and this strange T symbol engraved on the side of them.

Then, all of a sudden, the man's eyes enlarged, his back straightened, and Pulie heard a large thump as he dove for the hat as if it were gold. His light brown messy hair flopped against his forehead as he hit the ground. He got up and scanned the field and examined the hat for some time. In a low tone, he muttered 'Top hat' as if it were a threat to humanity. Soon after, a very peculiar expression appeared on his face.

"What?" He cried, trying to get his boots out of the glue puddle Piden had spilled onto the gravel. In a desperate effort, he itched and yanked, but the glue had dried and dried like a stone. Pulie clamped her hands around her mouth to keep herself from laughing loudly.

But then, the man stopped trying to save his boots and reluctantly slipped out of the boots, stepping onto the dirt trail with—another pair of shoes. They were black slippers, with the same T on the front in gold. The man had worn shoes inside of his boots. Pulie's eyes grew wide. Thereupon, the man scrambled straight down the steep path to the village, as if he had never used his cane before.

"We better go home before anyone recognizes and reports us. Especially if *he* comes back." Pulie squinted at the faded figure of the unusual man down the hill.

***

It was the next day. The sunlight beat down on their sunburnt foreheads as they swung to and fro on their hammocks, melting to the ground in the heat. Pulie adjusted the shade to cover herself from the daylight. Her necklace shone like a turquoise diamond in the sun. The hours without her parents seemed monotonous, so she read the newspaper's headlines they had *earned* in the morning.

They could not find any information that might help find where their parents were, but the village news caught their eyes.
Fifty Dollar Top Hat stolen from Delilah's Hat Store.
Pulie and Piden fist-bumped.

Woman Killed in Bank Robbery.
There was silence.
"Oh no…"
Pulie fingered the page in search of more information. Alas, she found the words.

Two criminals were arrested. Probin and Macuta Jake. Brothers. Age 37 and 41, respectively. Found handcuffed with strange devices to a tree. Police are searching for the peacekeeper to acclaim him or her with a reward.

Pulie scrunched up her face. "Don't you realize? That this might relate to our parents?" Pulie jumped up and down.

"Don't be silly. You can't just relate every single crime to our parents," Piden smirked.

Pulie knew her brother was right. But what if… no… it wasn't possible.

MR. WACE

Only minutes later, there was a knock at their front gate.

Behind the entrance stood a man. Brown fuzz sat at the top of his head, and a brown mustache hung from under his nose. His cane clinked across the marble pathway. In an instant, Pulie recognized him. She enclosed the turquoise pendant of her necklace in her palm. She always did when she was anxious.

The man glanced at the lock on the gates, rolled his eyes, and drew a small long metal stub from his pocket in which he fiddled with the latches with ease until Pulie heard both the gate unlocking and the jaw of her brother dropping. Yet, neither of the two made any attempt to stop the man from entering through the gates, and he did so with graceful confidence.

He did not walk any further than the front step and instead glanced around the front yard. His blue eyes twinkled in the rays of the sun. There was a silence when no words left the lips of the three.

The man began tapping his foot impatiently as if Pulie and Piden had explaining to do. And when Pulie stared at his feet, it all became clear to her. Black slippers. Golden T.

"I haven't introduced myself yet," the man interrupts the silence. "My name is Mr. Wace."

Pulie took a step back, glancing at her brother, slightly regretting that she had only put a lock on the gate instead of advanced security. "Who—"

"Pulie," Mr. Wace said flatly. "And Piden. I know who you are. Boot gluers."

"That wasn't us," Pulie said.

"Yeah, that wasn't us." Piden piped in.

"Oh?" Mr. Wace's eyes twinkled as he scratched his chin. "That was quite a steal from Delilah, I must say. *You are* quite the thief." Mr. Wace's finger jabbed at Piden.

Piden swallowed hard. "You know?"

"*But—*" Mr. Wace stated finally, "I will only report you unless you both come with me to this—place—" He raised his hand. "Don't ask any questions on the way. Our stay might take long—in fact, very long."

"What?" Pulie asked, squinting at him. "We? Go with you? You think we'll go with you?"

"If you do not choose to tag along on my journey, all I can tell you is that theft in the village down there is not taken lightly. And you might as well pay the price for those priceless boots. But if you choose to apologize, then come with me. I know your parents are gone, and I will take care of that."

How does he know that?

"We don't know you," Pulie said.

"Ah, but you will know." Mr. Wace said.

Pulie and Piden just didn't know what to say after that one.

"Is that a *yes?*" Mr. Wace asked impatiently. "I don't want to force this on to you. Say an answer, and either way, I am leaving."

Pulie looked at Piden. Piden looked at Pulie. They were thinking about the same thing.

This just might be the surprise their parents told them to wait for.

"Yes." Came the unanimous reply.

"Very well then," said Mr. Wace with satisfaction on his face. "We'll be leaving in ten minutes. Get *ready*."

∗∗∗

"We're here."

They were at the bottom of a hill, looking up at the peak that seemed to glow under the sun. Never in her life had Pulie gone this far away from home. She tugged on her backpack straps and followed her brother and the man up the hill.

Midway in ascent, as the air pressure proceeded to drop, Pulie began to grow anxious. What was she doing? What if this was all wrong? Her father had always warned her about the outside world. Full of villains, murderers, and evil-dare devils every corner of her way. That's why he told her to never go outside.

"Sir, tell us where we are going," Pulie said, catching up to Mr. Wace.

There was no response.

A gust of wind danced across Pulie's face as she finally reached the top of the hill, her shoes digging into the dirt and withered grass. There was nothing up there but old dried shoe prints and the flat octagonal stone on the highland center. Pulie carefully watched Mr. Wace as he stepped onto the rock and felt the indigo T shaped earring clinging to his ear. Pulie was beginning to feel queasy.

What if this wasn't the surprise my parents gave us? Is this just plain kidnapping? She searched for the word. *Abduction?*

However, Pulie waited, although she was gradually getting ready to outrun the strange man down the slope of the hill when necessary. Nothing about him made sense so far.

But suddenly, Pulie flinched. Then she squinted. As if the dust around her began to collect and move towards the stone where Mr. Wace's slippers sat upon, not long after, Pulie started to see steps. And soon, it was no longer like dust particles but a concrete step staircase.

"How—"

"We have our ways through science and technology, although this one is a genius idea." Mr. Wace paused. "Now, now, you must remember that everything is an illusion. Take caution in what you believe is real, although I'll give you a hint. The staircase here is mostly real."

"Mostly real?"

"Wait till the seventeenth step."

The seventeenth step?

The staircase in front of her seemed endless. It seemed to wind up to the moon. She could not see the tip of the stairs because they were so far up. Still, nothing about this trip made sense. Perhaps, if this strange Mr. Wace was the surprise her parents had sent them, he would've mentioned her parents in the least. Or about their work. But all he was doing was taking them to a place they had never been to before.

That was it. Mr. Wace was taking both of them to the place her parents worked at! It was all part of their plan. Of course, her parents had devised such an idea. Suddenly, the urge to dash up the long stairs up to the mysterious place and fall into her parents' arms once again was—irresistible. However, the slow, unhurried walking speed of the man in front restrained her impatience. Thus, she reluctantly calmed herself down and followed Mr. Wace up the stairs that showed no signs of ending.

Pulie had no idea what Mr. Wace meant by the seventeenth step. *Perhaps, no, it can't be.*

She counted the steps until Mr. Wace reached the sixteenth step, and as she predicted, he halted. And at the same time, the three stepped onto the following tread in unison.

No longer was there a staircase ahead of them, but a door.

"An illusion. Not an everlasting staircase but a master plan in case of an invasion; a test to trick the ill-witted and separate the cunning."

"Invade the hill?" Piden asked, puzzled. There was nothing unique about the door. Unless something quite magical lay behind it, Pulie saw no reason for anyone to want to invade the place Mr. Wace was taking them to.

But Mr. Wace made a face. "No, they will invade the palace if we are not careful."

"Palace?" Pulie asked, but she knew she wasn't going to get an answer.

There was a hushed silence as Mr. Wace scanned his T shaped earring on the top of the scanner, and the door clicked open.

They were no longer in the world below but in a new universe of technology. The door shut behind them, and soon, they were standing on a flat surface of transparent glass-like material. People, just like them, scuttled around in large numbers like they were behind schedule. There were buildings in front of Pulie and Piden, with thousands of windows and lights. It was the most bizarre thing Pulie had ever seen. Where was this place?

Mr. Wace left no time to explain. He walked straight through the see-through paths. Pulie looked below her and saw the hill far below her. How was this even possible? She and Piden kept close to Mr. Wace, trying not to get lost in the crowd.

Finally, after a short walk, they reached a bus-stop looking point where they waited for a while. Several long tube buses whizzed by them as fast as light. It was so fast; it became a long blur.

Pulie and Piden had not said a single word for a long time. They were too busy admiring the spectacular experience they had stepped into. It seemed to Pulie that she was standing in a world of light-colored blue. Even the glass below her was the same tint. Although the people were regular, the buildings, lights, and paths seemed to be the same color.

The speaker at the top of the bus-stop buzzed. "Tubus 743 arriving in ten seconds."

And the bus *did* arrive. One of the long transportation tubes halted right before them. *Tubus* was the name of the tube-like vehicle. It said so on the sign above their heads. They stepped into the compartment, and the doors slid behind them.

Other passengers stood by the compartment, taking no notice of the newcomers. There were so many people. New people. People Pulie had never seen before. There were no seats on the bus, and there was no need for them because every few seconds, a group of people departed the bus, and a new group of people boarded.

"Trickies Palace." The bus lurked to a stop, and this time, Mr. Wace hopped off. So did the two siblings.

They were still in this blue-tinted land of crazed advanced technology, but this side of the new place was quieter and less populated. In fact, there were barely any people standing around them.

Mr. Wace led them to another door, scanned his iris and earring, and was allowed through the entrance.

Another set of stairs.

"Where are we?" Pulie asked, before descending. "You need to tell us what we're doing. What was *that*? That place above the ground with tubes and buildings and people. Where was that, and where are you taking us to?"

Mr. Wace shrugged. "Why don't you go down the stairs and find out for yourself."

At the bottom of the staircase was *another* door. Mr. Wace scanned his earring again and heaved it open.

They were back on the ground; it appeared so. Up above, there was the familiar sky Pulie remembered ago at home. A vast stretch of land in front of them. And straight ahead, far in the distance, a massive building in the fog.

"And *no*, this is not magic," Mr. Wace assured them. "But it is a beauty."

As they approached this massive building, Pulie realized it was a significantly misshapen palace of enormous size. First, around the palace walls, there was a moat circling all around, filled with creatures glistening in scales, so shiny and slick, their eyes gleaming, murky yellow.

Plastic alligators. The entire moat was floating with rubbery gators.

Behind the moat was the vast green wall that towered before her. Well, Pulie could barely see the outlines of the wall because it was completely wrapped in a sea of long ivy vines that continued to grow in all directions. And behind those walls was a large shadow. It was tall—taller than anything Pulie had ever seen before. It was huge. And it was moving. It was a building for sure. But the shadow of the facility assured Pulie it was no ordinary building. She would have to wait and see.

She turned her gaze to Mr. Wace, who approached the tip of the moat, the water only inches away from his slippers. He squeezed his earring with his thumb and watched a part of the ivy building across the moat fall off and collapse into a bride, revealing a safe passage to the palace entrance. The bridge plank landed with a thud right before Mr. Wace's feet, a gust of air pushed up against them. It was an alluring bridge composed entirely of intricate tiles.

"I warn you not to step on the colored tiles unless you want to fall into the moat," Mr. Wace informed, skipping over the dazzling emerald and ruby ones and balancing on the white tiles.

"What happens when I step on the ruby ones?" Piden asked, inspecting the tiles with his nose.

"They were never really glued. It's somewhat like a falling trap. Your foot sinks right through and into the water you go!" Mr. Wace grinned at the sky, while it was quite evident that he recalled moments of revelry.

Now at the other side of the bridge, Pulie could see the squint and see what wonders lay inside, like the shadows of people, hanging and dancing on the vines. It was like a jungle.

The entrance of the palace was a metal door. As if there weren't enough doors.

Mr. Wace banged on the door and shouted, "Mr. Wace is here! Hurry up! Today is my Kitchen Duty day, and it starts in four minutes!"

A little flap of the door opened, and a wrinkly woman's face appeared through it. "Sorry, I can not let you in just yet. What are you here for?"

"Young trickies."

"Name?" the woman questioned.

Mr. Wace glared at the woman. "Wanda! I'm your boss!"

She shook her head. "Safety precautions, Wace. You made the rules. Earring?"

Mr. Wace lifted his earring impatiently. "Happy? You could've just let me in!"

"Not just yet, Wace. These two don't have their earrings," Wanda warned.

"They are new! Wanda, just let us in!"

Wanda crinkled a smile. "Security check?"

Mr. Wace waved his hand at her face. "No. No security check today. We're busy."

"They're from outside the palace, sir."

"I don't care. Pulie, what do you have in your bag?"

The bag on her back wasn't hers. It was her father's, in fact, but she had taken it along with her. Inside was a pocket knife and a notebook and a couple of other small things.

"Just the necessities, sir."

The old lady finally agreed to just let them in without the security check. She chuckled, "Yes, boss. I can't believe you *finally* caught the Jake brothers this time. They murdered a woman, I've heard?"

"What?" Pulie said with her mouth hanging open. "*You're* the person who caught those murderers? It's all over the news."

"You mean, *he's* the one?" Piden asked her, pointing his finger at the man.

"*Yes*, I did track down those two blockheads. They've always been meddling with my system and have only been getting nastier and stronger. It wasn't simple this time. Ended up with a cut right here." Mr. Wace turned his arm around, displaying a deep wound. Pulie grimaced when she saw the flesh still fresh.

"I'll have the nurses fix you up. But can you tell me how you caught them?"

"No, Wanda. I need to hurry. I'm against the clock! Can you please let us in?"

The door slid open.

Pulie and Piden both gasped again in unison.

Pulie's eyes were stretched out and open, her body frozen into a manakin. They looked around before even entering. The disguise of thick vines had surrounded the whole palace. But the inside was a completely different picture.

It was another world. The courtyard in front of them, bustling with people. Nearby, four maroon large mushroom-shaped structures sprouted from the ground. To her left was a small house with a chimney. And up ahead was the shadowy edifice she had seen from outside. It was a tree—or more like a building shaped like a tree. The massive trunk winded way up to the first of the eight branches. And at the tip of each stretched out unit-branch was an enormous beehive looking bulb—eight beehive structures in total. There was a large window up in the trunk and above all the beehives and branches was the canopy and the large crown of the tree.

Now everywhere else was confettied in emerald vines and tons and tons of little and large children who danced and swang from vines and leaped onto ladders.

There was so much to see; Pulie's eyes grew sore.

Mr. Wace brought them to Miss Ellie, who was sitting at the stand in the center near the mushrooms, and she entered both pulie and Piden's names into her computer and then spoke into the speaker, "Pulie and Piden Jark, entering Zive two." Her echoes crackled throughout the palace. Then she turned to both of the siblings and said, "Welcome to the Palace of the Trickies. Mr. Wace will lead you to Larry."

Larry?

She then handed each of them a plastic object, the shape of a T, and a thin needle.

Mr. Wace took care of the rest.

MR. LARRY

"Mr. *Wace?* Mr. Wace? Can you help me out a bit?" Pulie asked, catching up to the man who was walking towards the little house in the courtyard. "Where *are* we?"

Mr. Wace nodded. "Let me first start with the beginning. The place up there—where you boarded the Tubus? That was the SkyClouds."

"Huh?"

"This is the Palace of the Trickies."

"And?"

"You'll see."

Pulie was beginning to get irritated with the simplicity in his answers.

"Do you work here?" Pulie asked Mr. Wace. She knew it was a foolish question because he seemed to know the campus by heart.

"Yes. In fact, I am on the Leading Board of this entire school. There are three leaders total, and we lead the entire palace. Me, Ms. Tory Borthwick, and Ms. Ivanna Awolo." He winced at the last two names. "I'm the nicest of the three."

He said no more.

The house was the only normal feature in the entire palace. The inside smelled of sweet ginger cookies. There were warm lights, candies stacked on the shelves. Tiny sofas sat around a glass table. On the counter sat a little man with a white beard and the most miniature glasses ever. They sat on the tip of the man's nose, jiggling about as he hummed. He was carving a little wooden skull.

"Larry." Mr. Wace waited for a response.

No reply.

"Larry!"

Larry, the odd man at the table, threw off his muffs, looking a little shaken and muttered, "You scared me there." Then he peered at the siblings, closely. "Why, why, have we gotten more, eh?" He studied the siblings through his tiny round glasses. Then, he continued with the skull carving.

"Larry, we're *here* for the *earrings*?" Mr. Wace tapped his foot against the floor.

"Me too?" Piden exclaimed. "But *I'm* a boy! I can't go around wearing an earring!"

"Young man, earrings are for *everyone*." Mr. Wace tapped his own. He only wore one on a single ear. "You won't be able to go anywhere without it." Then, Mr. Wace turned to Larry. "And can I order one of those canteens for water tomorrow? I need a bottle," Mr. Wace added.

"Oh, right. And, yeah, I'll get you one of those." Larry handed a dusty brown sack to Mr. Wace. Then, after *years* of scrummaging through his desk, Larry finally found two empty tin cans.

Pulie glanced at Larry's ears. An earring dangled on one side as well.

Larry hobbled over to the sink and twisted the knob of a peculiar looking faucet. He filled the tin spray bottles with thick purple liquid. When Larry tried to climb onto his chair, it was then

Pulie realized he was only about four feet tall. He managed to heave himself up to sit on the high stool; his beard sprayed with purple dots. Larry took off his glasses.

"So, you want an earring or no?" Larry asked, tapping his tiny feet on the ground.

Pulie looked at Piden. But Piden didn't return her glance. He was thinking. It was an odd silence before the little man started hollering,

"Come on! Give me an answer. I don't have all day! Give me a *no* or a *yes*! Hurry up!"

Flabbergasted, Pulie and Piden both answered yes. Neither of them expected such a loud voice from a tiny man.

"Step up to this line. Come on." Larry nodded at Piden. "You and your little sister," he said.

"I'm his older sister—"

"I don't have all day. I have things to do and places to be!" Larry, by no means, had an ego smaller than his height.

Frustration gurgled in Pulie, but she was intimidated by the man. In fact, she was frightened of every human being, or so that walked the floor of this incredibly strange palace. Thus, the derogatory commands forced Pulie to obey.

Larry ordered, "Hand them over."

"What?"

"The needle and the plastic! That's what!"

It was clear to Pulie that the man lacked what was called patience.

After receiving the materials for the earring, he slipped the needle through the top of the bottle and the plastic piece through another slot. Then, he closed the cap. He shook his can so hard, his little pot belly jiggled up and down and he looked as if he were to fall over.

Finally, he rested the base of the bottle on Pulie's shoulder. Pressing the white button at the top, purple liquid showered over the bottom part of her ear. She felt the slimy cold mixture, a splat, and a glob of purple on her ear. Slowly, it transformed into a dark purplish-black earring, the shape of a T, identical to the rest. No pain. Not even the slightest. Her fingers patted the backside of her ear and the needle had definitely gone through.

The same procedure was executed on her little brother, who soon possessed a smooth glass-like T earring, purple with a black shiny outline that dangled like a freshly polished diamond in the dull light.

Larry reverted back to fiddling and carving his skull nonsense.

Leaving the quiet dollhouse, Pulie clutched the earring as tight as she could, hoping for an answer to the reason she came here soon.

THE NICKY AND THE EMA

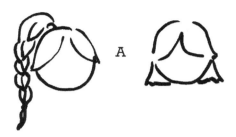

"Piden." Pulie nudged him in the arm as Mr. Wace went to talk to a boy. "Don't lose focus."

"Yeah."

"I'm serious." Pulie eyed Mr. Wace from afar. She leaned over to whisper in his ear. "We're in a completely different place in a completely different atmosphere with completely different people. This is not *normal*. We could be murdered here if we aren't careful."

"I know."

"Do you have an idea why he gave us earrings?"

"Fashion trend?" Piden asked.

"No! Obviously, a tracking device," Pulie turned Piden around with her, so their backs were against Mr. Wace. "And why do you think he said students, and why are there a bunch of buildings, and why is there a moat, and why would there be an invasion, and why is that man in there calling me a little *sister?*" Pulie threw her hands up as she gasped for air after her long tirade.

"Calm down! You suspect *everyone* of *everything*! For once, just calm down," Piden exclaimed.

"Jarks, may I speak with you?" said Mr. Wace.

Pulie and Piden spun around. Mr. Wace stood a boy with light hair and a bright face. "Miss Jark, this is your guide. Colin, this is a new student. You are both on the same level. Take her around the school. Make sure Pontz stays out of the Miralmalma for today. Can you do all this before evening sharp, Colin?"

"I think so, sir." Colin scratched his hair.

"Good, and Piden— hold on one second." Mr. Wace turned around and called at the top of his voice, "Alexander Walter!"

Pulie could see his Adam's Apple vibrating vigorously.

A pale and thin boy fast-walked on over to the group with his arms flapping at his sides. His dark brown curls bounced up and down, almost covering his large sunken eyes.

Mr. Wace pushed him towards Piden. "Alexander, do you mind giving Piden a tour around the palace?"

"Alex, sir. Uh, I—"

"I wasn't asking a question. I am already late for my kitchen duty and don't have much more time to waste, so have fun, everyone! Pulie, Piden, meet in my room today at exactly seven-thirty!" he hollered, speeding away across the quad.

"Technically, it *was* a question," Alex said.

Piden nodded. "*True*. Funny how sometimes grown-ups can't get that right."

"Yeah, come on, I need to show you the Zives. What's your name again?" Alex began to lead the way through the crowds of people.

Soon, Colin and Pulie were all alone.

"Colin," Colin said as he held out a hand. "You are?"

"Pulie," Pulie said, very slowly. "I have a question—"

"Colin! Oh my god, there you are!" A girl's voice cried.

Pulie saw two girls hurrying towards them and immediately shrank. More people? Where were her parents?

"Colin, earth to the lord, where were you?" One of the girls cried, wiping sweat from the top of her forehead.

"Mr. Wace asked me to take—" Colin turned back to Pulie. "Pulie, right? Yes, Pulie— on a tour. She's new."

"That's nice of you," the same girl said. She had a large puffy braid at the top of her head. She had bold features and a fire to her eyes. "Anyways, I realized it could be her. Give this to Livia so that me and Ema can to go Larry's to get the—thing. You need to do this quickly."

"I already told you, I'm sorry, I have an appointment." Colin sputtered, "I need to do this tour— Mr. Wace himself asked me to!"

"Well, I'm sorry, this can't wait! I will tell Ms. Awolo what you did last year," The same girl said again, retying her braid.

Colin made a face. "And she'd believe *you*. Oh, please."

Nicky glared at him.

"Oh, fine. Then, take Pidley on your way to Larry's, will you?"

Pidley?

"I want to send the message to Livia *privately*, okay?" Colin took a small packet from the brown-haired girl's hands. He concealed it by sliding it down a secret pocket inside his jacket.

"Very well. But if I don't hear from Livia that you—" The brunette's eyes met Pulie's. It was a split second of hesitation. "Never mind, come on, we need to go fast. Hurry up, though, Colin. I need to find who it was."

Colin mumbled something, but sprinted deeper and deeper into a sea of children and soon was out of sight. The red haired girl turned to Pulie.

"I'm Ema—"

"Sorry, we don't have time introduce ourselves right now!" The brunette interrupted. "Is it Pidley? Sorry. Really, really need to hurry," the brunette apologized, "Your tour guide will be right with you in a minute. But come with us."

"No, but—"

In a short period of time, Pulie was dragged by the brunette and the other red-haired girl to Larrys' once again. But this time, through the back door. The other girl unlocked it with a passcode.

"Okay, first of all, Pidley—"

"My name is—"

Nicky turned to Pulie. "All *you* need to do is follow us and stay—" Nicky put a finger to her lips. "Dead silent. Follow me."

First, Nicky, the other girl, and then Pulie. The door creaked open, and they snuck in through the back, tiptoeing around the boxes and avoiding the musty smell of bottles and tubes. Nicky halted in the darkness at the corner of the room opposite the door to Larry's chamber. She put a finger up and slid a small paper clip key through the hole. Something clicked, a small part of the shelf swung open. Nicky beckoned for the other girl to bring out a cotton bag to lower the large item in. The stand was locked and they snuck back out the door.

Nicky tied the laces of the cotton bag so tightly Pulie could not see what was inside. "Finally. Done," Nicky muttered.

"What's that for?" Pulie asked, pointing to the bag. "What's inside?"

Nicky shrugged. "It's an important business."

They were back in the center of the courtyard. Pulie longed to be up in the vines and the walls or up in those beehive bulbs or up in the tree trunk, free and happy, but instead, she was standing in the heat with two strange girls who had just stolen something from Larry's shop. Was she being kidnapped too? Was she dealing with robbers?

"Where can that boy be?" Nicky groaned, laying the bag on the floor with caution. "If we had ConnecT, we wouldn't be having this problem."

"Just wait till next year, and you'll be swimming in gadgets," The red-haired girl, called Ema assured her. Although her flaming, almost fire-like hair was mostly light scarlet, there were a few marigolds and light yellow strands. Her large round spectacles sat at the end of her nose.

"But really, where is that boy?" Nicky threw her hands up. "If it takes this long to ask one question, I'll never have him again help us on such an easy task. Just imagine how long it will take him to do something in the mission. And just imagine if he gets into the mission, and I don't. That would be a nightmare—"

"Let's try staying on track." Ema squinted through the crowds of people, searching for the yellow-haired boy.

Pulie asked, "Can I ask a question?"

"Sorry. Colin will help you with your questions," Nicky answered, not turning around and instead waved to Piden and Alex, who were walking towards them to the middle of the courtyard.

"Hello," Alex looked at Pulie, "I believe I've forgotten your name. Hello, Ema." Alex waved while smiling brightly.

"I'm waiting for my hello," Nicky pointed out.

"Hello, cousin Nicky," he mumbled less cheerfully.

"Did you finish the tour, Pulie?" Piden asked.

"Your name is Pulie?" Ema asked, a terrified expression on her face, as well as Nicky's.

"Yes, well—" Pulie said. "It doesn't matter now—"

"What doesn't matter?" Alex piped in.

Nicky turned to him, "We've been calling her—Pidley."

Piden and Alex both looked at each other and burst out laughing.

Pulie's smile quickly vanished after her brother commented.

"Pidley?" Piden shrieked with laughter.

Ema cleared her throat, "That's a pretty—"

"Unusual name. Both of our names," Pulie pointed to both herself and her brother. "—are quite peculiar. We get it a lot." Pulie tried to ignore that loud giggling from her brother. *Why was he having so much fun?*

"Actually," Ema began, "My name is spelled with only one *m*. That's not common."

"Yeah. My name is spelled with only one *n* as well," Nicky added. Everyone exchanged glances after that one.

"It has always been spelled with one *n*, Nicky," Ema said.

Alex changed the topic. "I took Piden around the Zives and the borders." Alex then turned to Pulie, "I thought you were doing a tour with Colin."

Nicky looked at Ema. Ema returned her gaze.

"Well, I *think*—" Ema began. "I think *we'll* just do the school tour."

"Yeah, and besides, we owe *Pidley* an apology for calling her whatever we were calling her. Come on, Pulie, let's begin our tour."

Zives? School tour? What kind of a mess am I in?

STRANGE

"First, what questions do you have?" Nicky questioned.

"*Everything*, really. But one thing I want to ask— what *is* this place for?"

"Haven't your parents told you about this place?"

"No, maybe—" Pulie paused, "Maybe it was a surprise."

Nicky continued, "Anyways, an excellent question to start with— it's like a school where children are selected to come and train for Tricky Trials, Leagues, missions, and basically fighting our worst enemies. We're the Trickies; spying, tricking, and stealing is kind of our thing."

Boy, this girl can talk.

"The Trickies is one-third of the power group that defends against the CAOT. We, the Trickies, have our specialty— the vines…"

So this was where her parents worked. All this time, here? At a palace, full of tricks and trickery and more tricks and trickery.

Meanwhile, Nicky continued to chatter.

"Everyone arrives at the palace a day before the school begins to adjust and become familiar with the campus again," Ema told her, "And to make sure everything is set. You're just on time to start like everyone else."

"Do you know how to read?" Nicky stopped all of a sudden while walking. She had a doubtful and judgmental expression on her face that did not please Pulie in the least.

"Of course," Pulie answered, beginning to feel a bit aggressive. She was a fifteen-year-old girl. Of course, she knew how to read. Her parents were great teachers.

"How?" Nicky asked. "You never came to this place when you were little, right? I can tell. Were you in a different Zive?"

"No."

"Nicky, people can probably come from different schools. You came from a different palace, right?" Ema looked at Pulie.

"No, I haven't. And I don't know anything about the trickers or trickies or whatever."

Nicky lowered her eyebrows. "Then surely you don't know how to read."

"My parents taught me."

"Your parents taught you?" Ema asked, surprised. "Can you do that?" She paused. "Not that it matters."

"Apparently," Nicky muttered, not looking Pulie in the eye.

Pulie crumpled her fist. "Do *you* know how to read?" Pulie asked. "Is that why you're asking me all these questions?"

Nicky opened her mouth and then closed it. "Of course, we do." Nicky sighed. "Okay, okay. I'm sorry. My mouth goes a little crazy sometimes. I didn't mean to interrogate you or anything."

"Well, you did." Pulie glared at them. "I need help right now. I don't know what's going on right now and why I'm here, or where my parents are. But if you can't help me, I'll be on my way."

Nicky shook her head. "We want to help. We just felt a a bit—"

"Your parents?" Ema's eyes grew large. "What happened?"

"I don't know," Pulie said, wondering whether she should tell these girls everything. "They went on some trip."

"A trip? To where?"

"Somewhere. I told you, I don't know."

Nicky shrugged. "Late honeymoon?" Pulie could tell she was trying to lighten the mood.

"No, they had theirs years ago."

"Then, it must be scouting." Ema glanced around and whispered. "Your parents must be on a secret scout mission."

"Of course!" Nicky added. "My parents left on a scout mission years ago without telling where they were going. Your parents must've done the same thing."

"You're right!" Pulie was relieved. So they weren't kidnapped? And they weren't at the palace but instead somewhere else? Why was *she* here then? At least she knew what her parents were doing. But the feeling halted. *But a mission for two years?* She didn't say it aloud; she didn't want to hear what Ema and Nicky would say if they knew.

"Look, I'm sorry I was rude or whatever," Nicky said. "I just wanted to know more about you. You were just different from everyone here."

"Yeah." But Pulie could tell Nicky wasn't sorry at all.

"This is not the first time someone is going to ask you questions, though," Ema reminded Pulie. "The people here are not the nicest to new students. Especially if you don't know much about this place."

Nicky added, "I'm still surprised your parents haven't told you about the Trickies, though."

"Likewise," Pulie answered. *Why didn't they?*

"Well," Ema said. "We'll fill you in on the information you missed out on. Go ahead, Nicky."

"Okay, this is the courtyard. The courtyard is where most of the main events happen. Around the courtyard is the big vine wall. I like to call it the Ivy Barricade. You're allowed to go up there and hang around or slip down the vines. Teachers don't care because it's already been two years since a boy cracked his head on the moat, but it's alright."

Then came several big *booms* from a distance, followed by a bunch of revelry cheers erupted from outside of the walls.

"*That* — is what happens when you slip into the moat," Ema chuckled.

"Uh, huh. Anyways, on the main courtyard, there's little Larry's house, which you're probably familiar with." Nicky pointed to her right. "And to your right are the ELSE domes."

"The mushrooms?"

"Yeah, the mushrooms. Sure. They're classrooms. You climb up the ladder attached to the mushroom's stem, and there's a door you go up into. They're called ELSE. Environmental Learning Stations Edge, where you are taught about water, fire, and Rangs— for us, Mrs. Wapanog teaches our ELSE class."

The girls strolled to the other side of the courtyard in front of the large tree trunk.

"And you see up there—" Nicky tilted her head up and up until her gaze met eight ginormous bee-hives structures. "—the eight little bee-hive looking things? Those are the Zives. They are designed to act and look like an actual beehive. All those windows for the rooms represent tiny holes in a beehive. We're just missing the honey. The four outer beehives are dorm rooms, and the four middle Zives are the main course classrooms. We have all of our classes except Wapanog in that one over there. We don't need to go anywhere else. Oh, and Señor Rodriguez is amazing. He's the gear teacher—"

"Yeah, but now, he's also the *spy* teacher!"

"You are going way too fast!" Pulie cried.

"Well, hey, *we're* just giving you a tour. We thought you'd already know a majority of this place. But it's okay— oldest siblings have to suffer the first part always," Nicky agreed. "Oh, and the four outer Zives are the sleeping dorms where we sleep. Did I say that already?"

"I think so."

"Okay. Are you staying here overnight, or are you gonna go back home like a regular school?"

Pulie had no idea what they were talking about.

Was she staying here overnight? This wasn't a day trip?

"I believe I am going back," Pulie answered quickly. "Mr. Wace said it was only for—"

He did say it would take long. The thought hit Pulie in the stomach. *I didn't know he meant this long.*

"I didn't bring anything with me except this backpack." Pulie pointed to her small bag. "And it doesn't have anything in it but a pocket knife and a—"

"A knife?" Nicky made a face. "I didn't know that would get past security."

"Security?"

"Yeah, didn't they scan you and dump out your bag and stuff?"

"No, why would they do that?"

"To make sure you don't have knives and stuff!" Nicky exclaimed. "And paper. No paper allowed. You don't have paper, right?"

"Nope." Pulie felt the notebook at the bottom of her bag.

"Don't worry," Ema interrupted. "We won't tell anyone that you have a knife."

"No promises," Nicky muttered.

There was a constant tension between Nicky and Pulie. It was like a rubber band stretching and stretching until Ema came along and snapped it in half.

"Don't worry," Ema reassured her, "If you forgot to bring your luggage, there's a shop—the log-shaped building behind the Miralmalma. You can buy what you need there."

"Do you have credits?" Nicky asked.

Pulie shook her head, wincing when Nicky sighed.

"Mr. Wace will take care of it. Now, let's continue our tour." Ema talked about the new rules and systems, where to go, and where not to go. Information poured into her head like water as she tried to stuff and stuff information into herself.

"The tall trunk you see in the middle… that's the main room, where the staff is and where Mr. Wace and all the teachers sleep and live. The Miralmalma is four hundred five feet tall, which is also the height of the Zives." Nicky explained.

"Don't try to end up there too often. Not a good thing… Right, Nicky?" Ema chuckled, softly.

Nicky turned around. "What?"

Ema whispered, "She goes there too much."

The next part of the tour took place at the base of the Zives themselves. Pulie was finally looking at the vines from close up. Two vines were leading down, both thick and green with leaves and thorns protruding from the sides. The vines led up to the bottom of the beehives in the sky.

"So, how do we get up?" Pulie asked. She was two feet away from the first vine. The base of the vine was attached to a large platform with steps. Indeed she didn't have to climb it with her bare hands. That was impossible.

"If you're thinking about climbing it, good luck," Nicky answered. "This is the greatest invention ever. It's like a drop tower."

"Drop tower?"

Ema nodded. "Yeah, have you ever seen one of those? In amusement parks?"

"Amusement—parks?"

Ema and Nicky stared at Pulie with their mouths open.

"Okay, whatever. I don't know what that is, but what do you mean a drop tower?"

That moment, there was a whoosh. From the second vine, a boy, strapped to a seat attached to the vine, descended quickly, and once his seat his the platform, he unbuckled and got off.

"That's the way down. That vine over there operates downhill." Ema explained. "The way up, you wait for a seat to arrive, you strap, and go up."

When the first seat arrived, Ema got on, buckled, then waved, and then shot up into the sky.

A few seconds later, the next seat arrived, and Nicky followed the same procedures.

Finally, it was Pulie's turn. She sat in the seat, tightened the straps, and squeezed the handles as hard as she could with her eyes closed, waiting for her turn up. And *whoosh!*

In an instant, she was up! In the sky! She could see the entire palace and the moat and far past the ivy walls. The air was thinner up here, and the next moment, she unbuckled and was in the lobby of the gigantic beehive. Pulie winced at the sound of her ears crackling and popping. In an instant, she realized how high above *home* she was. She shuddered and tried to stop her ears from parading with fireworks.

"This—is Zive two." Nicky spread her arms. "Welcome." She then slid across the carpet and down the hall. Pulie shut the door of the Zive. The wind stopped howling, and the lobby was quiet.

It was a maroon carpet that stretched down the long hallway with countless doors and room numbers on each side. *Is this where they sleep? Am I going to sleep here?* She tried not to lose sight of Nicky and Ema up ahead.

"This is our room." Nicky stopped at the door.

"Our room?"

"Yes. Look at the message on the door."

There was a hologram message drifting in the air.

This is your room, Pulie. It said. Mr. Larry informed me that Nicky and Ema took you on the tour, so you must be quite familiar with them. You will be sharing this room with them. Your welcome. Hard to find such good roommates.

Mr. Wace

Pulie winced. As much as she liked Ema, she wasn't so sure about Nicky. That brown-haired girl hated her gut.

Nicky bent over and scanned her earring on the sensor above the door handle, which, in fact, was very high up, almost up to her neck. A whizzing sound beeped, and the sensor glowed green. The door unlocked.

The room inside was the complete opposite of what she had imagined. The floor was carpet. Hammocks hanging from strong irons hooked tightly from the ceiling for beds. A small silver sink stood by the door while on the other side of the room was a large purple curtain with the T's symbol embedded every inch of the cloth. And next to the curtain, was a small wooden desk.

On the desk was a large hologram base that displayed a message floating in the air with a stack of thin sheets of metal below it. The message read,

Inside is your allowance to buy clothes, soaps, and other needed supplies. I will generously give both you and your brother a small sum every once in a while. Spend it wisely.

Mr. Wace

"Nice. Those sheets are your credits. You're lucky he gives you a monthly allowance. Only a couple of people get that," Nicky said. "Oh, that's our hologram, by the way. It's the message and connection base we have in our room. And you can drop your stuff over there. Like your bag."

Pulie unpacked the minimal belongings she carried, folded up the sheets into her pocket, squished her pocket knife in the other, and strode out of the room with the girls.

When they entered the lobby, they saw Piden and Alex arm-wrestling on a couch.

"What are you guys doing?"

"Hold on… just need to…" Piden's arm was trembling. He was on the verge of losing. His eyes, a bit red, were about to tear up. And then, the back of Piden's hand touched the couch.

"Yes! That's a streak of seven," Alex shouted.

Nicky chuckled. "Well, boys, we're off to the shop. Want to tag along?"

Alex shook his head. "I'd rather be eaten by a Woolly Rhinoceros."

***

The store was a little market full of everything a person might *not* need. At least, that was what Pulie thought when she first entered. In the front, all she could see were odd-looking clothes, some tattered, some ornate in strange logos and symbols, and they sat perched on the hooks. Yet as she walked deeper into the forest of unwanted items, she came across frozen food in refrigerators, drinks, candies, and cosmetics. Nicky helped Pulie pick out a couple of clothes from the back room, and Ema collected all the soaps.

"Where'd you get that from?" Nicky asked, pointing to the necklace on Pulie's throat after taking off a fluffy scarf.

"This?" Pulie asked, holding up the gem charm dangling on the silver chain.

"Yeah, it's so pretty!" Ema exclaimed in awe.

"It's nice," Nicky said casually. "Where's it from?"

"My parents gave it to me when I was born and told me never to take it off. It's like a part of me now."

"Turquoise?" Ema asked, inspecting as well. At the center of the golden chain hung a circular smoothed gem of special turquoise, a glimmering jewel in the light. It had thin black lines spread all across the stone in uneven patterns, like a spider web.

"Um—some kind of turquoise," Pulie answered.

"Wow," Nicky said, looking down, "I wish I had something like that. The only thing I have to keep living with is my cousin."

They all laughed.

***

"Well then, *here we are*." Ema stood at the platform of another zine leading up to the classroom Zive. Pulie had already visited one of the beehives.

"This is our *classroom* Zive," Nicky explained. "As I said, there are four dorm Zives and four classroom Zives. We're in Zive number two, which means all our classes are here, except for Wapanog. Let's go see who is up there right now."

Once again, they shot up the vines and hopped off the ride at the base of the Zive that was filled with classrooms.

At the other end of the hall was a door. Nicky was sure that Señor would be there because he usually was. They peeked inside.

"Oh." was the word that flew out of Ema's mouth, as soft as water. Disappointed, Nicky recoiled behind the door.

At the desk inside the room sat a teacher with blond hair slicked up in a bun. She was clad in a tight red sheath dress, and thick red shiny glasses sat perched at the edge of her plump nose. She had long eyelashes and a heavily caked face, smeared with lipstick the shade of rich dark strawberries, and shoes the color of shiny blood.

"I can tell she likes red," observed Pulie.

Nicky shut the door. "*That*—was Mrs. Idadosi. One of the most hated teachers here. But don't worry, you won't get her unless you choose her class for an elective next year."

More than one year? Here?

Nicky declared that they go see Señor Rodriguez if he was in the other rooms at the moment.

They scavenged most of the rooms on the first floor until they heard whistling from the last room in the hall.

"Shhhh," Nicky shushed as she crept towards the doorknob. "That's him. That's his whistling."

Señor Rodriguez was all alone in his room, sitting in an iron chair. He was skinny yet buff. He had a few scars on the sides of his faces, and a black french style mustache, followed by his black hair. He had a long nose, and on the sides of his faces, he had little mechanical items. One of them ticked beside his ear like a clock. On his neck was a collar with spikes. He looked like—a *gear guy.*

"Señor Rodriguez! Nice spring break?" Nicky exclaimed as she burst through the door.

His smile lit up when he spotted her and ushered the three into the room filled with decorated walls, a museum of magnifying glasses, spears, and computers. His desk was even more amusing. There were about a million tiny odd gadgets.

"Señor, she's a new student. We're showing her around. At first, Colin was supposed to do the tour because Mr. Wace absolutely adores him. But then, Ema and I kind of took over, and now we're the tour guides."

"Good for you, Nicky." Señor Rodriguez stroked his beard. "What's your name?" He pointed at Pulie.

"Pulie," Pulie answered. "What do you teach?"

"I am a spy gear teacher." Señor Rodriguez raised an eyebrow. "Pulie. I know another strange name, just like yours. What was it? *Piden*. Right, Alex came up here to show Piden around here."

"That's her little brother," Nicky said. "Wait. Señor Rodriguez, where's your new office now that Mr. Berger left?"

Señor Rodriguez grinned. "It's in the main room now. I get my private room in the *Miralmalma*," He said excitedly.

"This isn't your room?"

Señor Rodriguez chuckled. "*Yes*, Pulie. This is not my room. This is *your* classroom. My office is in the building in the center; we call it the *Miralmalma*. You'll get used to saying *that* word."

"Bring," cricketed a phone bell sound. Señor Rodriguez jumped from his seat. "Ahh, alarm sound. I need to contact someone right now. I do believe it is Mr. Wace. I hope you all have a great time and see you tomorrow! And, Pulie," He turned to her as one of his hands touched the glass watch on his wrist. "You and your brother look very familiar. Anyways, Cheerio! Nice to meet you."

Familiar? She and her brother were familiar to him. His words seemed to echo and carve into her skull. Her confusion and vertigo were washed away. So her parents *did* work here. But they were in a scout mission. And it wasn't a coincidence that Mr. Wace had taken them here. This was *the* surprise—a surprise to another secret world. So far, she learned that this palace was a training school to fight—what? The invaders? But if she and her brother had been sent here by her parents, that means everything was fine. But the only question that lingered in her mind was, where exactly were her parents?

Before she knew it, they were back in the courtyard continuing the tour.

"Mrs. Wapanog is the one in the—you called it a mushroom? Yeah. The *mushroom* things over there. Called ELSE, but whatever," Nicky said. "There's a lot of weird names around here. Like the Miralmalma."

"Who's Mrs. Wapanog?" asked Pulie.

"The strict ELSE teacher," Nicky answered as they walked over to the mushroom. "She seems to be a ticking alarm clock. Do this. Do that. At this time. Right now." Nicky jumped up and down as she said this and stopped. "But I can't argue about her impatience though. She is the reason how I get all my tar."

"Tar?" Pulie questioned. "What—what would you do with that?" She loathed the fact that she had to inquire about every little thing.

"She tars people—" Ema sighed as she said this, "She's known in this palace as the *tar girl*."

"Tar girl?" Pulie smiled, hoping for one from Nicky. She didn't get one.

"She ended up in the Miralmalma every day last year. But towards the end of last year, Ms. Awolo and Ms. Borthwick started their *game* of theirs to *stop* it."

"*It* as in—"

Nicky cut Pulie off. "I use tar on other people. I pour it inside bags, shoes, clothes, and the list goes on. It's my specialty. I especially—"

"Got it."

"But, we have to tell you this, Pulie." Nicky paused. "You have to understand that this is not a regular school."

I can tell—thank you very much.

"Like Mr. Wace said in his Halloween speech last year. We are highly encouraged, but not necessarily needed to trick."

Pulie tilted her head. "So, what's the deal with tricking people here anyway?"

Nicky twisted her braid into ringlets. "It's a bit complex and more *sophisticated* than you think." She seemed to be very happy after saying such a hard word. "It's like a numbing process of disturbing other people. The leaders want us to get used to using our brains and making other people you know… well… suffer? That's not what Wace said, but you get the idea."

Pulie scrunched her forehead, not understanding. "So, how does that help us? Like hurting other people?"

"It's how you develop to be agents and spies. You know, the missions are all about the sacrifices we make along the way. Sometimes, we will hurt people like the CAOT. Basically, Mr. Wace just wants us to get the feel of what happens in Scouts or just out there. Of course, Mr. Wace or Ms. Awolo don't want us to break any rules. Like stay after curfew or don't steal things from the shop, but it's inevitable, and that's how we learn.

"Of course, as long as you aren't caught," Nicky added. "Especially by the Borthwick and Awolo. They are so—"

"If you are caught, you are sent to the Miralmalma. Not fun. Nicky can tell you all about it." Ema grinned, poking Nicky in the ribs.

"Long story short, you don't *have* to trick people. But everyone is here at this academy for a reason. We are all talented in a different way. Mr. Wace has to approve of you to enter though, and he chooses people who have wily blood in their veins, which makes most of us. Maybe except for Moto."

"Who?"

Nicky grimaced. "She doesn't matter."

"But what does matter," Ema interrupted, "is that you're going to end up tricking people."

"Why is that?"

"You won't survive. It's crazy and scary what people will do to you here." Ema shivered. "You have to fight back. To people like… like… Erik Pontz."

"And he's right over there." Nicky pointed to a tall boy who was pouring tar onto the handles of a basket. "Wait a minute, that looks like my tar jar. How dare he? First, stealing my credits, and now that? What else is he going to take? I'll teach him." Nicky growled.

Ema grabbed Nicky's arm. "Not every jar of tar is yours. And Pulie, that's Erik Pontz. Try to avoid him your first couple days," Ema whispered.

Squinting proved to be useless and Pulie could only see the outline of the large muscular boy. But everything else around her suddenly caught her eye. She realized how different the palace seemed from when she first entered. All the people that terrified her, cawing, dancing on vines, jumping from roof to roof, now made sense. They were all in some way, making mischief or planting tricks.

Like from the vines up above she noticed that three girls were taping tacks on the steps. Pulie winced. To her left, a boy was putting a dark brown mixture inside a backpack that was left sitting on the bench for a while. Now, all of a sudden, she could see things that were really happening. She could hear the complaints and laughter and screaming now that didn't make sense to her at first. Pieces were starting to come together now.

"Don't worry. You'll be fine. Just don't get caught."

***

A loud bell sound trickled throughout the courtyard. Students from all corners froze and began sprinting to the center of the enclosure.

"Dinner time. Let's go to the eating room."

In a flash, Pulie nearly got lost in the pushing and shoving of a thousand students, trying to get to somewhere Pulie had no idea of.

Nicky? Ema? Where were they?

And then, there was a squelching squish, unpleasant and unsatisfying.

EVENING

I

Someone had poured a puddle of transparent tar in front of them as they walked to the center of the courtyard. So they were stuck in the clear mixture until they reluctantly decided to give up their shoes. They weren't the only ones; a couple of other students were also trapped in the paste. It reminded Pulie of the time when she and Piden had glued Mr. Wace's boots to the ground.

"My beloved shoes—" Nicky sobbed. "They were so precious. I will *kill* whoever did that to us. And they probably stole my tar! Rosetta and Floretta are now buried in the betrayal of the three of us and our need to eat."

"You named your shoes?"

"Rosetta Starlin' and Floretta Smith," Nicky answered, a smile spreading across her face.

"Hey, Nicky!"

Pulie tweaked her head around and saw a very tall girl with half of her hair combed to the side. Her shoes were also stuck in the glue.

"Celena? You stuck too?" Nicky asked, trying to reach over and high-five her. It didn't work.

Celena commanded, "We have to lose the shoes, Nicky. Right now. The food's going to be gone by the time we wait for the glue to harden." The girl had a husky voice and white teeth—very white teeth.

"Why?" Nicky muttered, slipping out of her shoes and stepping over the puddle of tar. "Why always the shoes?"

By the time they slipped out of their shoes and reached the center of the courtyard, it was silent. Everyone had disappeared. It was just the three of them and Celena. Pulie felt the cold stone floor on her bare feet.

"Hey you," Celena pointed at Pulie. Pulie stepped back and smiled uneasily.

Uh oh. I'm the new kid.

"Who are you?" Celena, who was a foot taller, poked at Pulie's head. Celena glanced at Nicky. "New kid?"

Nicky nodded.

"Name?"

"Pulie."

Celena knelt until her face was leveled. "Pulie?" She chuckled. "Go on, Nicky and Ema. Let's give this little rookie a little fun.." The tall girl grabbed Pulie's arm. Not in a friendly way.

Ema frowned. "Come on, Celena. Not today. We don't even have shoes." She glanced at Nicky, who didn't budge one bit, although she had a strange look. There was a pause, and it seemed as if the others were all communicating with their eyes.

Celena tightened her grip on Pulie's arm and said, "Well, what are you waiting for? Dinner time."

Ema uneasily nodded and started walking with Nicky in the other direction. Celena dragged Pulie the other way.

"I'm hungry, too. Let go of me," Pulie muttered, wrestling her arm out of the massive grip. She tried kicking and biting, whatever could help her escape. Pulie gritted her teeth as she tried to wriggle out of the trap.

Celena dragged her across the courtyard and tied Pulie's hands around a pole behind her. Then her mouth with a bandana. It took a while, because Pulie squirmed uncontrollably, gnawing and snapping at the red-spotted bandana pressed against her mouth.

Celena took a step back, her eyes glittering with delight. Then, she ran back to the center of the courtyard. From afar, Pulie could see her halt at a certain point in the quad, stoop down and flip a latch open, leading to a trap door. Celena disappeared into the ground.

An ungrateful growl aroused in Pulie's stomach, but she seemed to be stuck here until someone came to help her. But she was sure no one would unless it was her brother. *Or unless she got herself out*—to eat some dinner.

Pocket knife. Snug in her back pocket. Like always. The cloth-covered the grin on Pulie's lips. Her hands could still move, although her wrists were knotted. With one *flick! And another flick!* The rope unraveled and collapsed at her feet. She pocketed the handkerchief in her pocket and sprinted barefoot to the trap door at the center of the courtyard.

There was a wide square outline on the floor, and Pulie popped open the latch, and a staircase sprang downwards. The deeper she walked, the lights appeared, and soon, voices echoed. Then, she entered a hallway that extended from her right to her left. There were a total of four doors in this hallway, all in line horizontally. Arrows with Zive two on the boards pointed to her left. So she walked down the hall until she reached the second door. She opened it and finally arrived in everyone's beloved eating room.

Creatures of humanity buzzed around with plates piled with foods fighting for the right to sit and enjoy their meal in what is said to be one of the busiest rooms in the entire palace.

"Chef Raynott today! Let's go ransack this place!" said one kid, spreading the word, and soon, everyone was in the state of extreme rapture. Pulie was lost in a vast room that left little space for her to move in.

Her stomach grumbled some more and it made Pulie forget about everything that had happened to her in the past couple minutes. Her tour guides' betrayal, the tall girl's mischief; it was not time to get revenge.

She piled food onto her plate and desperately searched for a place to sit—so many unfamiliar faces and so many sneers. Pulie looked down at her tray of food as she walked through the bustling tables.

"Pulie!"

Pulie froze. It wasn't her brother's voice, but instead, it was Ema's. Pulie took a deep breath as she watched all the other tables around her fill up. So, she reluctantly turned around and headed to Ema's table. Ema wasn't alone, however. She was at one of the long tables with Nicky and many others.

Pulie's tray was across from everyone else and she didn't look up. How long was she going to stay in a relentless unfriendly place like this?

"How'd you get out?"

Pulie didn't respond; she knew who the voice was. Nicky had not been the best company. At the moment, Pulie hated each and every person that was breathing the same air that she was inhaling. She missed home, and she missed her parents and everything how it used to be.

"This is the cafeteria for Zive two," said Ema, munching on her food. "It's basically one large eating room, but the leaders decided to cut the room into four parts and divided it with removal panels. See that wall over there? On the other side is Zive one."

"Yeah. We also have different cooks." Nicky joined. "Raynott has the best hamburgers. You're lucky that Chef Susie isn't the cook for your first day," Nicky said, shuddering. "Her cooking makes you want to never come back despite everything else here. She has a mind of her own when it comes to cooking. She cooks an omelet without eggs and toast without bread. Her pasta is cold with thick stale dressings of Alfredo. Her nachos are hard, and her chips are bendable."

Pulie didn't respond. *Was that supposed to make me laugh?*

"She's the only bad cook, though," Nicky continued. "Thank god. On the other hand, we have Chef Hickle-Pumpkin, Cook Raynott, Chef Cabello, and Cook Ma. Hickle-Pumpkin prepares the best Italian food. His pasta melts in your mouth, his garlic bread toasty and warm on the outside, and is stuffed with cheese on the inside. Cook Raynott is the best hamburger maker in the palace. Soft beef, crunchy lettuce, warm cheese, and a nice toasted bread on the outside with a pinch of hot sauce, his meals usually came out on Fridays. Chef Cabello is the Mexican Food Mistress. She makes the best burritos, tacos, salsa, nachos, and all the Mexican food you can search up. And Chef Ma makes good sushi, barbecue, and dumplings," Nicky said effortlessly in one breath. "Oh, and don't forget Chef Appleton. He makes all the stuff, even seafood and everything you could imagine. I wonder why he isn't the only chef here. He can cook everything. Oh, and his son goes to school here—Gus? Gus Appleton. Yeah. He's in the Zive next to us."

Pulie remained quiet although Nicky was mostly doing the talking until Piden and Alex made their way over to their table.

"Auntie told me to tell you that you left your secret tablet at home." Alex grinned. "I found out that all last year, you had it in your room. It's illegal to possess a message sending device in this palace!"

Nicky bit her lip. "I'm telling your mother that you keep stealing books from the land sacks with paper in them."

Alex's face grew pale.

"And that you don't do the laundry."

Alex's eyes grew wide.

"Are you siblings?" Piden asked.

Nicky and Alex cracked up. "Siblings?" Nicky smiled a goofy grin Pulie had never seen before. "No. But we're cousins. If I was related that close to *him*, I would die."

"Same here." Alex waved his hand.

Shortly after devouring her meal, Pulie sat back in her seat, eyeing her table. Everyone was busy talking and stuffing the food into their mouths and paid no attention to her glowering glares. But the next person who joined the table made her freeze in an instant. *Celena.*

Celena sashayed to the table with such a pep in her step that it was apparent she had no idea Pulie was sitting at the same table. Celena announced something to the long group of people at the table, and everyone laughed. She greeted everyone at the table, and by their responses, Pulie could tell everyone liked her. She heard what Celena was saying as she walked closer.

"Where's Nicky? Ah, there you are—"

Celena's gaze met Pulie. *Shoot.*

Celena's eyes grew wide. But instead of dragging Pulie out for more trouble, Celena just laughed and pointed at Pulie. "I like that one. She's a fighter. Pulie, you say?"

Pulie nodded and caught the grin on Nicky's face.

Celena smiled. "Welcome."

***

Piden's room was a story above Pulie's room, which was on the first floor.

"Bathrooms to the left. Exit on the right. And danger zone Selma to the right as well." Ema pointed out all the directions and pathways in the Zive.

"Who's Selma?"

By the grimace on Ema's face, Pulie already knew it wasn't good.

"Snarky and dangerous, but not very clever." Ema frowned. "I don't do the talking, though. Nicky does. She'll explain, and she'll show you who she is later, but first, let's wash up and get ready for bed. Curfew is at nine-thirty—" Ema handed a bag for all Pulie's toothbrush and shampoo and some of the items bought at the shop. Pulie stuffed an extra pair of clothes in, just in case.

"Sorry I can't come with you." Ema said, "I have to go submit my spring forms with Nicky. But it will be fine because the shower lines are way shorter at this time."

"It's all good. Do I need towels?" Pulie searched for a towel in the room.

"No, there are towels in the bathrooms. And Pulie?" Ema stopped Pulie from walking out.

"Don't talk to a thin, thin teen girl named Selma with a mean face and lots of makeup. Oh, also, watch out for a chubby short one named Bonnie too."

"That's very reassuring." Pulie smiled uneasily.

Ema sighed. "As long as you listen to that, it'll be all good."

Pulie departed with Ema as she walked off to the girl's bathrooms. She saw a line of people waiting for only five shower stalls. In the long line, as she waited, she heard a tiny yell from inside the shower. Pulie perked up from her daze of the steam. She looked around. The two girls by the corner near the bathrooms stood snickering and pointing to a stall, holding a large bag. The taller one had a big blond bun and a face caked with makeup, while the other chubby with straight brown bangs. Pulie instantly recognized the descriptions.

  The shower curtain was thrown aside, and a small, frail girl excited, wearing only underwear, her curly hair a wet steaming mess, and she covered her chest with her towels. Her face was all red and puffy. She shook her fists angrily and hollered, "Where are they?"

  Pulie knew who the little girl was looking for. Selma and Bonnie. The two girls in the corner. Unfortunately, they had already left.

  "What happened?" Pulie asked the girl in front. The room was especially warm for the heavy thick steam from the shower stalls refused to leave and dampened every bit of fresh air that entered the room occasionally.

  The girl in front spun around and explained, "Anne. The little one is Anne Truo. She has to walk up naked, you can say, up to the fifth floor where her room is. Selma and Bonny are the ones who steal her clothes."

  "This is the only girl's bathroom in the Zive?" Pulie choked on her spit.

  "Unless you want to use the haunted bathroom all by yourself when the lights don't work, then yes." She squinted as if Pulie should've known before.

  "Oh." Pulie began feeling pity for the little Anne; she knew the pain in being attacked in such a palace of thieves and pirates.

  As the distressed girl passed her, Pulie stretched out her arm and tapped her on the shoulder.

  "Do you want to use mine?"

Anne stared at her with her deep blue eyes. She looked exactly like Goldilocks. Her response was a bit startling. "Do you work for Selma?"

Pulie stepped back. She realized that no one trusted anyone at this school. Especially strangers.

"Oh, no, no." Pulie shook her head, bringing out her extra pair of pajamas. "You can borrow mine because I have extras."

Anne took the clothes and inspected them. "For *real*?"

A sudden spray of water bolted from the top of one of the stalls. Pulie's legs were damp now and the entire floor was a swamp.

"Olivia!" The girls hollered, raging about their wet pajamas. Another tiny girl came out with her warm clothes on and smiled. "Sorry that was an *accident*." She high-fived Anne and left the room.

Anne shook her head. "That's my friend, Olivia. And she never creates accidents."

The little Goldilocks came up to about Pulie's shoulder so it was awkward to look down so much.

"I'm Anne, by the way. Anastasia is my real name, but no one uses that. Are you new?"

"Yes. My name is Pulie, and I came here today. Apparently, my parents enrolled me here."

Anne nodded. "Welcome."

"Anne!" A voice called, and a sweep of fresh air from the halls entered the bathroom. "I got your clothes today. See?" Nicky burst into the room, holding a pair of clothes, and froze when she saw Anne's hands.

"They didn't take it?"

"Oh no, they *did*," Anne said. "Pulie gave me hers for today."

Nicky opened her mouth to speak and frowned, although there was a hidden smile between her lips. She extended her arm and shook Pulie's hands. "Pleasure having business with you."

There were chuckles in the restroom.

"Good night, everyone!" Anne cried as Nicky walked out of the restroom to help Anne go back to her room.

"*Good night, Anne Truo.*" Everyone in the showers called in unison. Then they resumed their actions.

Suddenly, all the girls in front of her in the line ducked, and Pulie followed.

A bucket came flying from the corner of the bathroom. It whizzed by her hair and Pulie could feel the wind rushing past her. A girl three spots behind her hence received a smack in the face with the metal pan.

Slipping on her flip-flops, Pulie got into the shower stall when it was her turn, and to her surprise, found a large hairy black spider the size of her ear. She kicked and kicked, and her body dampened with sweat. Her eyes bulged at the sight of the enormous arachnid.

Finally, feeling the voice to scream, she let out a yelp and received chuckles outside her curtain.

This is not funny. Pulie thought, nearly choking in tears, trying not to breathe the same air the spider was intoxicating. But then, when she bent down, she saw a tag—a tag on the spider. Because the spider was rubber, someone had placed a rubber toy spider in her stall, just like Piden had done *years* ago.

Although she grew distraught, she pondered why Anne had never reported her situation to the leaders, like Mr. Wace. Surely he would put an end to it. Was it hard to explain? Or was it because this was an entirely different place. And these were not ordinary people. Thus no normal rules existed. So, if Pulie desired to figure out where her parents were, she would have to follow these rules; she would have to adapt.

The spider was tossed outside the stall, and after Pulie turned the shower off and dried herself with a towel, she glanced at the drain. The *glue* was all she could think of. Immediately, she rummaged through her bag, hoping she had not taken it out. And at last, she clasped her prize object in her fingers. She bent down with caution and poured high-quality sticky paste around the rims of the drain.

After changing, she opened the curtains, and a nice breeze of refreshing air filled her nostrils. The next girl walked in so fast, so Pulie could barely see her face. And when Pulie reached the exit of the shower room, she heard a ridiculous yelp, and the entire room burst into laughter. The shout had come from her shower stall. Her plan had been successful.

I guess it won't be that hard to fit in here, after all.

She stood in the main hall, waiting for Piden, snug in her warm pajamas, with a smile of satisfaction on her face. But the clock read eight twenty-five. And Mr. Wace was not a patient man. *Come on, Piden. You shower like a girl.* When two more minutes passed, she decided to go on her own.

She stood at the door of the Miralmalma. The trunk was bronze and the color of cinnamon with the wide eight branches and the Zives dangling from the tips. It was really all quite beautiful.

The door slammed behind her and pushed her into a circular room. To her left was an opening to a long spiral set of the staircase up to the top. But surely this was not the only way up. The light from the Miralmalma's main room shone down from an opening onto the center of the room. And certainly, the opening wasn't just to let light through.

Her instinct forced her to the center of the circular room and onwards. She felt the smooth bronze walls that curved all the way around with her fingers until there was a stud. Letters were engraved on the wall so tiny that Pulie had to squint to read them. *Ladder descending. Slide to activate.*

"*Slide*—" Pulie said aloud to herself. "And everything here works with the earring—" Pulie bent over and slid her earring across the words.

Then, a buzzing sound hummed, and from the very very top, a white ladder was lowered to the floor.

There really isn't any other option. She looked around. And besides, Nicky and Ema never explained about the Miralmalma.

She took a step forward into the circle light above her head. She set her foot on the ladder with a *clink* and her hand on the sides with a *push*. And then she was off. She began to climb as she had done at home. She would climb all the way up to the ceiling... like a little spider.

She went up and up and up very quickly. The walls were dark, and she couldn't see anything except the halo of the bright light above her.

Finally, she reached the top and pulled herself out of the hole and into the hushed room with all sorts of extravagant decorations in every direction; large paintings, little bowls of spices, a boar's head hanging to her right, and strange glass cased tubes of plants arranged in a line to her left. The ground was a maroon-colored carpet and a vast window stretched across the entire curved wall to her right. She ran to the window, pressing her nose against the glass.

She was in the *Miralmalma*. The view was so different from the one below on the courtyard. Everything seemed so small below.

On the other side of the room were ten identical doors; the last one had Mr. Wace's name engraved at the top. And Pulie knocked.

"Who is it?" Mr. Wace emerged. "Oh, Pulie, come in. We were waiting for you." He motioned her inside.

"Waiting for me?" Pulie said, confused.

Piden was *already* sitting on the couch, and Mr. Wace settled in on his armchair. The bed was folded cleanly, the closet organized, and the tables wiped. Not a speck of dust layout of the place.

"We have come here to talk, haven't we?" Mr. Wace said. "And I will assure you we will many more times."

Pulie smoothed the chair before sitting on it.

"We are going to discuss the matter regarding the whole situation. Although it wasn't very smooth in the beginning, it will be better. Most cases, in fact, every other case, the parents enroll and drop off their children on their first day at Level one or most of the time in the Punke classes." He sipped some more of his coffee. "But for you two, it's quite different. Pulie, for instance, is beginning at this palace at Level Two. I have placed you at this level, not only because this is your age group but also because you know how to read and write."

"How did you know?" Piden asked.

"You read the newspaper, and you were able to speak with correct grammar and fluency. Our program trains students from ages 12 through 19, no younger and no older is allowed, due to the missions and the physical capability rules of the Trickies Foundation. Luckily, you are both in that age span, I suppose?"

"Uh-huh."

"Everyone starts at the Punke level to learn how to read and write during those years, and when you start the actual levels of the Trickies, you practice other tasks, not academically. This means it isn't necessary to place you in the Punke level or in an age group the same as her brother, Pulie. That is why you are in level two. As for you, Piden, you are at the first level, which isn't as big of a jump as your sister. Nevertheless, this will be an extremely difficult academy for you, especially because you have never been exposed to such an environment.

"Well then, the first question, do you want to attend this academy palace? At all? This is a training program for children of all ages. Here, you will not learn mathematics or chemistry here but instead such spying methods and the revolution of darts. Make your decisions. In all honesty, do you wish to attend the Trickies Palace?"

"Well, if our parents wanted us to stay here, might as well," Pulie responded.

"Is that a yes for you too, Piden?"

Piden's bangs flapped up and down.

Mr. Wace smiled. "Very well, are you staying in a room here or using daily transportation to go back home every day."

There was silence.

"When you go back home, we have drivers, and you don't have to walk." Mr. Wace assured them, "But most students prefer here. What is your choice?"

Now, this was a bit hard to choose. She still had to contact her parents, right? But if her parents were in the same league as Mr. Wace, was everything under control like he said?

"I like my room with Alex." Piden chirped.

"And Pulie?" Mr. Wace questioned.

"I like my room too." Pulie lied. She hated the thought of rooming with Nicky.

"Good. No one goes back home every day anyways. It's much easier to stay here." Hence, Mr. Wace went to his desk and scrolled through the device he pulled out and displayed a screen.

"The rules state that if at any circumstance you are injured under the hands of Trickies Palace, it is not our matter to be concerned about. This section—" His finger slid to the bottom. "discusses the safety in your parents' hands, although our medical program fixes and medicates the students. And—" His eyes drifted up to the top of the screen. "—you can just read through the rules," Mr. Wace said, sitting back in his chair for Pulie and Piden to read and sign the screen.

"Thank you very much," Mr. Wace said as he saved the files. "I will settle everything else, including the confusion earlier, so do not worry. Any questions?" Mr. Wace stood up, smoothing his clothes.

"Yes, I do have a question," Pulie answered. "I've been wondering for a long time. When we first saw you, why did you find the hat on the floor so interesting?"

"Oh yeah." Piden nodded. "It's just a hat, sir."

"Ahhh, clever children." Mr. Wace scratched his head. "That was an obvious prank I had fallen for. Rarely do I fall for tricks of any kind. You two wouldn't know, but particular top hats are prized messages."

"Messages?" Piden asked. "What for?"

"Spies slip tiny pieces of information all around and inside the hat. Since the hat is black and dark inside, spies have gotten accustomed to using the hole more often. They lend hats, and the messages are inside. Of course, this is not what the Trickies do, nor the Oddies. However, our enemy, the CAOT, has used this trick more than enough. I thought I had found one at last.

"It was a good laugh afterward. But, get up now. You have school tomorrow. Curfew at nine-thirty!" He hollered after them before they shut the door.

And when the clock struck nine-thirty, a quiet chime rang throughout the school, just as Pulie had finished sorting out her clothes. Ema ran to the window, and Pulie followed. She pressed her face against the large curved glass window and her vision was illuminated with the millions of other golden Zive windows lighting up the midnight darkness.

"This—" Ema whispered, her breath fogging up the glass. "This is the moment I've been waiting for all spring break."

The view was dazzling, like butterscotch fireworks exploding from every corner of the air, blinding Pulie's eyes. And when the excitement settled down, Pulie reached for her hammock and, using all her strength, heaved herself up onto the wobbly hammock, swaying at a steady pace and dizzying at first. Then Ema climbed in and so did Nicky after she turned off the light.

It was dark in the room. It was quiet too; an odd silence ruled the room as if everyone had already fallen asleep.

A few minutes later, another chime rang and echoed through the halls and rooms like a whisper.

"We're supposed to be sleeping now," a voice mumbled. Pulie perked up and shut her eyes right away.

When Pulie opened an eye, both Nicky and Ema were sitting up in their hammocks, swaying and chuckling.

"What—What are you doing?" Pulie asked, sitting up as well. "The curfew—"

"Nobody follows those rules," Nicky said flatly. "Get dressed."

"What?" Pulie made a face. "But Mr. Wace—we got to sleep—"

Ema wiggled her finger. "No, no. Nighttime is when all of the palace's students have their free time."

"But what about during the day? You have so much time to—"

"But we're on surveillance," Nicky said. "At night, teachers are off duty." Nicky tossed a tiny hexagonal bud gadget to both

Pulie and Ema and one for herself. They all caught it and slapped it on their wrist.

"At night, this place seriously lacks supervision." Ema pulled on a sweater. "If you just stay quiet, you can do whatever you want. But if we mess up, we might expose every single student on campus. The only rules you have to watch out for are, no killing, breaking, smoking, snitching—"

"Snitching?" Pulie asked.

"Don't tattle at this palace," Nicky answered. "No teacher will listen and you'll be the only one in danger. People *despise* snitches."

Pulie swallowed. So many rules to break and follow.

Ema seemed to notice this thought. "No worries, Pulie. I'm sure you'll get the hang of it. Someone already told me a dozen girls got their feet stuck in the showers with glue. They said it was the new girl."

Nicky's eyes grew wide. "You? Even Celena was talking to me about it."

Pulie nodded. "Yes. That was me."

"Alright, then. Let's go now."

MOTO

Clad in dark smooth leggings and a black cap, Pulie studied the hexagonal gadget she was given; a camera and flashlight all in one. One of Nicky's relatives had invented it.

They crept out of their room, locking it with the earrings. They weren't the only ones. Many silent shadows lurked about, up and down the halls.

Once reaching the first floor, they sped down the vines and took refuge under the lollipop stand, where Miss Ellie worked in the daylight. Nicky scanned the courtyard for teachers and then waited for students from each Zive to follow. It was pitch black, except for the light shining through the Miralmalma's glass opening in the foggy mist.

"Coast clear," Celena whispered as she joined them. Slowly, the people began to move around and find new locations to hide in.

Pulie caught sight of the closed and dimmed windows of Larry's house. She made her way there and pressed her face against the windows, admiring the candy through the glass. Suddenly, she saw a figure in the corner of her eye, spreading its arms and crouching on the floor. She froze. She couldn't see much, but the whites in the eyes glinted from behind the glass until the figure stepped out into a brighter space.

It was a boy with hair the color of night and his skin as pale as snow. She could not see the exact outlines of his face. So she retreated to the center of the courtyard to her roommates and Celena.

The courtyard had transformed into an area for all the students to gather under the shadows while all the teachers were up in the Miralmalma. All the whispers and quiet laughing created a more crowded sense in the courtyard.

"There—"

"Shhh." Nicky put a finger to her lips before Pulie could finish. "The teachers might hear us from the Miralmalma."

Pulie nodded. "I saw a person over there."

"Of course. Tons of people hang out at night. Colin and Dan are at the gym right now, but—oh no," Nicky said softly, wincing. Pulie followed her gaze.

A girl was walking towards them. Skipping. "Hello, all." She caught sight of Pulie, and her eyes narrowed slightly for some reason. Celena quickly escaped to another group of people.

"Moto, this is Pulie. Pulie, this is Moto," Ema introduced.

"Hello, nice to meet you," Pulie said, smiling slightly.

Moto had black wavy hair, huge eyelids, sagging over her eyes, and thick pink glasses covered her chubby face. One thing that stood out bright even in the darkness was her bright pink neon lacy socks piled up at her ankles.

"How old are you?" Moto asked.

What kind of greeting is that?

"I'm fifteen," Pulie responded.

Moto shook her head. "A year late. School starts tomorrow."

"I'm aware. But why do we start school in the summer?"

Nicky was about to speak when Moto interrupted, "The reason is that we end school in the spring, so we start in the summer. How do people get confused?"

"Well—"

"It's not that hard."

Nicky insisted they go to the shop in the middle of the conversation. It was a blatant attempt to ease away from Moto, but the girl simply tagged along.

When they were midway in the courtyard on their way to the shop, suddenly, the busy jittery area dropped dead silent. Frantic whispers arose, and everyone around them sprinted and dove for the nearest refuge.

"Oh no," Ema whispered. Nicky muttered something as well.

"Run, idiots, don't just stand there!" Moto snarled. They all hastened to sprint towards Larry's house and waited behind the brick walls.

In the evening mist, one could only hear the sharp clicks of the black heels striding down the courtyard, full of shadows of shivering and frightened children. Two women, hand in hand, strode through. One had darker skin, big lips, and large eyes. She was an extremely tall twig whose neck seemed stretched out too long. On the other hand, the other woman had brown hair up to her stomach with odd bangs, a pink plaid dress, and was shorter. Ms. Awolo and Ms. Borthwick.

From the front, Pulie could hear the thumping of hearts from Nicky and Ema. The courtyard was silent. Pulie was so frightened; she didn't even know she was holding Moto's hand. Never had Pulie's breath felt so heavy and hard. It was like she was stuck in the shower room again.

Something tapped her shoulder. Pulie knew who it was already.

"What?" Pulie whispered.

When she didn't get an answer, she turned around and saw Moto tilting her head back, and her arm bent in preparation.

"No. Moto, you can't—" Pulie clamped her hand under Moto's nose, preventing the sneeze from occurring. Moto nodded and wiped her nose with her sleeve. Everyone smiled in relief and turned back to keep an eye on the two leaders of the school.

Then, Moto spoke again. "Pulie—"

But before Pulie could spin around, she heard the repulsive sneeze crack, and it echoed like a squealing trombone across the courtyard.

Nicky slapped her hand on her forehead.

"Sorry," Moto squealed, blowing her nose.

Pulie cried in fright. "Please, Moto. Don't make any more noise—"

"Who was that?" An elderly voice barked. "Show yourself!"

Moto began to whimper. "I sneeze when I'm nervous—"

Nicky snarled, "Don't make it any worse than it is."

Surprisingly, Moto stayed silent for a while.

So when the two women walked towards the spot they were hiding, the four crept back out to the middle of the courtyard. When Ms. Awolo and Borthwick walked out to the courtyard, the students were right around the corner. This continued until the teachers finally decided to split up and corner. Now was the chance.

"Cover your face," Nicky said. A few seconds later, the keyword was said. "*Run.*"

And run they did, sprinting like they had never done before. And all at once, everyone in the courtyard began sprinting in all directions to the zives. A mass diaspora of shadows circled the two women as they tripped about on their heels. Meanwhile, Pulie and her friends safely made it all the way to the shop.

"There's a million of them! Where'd they all go?" hollered Ms. Borthwick.

Ms. Awolo shrugged. "Don't ask me. They got away with it this time, but next time, it won't be that easy. We should come down more often and catch those slippery eels by the ears."

"Eels don't have ears," Ms. Borthwick reminded.

"Well, then I'll stick 'em on if I have to. They'll all pay for it later. Come on. There's a Council Meeting at twelve in the Eating Room."

So, the four were safe for now. After the two leaders disappeared underground, Pulie opened the door to the shop and ushered the three in.

"We made it," Ema cried in relief. Pulie collapsed on a cardboard box.

"We *certainly* did." Nicky glared at Moto.

"Well, I'm going to bed now," Moto huffed. "And I don't even care if you miss me." And with that, the door slammed.

"We won't!" Nicky hollered. "That was close."

"Too close," Ema muttered. "I knew Moto was going to cause trouble."

"We all did." Nicky knelt behind the shelf to avoid the cameras. "Ms. Awolo said we're gonna pay for it. We're done for. Only the first day of school, and she's going to punish us all."

"What punishment?" Pulie asked.

Nicky told her there were too many types of punishments to count. "It depends on what you do," Nicky said. "There was a time last year where a boy shut off all the electricity in Zive four, but Ms. Awolo made the entire school pay for it. She tied every single one of our legs together with strings and made us move around like that. Once she found the boy, she took him to her office and most likely lashed him."

"Lashed him? Is that even allowed?"

"Of course, it is." Nicky edged closer to the food aisle. She listened for people down the next aisle and began talking again. "That's one of the nicest punishments. The worst is her discipline weapon. She has this thing where she presses the button, and a taser shoots out. Your body freezes up, and it hurts—so much. It won't kill you though, that's why she's allowed to use it. But it *hurts*."

"Can't you tell your parents about this stuff?" Pulie threw her hands up.

"You can't! No one cares, first of all. Second, how do you think you're gonna tell your parents?" Nicky asked.

"With letters and emails and…"

"No letters." Nicky sighed. "We can't write to anyone outside this palace during our stay. The Leaders are afraid that some messages would be sent to somewhere else if double agents or traitors are disguised as students. Then the information might be sent to the CAOT, which will lead to disaster," Nicky explained. "CAOT, by the way, is the enemy group trying to kill us—and the rest of the world," Nicky added.

"Nicky, she probably already knows who they are." Ema rolled her eyes.

Pulie shook her head. "I don't. But thank you for the explanation. Then, how can I contact my parents during their scout mission?"

"You can't."

"Don't worry. You get caught up with all the work here, you'll forget eventually."

But I won't forget. It's the reason I came here.

***

"Storage room. Finally. Bingo." Nicky's declaration was a proud banner. She pushed aside the curtain and crept inside the *Employee* only hall.

"Shhh. The working lady is in *that* room," Nicky whispered. We have to steal her key."

"We have to what—"

Nicky shoved Pulie into the hallway.

"Steal the key! Don't get caught!"

Pulie swallowed hard, trying to imagine how it was going to work. She stepped on the wooden ground, followed by a loud creak. Pulie glanced back.

"Nicky, I can't do this."

But there was no one there. Nicky and Ema had disappeared out of nowhere. They had left her to do the dirty work. So much for being roommates.

Pulie crept up to the storage room door and peered through the small circular window at the top and was able to get a clear view of the inside. On the squeaky rolling chair sat a large blond woman who was sound asleep, snores blaring. A half-finished burger lay in her lap, and a coke dripped into a large puddle on the ground. And her security computer was active and operating.

The door was unlocked, so Pulie gently pushed it and slipped through, despite the loud squeak from the hinges. But the large lady was in a deep sleep. When Pulie reached the desk, she leaned over and thumbed the shutdown button. With the screen dead, no one else in the palace would be caught by the camera.

Now, where in the world is the key? She thought. Then, like a crown jewel, she spotted the object twinkling in the light of the rusty desk lamp, dangling from the listless lady's belt. She lunged towards the bottom of the chair and gingerly unclipped the key. From below the chair, Pulie could see this strange blood-red infinity on the back of her ear. Pulie could feel the grumbling of the fat lady's stomach vibrating.

The lady didn't notice her missing key, but just in case, Pulie scrambled to the door for safety, but tripped backward on a box and hit her hand against the picture frame against the wall. An alarm rang.

The fat lady sprang up in her seat and bolted straight to the picture frame and waited till the beeping had stopped; it was all quiet again. The lady scanned the room and took the box into her hands, and left the room.

Too close. Way too close. Pulie was in the corner of the closet with the door shut. She had managed to jump in at the last minute. *Was the picture frame an alarm?* Pulie creaked open the door. No one insight. Pulie toppled out of the closet, her foot hitting another cardboard box inside the closet. Glass bottles inside the box clattered and rang.

Like a rabbit out of its burrow, she dusted herself off the dust, clutching onto her. Kneeling to the floor and bowing down, she examined her foot. There was a slight throbbing, but it was fine. Pulie turned back to the closet full of dust bunnies, and she flipped open the sides of the box to find a little bottle of olive-colored liquid with a syringe and a small metal box. Next to it was a tiny star-shaped package.

She heard the flush of a toilet and the squeak of a nearby sink. Pulie knew she had no time. And with that, she sprinted out of the room.

Pulie had expected to find Nicky and Ema with ease. She did not. She scampered all over the store, searching until she was exhausted. It was like finding a needle in a haystack.

The lights were beginning to whisper and mutter as the store started to dim.

Finally, Pulie saw the familiar shiny red hair rustling about under a shelf. And so, Pulie ambushed the prey and leaped up to tackle Ema. They both ended up cracking up, as Pulie went on, explaining what had happened.

"So, did you get the key?"

"Yes."

Pulie dug into her back pocket. She felt the small smooth sharp key rubbing against her fingertips like she was kissing the Trophy of Robbery.

Nicky popped out of the storage box, finally finding the entrance lock. Her smile widened to her ears when she saw Pulie take out the jingling shiny key.

"Not bad, new kid," Nicky chuckled, "Now, let's get down to business."

A box full of long strands of seaweed colored vines overflowed and spewed all over the floor when Nicky unlocked the large door.

The three stared at the mess.

Nicky put her hands up as if she were surrendering.

"I know what you're gonna say. But hear me out. Just scrap up the few healthy-looking vines, we'll clean up and head back. Simple."

"How are we supposed to clean this mess up?" Ema cried, pointing to the ground, an island of white shoelaces on a sea of juniper colored vines.

Nicky bit her lip. "Grab five long vines each—the fresh green ones, not the choppy brown ones. We don't have time. Any minute now, that fat lady will come out and report us. And if she reports us, Ms. Awolo will realize it was us sneaking about in the courtyard, and then she will torture us to death."

After their job was complete, the storage door was slammed shut, the lock clicked, and the keys were thrown outside the fat lady's door as it rattled against the stone floor.

Their next task was to sprint as fast as they could without being seen. However, it was difficult to run in a straight line with all the people running with her. Everyone seemed to be scrambling to get back up the Zives.

Pulie threw herself and collapsed onto the carpet.

"So, you going to tell us what all that was for?" Pulie waited for an answer from Nicky that would clarify the importance of the plants they had stolen.

"Tomorrow. For now, let's put them into the sink. Ema? Can you fill the sink with water?"

Ema obediently inundated the sink with water and sloshed the vines into the cold water. Pulie watched as they squirmed around as the water faucet poured and poured. Her eyelids felt heavy, and her vision became blurry. She rubbed her eyes. Soon, Pulie's pajamas were back on, and she plunged into her hammock bed that did not seem so uncomfortable anymore. Ema and Nicky dove in as well and pulled their covers over their heads.

The room was quiet despite the sound of rushing water pouring out from the faucet and into the bowl of squirming vines until Pulie asked,

"Is there a schedule I need to know?"

"You get them at breakfast. Your training starts at seven," Nicky replied, kicking her pillow back and forth like a soccer ball. "Have your bag ready?"

Pulie glanced at her bag, lying on the floor. "I have my gadgets, some socks, and a towel. The things you told me to put in. I don't have any pencils, though."

"We don't need pencils. We never *use* pencils. What would we use them for? Writing? On paper? We don't have those either.

Unless one of our teachers is replaced with a bizarre substitute, who might force us into any torture she wants—"

"Nicky! She gets it!" Ema cried, although laughing midway.

Pulie smiled. She stretched her arms out and snuggled into her hammock. It was warm and fuzzy.

Maybe tomorrow I'll wake up in my bed at home, Pulie thought. *Perhaps this was all a dream. But,* Pulie thought, *But maybe I don't want this to be a dream... Maybe... I want this to be real.*

Tomorrow was going to be one interesting day.

SCHOOL

"Dong... Dong... Dong... Dong!"

The bell sounded. Pulie rubbed her eyes and spotted Nicky and Ema tumbling off the hammocks and landing on the carpet floor.

It wasn't a dream. Her insides bubbled with joy. It was the first day of training. It was time for a new start.

Grabbing her new toothbrush, dressed in her new Tricky clothes, she followed Nicky and Ema out of the room to the bathroom. No one was there yet. It seemed so unusual already after seeing how crowded it got a night.

Later, they dropped their bathroom bags in their room and headed down to the courtyard. Today was the day everyone was starting school. People she had never seen before came down from the Zives and gathered around to catch sight of their schedule displayed on the screen at the lollipop stand.

"Room Twenty?" Nicky asked, eyeing the schedule screen.

Colin appeared behind them. "Zive two, room two. We're in the same rotation group, remember."

"Colin!" Nicky exclaimed. "We need to talk about—" Nicky looked right at Pulie. "Never mind."

Pulie could not help but feel her face grow red.

Tables for dinner from the day before were now arranged into long tables stretching across the rooms. Everyone was chattering in the mood of the first day of training.

Alex got in a conversation about elephants with Piden, and Ema had gone to the bathroom. Pulie was alone on the table with Nicky.

"So, what's your schedule?" Pulie asked Nicky.

Nicky was chewing on her bread. "We have the same schedules." She swallowed her piece of bread. "First, we have Wapanog in the Dome, Mr. Rodriguez for Spy class, Miss Cherry for EP, Mr. Eerie for Imitations, and Mr. Lizarstrang for RS." Nicky winced. "Celena said that Mr. Lizarstrang is tough on Level T2."

"T2?" Pulie asked.

"It means you're Level 2. The school is in levels." Nicky named all the levels. "The preparation level is Punke class. Then, it goes, Young Tricky, Junior Tricky, Tricker, Trickmo, Trickjack, and finally a Trickster."

Pulie's eyes grew wide. "Oh."

"Next year, when we're Trickers, we'll be in the *high school level*. We'll be getting so many advantages, like more competitions, free time, gadgets. Trust me, this life—" Nicky pointed at the air. "—will be street life. *Next year*, we'll be living the *high* life. I cannot wait until next year."

Ema returned to her spot while Pulie asked another question.

"Who are the teachers?"

Nicky slurped her glass of water. "Señor Rodriguez is, well, you know, the spy and gear teacher thingy. Mrs. Wapanog, the dome teacher. Ms. Cherry! She's the gym teacher, and she's so cool!

Mr. Lizarstrang is this yoga teacher. Mr. Eerie, he's like the *drama acting* teacher."

"Do any of them give homework?"

"A terrifyingly long list of daily exercises, if that's what you call homework."

Breakfast was finished in a hurry, and they strolled around the sunny courtyard before class.

Pulie cleared her throat. "Where's Moto?"

"You mean a *motto*?" Alex asked, very concerned about Pulie's pronunciation.

"She does the SDC every meal," Nicky interrupted.

"SDC?" Pulie interrupted again.

"Motto means a short phrase or sentence used to—"

"*Serving Dish Cart*," Nicky interrupted again, fidgeting with excitement as she spoke. "But we call it Zoom. It's a service where you order food, and it's delivered straight to your room. But you pay credits each time you order. Moto's parents are loaded, you know. Her father works at the High Academy of Tricksters."

***

Mrs. Wapanog. *Snarky and strict* were two words that students called her. Pulie was at the bottom of the mushroom-shaped ELSE classrooms before she climbed up the ladder to the cap of the mushroom. There was a door above her, and she pulled herself up and into the classroom. It was a regular classroom with rows of desks and a large desk at the front of the room in front of a screen. The woman at the desk had a bob cut and round glasses. Mrs. Wapanog.

When the three entered the room, Mrs. Wapanog looked up. "Why so early? Ema, not surprising, but Nicky? Is *early* even in your vocabulary?"

"It's called a New Year's Resolution, Mrs. Wapanog." Nicky grinned from ear to ear at what seemed to be a compliment.

"Keep your jokes to yourself. You won't be laughing when the second bell rings. Now, take a seat. There will be a seating chart, so stand wherever you want for the next twenty-four seconds. You'll be in a mourning state soon. And I'll have to listen to all your childish complaints."

Mrs. Wapanog continued organizing the collection of jars.

And when a chime rang, and students of all sizes and looks rumbled into the classroom. To Pulie, it was an elephant stampede, as stomping and pushing and shoving was done to get through the door. The floor seemed to tremble.

Mrs. Wapanog ushered Pulie and Ema and Nicky to stand up beside the rest.

"Everyone!" Her voice hollered, and the class silenced. "Great to see most of you again. I said *most*." And she glared back at the students. Some people gave an uneasy chuckle. Everyone seemed to stare at Colin and another dark-haired boy.

"I will call a seating chart. You must sit there for the rest of the month. Ready?" She glanced at the kids with her glasses at the tip of her nose.

"Anne Truo? Sit here. Lulu Wong? Here."

She went about listing the names and pointing to where they were assigned seats.

"Selma Dutchstill, Dash Dupupboir, Fiona March, Bonnie Johns? And then, Dunkin Boar, Ema Rafferty, Santiago Gomez, Pulie Jark, Nicky Oster, and Daniel, do you go by Dan or Daniel, again?"

"Dan, ma'am," answered the dark-haired boy, whose afro bounced up and down when he spoke.

"That's what I thought. *Daniel* Zipmore, sit right here, young man. Then Eleanor Gray, Lane Remington, Olivia Powell, Colin Strussmore, Tom Clay, and Livia Gulgorin. Orla Agatha Margery, right here... " And the Dome Lady went on barking everyone's names and forcing the children to their seats as fast as possible.

"Now listen up!" she barked. "I'm glad to see you all back now, but we have no time for introducing. I am fifty-six seconds behind schedule, and if you all get me another second behind, we're going straight to the moat and learning how to eat moss. Now, let's go right away to our lessons because Tricky Trials start a week earlier now."

In front of Mrs. Wong's desk, the light blue large holographic screen turned on, and the aspects were written for everyone to see.

"Now call out what CIIN means?" Mrs. Wapanog hollered.

"Crucial Important Items Needed," the students' voices echoed.

"Warm-up for today. *What is a Rang?*" Mrs. Wapanog scribbled on the digital screen. "The student who gets the answer correct won't have to do our annual cleaning session for two minutes."

Hands were raised in an instant as if the question were that obvious. Pulie glanced around nervously. She watched Mrs. Wapanog point up to Dan.

He answered, "They are vines that squiggle and cringe."

The class laughed. Mrs. Wapanog abhorred and almost tried to spit at his hair. Then, she shook her head sternly.

"Olivia?"

"The Trickies Foundation has biologically engineered regular organic vines into the Rang, a mutated living plant."

Dan scowled.

"Thank goodness someone didn't forget everything we learned last year. Now, let us begin our exercise. Answer the following questions." Mrs. Wapanog's screen changed the slide.

"First, if tar is stuck to some part of your body, what is the first thing you must do?"

Nicky's hand shot up, and before Mrs. Wapanog called on her, she began to speak, "You apply the special pumice stone and three drops of the Audistione Oleum. Rub it all over the skin. It'll probably be gone in about two or so minutes. And if your clothing is the one that is covered in tar, you'll simply have to forget about that. It's much more difficult, and you could just buy yourself a new pair of whatever you lost at that time. But if something valuable is stained, you shouldn't ask the person who tarred you to buy it, because that's unfair to me. And—"

"Next question!" Mrs. Wapanog clicked on the next screen. "Why should you always wear gloves while handling Rangs? Ema!"

Ema's face paled at this. She nervously fidgeted around. "Um… the Rangs might—cut and pass through into your skin because they are continuous—growing unless contained," Ema's voice trailed off.

"Correct. Good job, Miss Rafferty. Final question, tell me the main aspects of the Palace of the Trickies otherwise the palace you are in right now? Everyone say the answer out loud!"

"Spy, CIIN, Athletics, and Knowledge!" The class answered in unison.

Pulie had no idea what was going on. She felt like a coin in a well, sinking farther and farther away from the top.

The fastidious teacher opened a shelf, where their class period's materials and supplies were located. On the top shelf was a large box and a coat rack filled with suits for every student. The bottom bracket was a collection of jars and bottles.

"You have thirty seconds to come and scan your earring to *your* suit. And then, grab your ShooTers and line up. Chop, Chop!" The room was a beehive, the bees without any honey to present to their queen. "I want it now! Make sure to have extra toothbrushes by the end of the day! *Moss gets stuck in your teeth!*" Mrs. Wapanog barked from her desk. A certainly loud queen bee indeed.

Everyone was frantic when they heard the irascible teacher say the last sentence.

Soon, Pulie waited in line with a strange looking gadget, a dart launcher at the top of a bracelet wire. A button at the top was used to shoot and aim. But why would they need this?

Mrs. Wapanog snapped her fingers. "Very well then, first activity. You see that target area over there?" The old lady eyed the bull's eye and pointed. "Launch the dart at the bull's eye center."

"From here?" Dan asked, staring at the far distance from the wall to where they all stood. Pulie slipped the gadget onto her wrist like an ordinary bracelet with the dart above her hand.

"This is *impossible*." A girl named Livia groaned.

"There are other options! Moss, losing points, or what more do you want!" hollered the queen bee, and in a moment, all the students stood with their back straight, and their eyes glued to the bull's eye.

One by one, they stepped up to the marked line and aimed their dart, arms still shaking, and launched the tiny arrow forward. None of them hit the center. Watching everyone else miss made Pulie weaken inside. But she caught something. All of the darts landed to the right of the target, which meant that—Pulie glanced to her far-left and saw a fan blowing from the corner of the room, throwing all the darts off track. The fan was either for the summer heat or Mrs. Wapanog's little game.

After Ema's dart went flying into the wall a good four feet to the right away from the target, it was Pulie's turn. And she was last. But instead of stepping onto the blue tape, Pulie walked to the fan and switched it off. It was silent in the room. Then, Pulie returned to the mark and aimed with her eye, and launched the dart, almost bulls-eye.

The satisfying click of the tip of the arrow sunk into the sponge target. It was in the blink of an eye.

Mrs. Wapanog smiled; her face was glowing. "Finally!" She clapped. "Not one student could figure this out before, even from the morning classes. It's that simple. Yet none of you thought about the outside factors that might influence your execution." Mrs. Wapanog cleared her throat when the entire class had taken their seats. "None of you are skilled enough yet to shoot a dart with a fan blowing from the corner, so you must use intelligence to win the game. And, *Pulie* did that quite well. But the class as a whole, I see we have *a lot* of work to do before the Tricky Trials. You must master the skill of shooting a dart regardless of the situation. Especially because last year, so many of you complained that Zive four Level Twos weren't prepared enough."

The queen bee herself switched the fan on, stepped up to the blue tape, and flicked her wrist, shooting her own ShooTer dart. The arrow tip landed embedded perfectly in the center of the wall.

Bull's eye.

It took almost every student's breath away except for Dan.

"Bro! I couldn't do it because I don't have any muscles." He lifted his skinny arms and flapped them up and down.

The class chortled.

"*Silence.*" Ms. Wapanog interrupted the revelry as everyone got back to their seats. "Pulie, you got first place. Second, Colin, and third, Dunkin. We don't have a LeaderBoard yet, because that starts when you become a Tricker. Right now, you are still a tiny Tricky," she spat. She had a revolting habit of spitting. "The LeaderBoard, many of you don't know this, but it is one of the most important of all. It goes on applications and reports. It can get you out of trouble, and it can get you into Tricky Trials. This year, Señor, myself, Buckledoe, Miss Cherry, and Mr. Eerie have decided to make a junior LeaderBoard. It's a point contest. Top three is called the LeaderBoard, but really, each and every one of your names is written here," She said as she typed the list on the screen.

"How did Dunkin get in the top three?" Nicky sobbed. "How *bad* did I do?"

"Don't get too fuzzled up and come running to me when the class ends. The LeaderBoard *isn't* real, but we will be using this throughout your SIRE classes throughout the year. It's just *practice*," Mrs. Wapanog growled.

Nicky leaned over to whisper to Pulie. "Good job, new kid." She said with a smile. "Oh, and SIRE means Spy, Imitations, RS, and this one, which is Else. She likes acronyms."

"Talking already, Miss Oster?" Mrs. Wapanog raised a brow.

"No, Mrs. Wapanog." Nicky shook her head fast.

"Good, because I don't want another year like last year where I had to tape your mouth shut."

Dunkin and Dash burst out into laughter, simulating Nicky with a piece of tape on her mouth. Nicky's fists were curling tighter and tighter.

Ema leaned over in her seat and whispered, politely, "Nicky just received a new barrel of tar."

Those words shut them up.

"As I was saying," Mrs. Wapanog continued, "At the end of the year, all teachers will be calculating how many times you enter a LeaderBoard and who ends in the point system last. It's all the things that go up here." She swirled her fingers around her head. "Anyways, that was an activity for the LeaderBoard. When we do any activity, assume the points go towards the LeaderBoard. For trickers and levels up, the scores are posted at the Miralmalma door. However, since this is just a practice event, I will just write the scores of your Zive next to the rest of the other Zive's trickies."

"There's more than one group of trickies?" Pulie whispered.

"Yes. Each one of those dorm Zives has a rotation group of Trickies. There are four groups in total," Nicky replied, trying to speak without moving her lips.

"But today, let's start with a little bit of refreshment to our brains. Small review, what are the three key items of the Palace? Ema? You answered a question earlier. Answer this one."

"The three main aspects are water, fire, and rangs." Her face was bright pink and she shrank into her seat after she was done.

"Correct! The three main aspects are…" Mrs. Wapanog glanced back at the class after writing additional information on the screen. "Water, Fire, and Rangs. Repeat after me, students."

Pulie was paying attention, yet at the same time not. In the corner of Pulie's eyes, she eyed the cabinets and spotted a drawing on the wall. It was a spider. She closed her eyes for a moment. Spiders absolutely disgusted her. *It's only a drawing, Pulie.* And she glanced at the drawing one more time. The figure was so… so… familiar.

"These are the simplest yet most dangerous aspects. You can call rubber one minor aspect since it is not that important…"

So familiar, it feels almost alive. The spider was shaded in ink and had eight legs that stretched across the paper.

"Another example of a minor aspect is glass."

Pulie shook her head and focused on the lesson. But she needed information and fast. What if her parents were in danger?

Or what if, Pulie sighed. It was always the same conclusion. *You were sent here by your parents and not anything else.*

There was an odd silence in the room. Mrs. Wapanog had begun to dig through her desk for something.

I wonder if any of these teachers know my parents.

"Dunkin, stand up."

Pulie snapped out of her daze and looked around.

Dunkin stood up, straight and tall.

"What flavor gum do you have today?" Mrs. Wapanog glared at him.

Everyone burst out into howls.

Like a tomato, his face erupted into colors as he took off for the trash can to spit out his gum. Mrs. Wapanog had her eyes on his jaw for a while.

"We are to learn the three aspects thoroughly this year. Review and review it again until you're fed up with such talk! Like The class ends in one minute and forty seconds. Pack everything up and head to your next class."

They were outside the mushroom-shaped classroom.

"Thanks, Ema, by the way," Nicky said. "But I am *not* and will never be able to get another bucket of tar. Awolo is keeping a close eye on where my credits go."

Their next class was Señor Rodriguez. Everyone in the courtyard was buzzing like bees at work to find their classes.

"Come on! We have *Señor Rodriguez*. We *can't* be late." Nicky dragged Ema and Pulie across the courtyard to talk to Celena.

"Okay, thanks for the information, Celena. See you at the gym!" Nicky called out.

Ema shoved Nicky's shoulder, waiting for an answer to what was taking so long.

"I'll show you later what I asked for."

Then came the time to buckle up and shoot up to the Zives. The wind smacked her hair against her face. Up there, far past the walls of the palace, the sun was rising. It was a marvelous sight, and she had seen nothing like it before.

They burst through the door, assuming they were late, only realizing that they weren't.

Señor Rodriguez lolled in his uncomfortable-looking chair, smoking his cigar, humming around, as he was screwing a nail into his watch. His reading glasses sat at the ridge of his nose as he squinted through them. Nicky took a slow step, trying not to disturb him. However, her foot pressed against the chestnut carpet, making a loud creak sound as she tried to close the door again.

"Why, hello, young students!" Señor Rodriguez cried out. "For the *first* time, Nicky and Ema, not late to class. Well done."

Behind them, the class began to pile in.

"Señor Rodriguez?" Nicky hurriedly began. "Are we assigned seats? Sir, I have several reasons I should be put with my friends. First, they emotionally support me throughout the year. Second, we can all have great discussions—"

"About what, Miss Oster?" He raised an eyebrow, sipping his coffee. "I have already made a seating chart as well. So enjoy these couple of minutes of the three of you together."

Soon the chime rang and students clustered around in the classroom.

"Everybody!" Mr. Rodriguez boomed. "Line up near the Crocanic Wall of Doom."

All the students hurried over to the wall where shelves of displayed weapons of bombs, minuscular missiles, boxed gadgets, and rifles sat collecting dust.

"Lulu Wong?" Señor Rodriguez asked as a girl with black hair stepped out of the crowd. Pulie remembered her from her Dome class. Mr. Rodriguez pointed to the first desk in the corner.

"Olivia Powell and Eleanor Gray?" he pointed to a desk. A tiny girl and a tall girl stepped out of the students and headed towards their desks. Mr. Rodriguez went about listing the names as Mrs. Wapanog had done.

"Dan Zipmore? Livia Gulgorin? Dunking Boar? Colin Strussmore? Anne Truo? Santiago, where's my little nephew?"

Mr. Rodriguez said as he nudged Santiago on the head. Then, Mr. Rodriguez continued to call out names, "Nicky Oster, Pulie Jark, and Ema Rafferty? Your welcome, kiddos."

They were all sitting next to each other.

"Selma Dutchstill, Fiona March, Bonnie Johns?"

Pulie immediately recognized Selma and Bonnie from the bathroom. In the corner of her eyes, she could see Anne instantly stop talking to Lulu and begin glaring at her adversities.

Bonnie waddled around Selma, trying to follow her. Fiona was the girl Pulie had never seen before. She was very thin, with short-cropped blond and pink hair and thick eyelashes. Selma's group looked like the type of people Pulie didn't want to get to know. Unfortunately, that wasn't the case. Right as Selma passed Pulie's desk, the snob face tipped over Pulie's chair and sent Pulie on her back with the chair knocked to the side while Señor Rodriguez was searching for something in the closet.

"Oops, my mistake. Why, isn't it the new kid?" Selma snickered. Fiona and Bonnie chuckled from behind.

"Just because you didn't fail one task in Else, doesn't mean you belong here." Selma shook her head. "So let's see who's behind… "

Pulie's face grew red as she got up from the floor.

Nicky simply snorted from behind. "Let's see who's behind?" And then she snorted again. "All I see is your rear, Selma!"

"Nicky Oster, quiet please." Señor Rodriguez hushed.

Pulie smiled, trying to contain her laughter inside.

Selma's face had gotten bright pink, matching her skirt, as she marched off with the fat bodyguard, wobbling after her.

After she had left, Nicky and Pulie cracked up.

"Excuse me, ladies? Do I have to separate you three already? Nicky? I don't want to send you to the Miralmalma on the first day. I have many seats left."

Mr. Rodriguez was behind them, tapping his foot and touching his mustache.

"No, I think I am fine where I am." Nicky's smile disappeared.

Pulie pushed her chair back up and sat on her desk. Mr. Rodriguez returned to his desk and sat in his chair, folding his arms and staring calmly at the class.

The people who were once talking stopped talking. The people who were once laughing stopped laughing. The people who were once running around, stopped running around. Every single student stopped and sat at their desks, ready for the lesson. When the whole class was settled, Mr. Rodriguez stood up, clicking his boots on the floor. Then, he jumped up and grabbed onto the bar hanging from the ceiling. He pulled himself up and sat there.

Everyone was amazed. Pulie was in awe. Her eyes widened. *The teacher just did a flip in the air.* Then, the teacher jumped off the bar.

The class was gasping and shrieking as Mr. Rodriguez came soaring through the air. Pulie shut her eyes as tight as she could, plugging her ears.

Only, she never heard a single plunk. She peeked open and saw Mr. Rodriguez was upside down on another bar that had come down to catch him.

"Welcome to SPY class!" he roared.

Everyone stood up, clapped, and whistled. He flipped off and came down onto the floor with ease and announced, "Today's class, we shall go on an adventure! Line up at the door."

They were outside on the main floor. Mr. Rodriguez finally found a bench and ushered everyone to sit down. Selma, Fiona, and Bonnie scooted over the closest to Mr. Rodriguez.

"Settle down, and no, we aren't going to be doing anything like I did today. Last year, we learned about how we operate with gears. This year is Level 2. Everyone here is a Tricky, correct?" the teacher questioned.

Selma's hand swooped up in the air, "No, sir. Not everyone is *full* Tricky." She glanced at Pulie. Selma's eyebrows were hunched, and she stuck her tongue out between her thick red lips.

I don't even know you.

"Yes, maybe it's possible," Señor Rodriguez uttered. "But in this class, *no*. Everyone here is a full Tricky."

Selma frowned and sat back in her spot.

"And Tricky or not, everyone around you is here to help. That's the point of this class. We help *each other*." He cleared his throat. "In this class, we do everything from spying on Mrs. Wapanog to sneaking through the labs and running around outside the palace. Now, where was I? Today, we'll learn to spy, does anybody know how to spy?"

Ema's hand shot up into the air.

"Yes?"

"It's to watch over something, while the object doesn't know that they are being observed."

"Yes, and Pulie? You were not a student here last year. Do you know what a spy is?'

"Yes, Señor. I saw Spy Kids and like movies and stuff."

The people in the back burst out laughing.

Pulie bit her lip.

"Ah, yes, movies," Señor chuckled. "How about real life? Have you ever spied on someone?"

Selma's hand soared through the air, but Mr. Rodriguez signaled her to put it back down.

Pulie remembered that Piden and herself had always spied on the villagers, but she didn't feel like sharing any incidents. Dark thoughts arose throughout her head.

"No, sir."

It was like she had done something wrong in her past life when she heard the courtyard drop silent. But Señor waved it away and took them straight to the back of Larry's house. They stopped outside the back door.

Señor glanced around the house and peered through the back window. He tried the keys first, and it unlocked. He smiled.

"Today, we start off fun. No studying gears and videos, but we're going to try to break in and steal a pillow without Larry noticing. That is your mission. Do not steal anything else, and *do not* fiddle with computers and glass. It's just a pillow, the easiest of the steal system. Larry has no idea that we are sneaking in. If any of you mess with anything inside, you are immediately out of my class. Forever. No excuses. Or, if you are caught by Larry trying to steal a pillow, then you will receive a lecture, a deduction of points, and an additional hour in the gym. Groups of two or three. Line up, once you have your groups."

Pulie scanned the room, hoping that someone would ask her to be a part of their group. And someone did. Ema and Nicky and Pulie linked arms and marched to the entrance. Señor took a peek inside the storage room for a minute or two and then came out saying the coast was clear. Then, he let them in through the back door.

The storage room was dark and damp.

"I can't see anything. Where are you? What is this?" Pulie felt a stubby item in front of her.

"Uh, Pulie? That's my nose?" a voice squeaked.

"Sorry, who are you?"

"It's Ema. Guys, I found the door. Where's Nicky?"

"*I wonder where?*"

Suddenly, from behind them, a bright light turned on behind them and a pale face appeared.

"What? How'd you find a flashlight in the dark?" Ema pushed the object out of Nicky's hands.

"Celena told me this morning that during her second year, everyone went to the eating room tunnels, and it was super dark. Strangely, this year we're at Larry's house, but I still brought a flashlight."

They tripped and fell on the ground with not an inch of spare space.

"I can't see my hands," Pulie squeaked. "Turn the light back on."

Nicky grinned as she played a game of continuously flipping the flashlight on and off. Pulie could now see what she had tripped on. It was the large maroon rug covering half of the storage room floor. Pulie guessed that there were a lot of dead mice and collections of dust underneath the carpet because it was full of lumps.

Then suddenly, they hear a loud groan.

"Hide!" Nicky whispered, switching off the light. Pulie felt a doorknob of an empty closet and jumped inside.
They waited in painful darkness.

Shortly after, "Coast clear," whispered Ema. "Let's try not to get caught, though."

"Yes, but we don't have time! We need to win! Points! Leaderboard!" Nicky rattled like a snake in the dark.

"How about starting with turning the light back on?"

The light appeared again, and they found out the door to Larry's room. There was a tiny space between the door and the wall next to it. If they made some kind of noise in the storage room, Larry would most likely enter the room to check on it. Then, they could slip out behind him, grab a pillow, and flee for their lives.

Pulie was assigned the noisemaker, of course. She made her way to the nearest shelf and felt for any hard or metal objects. She wasn't supposed to touch anything. But if she could find what she was looking for, no one would ever notice. She felt the curve of a handle and the bottom ring. She had found it. A bell. A little metal bell. She crept into the closet next to the door and rang the bell three times. No one moved. Pulie peeked outside to check on Ema and Nicky. They were still there, two shadows waiting for the cue. Pulie ran the bell one more time.

Feet were shuffling, the shove of a box, and then a plunk. Then footsteps approaching the storage room door where Ema and Nicky hid to the left and Pulie to the right in the closet. Light flooded the darkroom, and the little man's shadow began to grow as he stepped forward. Pulie held her breath as she watched Nicky and Ema slip behind him and into the main room. Finally. Now all they needed to do was find a pillow and leave the front door. And all Pulie needed to do was not get caught.

Larry kicked at the boxes on the floor, humming the tune of a funny song. He had clearly entered the storage room to find out what the ring was, but he had forgotten already.

He left after a few seconds. Pulie was still in the closet. She creaked open the door a bit more. It was dark again. She dropped the bell in the closet, and the ring echoed. She heard Larry shuffling around outside, and her heart stopped. She was taking too long. She waited a few more seconds then bent down to pick up the bell. Her finger hit a tiny flat circle indent in the wood. Pulie squinted, although she could not see anything. So she pressed the circle. All of a sudden, the bottom of the closet below her unfolded and opened.

Thump! She landed straight on her feet, a shock spiking up her knee. The bell flew out of her hand, and it rang as it bounced down the metal hall and into the darkness. Meanwhile, Pulie was frozen like a sculpture in her position. What—had just happened? It took a few minutes for Pulie to realize that she had fallen down a closet trap door. And she landed, in the sewers? No, it couldn't be. But the musty smell of urine and old waste and the faint dripping of water confirmed her idea. She was in the sewers.

One thing she knew for sure was that Nicky and Ema were going to kill her. Mostly Nicky.

Pulie paced around at the bottom of the sewers, biting her lip. Surely Nicky and Ema had gotten the pillow and were out of the house already. She needed to get out of there.

If a button had gotten her down, would a button get her up? Pulie felt the ground for circles or indents. None. She felt the walls around her even though her fingers began to grow slimy and grimy. None. There was nothing—no nothing to help her get up.

This is just another prank, Pulie assured herself. Just another joke that the students created. There was a way back to the palace. She couldn't stay down here forever.

She paced some more, thinking, exhausting her brains with ideas or ways that might get her out. So far, she had learned that this place had no limits to what secrets lay in the air. If she could just think—Wait, she moved her fingers towards her earring and squeezed it hard. Everything worked with an earring here. Would it work?

And to her surprise, it did! The ground she was on began to elevate and ascend up the abyss she had fallen into and up and up until the bottom of the closet was right at her forehead. She pushed through and pulled herself up, collapsing and panting heavily. She was safe. Thank god.

Pulie was able to leave the room by the back door again, and she bumped into Ema on the way with a pillow in her hands. Nicky appeared shortly after, explaining that they had gotten stuck behind the couch because Larry had reentered the main room so quickly. Pulie didn't bother mentioning the closet trap door.

"Ema, Nicky, and Pulie." Señor Rodriguez smiled as he saw the pillow, then glanced at his timer. " Impressive. Mission accomplished in four minutes and fifty-nine seconds. How did you do it so fast?"

Pulie couldn't believe it either. The time she had spent in the sewers felt like hours.

She waited for the rest of the class to finish up their rounds. Señor Rodriguez continued time after time, sending kids in through the obstacle. At the end of the course, Mr. Rodriguez gathered the students and announced,

"Great job to all of you. You all succeeded in *not getting caught*," he chuckled. "All points go to the junior LeaderBoard. The winners of today's mission are…"

Everyone crossed their fingers.

"Santiago, Colin, and Dan. "

Nicky let out a heavy sigh as she watched in disappointment how the boys began to jump into the air and punch the sky. "It's only a game. They're so crazy about some game," muttered Nicky. "Especially, Dan. He's blowing kisses."

"*And*, Nicky, Ema, and Pulie!" Señor Rodriguez added. "Those two groups tied at *exactly* four minutes and fifty-nine seconds. Extra points to those people. Now, let's go back to our room, and you can head on to, which class is it? Miss Cherry? Grab your bags! Cheerio!" Señor Rodriguez hollered as he disappeared back into the back door of Larry's house.

"Nicky, Ema, and Pulie *won*! We won!" Nicky danced around the pile of pillows, erupting into happiness.

Bonnie clapped her hands, smiling until Selma slapped her arm. The clapping ceased and Fiona rolled her eyes.

Nicky began to blow kisses back to Dan who was on the other side of the pillows, bowing and saluting. Everyone laughed. Pulie laughed too, especially because of Nicky's funny spirit.

MISS CHERRY

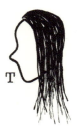

T Their next class was in the classroom zives, next to the right side of the hall, while the apparent gym was the tall door on the left. The gym was also called the cluster gym because it was a collection of many work out areas.

The main room was a vast wide space with shiny floors with intricate and curved long line marks. The ceiling above swarmed with metal bars, vines, loops, and obstacle courses hanging upside down. Pulie was in awe, her mouth hanging open with amazement. She joined the others on the silver bleachers on the other side of the room, sitting beside Nicky and Ema, and waited for their teacher. Everyone waited and waited and waited.

Finally, a slender woman clad in black glided down the steps of the left staircase. In between her arms was a digital clipboard while a stopwatch dangled from the side pockets of her leggings. Her night colored hair flowed down to her shoulders like water.

"Good morning, everyone," she said in a hushed voice. She was a beautiful woman, at least that's what Pulie believed, and she knew quite well that the rest of the class thought so too. But strange enough, her coral lipstick and her rosy blush seemed to disappear like melting ice behind the blue in Miss Cherry's face. Not that she was actually—blue. Yet, her large eyes seemed to cry when they were dry, and a smile to her face seemed to exhaust her.

Nonetheless, the class sweetly chimed back, "Good morning, Miss Cherry."

"Yes, yes. Welcome to another year of EP. As many of you know, my name is Miss Cherry. I am going to check for *miserableness*."

She certainly sounded miserable, too. And apparently, miserableness to Miss Cherry was known to other people as attendance. After she had finished calling out all the names, she set her clipboard aside and commanded all fifty students to run laps on the gym floor.

"How many times?" the kids asked in unison.

"Nineteen would be nice. But twenty would be even better. Twenty. Yes, that is a splendid number. Let's do twenty laps."

"But, Miss Cherry, we don't even have our EP clothes. They come today at lunch!" one girl shouted.

"Oh, what a pity." Ms. Cherry looked, sincerely sorry. "I guess you'll have to wash those clothes after this class."

No one could resist or retaliate against her.

"Marvelous effort to all of you," Miss Cherry remarked after the students collapsed onto the shiny floor in exhaustion. All Pulie would see was sweat and stars. Her new clothes were drenched; the air smelled of a stench so putrid to even think of.

Miss Cherry slid into the splits. "Now, we shall begin class."

"*Begin* class?"

"Today—" She sighed. "Today shall be easy, pumpkins. Just stretching."

Nicky sighed with relief. "Oh, thank goodness. If she made us do another cardio workout, I was gonna throw up. Last year, when she made us do those flipping bar pull-ups, I was gonna puke. I was only able to do fourteen, and I collapsed. It was quite —"

"Nicky, we don't stretch with our mouths," Miss Cherry noted as she twisted her leg over her arm in a swift way.

The bell rang.

The next minute, Pulie, Colin, Piden, Nicky, Dan, Alex, and Ema were at the table, licking their plates clean.

"Is it just me, or does Miss Cherry seem very sad?" Pulie asked, wiping her mouth.

Colin shook his head. "She's always been like that. For as long as everyone's known her. They say she's got—depression."

Pulie raised her eyebrows. "That's quite a guess."

"No, it's widely known. No one knows why she's like that," said Nicky.

Alex wiped his mouth and cleared his throat. "Her mother was diagnosed with Alzheimer's one year ago."

"What does that have to do with anything?" Nicky asked.

"Everything. Family impacts our lives greatly."

"He's right. There must've been something in her family to make her life hard. It's not normal. She seldom laughs or smiles.."

"She's like that character in Moose Boost, the one who's always mopey," Piden added. "Remember, Pulie?"

"Yes."

"What's Moose Boost?" Dan asked.

"You don't know what Moose Boost is?" Pulie exclaimed. "That's crazy."

"Is there television here?" Piden asked.

Ema shook her head. "Nope. Not that I know of. Too much hacking and illegal communication in the past. Although our teachers occasionally show videos of some sort. Television is regarded as a brainwasher here."

Pulie widened her eyes. "That's unfortunate. You *have* to watch *Moose Boost!*" Pulie swiped her arms around and imitated the commercial.

Piden turned to the rest of them. "She's in *love* with that show."

Pulie turned bright pink. "No, I'm not. I simply prefer it above all the other shows. And that's not the point. I watched the last episode last week, and a *new villain* came out, and I was angry because they replaced the old character."

"Ahem—" A teenage boy stepped up to their table. "*Clothes.*" He pulled out seven pairs of EP clothes and tossed them on top of the dirty plates.

"Erik!" Nicky picked up each outfit one at a time. "No, no, no. Our clothes are stained in marinara! You know we only get one pair till Tricky Trials!"

"C'mon Erik." Dan ran his fingers over the plates. "You know there was a lot of space over there." He pointed to the table.

"Yeah. Why over here?" Nicky cried.

"You should've cleared your plates like a good girl then," huffed the *Erik* before he stormed to the tables nearby to pass out more clothes.

"Oh, dear." Ema sighed. "My pants are red." She held up her white leggings smothered in sauces and pickle juice.

"He can't get away with this." Nicky furiously shook her fist. "*Clothes?* No, he will never get away with clothes. *Never.*" She blew her hair out of her face and sat glumly in her chair.

A melancholy wind replaced the lively atmosphere. Attempting to change the topic, Pulie continued about the villain on *Moose Boost*. "Anyway, that villain. One dreadful man—hasn't got a brain in him, revolting black hair and a crooked nose. A scoundrel is what I'd call him. He's like the type of person to think he's good at everything and he just ends up burning—"

Pulie halted when everyone in her table stopped talking. She felt hard breathing coming down on her head. Nicky and Ema sat like frozen gnomes in their seats. Slowly, Pulie turned her head to see who it was.

The Erik boy.

Standing behind her, shaking his fists, he grabbed Pulie's shirt and lifted her up, feet dangling in the air. She had no idea how he did this.

"What did you just say about me?" His breath smelled foul. She was an ant squirming beside an elephant. An enormous smelly elephant.

"Erik, you put her down." Pulie heard Nicky clearing her throat.

"Come on, Erik. Seriously?" Colin groaned.

"Answer! What did you say?" Erik barked at Pulie, not even glancing at Nicky or Colin. The room had now tuned down, such a deep silence, that Pulie heard eyeballs in the room twitching. There, Pulie and Erik were. A giant choking a small child to death. Soon Ema and Piden were hollering with their fists in their air. "Stop, you blockhead!"

"Answer, or you die," he gargled, his grip tightened, and Pulie's eyes watered a bucket before soaking into her shirt.

"Hey! Put her down! You don't even know who you're holding."

"Yeah, I didn't say a *thing* about you— I don't even know you—" Pulie snarled, trying her best to sound fierce, but nothing more than a squeak was produced.

"Put her down!" Nicky hollered, narrowing her eyes. But through the narrowed eyes of her friend, Pulie saw fear.

What have I done?

Yet, Nicky insisted on fighting. "Put her down, you moron! You don't just go around choking students! You're not that great. What did she do to you, huh?"

Erik turned from Nicky to the wincing face of Pulie. "This piece of oyster dung was just talking behind my back."

"What—" Pulie choked again. Her thoughts finished her sentence. *What are you even talking about?*

However, Pulie opened her eyes and locked with the giant teenager; she gasped in her head.

Black hair. Crooked nose! A lump went down her throat.

"See?" Erik spun around to face the rest of the kids in the eating room, swinging Pulie around like a doll. "What'd I tell you? She knows she did it. She's even guilty that I caught her red-handed!" The room was still silent, and he lifted Pulie higher up into the air.

Pulie had always wanted to be taller, but this was not what she had hoped for.

"Please…" Pulie gasped for air. "Let me go."

"I'm gonna turn you into Borthwick or maybe worse—Awolo," He sneered. There were a couple of gasps.

"And you think they'll believe you?" Nicky snapped over and over, trying to get Erik's attention.

"I can just make up anything to punish her. They'll believe me just fine." He flashed a grin at his friends. They hooted and smacked their thighs—those *scoundrels*.

Her friends' ongoing shouts tried to stop him, but mercy wasn't a word in Erik's dictionary.

"I wasn't talking about you." Pulie's voice was raspy, her body sweating with the large hand tight around her throat. She closed her eyes.

Suddenly, the grip loosened. Pulie opened her eyes. *Was it what I said?* Everything was silent. Erik let go, and Pulie fell to the floor, a long way down. She glanced up at the lower half of the giant's body, which was now encrusted in food. He was a piece of art, pied with leftovers and strings of pasta and pasta crusts. It was like painting a picture, smearing sauces gracefully over his trousers, and gleaming white shoes. Lemonade dripped from his belt, and marinara drizzled down his knees. Colin, Dan, and Nicky were on one side of the table, throwing meatballs at his left side, and Ema, Piden, and Alex on the other attacking him with salad leaves.

"Food fight!" A boy hollered from across the lunchroom. Then, like the signal for the start of a war, from all corners, chunks of food soared over the large eating room and splatted straight on Erik's back. And just like that, soon, the food rained from the ceiling. The floor began to grow slippery from grease, and the walls were painted in different colors.

Erik and his friends retreated and fled out and up to the courtyard, roaring about their clothes. And meanwhile, food flooded the floors, and the tables were stained and dripping.

Nicky dusted her hands after she dodged a bread bun. "That's right," she said sarcastically. "You *never* mess with *my friends* or *my clothes*."

***

Everyone in the escape room fled for their lives after that, abandoning the underground deserted eating room. No one wanted to be the last one there.

Colin, Dan, Piden, and Alex left for their rooms up on the second floor. While back at their room, Pulie, Nicky, and Ema were met with a surprise. Taped onto their door was a large cardboard poster with words as big as boulders.

Watch out, you three. Death awaits you. I'm waiting. And for you, Nicky, remember, Theo died because of you.

The hall was silent.

Nicky stammered. "How—"

"Forget it, Nicky." Ema hurried and snapped the poster in half. It crumpled in her hands. "We don't need to listen to what they say."

"How did they—"

Pulie knew something was wrong with what that poster said, and she knew exactly who it was written by.

"Erik doesn't know who he's messing with, okay?" Ema assured them. "We didn't see *anything*."

When they unlocked the door, Pulie let out a frightened shout. Posters everywhere. Upturned desks. Cut pieces of vines. Their room was a mess. And on each sign, a tantalizing message was written across like blood smeared across classroom boards.

Rafferty doesn't belong here. Ema tore this one down immediately.

Most were about Pulie and Nicky, though. **Talking behind backs is rude—filthy slug. None of you belong here. Stay out. This is only for the talented. Your family was a fool to kill their own son.**

"My family did not kill my brother!" Nicky roared, and she shredded the poster into bits.

"Nicky, calm down. They're doing this on purpose. They don't know the truth, and they will never understand. If you get upset, their trick is working!" Ema waved her hands around. But this was not enough to make Nicky feel better.

"They will not talk about my family like this!" Nicky went from cardboard poster to poster tearing them down from the walls. Ema tried to reassure Nicky and coax her into settling down, but nothing could stop Nicky.

She soon calmed herself down, the room a sea of ugly brown posters and a lake of tears. Nicky was a melting piece of broken glass.

"I'm sorry—" Nicky finally said.

"For what?" Ema replied.

"For being so sensitive," Nicky whispered, she glanced around the room as if someone were listening, "You were right, this isn't a big deal. If he's gone, he's gone." She collected herself, like gathering shells in a bucket.

"How did they even get in here?" Pulie asked quietly. Her voice trailed off, scared it might trigger another tantrum or sob.

"Erik's not the worst student in the class. He and his friends are clever. Mostly everyone here is. Opening a couple of locks on a door with a fake key isn't that hard."

"So, anyone can sneak in to anyone's room?"

"Yeah. That's why you have to change your lock codes and add different locks weekly. Your earring lock is the hardest one to hack, but it's possible. We have a total of five different locks at that door. Five is not a large number."

"You are experienced."

"Indeed."

"Nicky, is it alright if I tell Pulie about Theo?"

Nicky nodded, then buried her head in her shirt.

So, Ema began, "Nicky's father was sent on a mission. He and his team did well. But one person betrayed them after it had succeeded. The CAOT was able to locate where Nicky's home was. They took everything from her, including Theo."

"Did Theo—die?" Pulie asked softly, in disbelief.

Nicky nodded. "He was found dead on the streets nearby. No child could survive in the hands of those malicious people. They stole all our credits and our stuff. We were left with nothing. Nothing at all." Nicky sighed. "Part of me is thinking—no, I mean, it's just a guess. Don't take me seriously. But what if that *person* wasn't the only one who betrayed us. Like we were betrayed by more than one person… But either way, they somehow were able to take everything from us. All that credit money my parents worked for many years—gone. Like that."

"Were you the only family?"

"No. But only three more."

"I'm sorry."

Nicky stood up and dusted her pants. "It's alright. But enough, crying. I want some revenge."

Minutes later, they were scuttling around in the hallway, quietly.

"*Shhh*, quietly," Nicky whispered when Ema made a loud creak with her foot. "We can't be caught."

"Are we allowed to whisper?" Ema asked.

Nicky nodded. "But *quietly* or you're both going down the drain." Then, she flashed a grin.

"Okay, I'll whisper." Ema turned to Pulie as they snuck down the halls of their own Zive. "Erik Pontz, a couple of things you would like to know about him is, he's a bully."

"Could tell," Pulie said.

"He is pretty tall, so never play *Kick me off the Schoolyard*," Ema added, "And *never* play *Monkey in the Middle* with him either."

"I know *Monkey in the Middle*," Pulie whispered. "Isn't it that game where you toss a ball to your partner, and the middle person can't catch it?"

"Almost," Ema said, "The ball is a piece of tar that was frozen, and you have to throw the ball straight at the middle person's face as hard as you can."

"Oh." Pulie stepped back.

"Another thing to remember, Erik is one bitter guy to students and one lovable boy to the teachers. Never think about telling on him or snitching on him—" Ema shook her head quickly. "It never works, and the teachers backfire at you. Unless it's Mr. Wace or Señor Rodriguez."

Man, this guy's invincible.

"But the only way to get revenge, like we're doing is to use clever tricks on him. Many students try to sneak into his room to prank him. That's why he has sixteen other padlocks. Smart trickies can hack into the original key lock. But I wonder how they got into *our* room this time…"

"Does he like you?" Pulie asked.

Ema shook her head. "Nope. I believe he doesn't like anyone at our level or below. But there's a reason why he hates me specifically."

"What?"

"There was a Hacking Clash last year, and I got into the contest. It's a computer hacking thing. It's not a big deal. Erik, *somehow* go in, too. And I beat him in our Zive. He got mad and started spreading rumors that my father was an illegal contributor —someone who only got a job by paying credits and stuff. In return, I hacked through the school system and sent him messages to his hologram about death. He doesn't know it's me because I wrote *From, Boar's Bottom* after each message. Either way, he doesn't like the Rafferty blood as well as the Oster blood."

Nicky stopped in one room. "Guys, we're here."

Pulie lost track of how many floors they had climbed. They stopped at a room that was like every other room.

Nicky smiled. "There's nothing better than a pillow stuffed with eggs." From her bag, she pulled out a cart of eggs. "We stuff only Dash and Erik's for now."

"Did you steal the eggs from the kitchen again?" Ema opened up a tiny key lock kit from her pocket.

"Yes, but hurry. We don't have that much time."

Inside the kit were a hundred metal odd shaped tools. Some were shaped like keys, others shaped like stars, knives, hooks, or strings. It took about fifteen minutes for Ema to figure out what

120

keys were needed. Then she needed to find how to hack the earring lock.

There was a satisfying final click when the door creaked open, and there was a gust of stench blown at them.

Ema squeezed her nose. "Erik hasn't done his laundry yet."

Stuffing the eggs into the pillowcases proved difficult because of the height of the hammocks. But soon, Erik's room consisted of two fluffy pillows packed with six farm eggs in each.

"Done," Nicky called from above. "I cannot wait."

"Just one last thing." Ema snatched a tiny knife-shaped key from her kit and scratched onto the wall letter large enough to see blindly.

Boar's Bottom, she had written.

They all cracked up.

"The bells going to ring any minute," Nicky whispered, "and I don't want to be caught in Pontz's corner."

IMITATIONS

The bell rang.

Pulie's bag slapped against her back as she sprinted away.

Mr. Eerie's classroom was two doors down from Señor Rodriguez's. The three girls burst through the door, as Mr. Eerie was calling the first seating arrangements. It was an extravagant room with black, white, and gold theatre masks dangling from streamers on the left wall. To her right were large portraits of women in bodices and elegant textiles and men in red cloaks. On the shelves were filled with clothes and wigs and fake mustaches and masks and makeup arrangements. It was like the backstage of a theatre.

Pulie sat on the right corner, Nicky on the left, and Ema at the very middle. It would take hours just to walk over to each other. Their sweaty smiles had been erased completely. Nobody, in fact, looked happy. Except for the slender man at the front of the room, grinning from ear to ear and spreading his skinny arms towards the class. Mr. Eerie looked around twenty, with a mustache under his long nose and a strange sailor's cap perched on his head.

"Hello! Hello! Good day, class! We are in another year of Imitations, and I am so very pleased. This will be a fresh start—a new start—to become one of the world's greatest imitators! Now, we will first start off by introducing our names, age, and how long we've been here." His petite brown mustache jiggled up and down when he spoke. "We'll start with… you." He pointed to the boy sitting next to Pulie at the edge of the room.

He stood up and introduced himself, "My name is Lane. I am fourteen years old and have been here since I was four." He then sat down, and the class waited for Pulie to stand up and speak.

"My name is Pulie, and I am fifteen, and I have been here for zero years."

Murmurs arose.

"I meant that this is my first year here." Pulie changed her sentences and plopped back into her seat as quickly as she could. She was relieved when the next person began, and she was soon forgotten.

Soon, Selma stood up and curtseyed, whipping her hair. "As you all know, my name is Selma, which means peaceful, like myself!" Her silk skirt bounced up and down. "I am fifteen, the age of beauty, and I have been here for over eight solid years."

That was a moment Pulie hoped to erase from her memory.

Nicky was last.

"My name is Nicky, spelled with one *n*. I am fifteen and almost turning sixteen— at least I think so because it's been more than half the year. Otherwise, I am still fifteen. And I have been at this palace for three years, and my favorite memory back then—"

"No one asked for your favorite memory!" Selma barked from across the room.

"No one asked about your age of beauty either! Or what your name means!"

"No one even—"

"Silence." Mr. Eerie smacked his hands together so tightly, all the color in his hands drained away. "Ladies, let's not repeat what we did last year. I don't want a bloody year again." He shuddered, making Pulie really wonder what chaos Nicky and Selma had caused last year.

"Now for me," Mr. Eerie announced. "My name is Mr. Eerie, scouted by the AT Tricksters and Academy Tricksters for Imitations and Disguise. I was a part of the greatest scout missions of all time, but I fell in love with teaching five years ago. And now, I am an Imitations teacher at the greatest training camps of all time. Now, this fantastic blood did not appear out of nowhere. My mother was also a professional Imitator her entire life, and my father was an actor up in America. They fell in love and had me. You probably wondered where I got this success in my veins. We were one of the greatest Imitating family of all time. I was always top in my class. However, my parents both died on a mission during the Great Death."

Pulie's eyes grew round. Great death? She looked around and saw everyone with their faces looking up at the ceilings with obvious signs of boredom. It was clear that this was not the first time Mr. Eerie had given them this speech. But his parents had just died? Wasn't it quite rude to not care when he was talking about his dead parents? How hurt must he be?

"But I don't care," Mr. Eerie said flatly. "One must die at some point, and their time had come. Like the Fortunate Man, King Admetus of Pherae of Thessaly. Although, he did not die thanks to his wife and with the help of Apollo—Aha! I am going off-topic. Here we are. Let us discuss what we are going to achieve this year." He prepared to walk over to the wall with the tall mirror embroidered in rubies, but the moment he saw himself in the reflection, he halted and skipped back to the front of the room. He rubbed his hands together in glee.

"I almost forgot." Mr. Eerie smoothed down his long coat. "Can anyone shout aloud what I am wearing?"

"I don't care," Selma groaned. Mr. Eerie shushed her and continued waltzing around the center of the room, showing off his costume.

It was a bright white sailor's suit with little button badges and a blue-collar.

"Cooking apron?" Dan asked. Nicky and Colin snorted loudly from the other side of the room.

Mr. Eerie frowned disappointedly. "No, it is a sailor's suit of my great grandad. He was one hundred two when he died on a sailing ship, trying to catch a foolish sneaky fish at sea. He fell off the boat and—"

All of a sudden, a loud thud hit the floor and the room silenced.

"What—just happened?" Nicky stood up, panicking.

"The teacher just fell down!" Anne squealed.

Dan climbed over Selma's desk to see the commotion.

"Oh my gosh! He fainted! Guys! Come over here!" Dan hollered, waving his arms around in the air like a bird.

Already, a U shaped crowd of students hovered over the man. The pale motionless face of the teacher didn't twitch in the least. His body was sprawled on the floor, almost lifelessly.

"What should we do?" said one student.

"We should tell the Miralmalma?

"*No*, don't tell anyone. We could have one whole free period of free time!"

"Blockhead, that doesn't mean we're going to get *free time*."

"Pour water over his head, maybe?" Anne recommended.

That moment, Mr. Eerie awoke from his faint.

"Mr. Eerie!" the students cried.

Mr. Eerie clamped his hands over his head. "Stop this nonsense shouting and whistling, please go back to your seats!"

Seats rustled obediently.

Mr. Eerie stared at everyone suspiciously. "What just happened?"

"You fainted, teacher," Anne replied. She even looked like Goldilocks from behind.

Mr. Eerie had a perplexed expression.

"Faint, you say? How many thought I—*fainted*?"

Most of the class raised their hands. Selma pretended to snore.

Mr. Eerie grinned. "Well, this is an Imitation class. This class is where we *imitate*."

There was still a confused look on every student's face.

"I did not *faint*, children! I faked it! It took long enough in this class; the other classes caught on perfectly after I said the word *imitate* so I could perform my magical bow."

And with that, he took an exasperatingly long bow.

"Well, at least you children did a good job *trying to* think of a way to save me. I awoke because I did not want Anne or anyone pouring water over my fresh, clean suit of sailing from my great granddad. And who was the boy who wanted *free* time?"

Fingers pointed at Dan.

"I'm sorry, Mr. Eerie, I thought you were really dead," Dan explained.

Pleased by this compliment, Mr. Eerie chuckled. "No need. I hope you enjoyed the first couple of scares. We will try to finish our lesson because we wasted quite a lot of time. First, why is there an Imitation class?"

"Because we need to imitate?" Dan asked, scratching his hair.

Mr. Eerie made a face, "No! There is a lot more to this class than just *imitating!* When you are a spy, you need to be able to keep a straight face, control your emotions, handle situations like your enemies, so you aren't discovered or, worse, identified. When you need to play dead, you will need to have the ability to drop down in an instant and make your face very pale, eyes sunk, and dry."

"We have to learn *all that?*" Dan asked. Colin nudged him in the side of his stomach.

Mr. Eerie answered, "Yes. In your first year, all we did was watch movies to get you a sense of what real imitations are! The actors! They are all imitations! Take, for example, Shakespeare! In Romeo and Juliet, he was merely submerging an actual event into a romantic fairy tale. The Capulets—they are the CAOT. The Montagues—they are the Montonos in the sea."

Pulie scrunched her nose, wondering if anything the man was saying was true. She had read Romeo and Juliet, and she was sure they did not have anything to do with the—CAOT or whatever.

For the rest of the class period, they spent their time focusing on their vocals and facial expression. Mr. Eerie would put a person from a movie on pause, and they would have to imitate their reaction and movement. They also were given pitch control retainers, which you would fit in your mouth and adjust the octave of your voice.

When this wrapped up quickly, Mr. Eerie put his leg on the table and sat back in his chair with a gratifying look.

"Class! Since there are only a couple minutes left, sit down and let me tell you a story."

Everyone scrambled back to their seats.

And so he began, "My grandfather always told me about the Tale of the Island. Now, mind you, it's a tale. A tall tale indeed.

And it all started with a strong and powerful man who collected and sold something so extraordinary that he became an outlawed tycoon."

"What'd he sell?" Dan asked.

"No one knows. But every part of his extravagant business was going so well, until one day. The fog had poured in, all around his estates, but he refused to listen to orders and took his right-hand man on a trip. His helicopter crashed in the mysterious island, and although the man died, his right-hand man survived. But he was also stranded."

"And?" asked the whole class in unison, anxiously.

"I will only tell a portion of the story on the days each, and every one of you behaves well. It's a long story that has been passed down for generations."

"Why not tell us some more?"

"Not today."

Pulie sighed. She wanted to know what happened to the right-hand man. Or where the island was. But Mr. Eerie could say no more, for the bell rang, and everyone made for the door.

***

Mr. Lizarstrang. He was the shape of an ice cream cone with broad, thick shoulders with large muscle bumps all over his arms. Only looking at his body, you could tell her was a bodybuilder. But his face was a completely different picture. He had thin circle glasses, a square face with a butt chin, and a curtain cut. He was too busy observing how filthy his hands were, blowing at his fingers to even notice that his students had entered the classroom for their first day of school. Pulie could tell he was quite oblivious to the things he didn't quite care about.

There was a screen at the front of the classroom, ordering the classroom to remain silent until asked to.

Therefore, the room remained quiet until finally, words escaped the lips surrounded by the bushy forest on the man's face. "Vell, vell. Zou are zall here." He opened up a briefcase and tied a bandana around his floppy hair. He walked out from behind the desk and stood in front of the classroom. It was then Pulie could see the scars on his body. He had a dark keloid scar across his neck, several slash marks across his arms, and a large red stitch across his knee on one of his legs. But his face was not much better. He had what seemed to be a black eye settling down a bit, and his lips were bruised and his nose was crooked. In addition, he had more scars sprinkling across the left side of his face.

Everyone was still silent, not out of respect but of pure fear for the man at the front of the room.

Mr. Lizarstrang clapped his hands twice. "Very grood. Tis class has done vell! Ye all has done amazing, vetter than all the other classes. Self-control ves very important especially here at vis palace. Learning to not speak vhen asked to vand keeping inner thoughts vis— well important.

"Let first introduce meself. Ma name is Buckledoe Lizarstrang. I teach what zou all know as RS, reflective stretching. Last year and this year vill not be very different. In this class, ye will learn how to control crying and emotions and stretch zour body out. It is me and Cherry who vill give zou zour proper exercise lists. And I have purposefully not arranged a seating chart, partly because me want ye to be with yer friends, and partly because me was too lazy to."

A few people laughed.

"I vill zend zout the list to zour holograms. Zou must do every single exercise every single day. No exceptions. Zou have a lot of time and zou will submit zour status at the end of each day. Very simple. Like last year. Remember, zis is for the Tricky Trials. Zand for zour future. Zou cannot enter Tricky Trials with a body made of wood, eh? You'll snap like *that!*" He snapped his fingers. "Now, pack up!"

***

Mostly everyone in Pulie's class headed straight to Miss Cherry's gym once again. But this time, they took the staircase up from the gym to another room, which then branched out to several other rooms. Other students were already there, working out. Pulie set her bag with the others by the hooks and followed Nicky and Ema into another room. It was the running room.

They spent an hour running on the mountain treadmills, and after that, they grabbed their waters and moved to the weight room for another thirty minutes. Afterward, they grabbed a quick snack at the Nibble station. They proceeded their work out as students gradually began to pour in. But there were enough rooms to fit almost a thousand kids all at once.

About an hour later, they headed back to their dorms. But they had no time to rest, for time passed quickly as the three spent the rest of their day in their room, moving accordingly to Nicky's plan, gluing the stolen vines onto the ceiling.

"Why ceiling?"

"Can one of you move the vines into that box?" Nicky swiftly ignored Pulie's question. "Wrap them in a towel but do not dry them!"

Ema and Pulie stared at her, confused.

"Don't just stand there!" Nicky hollered, almost losing balance on her hammock.

"Careful, you might fall off like last time!" Ema cried, quickly soaking the dripping vines into the towel.

"I don't care and Ema, when do you ever have some fun?"

"I have lots of fun. But I'm never stupid."

Pulie stared at the wet plants. "We have to touch that?"

"No, Pulie. We use the force and make them stick to the ceiling." Nicky was beginning to grow impatient.

"Nicky, this is never going to work," Ema said, "How are these—"

"Hand the thickest vine to me!" Nicky shouted, nearly falling off the hammock again.

Pulie jumped to her feet and untangled the juiciest and plumpest of vines and handed it to Nicky, who was the monkey, leaning down to grab the slippery vine from Pulie's hands.

"Careful, Nicky!" Ema cried. "You're getting impatient again. Imagine you fall down. You can't apply for Tricky Trials!"

"What?" Nicky asked from the hammock.

"Never mind, do whatever you want—" Ema grumbled in a low voice. "Fall off the hammock and break a bone and never be able to enter Scouts."

"I heard that!" Nicky sang in a childish voice. "Now, come, look!" Nicky was swinging from the hammock and leaning upwards, pressing one end of the thick vine to the ceiling, the remaining water dripping onto her forehead. She held the vine in that strict position, limiting movements for a couple of minutes.

"Just wait—a few—seconds—" Nicky muttered. And finally, Nicky lifted her hand off the vine, the plant dangling from the ceiling, cemented firmly.

"No way."

"How out of all people?"

Nicky smiled. "Now watch this."

And she continued the process for the other end of the same vine until the plant was a hanging U loop from the ceiling. Then, she leaped from her swinging hammock and grasped for the vine. The vine held her weight, and Nicky was able to sway six feet up in the air, laughing and grinning down at Pulie and Ema, whose jaws hung low.

The vines created a jungle of plants, dropping down from the top of the room. And now, with freedom and ease, they could all use the momentum of a vine from the floor and launch themselves onto their hammock. Compared to their old method of jumping countless times to perhaps grasp the tip of their blanket from below.

Only a couple of minutes later, there was a buzz from the ceiling speakers.

"Students!" A voice crackled.

Nicky froze midway dancing. Her eyes grew wide, and her mouth hung open. Nicky and Ema both locked eyes with each other.

"Ms. Awolo," They gasped in unison. Then came panic.

"Students! Stop what you are doing—right now!" The voice screamed.

Nicky clamped her hands over her ears. "Gosh, you don't need to scream. You're speaking into a *speaker*!"

"Students in Zive two!" The voice hollered even louder. "I want *all* of you to come down from wherever you are! Stop what you are doing! And come down to the eating room. Right now!"

Then there was a loud smash, and it was clear that Ms. Awolo had thrown the speaker piece onto the floor.

At once, everyone in Zive two began to drop what they were doing and speed down the vines. Nicky could not open the door because of the flood of people who were pushing and shoving to get down the ball behind it.

"God damn it!" Nicky shoved at the door. There was a loud thump outside. Nicky pulled at the doorknob. "We can't get out!"

"We'll just have to wait. There's no use in pulling at the door, Nicky." Ema peered through the crack. "Wow, that's a lot of people."

"We can't wait," Nicky groaned. "Not when Awolo's mad on the first day. We're doomed!"

They waited awhile until most of the students had passed their hallway. Then, it was silent. Finally, they made it out of their room and into the quiet and empty hallway. They scrambled to get back to the crowd.

Everyone was quiet. Everyone was scared. And everyone was desperate to get to the eating room on time.

"What have we done?" Nicky whispered. "Why is she so mad on the first day?"

Ema shrugged. "I don't know. But it looks like we're all going to be punished."

But when they followed the crowd into the eating room for Zive two, Pulie, Nicky, and Ema nearly fainted.

Tomato juice still dripped from the lights up above. The room was coated in food from the floor to the top. The revolting smell of rotting food pervaded the damp and squished room. It was the food fight. No one had cleaned it up.

Nicky closed her eyes and covered her face. "No, no. This is all my fault. Please, please help me. My only wish for the rest of my life is that nobody in this room snitches on us." Nicky blessed herself afterward.

Awolo was standing up on the steps of the front of their eating room, hands on her hips, her face throwing a nasty look at all the students.

When everyone settled in and sat on the slippery floor knowing that Ms. Awolo's tirade would last awhile.

"First day of school." She paced around the front in her silky dress. "First day." She picked up a piece of plum and chucked it at the boy in the front of the crowd. It splatted on his face, but he remained as still as a soldier.

"First day of school!" She screamed, grabbing the boy by the collar. "You imbeciles! Which one of you started it! Say it right now! Which one of you started it!" Her voice was a sharpened knife to the ear.

Pulie felt Nicky trembling beside her.

The room remained quiet.

"Which one of you started it? Huh?" Ms. Awolo grabbed another piece of food and chucked it at a girl to her left. "Was it you?" She squinted at everyone's faces. "If you don't speak up now, you will get a punishment for the rest of your lives! I will find out who it was, and you will suffer! Die! Split your bones in half and tear the hair out of your scalp!"

The entire floor trembled.

"Who was it?" Ms. Awolo barked. "Do you want me to list out each and every punishment possible? Starting with removing your toenails! Then sizzling your—"

"It was me!" Nicky shouted, her eyes on Awolo.

Awolo turned her head and smiled once she saw Nicky.

"Ahh. Nicky Oster. I was looking for you in the crowd." Ms. Awolo cackled. "Come up here, this instant."

Nicky obediently followed directions. Pulie began to feel immensely guilty. This was all her fault, too. If she hadn't gotten into trouble with Erik, Nicky would never have started a food fight.

She watched Nicky take the long route up to the front.

Everyone was still quiet.

"Miss Oster," Ms. Awolo announced, "You are permanently suspended from class and will be removed from Zive two."

What? Pulie gasped. So did everyone else. Ema had frozen in her spot the moment she entered the room.

"You will never see your friends again or this room either. You will eat in eating room four down the hall, and you will attend class with Zive four. Have I made myself clear?" Ms. Awolo bent down to be eye level with Nicky, who was looking down at the floor.

"Yes."

Ms. Awolo squinted, then stood straight, then raised her hand and then *Crack!* She slapped Nicky across the face.

Everyone gasped and trembled some more.

"You filthy spoiled girl, you are the stupidest student in this entire palace. I don't even know how you got into this palace, but I hope that you will not stay here for long. You have only brought chaos and trouble to these grounds and you will pay for it. You will meet me in my office after you help the rest of your zive clean up the mess you made."

Everyone in the crowd groaned.

"It was me too!" Pulie finally hollered. "I did it too." Pulie saw Nicky's eyes widen at her and shake her head frantically.

"Who said that?" Ms. Awolo silenced the crowd. "Who was that?"

"Pulie Jark!" Selma shouted from across the room.

"Pulie Jark?" Ms. Awolo smiled devilishly. "*Jark?* Please come up to the front of the room."

Nicky was mouthing, *no, no* at Pulie, but Pulie did not stop.

Soon, she was at the front of the eating room with the crowd in front of her, gaping and in shock. She was like the star of the show; only the show was a humiliation contest.

"Jark." Ms. Awolo flashed a nasty grin. "You and Oster will both meet me in my office—"

"It was me too!"

Ms. Awolo froze and turned back to the crowd. "Who is it now?"

"It was me too."

A blazing orange-haired girl stood up from her spot. Ema.

"And it was me too." Piden slowly stood up.

"And me." Dan jumped up to show off his afro.

"And it was me too." Colin also came forward.

Ms. Awolo's eyebrows narrowed, and she opened her mouth to speak but she was cut off.

"It was me."

"It was me."

"It was me."

"It was me."

And then the entire crowd stood up and said in unison, "It was me, too."

Pulie glanced at Nicky, who was in complete shock. Ms. Awolo was quite surprised herself.

"Shut up!" She hollered, bringing out her taser.

Everyone began to panic, although still chanting the same three words.

It was me.

"Shut up! You! And you!" She activated her taser, but she was stopped by the next person who walked through the door.

Señor Rodriguez.

"Ah, Ms. Awolo, they want you in the Miralmalma. The— mission?" Señor made a gesture with his eyes.

Ms. Awolo nodded, returned her taser to her pocket, and stormed out of the room.

"Students, I will take the punishments from here. Ms. Awolo has already given me—" He looked at the gadget on his wrist, reading a message. "She ordered that every person in Zive two stay as long as it takes till every inch of the eating room is cleaned and—*immaculate*." Señor Rodriguez whistled for someone outside the eating room. A tall, lanky looking guy walked in, juggling to hold a stack of broomsticks. He had a working apron, a mask, and a large black afro. He began to hand out other items such as rags and mops and buckets of water.

He handed the items to Nicky as well, and when he turned around, Pulie caught sight of a red mark behind his ear. It was a tiny tattoo in the shape of a dripping infinity sign. She had seen it before. But where?

She didn't have time to think because the next moment, she was under the table, scraping the muck off the chair legs.

Señor had never ordered for silence, so the room began quite loud as all the students began to wash and clean the room. Nicky took her place soon next to Pulie by the walls. Ema soon joined.

"I think—we just made history," Nicky whispered. It seemed she had still not been able to understand what had just happened.

"History?"

"Yeah." Nicky stopped wiping the wall. "Never—ever has anyone confessed at this palace. And never has anyone taken the blame."

"Take the blame?"

"Yeah! You didn't start the food fight. And now everyone was like, *me too*."

"Is that a good thing?"

Nicky shrugged. "Good thing or not. You all *saved* my life. I don't think I would've survived a minute in her torture on the first day of school. I wonder if I'm still moving zives."

"She can't do that," Ema assured her. "She can't just move people around. The kids have to choose."

"Nuh-uh." Nicky scraped a big pie crust off the corner. "Awolo always moves kids around. She's a monster."

Pulie glanced over at Señor Rodriguez, who was at the front of the eating room, talking to the tall guy who had distributed the washing items. Señor seemed extremely distressed in the conversation. He would constantly point at the floor around him, which was the area of the eating room lifted up like a stage. The other tall guy would, in return, shake his head and say something Pulie could not hear.

"Hey, did y'all hear about Uma Bahati? It's crazy!" Dan asked, walking over to the wall with Colin.

"The *what?*"

"Uma Bahati."

"Nope."

Colin rubbed his rag on the stains. "Uma Bahati was one of the leaders in a mission tribe down in Bujumbura. Great man. One of the most skilled members of his area. He was both a Tricky and an Oddie. They say he has eyes on the back of his head. My brother told me that about a thousand men have tried to kill him, but none had succeeded. But he was found dead just last night in his garden with no blood, no weapon, no nothing."

"Could be a health issue," Ema said. "Heart attack? The man was almost seventy years old."

"I don't think so." Colin shook his head. "I mean, it's possible. But I think it was murder."

"Where'd you learn about this?" Pulie asked.

"On the news."

"The news? Where'd you learn the news?"

"Usually on the holograms, but I went up to the computer labs yesterday, so I got the news *fast*."

"Computer lab?"

Nicky slapped her forehead. "We forgot to show her the computer lab. We'll go tomorrow. Wait, Colin, do they have suspects?"

"Yes. The CAOT."

"Of course," Nicky mumbled. "Always them."

Pulie remembered that they had attacked Nicky's own family. She shuddered at the thought of seeing her own house robbed and her family taken from her.

Dan added. "Oh, and the Deck family is going to the Factory."

"Knew they'd end up there, too."

Pulie picked at the food pieces on the ground now. Slowly, the eating room was draining from a vibrant color.

"So, the computer lab? Where's that?"

"In our classroom Zive. I'll show you tomorrow. It's not too much, but it's where we get most of our information for our research projects."

"Information?" Pulie asked. "Like what information?"

Nicky shrugged. "Like where people in our foundation are located. You can also search up facts like how many tons of tar and glue products do Adhesive produce every day."

"Wait, hold up. You can track people?" Pulie exclaimed.

Nicky nodded. "Uh, yeah? As long as you wear an earring. Or if they have other trackers like shoes and equipment, that's theirs."

Bingo. Pulie could track her parents and see where they were at. They didn't have earrings, but they surely had some equipment she could track. She was pretty sure they were just on some scout mission—but just to make sure.

"Mr. Diablo also sent an executive order to get rid of all markers in every school," Ema said after awhile. "I saw it on the hologram yesterday. I mean, pencils can be dangerous, but markers? They smell so good."

"At some point, he's gonna get rid of everything in this palace. Imagine he gets rid of toilet paper because it's *paper*. And then, he's going to get rid of all the students too, because technically we can pass on information when we leave for spring break. Or maybe even computers in general."

"Mr. Diablo?"

"Yeah. He's the Commander of the Agency. Top secret agent organizer. Top in everything. He's a good man, though. My parents really like him. They say he's got guts and he makes daring choices. I know he's the reason we have decent food."

"Of course, Mr. Diablo is one of the greatest Trickies of all time. I mean—" Nicky scrunched her forehead. "How do you do full top scores in all years of school, then get scouted into one of the best mission leagues of *all* time. Then, get bored with all of it—"

"He got—bored?"

"Yes. He got bored of all the missions. Apparently, all his missions were too easy. He settled in at home in Wisconsin and just disappeared for a while."

"What are the missions like?"

Nicky squeezed the wet towel over the bucket. "I don't know. My parents told me they used to do the real stuff. My father was scouted one time for a mission in a museum. There was a CAOT inside the museum trying to find a Wanderer for some reason. He said it was all dark except for the crowds of people and the glowing water all around him. His team had to hack into the security to track and pin the Wanderer. They lost the Wanderer—and they all got fired."

"Oh, dang."

"It's *hard*." Ema patted the towels. "My parents failed both their first missions, and they were suspended for a year. That's when they met each other and grew determined to get on the same mission together. And now, they're doing well with it."

"My brother's now getting hired for the scouts," Colin said. "He's back from his other trip to Louisiana. I think his dream is to work for Mr. Diablo. Don't know if that's even possible."

"Mr. Diablo requested for my mother once," Dan sang. "Which is like an *honor*. But she had to take an interview before working for him, and she couldn't go to the interview—because I had just thrown up all over the house. She lost that chance because of me."

"*What?* Your mom got called into work for Diablo? Yeah, right!" Nicky hollered, then lowering her voice. "I hope we at least get dinner after this. My stomach is really angry at me right now. It's why they tell you to never waste food."

NEW PLACE, NEW PEOPLE

The following day was no less interesting.

The previous night, everyone in Zive two had stayed up late after cleaning up all the mess in their eating room. They were each given crumbly peanut butter and jelly sandwiches with a cup of milk for dinner because Chef Susie was working the night time job.

However, in the morning, they were greeted with a plethora of food waiting at their tables.

In ELSE class, Mrs. Wampanoag explained all the fundamentals of hurling the dart onto the target, even with the fan blowing. Surprisingly, Pulie's dart was second closest to the ever so small red dot in the center of the whiteboard. And Pulie could only help smiling at the sight of the fury on Selma's face growing extremely strong.

Throughout EP class, Pulie realized that she wasn't the only one suffering from Erik's tricks and dagger-sharp comments. In fact, *every* student in Zive Two prayed every night not to meet face to face with the tall, arrogant teenager.

In Mr. Lizarstrang's class, everyone was forced into the splits for an entire class. Only Dunkin Boar couldn't manage to, and he knocked over the mug on Mr. Lizarstrang's desk while doing so.

After their second day of training ended, like yesterday, Pulie and her class immediately went up to the gym again. They started with the weights in the heavy lifting room and worked their way down to the running machines. In between, they stopped at the Nibble station for a break.

"This is my favorite. *Vitality*." Nicky held up her green bottle of juice after she gave her quarters to the station.

"I don't like that one," Colin said, sipping his vitamin water. "Pulie, I wouldn't recommend that one."

"I wouldn't recommend it either," Dan said, shaking his head. "It tastes like—like—juice."

"It *is* juice!" Nicky shouted, licking her lips. "It's delicious."

"Eh." Dan shrugged. "I prefer T-Nectar." His drink was a cylinder bottle with a pull-tab on the top. It made a pop and a soft sizzle after he opened it. He chugged half of the drink in two seconds. His eyes bulged out with satisfaction. "I'm telling you. It's the best."

Ema had her bottle of plain water but also a bag of little sphere-shaped jellies. They were called Herbies and were good for working out. Other than that, the Nibble station was full of all kinds of snacks and drinks, although you could only buy a maximum of two items per day.

They finished up their exercises and headed back to their rooms.

Minutes before dinner, Pulie hurried through the halls alone to change her sweaty socks, when she forgot to be cautious in the narrow walkway and mistakenly stepped on a piece of rope that connected up to the ceiling of the halls. A bucket of ice-cold water was dumped straight onto her head—a perfect bull's eye.

She froze, her arms spread out and stiff. She was a sponge dripping with water, with forest goosebumps and metal cowbells for teeth, clacking away at each other. Pulie looked straight up and possibly saw her reflection in the silver bucket that hung from the ceiling with the rope tied to the handle.

Nicky had warned her not to step on any ropes or buttons in the halls. Pulie huffed.

But her bitterness was sugar-coated when she began to laugh, the iciness melting away in her eyes. She intertwined the rope in her fingers, thinking about how funny things worked here. She had never *imagined* a place like this would exist.

Pulie filled the bucket to the brim for the people yet to come.

During the evening, Ema and Alex took Pulie up to the computer lab, which existed in every classroom Zive. It was a vast dark room with rows and rows of large monitors and keyboards. There was a large screen at the front of the room, which was very far away from the door.

Ema settled on one computer near the corner. She clicked through the main screens, showing Pulie how to use it.

"This is the web search for like general information." Ema pointed to the button. "This is the *people search*. And this is the *location search*."

"*People search* is *that* one?" Pulie asked.

"Yes. And the location is this one. Oh, also, there's a database for—"

"They also monitor what you search up," Alex interrupted. "So be careful. I wouldn't try to search up stuff about the CAOT or anything. A kid from Zive One did that and got was forbidden to go to the computer lab again. They might think you're a spy."

"Who's they?"

"The Leaders."

But Pulie knew she didn't have to worry. She was just going to search for her parents, who were on a Scout mission. She could not be expelled for *that*.

"Don't worry, all our news about the CAOT come through the holograms," Ema added. "Whatever you want to know, it will be waiting for you."

The very next day in Miserable Miss Cherry's class, Pulie was taught how to balance on a two-inch ceiling bar, ten feet above the ground, which was quite terrifying. But soon, Pulie could jump down from the poles, swing onto a vine, and land safely on the ground.

"Miss Cherry," Selma said sweetly after the instructions were given, "Anne has been chewing gum. May I accompany her out of the gym to the bathroom trash can?"

Miss Cherry, too busy to see, nodded quickly and then ordered everyone in a line to do pull-ups. When the bell rang, Anne had a black eye, and her shirt was torn.

In Señor's class, lessons went from learning the trick to picking locks with only a flashlight and a watch, from being taught how to shoot blow darts, to learning the landscape of the land field around the Palace.

"Señor, is it true that we're going to go to the sewers?" A boy in their class asked. "Someone told me that there are—"

"No, we are not. Why would we go to the sewers? There are just pipes and waste and—nasty smelling things. Sorry. That's not a place for *us* to go."

The hardest task in his class was learning how to hide in unreasonable spots for a long period of time.

"*Imagine*. The world around you explodes the moment you make a single sound or move a single muscle. I would certainly like to keep still." Señor Rodriguez had said. "It will be no different during the Tricky Trials. Silence is key."

Inside the dome with Mrs. Wampanoag for ELSE class, they studied substances and chemicals used in missions and everyday life. They also mastered dart throwing and even trained with actual lethal darts.

Every other day, Mrs. Wapanog and Mr. Lizarstrang took them to the outside land around the palace walls, where a vigorous training camp was set up. Rings of fire, pools of water, real-life Rangs, tracks, hurtles, and snow lands. Pulie's hair was burned slightly, and she was slashed across the back while dodging a Rang and while climbing the swinging ropes. She wasn't alone in the pain. Colin was continuously smacked by the Swinging stones right below the stomach and needed to wear bodysuits to Else Class.

Everyone learned to swim and how to avoid drowning. On pool days, Selma occasionally tried to drag Pulie underneath the moat, so it was great practice. Booby traps were a difficult skill. Pulie had to check for every single possible outcome. Sometimes, the letter *A* carved into a paper meant that the second step was a drop but also that if you touched an item on a shelf, they would burn. Nicky's finger was cut when she pressed the wrong button, and she couldn't stop talking about the pain in all her classes; she was sent to the Miralmalma for the next few days. When she came back, she began to talk about how Awolo would stab and poke at someone until he or she died. Nicky was sent to the Miralmalma for another day.

It was midnight when Pulie opened the door of the computer lab. Her face grew damp with sweat, and her hands were slippery as she tried to fiddle with the keyboard. She could only think of her parents' location popping up on the satellite map on the screen in front of her.

She pressed the *people search* and then entered her father's name, Samuel Jark. Enter.

The screen loaded for a second and then came up with a list of locations.

Pulie scrolled through each one, although none of the places were related to Samuel Jark. There was a Samuel Jackson. Samuel Jess. Samuel Nate, Jr. But no Samuel Jark.

Pulie's eyes grew wide. Surely she knew how to spell her father's name.

Was it Samual? She tried that name, but nothing came out. She began to grow anxious. What had happened? Was he not wearing his earring?

Then it hit her. He *didn't* wear an earring. Neither did her mother. Then how did they get into the palace? How did they communicate? Pulie was muddled but had to return to her room when she heard a door upstairs slam shut.

The next day, in Imitations, Mr. Eerie taught them how to fake an ID and pass security under a different person's name. He had a scanner the size of a door frame that would have a pre-selected identity in which you would have to imitate.

"Look at the picture, and you can learn countless things," Mr. Eerie said, holding up a picture, "Here you can tell he is gruff, loves hockey, and speaks in an awfully low voice. This is going to be good for the Tricky Trials."

And even still after the first day, Mr. Eerie refused to succumb to the student's pleas for hearing the rest of the story about the island. He said that only on special days would the tale leak from his lips.

Everyone was quite glum. How could one start such a tale as that and leave it off the hook?

All classes continued to grow more difficult by the hour. Soon, barely anyone had time to stay up past nine to hang around in the courtyard. By the time they finished classes and training, they were exhausted and headed right to sleep.

Pulie started to go to the computer lab during lunch. She had already asked Señor Rodriguez about the earrings. Apparently, not all Trickies needed to wear one, especially if they were on a mission. They *did* need the earring to enter the Trickies, but if they were somewhere else, maybe not.

This relieved her greatly. She continued to search up her parents' names and the possible scout teams that had *recruited* them. Nothing. Nothing at all. There was no last name Jark let alone Samuel or Natalie Jark. There was no scouting that recruited a team for almost two years either.

But aside from not have a trace of her parents' locations, what she did realize was that *she* herself was not listed on the list either. Pulie Jark nor Piden Jark appeared on the person list, which greatly confused the situation even further. Was Nicky wrong? Was really *everyone* on the list?

However, Nicky, Colin, Ema, Dan, and Alex were on the list. Clearly visible on the location titled, Palace of the Trickies. Was it because she and Piden were new to this place? Or was there something else?

***

"Cat Wallis. Found dead at the Lucas Lee mall. Knife in her throat. Age 29. Scout mission #45. Recruited by AT Tricksters," said the hologram as the message hovered in the air.

It was no surprise. There seemed to be a murder every day now. It was only yesterday that an innocent non-Tricky normal couple had been found dead on a beach. Both were diagnosed with obesity. The Trickies detective group had worked hard to find what was the cause and revealed the main suspect—the CAOT. Pulie didn't know that the CAOT killed innocent people too.

Even all her teachers would talk about the deaths in an angry but motivational manner. The CAOT, pronounced like *chaot* in *chaotic*, was taught to be a cruel, ruthless, and murderous organization of people. They "split the blood of the innocent and swam in gold," according to Mr. Eerie. "But, *we*—are the CAOT's strongest enemy. We are the reason why they fail to destruct the world.

"One of their main goals has been set to wiping out the entire Tricky population. Because, if we weren't here, many more people would've died. Train hard because this world needs you."

These words circled Pulie's head, day and night. In addition, finishing Mr. Lizarstrang's long list of exercises every day was no easy task and proved difficult, requiring persistence and determination.

But the thought of the Tricky Trials and the CAOT brought the will to everyone to train vigorously.

***

"Now," Señor Rodriguez rubbed his hands together one day, "the day has finally come. All volunteers who wish to sacrifice their talents and lives for the Tricky Trials, please take one of these devices."

He held up a thin rectangular clip in the air. "Want to enter the Tricky Trials? Come and get your flash drive up here."

Every single student in the room perked up and scrambled to get a clip from the box. They fingered it with great pride and hope.

Confusion swarmed Pulie's head. Sacrifice life? Surely he meant in figurative terms… right?

Pulie was the only one in the class seated still, and she felt the embarrassment burning in her stomach as she got up from her seat in a hurry to bring back the device which everyone had so admired and carefully set on their desks.

"Please sit now and stop talking. I cannot hear what Olivia is asking me, and she is right in front of me," Señor Rodriguez hushed the class. "Now, now. It is by the order from the Leaders that every teacher who distributes the clips must read the instructions."

He pulled up a slide show at the front of the room.

"Number one," he read. "You will take excellent care of this item. It is not to be lost, and it is not to be broken. If any part of it is damaged by the time you bring it back, you will pay the price directly from your pocket money. Understood?"

Everyone nodded.

Señor smiled. "Okay, good. Enough with the tough talk. Let's get to the fun part. I know you all are extremely excited right now; I need you to—Dan, please do not lick the flash drive. As I was saying, you will take the flash drive to the computer lab. Everyone knows where that is, I'm sure. Then, you will plug it into the computer and log in. A digital form will automatically pop up. You will then enter your name, age, and the rest of the information asked for. Be careful with your decision. It is *okay* to not enter. It is your choice. But if you want to help our world, I highly recommend participating."

Heads bobbed.

"And do not hustle. This is meant to be *thought* through clearly and with precision. Bring back the clips by the end of the week. You will *directly* give me the clip and not to anyone else. Do you understand? And, once you submit, there is *no* turning back. Did I make myself clear?"

Pulie packed the device into the front pocket of her bag and patted it securely. She lifted her bag to make sure there were no holes underneath. She surely didn't want it to fall out on her way out. Before she set the bag down, she saw a tiny marking on the floor underneath her bag. Her eyes grew wide. The mark was in the shape of a spider. *Spider.* She had seen it too many times.

"Now, we shall proceed with our lesson." He pulled out a large metal object with thousands of gears and switches hanging from the outside. "How do we *decode* a code?"

Pulie brought out the tiny notebook from home she found in her bag and began to draw the symbol on the first page. The abdomen was larger than the front part, and the legs were curved in a strange way. She tried to sketch it with her marker but the ink smeared along the way.

"Oh, my gosh! Is that paper?" asked an unfortunately familiar voice. Selma snatched the notebook out of her hand.

"Give it back!" Pulie said, trying to keep her voice quiet. Señor was still talking about the codes, although most of the class had gone silent. Pulie gritted her teeth. "Go back to your seat."

Selma flashed a grin. "*I* get to do whatever *I* want! *You* have *paper.*"

There were a few gasps.

"Hand it over. That's all you have to do. And we both don't get in trouble," Pulie said calmly.

Selma began flipping through her notebook.

"Selma, just give the paper thing to Pulie, for heaven's sake. Don't be such a Dutchstill!" Nicky hollered.

"*Silence.*" Boomed the voice of Señor Rodriguez, louder than ever, "You three will meet me during lunch." His face was stone cold.

Great. The last time Pulie got in trouble was only last week. Mr. Lizarstrang wasn't lenient because it was a disciplined exercise. And when the school bell chimed, like an ungrateful signal of distress, the rest of the class were freed of trouble.

"I'll save us a table for lunch," Ema whispered, zipping up her bag and disappearing through the halls.

Pulie saw the nervous expression on Nicky's face, knowing when Señor Rodriguez was angry, there were no excuses.

"Pulie, Nicky, and Selma step up to my desk, please," Señor said, as Selma set the notebook down on her table. "*With* the notebook."

Pulie's thoughts raced, hoping that Señor wouldn't see what she had drawn on the first page.

Selma slammed the notebook on Señor's desk and patted the cover. "This is paper, sir. We have the evidence right here. Pulie is smuggling something we don't know about because I don't—"

"Selma—" Señor raised a hand.

Selma's eyes narrowed. "Sir, I clearly do not understand why you are seeing me after class, *clearly*—" She narrowed her eyes, "Clearly there has been a misunderstanding. It's all Pulie's fault."

Señor Rodriguez shook his head. "No. *Clearly*, it is the fault of both of you. It takes two hands to clap and two people to start a fight."

"*Clearly* not with Selma," Nicky muttered to herself.

"What's that, Miss Oster?" Señor peered at Nicky, standing in the corner.

"Nothing, sir."

Señor turned back to Selma and Pulie. "Now, ladies, give me the paper, which is what started the fight, I'm sure?"

They nodded glumly, Pulie the glummest of all.

He opened the book, and—he skipped the first page.

Please don't turn back. Pulie squealed inside. *Please continue.*

"Nicky, you may go now," Señor commanded.

Selma raised her voice, "What? Sir, that is not fair!" But she was silenced by the teacher.

"Which two started the fight?" He asked, voice steady and clear.

Selma lowered her head as the door shut quietly.

Señor continued to flip through the pages in silence.

Selma began, "But, Señor, have you gone out of your mind? Paper isn't *allowed* here at the palace. It's illegal, almost. Aren't you curious how Pulie got it? Rather than just flipping through the pages, why don't you just interrogate her? Find out what she knows? What if she's a—"

"Now, we know that our possessions are ours to keep?"

His eyes were on Selma.

"Yes, sir."

"Then, we will promise not to take another's items again?"

Selma nodded, "I won't do it. Not in front of you." The last sentence was in a whisper.

"Very good. Selma, you may leave."

Pulie was shocked. Was paper really that bad here?

"Miss Jark?"

"Yes, sir."

Señor scratched his bear with his index and thumb, glancing up at Pulie. "If I may ask, where'd you get this paper from?"

Pulie nervously fiddled with her shirt. "From home, Señor."

Señor nodded, although he seemed to be in a daze, staring down at the notebook. "Very interesting. And your name is Pulie Jark."

"Uh, yes, sir?"

"Interesting. Very interesting." Señor nodded, sticking out his lower lip a bit. "I skipped the first page on purpose. I assumed you didn't want others to look at it?"

"Yes, sir." Pulie bit her lip. His intelligence awed her.

"And I respect privacy. I don't know how you managed to get the notebook inside the palace from home because we do security checks. But I'd keep it more concealed next time. I am extremely kind enough to return this to you. Usually, it is confiscated. Pretend I have never given it back to you. Selma will not take it lightly the next time on both of us." He handed the notebook back and added, "But is there anything you want to tell me?"

Spider. The spider.

"Yes, sir. It's about a spider."

His eyes enlarged like pupils dilating in light. "Continue, please." He was sitting at the edge of his seat now.

Pulie began to wonder why everywhere she went, people acted strangely when she said the word, Spider. She led him to her desk and showed him the mark next to the table.

Señor gasped, "This—you did not make?"

Pulie shook her head, her eyes on Señor's startled face.

Consequently, he pulled up his sleeves, revealing many gadgets of all sizes, some squared and some triangular, clipped to his shaved skin. He pressed on one and ordered, "Inspection, Spectra, Immediate Inspection." As he spoke, he rubbed the marking with his finger, then sniffed and scanned it.

When the machine clicked off, he turned to Pulie. "Great discovery. This is an important find. Do you want me to tell you —"

The door burst open, and teachers and workers she had never seen before came in with all their tools. *Was this little marking really that important?*

Señor was crowded by a number of staff members that Pulie was swept away by the sea of people and out the door. His room now swarmed with strange people, one. She was outside of Señor's room. The quiet chilled her spine. It was a great way to get out and run to the eating room.

***

One day, Pulie quietly entered the room and caught Nicky pulling out the same cotton bag that she had seen her steal from Larry's house on the first day.

"What's inside?" Pulie asked.

Nicky spun around, trying to stuff the item up to her shirt. "Nothing." Her face turned red.

"You know, after all those imitation classes, you don't know how to lie." Pulie laughed. "Well, I'll give you some privacy now."

Pulie turned back to the door and was about to close the door when Nicky shouted something.

Pulie popped her head back in the door.

"You can come in." Nicky set the kit on the carpet. "But shut the door and sit over here."

And when Pulie obeyed, Nicky began to talk.

"It's a complete secret. Don't tell anyone. Literally, five people in this entire palace know this and—and— this is all really important to me. I mean, it's not a big deal. But still. And I trust you, I really do. So, let's make it quick."

Out of the bag, Nicky pulled out a large square box. Inside was a jumble of strange items. From the pile, Nicky pulled out a plastic covering with a single piece of yellow hair inside.

"Second years, otherwise known as, you know—Young Trickies, are supposed to come two days before school."

"Even the ones who go home every day?"

"Yes, everyone. Just to get familiar with the campus once again. But, on the first day I got here, in my room—or *our room*—"

Pulie beamed; she felt a part of something for once.

"We found a hologram message activated in our room already. But it wasn't from the Leaders or the school. Not at least what I think, because it was telling us where to go and where not to go. Only that the places were written in *numbers*."

"*Numbers?* How do you write in numbers?"

Nicky shrugged. "That was Alex. He found a pattern within the numbers. We thought it was just a bar code or an ID number. And we still haven't been able to crack it, but at least we found out it was *something*."

"So, we're trying to figure out who wrote it."

Nicky then explained about how Colin and Dan had helped her as well.

"What about Livia?"

"Livia is where the mysterious hair comes in. She has horse-tail hair, no offense. People have all different kinds of hair. I mean, I never said my hair was that soft either, but hers is quite—"

"Uh—"

"Anyways, this is important because that same day, someone came into our room and opened all of our bags! I don't know what that person was doing but we found a piece of hair on the ground next to the bags. It was rough, blond, of course, and around the size of Livia's hair. That day we sent Colin to ask Livia something was to ask her if she knew about it—"

"So, the hair was what you slipped into his pocket that day."

"Exactly." Nicky's eyes twinkled, "But she said *no*. And Livia, no matter how angry or quick-tempered, *she's* honest. And she's not all that *smart* to write a code like that. And besides, her room's on the fifth floor. Why would she bother to put it here? You get what I mean?"

Pulie nodded. "Why'd you have Colin do it for you?"

"Colin is a cunning young man. Mr. Wace adores him, and so do all the other teachers."

"So have you finished the fingerprint investigation yet?" Pulie rubbed her hands together.

Nicky shook her head, "No one knows how to use it but Colin because his dad taught him and stuff. But he's been quite busy with all the Tricky Trial training. I have been too. We all have. I don't think we'll ever find who it was."

"Well, let's go to him! We have ten minutes till Imitations."

Nicky pursed her lips and then opened, saying, "I don't think that's enough time. Besides, Ema is going straight to the class from the Else class with Dan and Olivia and we'll meet Colin at Imitations anyway. We'll talk to him then and meet after classes."

***

"Click." Was the soft sound made when Colin pressed the button. The box sprang open. Inside, were a couple of alcohol pads, a thin brush, lenses, imprinting sheets, a digital scanner, tape, and a couple more items. Colin carefully placed the items on the carpet. Pulie, Piden, Nicky, Alex, Colin, and Ema were all huddled on the carpet floor of Pulie's room, holding their breath for the very moment beside the fingerprint kit.

"Of course it's illegal!" Alex had said, "No one wants children snooping around with evidence tracking devices that can expose them! It's a true miracle Larry even had the guts to sell you one!"

"Colin, what's that?" Pulie pointed to the bottle.

"It's water. *Special* water. My dad says it is only used for real emergencies though. I don't quite know why."

"His dad works at a manufacturing company," Ema explains. "It's the only reason he and his little sister, Cassy, have a pen recorder *and* stamps."

"So, what've you got?" Nicky said anxiously, "Go on!"

Colin handled the piece of hair with his gloves and carefully placed it on the carpet.

"In order to do this, I need all of you to help," Colin said, "I am no fingerprint specialist. I simply know and have seen it in progress. Okay, so Nicky—" He took out a bottle full of powder, and set to work, assigning everyone a job. He assigned *Pulie* to take pictures of anyone with rough blond hair with a camera he gave her. So, Pulie Pulie began walking around in her spare time to take pictures of anyone with blond hair. After she finished the task, Colin gave her the camera as a present.

But the case was left open because Ms. Awolo began to check rooms after Selma's room exploded with glitter and made a hole in the ground. The fingerprint case was too big and obvious to lay out in the open. It was placed in the shoe rack under the clothes.

***

The rest of the days, everyone's minds were so wrapped up about the Tricky Trials. It seemed like years ago she had entered her submission through the computer chip following the rest of the students.

Pulie had almost forgotten about searching for her parents. Once a week she was able to search through the files and locations, but that was not enough time.

She needed to focus on the Tricky Trials like everyone else was. She knew it was a tremendous honor and she knew it would please her parents. She wanted to get into the missions.

But she didn't know what she was even up for.

TRICKY TRIALS

At six in the morning, the speakers of the Zives crackled,
"Everyone who applied for the Tricky Trials, please wear your EP clothes and exit the palace to the left. The Tricky Trials will be held there."

"Today?" Nicky fell off her hammock.

Ema gasped. "It's finally time."

"What is?" Pulie followed Nicky and Ema in the procedure of changing into the leggings and t-shirt. When they had finished donning their new attire, Nicky began to bounce up and down to get her blood pumping. Soon, all three of them were flat on their backs, stretching out their muscles.

"Oh, my *god*." Nicky trembled as she spoke. Her face grew very pale, but her eyes gleamed with excitement. "I am so nervous. It's *finally* Tricky Trials time. Remember, it's what you applied for at the computer lab and turned in to Señor Rodriguez? Well, now, it's finally begun. Every person who applied is going to be dead-hard competing for the spots on the mission. Basically, *everyone* participates, which makes it thousands of students, all at once. If you earn the spot in the mission, it is *tremendous* glory. Right now, it's the Zive versus Zive competition where only one Zive at the end of the Trials is selected for the mission out of all four Zives. And once a Zive is selected, from there, students compete for individual spots."

"So, what's the first task?"

Nicky shrugged. "Who knows? The Leaders always keep that a secret."

***

It was a battlefield out in the open chilly breeze with the sun's rays penetrating the bubble that wrapped around the palace like a shield. The grass beneath their feet danced softly. Everyone knew that this tranquil land would be peaceful no more.

"Trickies!" Ms. Awolo's voice interrupted the silence.

All the students had been separated by Zive numbers into four large groups. Everyone faced the three Leaders who stood like stone statues, hands crossed behind their backs.

"This is the beginning of our annual Tricky Trials. Today, we will be competing for which Zive will be selected for the mission. I expect sportsmanship from all of you because everyone here has trained very hard, I'm sure. While there are short cuts and tricks in these games, no cheating and hurting are allowed. Oh, and absolutely no tricks today. We have cameras all around campus, so don't you dare lay a finger on the rule book." She glared at everyone as if they had already cheated.

"And to anyone who violates the code, it will be automatic suspension and removal of the *entire* Zive."

That put everyone's hair at end.

Mr. Wace took the microphone from her and managed a weak smile. "Ah, yes, yes. Now, for the fun part. Three games will be run in the next two days. Every game, a team will be disqualified. By the end of the Trials, there will be a total of *one* Zive left. Right now, I will read the list of games that will be held this year. The first one, Quarter Dodgeball. The second one is the Relay. And the third is one is the Ambush Game."

Everyone shifted in their spots, bobbing their heads. The games were easier this year, which also meant it was easier to get disqualified.

"You have fifteen minutes to discuss strategies with your group, and then you will immediately report back here. Ready... Set... Go!"

Then the silent meadow of grass was a jumbled mess. People were scrambling and squeezing to get into human circles. Pulie could not understand a word anyone was saying in the loud screaming and cheering. She was already so confused and she wished Nicky and Ema would've explained a bit more about this whole trial game. But they were far away in the middle of a circle, whispering tactics and pounding their feet. Pulie felt truly lost.

Fifteen minutes later, everyone reported back to their original spot, all split up into four groups.

Ms. Borthwick stepped up to the front of the students with a whistle in her hand. "Up first! Quarter dodgeball!" She snickered in the most absurd way. "This will be *fun*." She then whistled for the workers who hurried out and surrounded the large group of students and painted a circle that marked the perimeter and the boundary lines. Then they split the circle into four.

"You are to stay in your quarter of a circle the entire game. If you are hit, you leave the circle." She whistled again. Four large barrels overflowing with sticky black objects were carried out.

"Tar," Nicky whispered.

"Students!" Mr. Wace announced, "You have exactly thirty minutes, and when the timer ends, the team with the lowest number of survivors is *out* of the trials. Understood?"

Thick silicon gloves covered in another layer of clear protection were passed out, and everyone was given an oozing midnight tarball. Pulie regurgitated in her mouth.

Slowly, every Zive took formation. Everyone was in a low squatting form, balls ready, eyes darting back and forth. Unlike regular dodgeball, balls would be flying at them from three different angles.

"Ready."

"Aim."

"Fire!"

And the game began.

Within the first few seconds, a ball barely missed her and scraped the ends of her hair. She shuddered at the thought of tar all hitting her face. Would it come off? She didn't want to find out.

Her gloves somehow kept the ball from sticking to her own hands, but every other part of her body was vulnerable. Like arrows, the black balls showered over her head. Everyone was screaming and hollering, dodging right and left. One by one, people began to fall to the floor, then scrambling to get out of the circle while attempting to get the black liquid off.

Everyone was gathered in the center of the circle, trying to attack, but Pulie slipped between the charging mass of students and snuck over to the edges of the circle. There, she could throw with an angle.

And—Smack!

The ball spun with such curve and grace that it knocked a girl down from behind. Ball after another, Pulie shot at her opponents, hidden and safe from her spot. She could see the victims on the other side, falling to the floor. But her team was also draining of people. Especially when Erik Pontz was pummeled with about fourteen tarballs, Zive two went wild.

Pulie lunged for another tarball on the grass and blasted it straight up into the air. She watched it soar over a dozen people and pound upon a large boy who seemed dazed in a dream. His hair dripped with the black liquid. Pulie laughed. This wasn't as bad as she thought it would be.

Soon, time was running out. She launched as many tarballs into the air as she could until finally...

SMACK!

Right on her leg. Other people from the opponent Zives has started using the corners of the circle. The oozing ball was soaking through her white leggings, an ink pen bleeding on paper. She cursed under her breath but scampered out of the raging circle.

When the timer rang, all balls dropped to the floor obediently, and Mr. Wace and Ms. Awolo marched through the battlefield and counted the survivors.

Then Ms. Awolo grabbed the speaker and hollered, "Zive number four! You're out! With only twelve survivors left, it was an obvious loss. The rest of the Zives, like Zive number two, had ninety players left. Congratulations to the rest of the students. Go home, number four!"

The remaining Zives hooted and pounded their chests.

The remaining students were allowed water and a ten-minute break. Pulie, Nicky, and Ema were lying on the grass, recalling the funny incidents that had just occurred.

"Well, well." Selma and her group walked over to the three who were lying down. "Poor, *poor* Pulie got out before the bell even rang. What a pity. I don't know how long you'll last at this rate."

"Hah! Same for you, Dutchstill." Nicky sat up and said aggressively, "At least she didn't run away to the back to hide. You're just afraid that you'll get a—"

"Okay, let's stop now," Ema interrupted. "We're a *team* as much as you like it or not. If we don't work together, there's *no way* we're winning. And that's a loss for all of us."

The anger settled, although Selma stuck her tongue out one last time at them before marching away with her squad.

"What a loser," Nicky muttered. She stood up and stretched her legs. "Anyways, next up is the Relay. I hope I don't get moat jumping."

"Moat jumping?" That didn't sound pleasant. Pulie asked, "What is that?"

"Oh, god," Nicky mumbled. "It's just what it sounds. The relay winds all around the palace including climbing up there and jumping into the moat off the barrier walls—"

"You mean the really tall ones? Covered in the vines?" Pulie asked, pointing to the huge barricade.

"Exactly those."

At the sound of the next whistle, all the teams began to gather around and chant their names. It was a way to strengthen their teamwork and sense of unity. Zive two began to huddle in a large circle, stomping their feet.

Nicky stood up. "We better join them. We got to know what strategies we need."

When the team chants ended, Ms. Borthwick led the *remaining* three Zives past the meadow to an area where the ground was dry and dead. There was a flag planted into the dirt, bold and red.

"Now, only half the team members from each Zive are allowed to participate. The rest will stay here and watch. So now choose the members you want to put forth and have them step up to this line."

From Zive two, a Trickjack came forth from the crowd and stepped up to be the leader. She quickly assorted a team for the game.

"Y'all, settle down. Those who don't want ta participate, leave the circle and sit over there. Okay, then. I'll choose a handful of random fellas."

She began by choosing mainly her friends and the Trick Jack levels.

"Daria, you're only choosing friends," Dan hollered from behind.

"I'm gonna get ta y'all later."

Finally, Daria pointed at Nicky and Pulie but not Ema.

The participants stepped up to the line. Pulie looked back and saw Ema glumly take her seat next to Anne and the other *unchosen* ones. Pulie listened to Anne say,

"I'm not doing this game either. Last time, my sister fell off the moat's walls with her arms twisted when she hit a block and broke her arm. It took her so long to recover. It was a waste of time."

Pulie swallowed hard. *Please, oh please don't say moat jumping for me.*

Each Zive had their representatives lined up, facing the palace, as Ms. Borthwick walked down the aisles with her device, assigning different tasks and ordering them to their positions.

When Pulie was reached, Ms. Borthwick said, "Sprinting."

When it was Nicky's turn, Ms. Borthwick immediately recognized her and sneered. "Moat jumping."

Nicky erupted only after Ms. Borthwick was a safe and far distance away while Nicky and Pulie headed to their positions.

"Moat jumping? Moat jumping?" Nicky threw her hands up, her face turning red. "There are hundreds of tasks, and I get the *one* and *only* moat jumping? Pulie, did you see? Ms. Borthwick took one look at me and literally gave me this nasty grin and like *hissed*. Literally *hissed*. Like a snake. *Sssssssss*. Like that. And then she says, *Moat Jumping*. Of course. Of course. I should've known. She wants me dead and away from the mission group in all possible ways."

"That's her mistake then," Pulie said. "This is your time to shine. If you can pull off some good moves in front of the teachers and Mr. Wace, most definitely, they'll pick you if our Zive wins."

Nicky opened her mouth and then paused. "That's *true*! That is very much true. This is my time to shine. Just watch when I *do* get into the mission, and Ms. Borthwick sees me, and she'll be so *distraught,* and she'll regret ever trying to kill me."

"That's the spirit. Now go to your position. The moat is that way." Pulie pointed to the palace far away.

"Shoot. Okay, good luck! To both of us!" And with that, Nicky sprinted away back to the palace.

Pulie's position was at the flag where she was to sprint along the long pathway to the back of the palace. And then she was done. Two other people were competing with her. Both were boys, and one had a very serious look on his face, almost as if he wanted to murder Pulie and his other opponent, while the other boy looked almost happy to be standing near him.

Three lanes were set for them, and they were to *stay* within the lines. From far away, Pulie heard the faint whistleblowing and saw the starters twisting through the tracks and passing the baton onto the next people. Soon, the team members were racing towards Pulie's own flag.

And then, *Bam!* The two other boys took off with the baton in their hands. Pulie was still waiting for her teammate to hand her the baton. She could see her teammate, slowly approaching her flag… just a little closer… Then finally, she was off as well. She sprinted and sprinted, but the boys were so far ahead of her she could barely see them. There was no way to cheat this game.

The lanes intertwined at one point, and soon, the roads became one. Pulie was catching up, but she still had a long way to them. She saw the boys disappearing through the tunnel ahead of her, and she let out a gasp of air and groaned. Sweat drizzled down her face, but she kept going. Why was her task going for so long?

Then, when she reached the tunnel, she skidded to a stop. At the corner of the tunnel was an arrow engraving, which pointed to the tunnel's right, instead of inside. And the arrow's direction pointed to the grass path to the right. Was she just wasting time? Was this cheating? But the moment Pulie switched tracks and began sprinting through the secret path, she realized that this was a short cut intentionally created by the leaders.

Her legs ran faster than ever until she was out on the main path again with the next row of three competitors, extending their arms for the baton. Pulie shoved the baton to the girl in front, and she took off. Pulie stumbled to the side of the path and collapsed, barely able to breathe. The other two boys were still not here. Which meant it really *was* a short cut. Minutes later, the boys arrived in a sweaty mess, shocked that Pulie had beat them to it. Both boys headed back around the other way of the palace, but Pulie was still on the floor. She had done it. She had not run faster than them. But she had beaten them.

She lay behind the palace walls which meant that *soon*, Nicky would be moat jumping at the front. Pulie wanted to see it, but the paths were blocked off. Her only choice was to return through the path she came from and join the rest of the team.

***

"We—we won," Nicky said, breathlessly and then she and Pulie crumpled to the carpet floor once Ema opened their door.

Nicky's hair was a mess; water dripped from all corners of her face and down to her drenched clothes.

"Well, the moat jumping took a turn." Ema sat next to the girls who had completely given way. Nicky threw her wet socks into the closet. After a few minutes, all of them regained their energy, and Nicky tossed her wet hair back and forth, narrating what had happened in the moat jumping.

"The point of moat jumping is to dive from the top of the palace into the water. Which is like a sixty—no seventy—I'm not sure. But it's a high drop. And with no gear. My baton came first, so I climbed up the ladder, but my foot kept getting stuck. But then, Clarissa, the girl from the Zive, fell completely *flat* on the water, like this—" Nicky spread her arms out on the carpet like a starfish. "And then she couldn't swim past the pole. The other boy was pretty good at swimming, but of course, my dive was perfection. It was so smooth. Not to brag."

"Oh, and there was Zive three. Apparently, the fastest boy there, his name is like Aaron, went complete berserk! After the game, he went straight to the leaders and ranted about how *you* cheated and stuff." Nicky pointed to Pulie. "Did you?"

"I guess so," Pulie admitted, feeling very shameful all of a sudden. *So, it wasn't part of the games?* This was not looking good.

"But then the leaders told him that you had not cheated."

"Really?" Pulie made a face. "Why?"

Nicky grinned. "You found the first shortcut. There was apparently a short cut in the first game too, but no one could find it. I assume the leaders will tell us after all the games are done."

"How do they know? Like how do they know I took a short cut?"

"They monitor everything with drones. Didn't you see them flying above you?"

Pulie shook her head. "So, that secret path I took wasn't called cheating?"

"Nope. I thought we were done for after Selma started her sprints. She slowed us down so much. I don't know what she was doing—dancing and singing combined. Whatever it was—it wasn't running. And then it was your task, which I think is the longest. We all thought it was over. But then you came in first. Nobody knew how. And then Erik and Celena finished the obstacle course super fast as well, and we ended up winning."

The three lolled on the floor in satisfaction for a while. They were *exhausted*.

"What time are we playing tomorrow?" Pulie asked.

Nicky rubbed her hands. "One thirty. Against Zive number one. They are one dirty team, but they are pretty good."

"How so?"

"They have Wallace Sulligan, Alexa Quin, Melissa Pallart, *and* Michael Roberts on their team," Nicky paused and blushed. "I can't believe we're playing against Roberts."

Ema chortled. "Nicky, stop daydreaming."

Pulie laughed as she saw Nicky's face glow red. "But how do you even know who he is? Isn't he from a different Zive?"

"*Everyone* knows who Michael Roberts is. It's like how everyone knows who Erik Pontz and Daria Chwala and Ria Sai are," Ema informed Pulie. "They're just known for being really good at things. Or for Nicky, really good looking."

They all laughed.

Ema said, "All of our Zive team members are meeting at the gym today at seven-thirty after dinner. To plan out our game."

"The Ambush Game." Nicky's face grew dark. "Scary game. I mean, this is all just a *game*. But everyone's so desperate to win that it really does get *scary*. We are taken to this large closed area outside of this Palace and out of the land and up to the Sky

Clouds. We take a walk to a nearby station. Inside, there are walls and doors all around us and long thick poles like forest trees surrounding us. We each have small laser pointers with triggers. Each time we see an opponent, we fire. Then that person is out."

"How do you know if you're out or not?"

"You wear special clothes when you enter the room. You will be a walking target. On the uniform, there will be a lot of circles that are where you aim for. If a laser is shot at the target, you will be notified."

"It's going to be really dark," Ema said. "Like pitch black and—"

"And plus," Nicky interrupted freely, "Mr. Wace, Awolo, and Ms. Borthwick will be monitoring us with surveillance cameras at the top of the room. But imagine bumping into Michael Roberts in there..."

"He'll get you out of the game then!" Pulie exclaimed.

"But, it's *him*!" Nicky cried, burying her head into her arms. "This is my only chance to meet him."

"Listen, Nicky. This is also your only chance of the year to get into the mission. You have a clear shot at it because you're in the finals. Why risk it?" Pulie reminded her.

"Of course. What am I talking about! I am off track." Nicky chuckled. "But you talk like you're not going to participate in the game with us."

Pulie rolled her eyes. "I am. But Michael Roberts isn't my goal tomorrow."

They all laughed.

***

"Zive number two, please follow me. Zive number one, follow Mr. Wace that way," Ms. Awolo announced when they reached a large rectangular flat building. They had left the Palace borders and up the stairs and into the blue world of the Sky Clouds up in the sky. The Ambush game station was a walking distance, so they arrived shortly.

It was one-thirty already. Pulie was starting to get nervous.

"Michael Roberts. There he is." Nicky pointed at a tall, muscular boy, marching behind Mr. Wace, his teeth gleaming and hair moosed back.

"Nicky. Focus. You'll see him *after* we win this game," Pulie assured her.

"Oh, fine."

They followed Awolo through the second door while the other Zive entered through the first one. Then, Pulie's group was given special instructions along with their gears.

Ms. Awolo read from her device. "Let's see the rules rules rules. By the end of this thirty-minute game, we will see which team has more survivors. Shooting the laser at someone is the only way to get them out. But, think *outside* the box. And *yes*, physical contact is allowed. That doesn't mean punch random people. Just be careful. You remember the rest. Some part of me wishes you good luck, and the other part doesn't." Ms. Awolo walked away. The door closed behind her, and Pulie's entire Zive was alone in the dark, cramped room, waiting for the game door to slide open. She was squished between so many people she couldn't breathe. Her new clothes made her sweat uncontrollably in a strange environment.

"3, 2, 1. The game begins." The monotonous voice in the machines around her said.

The door in front of them slid open, and she was swept away in the crowd of anxious people into the vast open space. She almost slammed into a large pole. There were many poles. Just like forest trees as Nicky had described. The room was so dark; all Pulie saw was black and black and more black. She fiddled with the small laser gun in her hands. She heard someone behind her. She spun around and pulled the trigger. With a small beep, a red laser beam was shot out of her weapon. Nothing happened. She had missed.

She continued walking. She felt as if she were all alone. So many people around her but she couldn't see anything, nor could anyone see her.

Then, she heard the symphony of beeps as people all around her fired. She began to run. But she wasn't the only one. She could feel everyone around her sprinting with her, not knowing if she was foe or kin. But her laser was red while the other team was green. The more she shot, the more vulnerable she would be.

"Gomez, Lim, Gray, Bauer, Schuman, Lee, Nguyen. Out. Please exit the room."

Pulie stopped. *Had people already been attacked?*

A couple of minutes later.

"Oster, Truo, Miller, Hernandez, Wang, Scott. Out. Please exit the room."

Nicky? Anne? Already?

Then, someone began shooting at Pulie. She dodged the laser beams and landed on her back. The lasers stopped. But someone had found her location. She held her breath for a few minutes and then, it became very silent.

There's got to be another way to win this game.

Then, Pulie's eyes grew wide. She felt the wall beside her and traced over an arrow engraved on the surface. It was another signal like the shortcuts for the relay. She had to find where it pointed to.

Pulie sat up and silently crept along the floor, following the direction and forgetting about the laser shooting itself. Then, when the laser firing again, Pulie, unprepared, dove for the floor, hoping that no one heard the thud she made. Lasers shot across the large room in every direction. Pulie remained low and continued her journey.

Soon, there was another arrow. It was pointing at a tilted direction this time. And so, Pulie followed it as well. She continued this, finding arrow after arrow.

This room must be ginormous. I keep going and never reach a dead end.

Finally, the arrow pointed downwards to the floor. Pulie immediately searched the area around her and found nothing. Not another engraving, not a secret latch, not a lump or bump on the floor—nothing.

Pulie winced and then sighed. All her hard work during the game was useless. This was just a fake signal—a trap. The laser shooting began again, but Pulie lay flat on the ground in the far distance. But the noises grew louder and louder. She had to hurry.

But there was one thing Pulie hadn't tried. She thumbed the engraving of the downward arrow. The space around the arrow was pushed back into the wall and, in its place, popped out a gadget.

Think outside the box!

She slapped the gadget on her wrist and activated it. It was a map—a map of the ambush room itself. There were also tiny green and red dots moving around the room. She had access to the location of every player at the moment.

A green dot was approaching her area. The person was behind the left pole. Pulie aimed and fired her laser, and a red beam was shot out.

"Ray. Out. Please exit the room."

Pulie grinned. This device was magic. She snuck around, shooting at the green dots that were in motion on her screen. Only a few times did Pulie miss the target. Most of the shots landed bull's eye on the person's chest.

Countless names continued to be called on the speaker.

"Rafferty, Walter, Pontz. Out. Please exit the room."

She heard gasps around her. *Erik Pontz. Out of the game before me.* Pulie grinned. Her gadget detected another *green,* and she fired, hoping for yet another win. There was a beep.

"Gulgorin, McCallen, Dutchstill, Trucker. Out. Please exit the room."

Pulie shook her head. Selma was also out of the game before her. Red beams never stopped shooting out of her tiny gun, and the speaker continued to announce the victims' names. Even Hailey *and* Sana were gone too. And soon, the sound of stomping feet and tackling settled. It was silent now. She wondered if the game was over.

There were still a couple of red and green dots floating around, but no names were called on the speaker. Pulie slipped behind a pole with her back to it and her laser ready to fire.

Wait a minute. Pulie began searching on her gadget for a certain movement of a green dot. *Roberts's name was never called on the speaker.*

"There she is!" hollered a voice, very closer to her.

Pulie winced and began running again. She swerved around and dodged every object in her way in the darkness. Someone had seen her with the gadget. How? In this darkness? Was it the light from the screen? She could hear heavy footsteps chasing after her while the green beams were firing at her side.

"It's another one!" A boy behind her shouted while panting.

Another one?

"What is it this time?"

"It's on her wrist!" Said the voices.

They saw the gadget. Oh, shoot.

The chase continued, the group of students trying to find out where Pulie was at the moment while she knew *exactly* where they were.

She zig-zagged around the poles and made a sharp turn. Everyone else was in the far corner of the room. She had finally gotten them off her scent. She carried on with her task of shooting at her opponents in silence, lurking in the darkness and ambushing her prey. But then—

Bam!

Pulie was thrown onto her back. She couldn't see anything, not that she was able to before. Had she hit a pole? Her gadget flew off her wrist and fell to the floor.

But the object in front of her pointed a green light at her face, blinding her eyes. She thought it was the end as she blindly scrambled to get the gadget, but the huge stranger, instead of shooting her on the spot, recognized the glowing device as well, left abandoned, and rushed to pick it up before Pulie could.

She couldn't see where he was until he slapped the watch on his wrist. It glowed like a gem. And then, she shot him.

"Roberts. Out. Please exit the room."

Pulie clamped her hands around her mouth. She had shot the Roberts guy. She quickly fled through the forest of poles.

The speaker later announced that the game was over.

Which team won? She didn't have the gadget to see how many people were left.

She found her way to the exit door and squinted through the sudden bright lights of the SkyClouds land. And after returning her gear, she found Nicky and Ema, sitting on the bench, both looking quite soberly.

"Pulie! Where were you?" Ema stood up immediately.

"I was in there," Pulie answered, pointing to the building.

"You were still in the game?" Nicky's eyes got wide. "No *way.*"

"Yes, way, actually." Pulie broadened her smile.

"Oh my, I lost to the new student!" Nicky slapped her forehead, grinning. "Did you hide in the corner or something?"

"Actually, I didn't. I found this hidden watch that displayed where every player was and moving."

Nicky and Ema made a face. "What?"

"That's how I ambushed everyone."

"Where's the device now?"

"Roberts has it."

"Really? Why does he have it?"

"It fell off my wrist, and he reached to grab it, and then I shot him."

Nicky gaped. "*You*—you got Roberts out. He's the one who got *me* out of the game. And literally half the people in our Zive. He and Erik had a major battle, apparently. And everyone stopped to watch. But then Erik accidentally tripped while he was backing up and then Roberts shot him. How did you find the watch?"

Pulie explained to both of them about the arrows and the buttons and how tracking everyone made it so much easier to ambush and escape.

"Secret tools." Ema slapped her thigh. "Why didn't I think of that? Good job, Pulie." Ema smiled. "You got Roberts out of his favorite game. You're going to have to avoid him. He isn't nice to new students *or* talented ones."

***

"Where are we going?" Pulie squinted through her puffy eyes and allowed her friends to drag her out of the room and down the hall. They were back at the palace the very next morning. "We aren't going to class, right?" Pulie yawned. "Why'd you make me get ready so early?"

"For heaven's sake, Pulie! How'd you forget already? We are going to see who won the Tricky Trials. The announcement came out yesterday. You were so excited, and you spilled your water," Ema explained, questioning Pulie's memory.

"Oh yeah." Pulie couldn't help yawning again. She had stayed up too late researching in the computer lab again.

"There they are." Nicky pointed to the group of people, standing around Mr. Wace and Ms. Awolo.

"Gather in," Mr. Wace addressed the crowd. "I believe now that's all of you. If you do not belong in Zive number one or two, go back to your dorm or whatever class you are supposed to be in. This is only for Zive numbers one and two.

"This year, instead of attaching tools inside the laser gun like last year, our staff hid three secret tools inside the *room* to assist the game. When thrown, the first was a bomb would create a fog in which light is impenetrable. The second was a pair of listening buds to hear from which location the laser beam was shot. And the third and most helpful tool was the maps gadget that displayed the location of each and every player in the room. Only *two* of them were found. The listening buds were discovered by Diana Fernsby from Zive one, and the gadget was found by Pulie Jark from Zive two, *not* Michael Roberts. Nice try, Roberts. Just because the room is dark doesn't mean we can't see what you are doing."

Michael Roberts' group in the back of the gathering hissed and scowled, while everyone in Pulie's Zive stared at her with shock.

"Anyways, the scores were very close. The Ambush game left a total of twelve people remaining when the timer stopped. But *one* Zive had two more survivors. Which makes all the difference," Mr. Wace said. "So the winner of Tricky Trials is…"

There was a steady, quiet drumroll.

"Zive number two!"

Everyone in Pulie's Zive leaped up into the air and screamed with joy. Their cheers were loud enough to wake up every living or dead soul in the palace. The losing team frowned and stomped on the ground. But it was no use. The game was over. Zive number two was unstoppable.

Ms. Awolo's lips curled. "Now, losing group, leave the courtyard. Go on! Don't stand there making faces at them, or I'll dunk *your own* faces in that leftover tar bucket we have, *one at a time*!" Ms. Awolo barked.

That got their feet moving quickly.

"Now for you. We're not done yet," Ms. Awolo spat at the winning team, with an unusually dark twinkle in her eye. Mr. Wace interrupted,

"Although, *congratulations* on bringing your team all the way through Tricky Trials. But now, there are only a selected few that will go on to being mission members."

"How many will you pick for the mission?" Someone from the remaining crowd asked.

"That is not information I will tell you. The only information you get is when the mission takes place and what you bring and wear to it." Mr. Wace grinned. "And *today* is the day we will be testing each and every one of you."

"Today?" Nicky exclaimed. She turned bright pink when she realized her voice was too loud. "But today?"

"Well, Ms. Oster," Ms. Awolo grunted, "If you'd like to be disqualified before the testing begins, keep talking. I'd like to see your mouth open some more."

Nicky shrank but crossed her arms, muttering. "Who in their right mind raised this lady?"

People nearby tried to conceal their laughter.

"Anything you want to share?" Ms. Awolo narrowed her eyes.

"No," Nicky answered. "Not with you."

There was an unpleasant look on the lady's face, and it put a sweet smile on Nicky's own.

"Ms. Oster, let's settle down." Mr. Wace waved his hands. "Like I was saying, the testing day is today—surprise surprise. Please head to your rooms right now and bring your EP clothes, and if they were ruined from the tar or relay, extra pairs will be handed out in the bathroom. We shall meet in the gym because Ms. Cherry has generously moved her class right now to the courtyard here to practice sprints. So we have the entire gym to ourselves. Hurry up now. Time isn't in abundance."

***

Everyone was lined up against the wall, wearing fresh training clothes, and they listened for instructions in the gym space that had been entirely transformed and arranged.

"Listen up!" Ms. Awolo barked, hands behind her back. She was a general, a sailor at sea, with enough charisma to burn the sun itself. Her deep dark eyes glared at them while her lips were snarling.

"To see which of you are capable of the dangerous mission ahead, we will run you to the ground, force you into the worst situations and see which of you are able to push yourselves when you are feeling weak. *Pain!* There is no such thing as *pain*. You *feel* pain, but there is none. So, if you're scared right now, exit the room. You'll be sorry if you don't."

No one budged. Fists crumpled. Each and every one of them was willing to give it all they had. If this was all it took to receive the glory, the pride, and the honor, they'd be glad to.

"That's what I thought." Ms. Awolo crunched her nose. "Only fools run from here." She stepped up to the line beside Mr. Wace and Ms. Borthwick. "From now on, only talk when told to. Do not make noises: no sneezing, no coughing, no nothing. Do not move unless told to. Do not touch anything you are not supposed to use. Listen carefully. Every single move we will be tracking. Step over a forbidden line once you're out."

"And when she says *out*," Mr. Wace added, "She means you'll lose points. Everyone stays until the end of this test, no matter what. We will determine which of you will pass later on. Now, let us begin. Sixty laps around this gym."

"Sixty?" Nicky immediately smacked her hand over her lips. Ms. Awolo raised her eyebrows but said nothing. She didn't need to. She just needed to remember everything she saw. Ms. Awolo blew into her whistle and legs started running and hearts began to pump.

By the tenth lap, Nicky was ahead of Pulie, who was in front of Ema. There was no "waiting for your friends" today. They weren't here to be nice. They were all here to fight.

By the thirtieth lap, Pulie's mouth was full of blood. She wasn't the only one. In front of her, she saw a dozen students spitting out a red liquid from their mouths and continuing to sprint. Two students threw up, and another fainted. Pulie strongly believed one of them was Dunkin Boar.

On her forty-third lap, Pulie was third in the entire Zive, ahead of everyone else. It was a pleasing sensation, but her body didn't agree. Her legs were aching and a gooey fluid built up in her mouth. She took gasps for air on the last two laps and finished in fourth place, right in front of Nicky.

The ones who finished first collapsed onto the floor and waited for the rest to finish.

Pulie was lying on the floor, drying her shirt next to three students she didn't know, Nicky and Erik. It felt good. That was all Pulie could think. Of course, she couldn't say it aloud.

There was no air conditioner inside the room, so she was stuck with the heated damp breeze. Her hair was a sponge, dripping with the salted sweat and her socks squeaked in her shoes.

"Very well done," Mr. Wace announced, clapping his hands as the last runner finished. "However, three students have given up in this activity. They are gone for good. Giving up is the last thing you want to do. Perseverance is key in that drill. For a cool down, let us bring down the bars."

From the ceiling, long poles were lowered slowly with precise calculation so that they became steps leading upward. However, to get from one step to the next required a great air jump.

Pulie swallowed hard. Running was one thing. Heights was another.

All she had to do was pull herself up onto the bars and then balance her way up the skinny poles to the top of the ceiling and then slide back down.

Easy. Real easy. Pulie thought, trying to breathe.

"I don't think I can do this," Anne muttered, holding her stomach.

"Me neither. But we have no choice."

Pulie's foot had resisted the momentum she wanted, and she slipped on the top bar. She was dangling by a single sweaty hand. She let out a squeak. Everyone froze, gaping at the girl who could fall to her death.

She heard gasps.

"Pulie!" Nicky cried, trying to keep her voice as quiet as possible.

"Miss Oster, no talking," Ms. Awolo reprimanded, although she looked quite happy observing the poor girl dangling from up high and whose arm strength was giving up on her.

The arm that was holding her up had frozen like an ice cube. Pulie was panting and sweating and kicking. She had to get momentum or else she'd fall. Gravity would swallow her whole if she didn't get another arm up there.

Pulie winced and gritted her teeth, not once looking down. If she did, she was sure to let go. *Up, Down. Up, down.*

She swung her legs back and forth, one at a time until she got the back of her shoe hooked onto the bar. She was safe, for now.

"Everyone, continue your paths. And you, hurry up now. You have caused a distraction," Ms. Awolo grumbled. It was clear she was disappointed that a fourth student didn't leave the test.

Fortunately, Pulie got her body back on the bar, safe, and sound above the ground. She proceeded with her task with much more caution.

The next task was to hit the target set across the entire gym. Everyone was given a single tiny metal dart.

"One throw, one dart. Get the dart as close as possible to the red dot." The red dot, however, seemed to be no bigger than a penny from this far away.

Although Pulie did not hit the target, she missed by a centimeter. Mrs. Wapanog proved to be helpful, after all.

"Absolutely terrible," Ms. Awolo muttered after the last boy missed the target by a couple of feet.

The next several tasks included jumping, stretching, diving, hanging, and quick wit. Then, there was a hacking race with the computers set out. Only a few students were able to crack the code.

When they had finished those, Ms. Awolo ordered them to gather around her. "Not too close! Don't want to be around all your disgusting odors."

They made a semicircle around her and waited for instructions.

"Last activity and you are free to go. This is just common sense if you'll ask me. This activity requires nothing but timing and how alert you are."

"Line up on the line," Mr. Wace ordered, "When I say go, you will sprint through the cones and to the other side of the room. Ms. Awolo will time you on the other side. You will have two turns, and it will be the average."

On Pulie's first turn, she made it just under thirty seconds, right after Erik Pontz and Celena. She beamed although she could see a scowl on both Ms. Awolo and Selma's faces.

On her second turn, Pulie had her foot behind the line, back hunched, and arms forward. She waited for the signal to sprint.

"Go!"

She halted. "What?" She spun around and saw Selma with her mouth open.

"Ready, Set, Go!" Mr. Wace hollered and caught Pulie completely off guard. She almost lost balance but began her sprint. Anger burned in her throat, but she couldn't stop running. She would get Selma later for that.

"28.34.90." Ms. Awolo calculated.

With a sigh of relief, she followed the class out of the gym.

Results would come days later, and she decided it was too much effort to mess with Selma today. Besides, she pitied Selma because Pulie had beaten her in every single task.

"How'd you think you did?" Ema unlocked their door.

"Pretty good, especially on the last one." Nicky dove onto the carpet and heaved a sigh.

"What about you, Pulie?"

"I don't think I'll get in."

"Why is that?"

"Well, first of all, I messed up real bad on the poles. And I didn't do particularly good on any of them."

"You beat me in all the running," Nicky added. "That's a big factor they look at."

"Maybe. I don't know. The fact that I fell off on the poles itself might ruin all my chances."

MISSION ALMOST IMPOSSIBLE

Tomorrow was the day when all Tricky Trial members would be announced. And the night before, the students in Zive two would crawl to the floor, bowing and praying to the lord so that they might be selected.

Nicky and Ema as well were on their knees, almost crying as they whispered their entreaties to earn the spot in the mission. Pulie followed their behavior.

"Is the mission like scouts?" Pulie asked.

"Well, yeah. But the missions here are for juniors and scouts are for adults. Why?"

"Maybe if I get into the mission team, I could see my parents. I mean, it's been a long time."

Nicky shrugged. "I don't know, Pulie. Unless they work here, you won't see them till next spring. And if they're on some scout, they'll be far away."

The following day, the entire school gathered in the vast courtyard which was soon covered in thousands of squirming students, trying to obtain a good spot on the floor.

A metal platform upfront was installed so that Mr. Wace and the two other very despised leaders could speak and present to the school.

"Thank you, everyone, for volunteering—" Mr. Wace said, tapping his hands on the speaker chip afterward. There was a muffled sound and then a cough. "—it is already October first. Nearly half of our year has passed. And we have no time to waste. This year especially called for a dangerous mission. The mission will include both a teacher's mission and a student team. The teacher's mission will be held separately with confidential privacy. On the other hand, the student team members will be announced at this very moment. Our teachers have been quite conscientious this year with the winning Zive number. So please, do not sabotage the winning Zive or there will be extreme consequences for everyone. Furthermore, this year's chosen Zive is—"

A stern and stressed silence pervaded the entire palace.

"Zive number two!" He announced into his speaker.

The people from Pulie's Zive section erupted into a massive tumult. Four teams battling for victory, each Zive anxious to present this honor. And her Zive had won! Of course, it was no surprise because *they* already knew. But now, it was time to celebrate. Even Erik was dancing around— in a very disturbing and unseemly manner.

Ms. Borthwick's chubby fingers now suffocated the speaker. "Sit your rums down. The mission is to take place at Conto Island," She said, spitting everywhere. Murmurs arose. *Conto Island?* She glared at the first row of students and continued, "It's always covered in snow. A mighty large island indeed. There's the main dock or whatever your folks call it— ah! The big building where most of the CAOT information is stored—"

"And thanks to our head detective here," interrupted Mr. Wace, "We have finally located it." Cheers arose from the crowd. Ms. Awolo came from the side and set a tiny metal box in the center of the platform and pressed a green button on the side. A large green hologram was spewed out, showing a replica of what is supposed to be the CAOT Dome.

"Thoyos, one of the five standing CAOT buildings in the world will be burning under our hands soon." Ms. Awolo declared, sashaying around the platform in her new silk green dress.

"We have to do this carefully." Mr. Wace continued, now forming a line with the other two leaders, "It is the second most important mission yet, and we are to do it with determination. Right now, I will be calling the names that have been chosen to be executors of this plan."

Everyone could feel the heat of anxiety. Pulie's Zive was a bunch of potatoes on a pan, trembling and popping up in their spots, fingers tightly crossed behind their sweaty backs, biting lips, and praying for their names to be called.

"Erik Pontz."

The crowd exploded in cheers when his name left the lips of Mr. Wace. *Of course, him.*

"Celena Drone."

Another outburst of cheers, as Mr. Wace read through his list.

"Nicky Oster, Ema Rafferty, Maya Lee, Alex Walter, Piden Jark, Pulie Jark—"

Pulie, Nicky, Ema, Alex and Piden all stared at each other with their mouths open in shock. They had all gotten in! All of them!

"Dash Dupupboir, Dan Zipmore, Noel Waycott, Alexia George, Colin Strussmore, Daria Chwala, and Tilda Kisinger. Please come up and receive your folders."

"This is insane!" Nicky jumped up. "How did we *all* get in?"

Pulie brought back to her seat the document files she had not been expecting.

"And now! Hush," boomed Mr. Wace. "Ms. Borthwick, please announce the jobs of these people."

Ms. Borthwick began. "Erik, driver of the cart and network leader— Celena, cart leader, medication organizer. Also assigning vests and equipment. Nicky, Alexia, Maya, Piden, are Distractors. A very important job. Daria, leader of bombing…"

"… Dash, Ema, Tilda, and Alex, hackers. You will be the ones to hack into the system in order to disable and deactivate security. I expect very much from you. Dan, Noel, and Colin, bomber's helpers. And lastly, the bomber, is—"

"Pulie Jark." The moment those two words left Ms. Borthwick's chubby lips, the palace seemed to sit still in its end. So silent, the mice had dropped dead in the sewers.

Mr. Wace raised an eyebrow. Pulie felt the sharp disturbed eyes lasering through her back, searing through her muscles and cutting into her.

"Now, now," Ms. Awolo said, "All in favor, say *Aye*."

Pulie's heart thumped. The majority of the school echoed in agreement.

"All who disagree, say *Nay*."

Selma's *Nay* echoed the loudest of few, she jumped up in her seat, screaming that everything was unfair.

However, the majority rule came into place. Pulie was officially, the bomber of one of the most important missions in the palace.

"Very good," Mr. Wace said, "Mission group, please come to the back of the stage. The rest of you remain in your spots, we will dismiss by Zive number."

People shook their heads nervously. Pulie slowly walked behind the rest, receiving a folder of directions and other information. Then the fifteen people took a bow in front of the audience.

Mr. Wace led the mission group to behind the stage platform and dismissed them.

"Rest today, students. Your training begins tomorrow morning at five am in Room T4."

Five am? Pulie thought, *This mission is all around crazy.*

EARLY

    The imperative command of honor and responsibility forced the girls to be awake at such an early time. They had been snug and cozy in their hammocks, but now, they were walking through pitch dark hallways, searching for the bathroom. Nicky slammed into the wall, and the crack echoed through the Zive at four-thirty in the morning. She heard another crack on the fifth floor. Someone else had run into a wall.
    Somehow, Ema found the bathroom door. The door creaked open with a high-pitch squeal. The lights were on, although it stood empty.
    "Who's been in here this early?" Pulie asked, stepping into the room.
    "Probably the night trolls," Ema whispered.
    "Night... trolls?"
    "She means the people who sneak around the Zives at midnight, you know, how we got down to the quad. They just chill around in the bathroom," Nicky explained. "Lame, in my opinion. But *five*?" Nicky continued. "Five am? I mean, if they said the mission class was thirty minutes early, I would've been like, *Right away, sir!* Even though it would be quite painful. But *five*? In the

morning? Well, it is a tremendous honor, which is why I'm here up this early in the bathroom like a night troll, but I'm just saying, this is crazy." Nicky's chatty disposition had returned.

Ema had dark circles around her eyes. "So, we going regular— classes?"

Even her English skill was deteriorating. It was too early.

Nicky gaped at Ema. "Were you not listening to *anything* yesterday? We are in a special group now! I swear you grow to be like me when I was little!" Nicky cried, patting the lotion onto her cheeks, "You know, it's kinda exciting, though. I haven't been on a mission before. Last year, Zive Number One was selected. Just *imagine* what my parents will say after this year. And the best thing is, *all* three of us were accepted. What better luck than that? But can you believe that both Piden and Alex got in? It's pretty rare for Young Trickies to be selected. Although Alex *is* pretty talented with technology and Piden *is* a fast boy."

After wandering around the courtyard, completely clueless, Pulie asked, "Mr. Wace said to go to room T4. Where is that?" Pulie asked, staring at her paper, searching for answers. "I thought you would know."

There was no answer.

"Nicky? Ema? You've been at this palace for more than a year—"

Still no answer. Pulie stared at them with large eyes.

"Nope." Ema shrugged.

"I told you," Nicky said, "I haven't been on a mission before."

"Then, should we go to the Miralmalma? Ask Mr. Wace?"

"Good idea." Nicky constantly looked at her clock gadget as time ticked away.

They opened the Miralmalma door and glanced at the long staircase before them.

"Here were are." Ema sighed, "Go on, up we go."

"Seriously? Is this how teachers go up here every night for bedtime?" Nicky groaned as she took her first step.

"Why are you complaining, Nicky? You come up here like twice a day!"

"Yeah! That's why I'm complaining. Now we have to go up here every day—surely, this can't be the only way up."

However, Pulie strayed away from the stairs as her hands trailed along the walls. Taking one step at a time, she felt the wall. Then, she felt the familiar stud and pressed the engraving. A small square block popped out. Then she slid her earring against the button.

There was a whirring sound, and Ema squealed out of curiosity. A white ladder was lowering down from the top of the ceiling. It reached the floor and waited quietly.

"Ema! Nicky! This is the same ladder." Pulie felt the ladder with her hands, cautiously, "I've been on it before."

Ema cried, "Were you out of your mind, Pulie? It could be a trap!"

"A trap? Why would there be a trap?" Pulie laughed. "I already went on it last time, and it was perfectly safe. How about I'll go on it first, and you can follow. If I die, then you all go and fetch Miss Ellie."

Nicky grinned. "Pulie, you seem to know this palace better than the rest of us."

Pulie chuckled, "I hope that's a good thing."

Then, she set her foot onto the first ledge of the ladder. A buzzing noise erupted, soft and faint. She grabbed on with both hands and started her ascent.

"Be careful, Pulie!" a voice screamed down below. Most likely, *Ema*.

"It's okay!" Pulie hollered, "I can see the light above me!"

"That might be heaven, Pulie. Or maybe daytime in hell!" That was probably Nicky.

Pulie went up, and up, very quickly.

It felt like a funnel or a tube of darkness, but there was bright and beaming light at the tip.

Finally, she popped out of the hole into the quiet room. She ran to the window, pressing her nose against the glass. She was back in the Miralmalma. She had remembered seeing the window from below. She saw the little domes and the tiny lollipop stand.

"I'm alive still," Pulie shouted back down the tube, where her echoes were sure to reach Nicky and Ema way down there. Then, Pulie went back to examining the room. From the circle opening, again, she could hear the machine buzz start to sound.

Soon, from behind her, Ema and Nicky stepped out, gazing out at the strange room. Nicky closed the opening with the lever. Then, she glanced at the staircase leading back down.

"Finally, thank god. Now I have a short cut up here!"

"We're here! We're in the Miralmalma! Now we have to go find Mr. Wace."

Pulie tried knocking on Mr. Wace's door, but it appeared he was not present in his room from outside. There were ten other doors. Each one looked identical.

"Let's try this one," Nicky said as she turned the doorknob.

Ema shook her head, "Knock, Nicky, it's not polite to—"

"Who cares? If I woke up this early, them teachers better be up too!"

They popped their heads inside the door, like a fox out of his den.

It was just the cafeteria for the teachers. Quite small in comparison to the vast eating room.

The next two rooms were locked shut. Curiosity got the better of Nicky, and she peered through the hole in the doorknob.

"It's the women's dormitory. I can see Mrs. Wapanog's nose from here!"

"Nicky!" Ema cried, although slightly laughing at the same time.

Nicky did the same to the next locked door.

"This one is the men's dormitory, Mr. Wace wakes up at five. He should be working."

The next door was also locked. Nicky squinted through once more. Nicky whispered, "It's just dark and seems empty to me. Where in the name of the Lord, could Mr. Wace be?"

Pulie heard rustling from somewhere in the room; someone was watching them. "Guys, we're not alone."

Ema cringed and sank to the ground, but Nicky scoffed.

"No one's even *alive* this early. *Don't* worry. And we found the room anyways, T4, right here. Great, we're earlier than the teachers. *Where...*"

"What are you three girls doing around here? No students allowed here this early," a sharp voice said. They spun around.

A tall thin bony woman stepped out of the darkness. She tapped her long slender fingers on her skinny waist. Her eyebrows narrowed at the sight of them as she pointed to the sign on the wall. Ema and Pulie had frozen up.

However, Nicky, on the other hand, was different. "We need to go to T4 for the mission," She answered right away, "We were assigned this special position yesterday, at you know, *Tricky Trials*. I mean, it's an honor to be in this group. Not that anything here isn't. Of course, it is. I am so excited. My parents would be so proud if they heard, but this school doesn't allow communication, so I have to wait till the end of the year. But that doesn't matter because—well, there are many reasons. So— if *you* can't help us, we'll be on our way," Nicky muttered, grabbing Pulie and Ema's hands tightly. The three backed away silently.

Suddenly, the bony woman smiled, a warm expression appearing instead.

"Well then, you're in the right place. Call me, Mrs. Slendersan. Welcome to Mission class."

MRS. SLENDERSAN AND HER CLASS

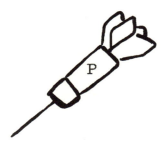

"I always knew that big mouth of yours would come in handy."

Nicky bragged. "I have many talents."

Their entrance was strange. The only light offered was the shallow lighting from the outside of the darkroom. The teacher refused to switch the lights on *yet*.

Mrs. Slendersan, a walking pencil, was so thin if she turned sideways, she would disappear. She handed each of them a pair of slippers to wear instead of their own shoes and ordered them to wait until the entire class was present.

One by one, the mission group arrived, each one with black circles under their eyes and an everlasting yawn imprinted on their faces. Colin entered the room, dragging Dan by the arm. Alex and Piden both marched into the room with even their feet matching each other's beat. Erik came in last, wearing a sport's set of clothes, with his hair slick. He walked up to the teacher and said something that made her smile. He walked off, grinning, and sat next to Celena. That boy meant business.

"Who are the other people?" Pulie asked Nicky when she saw many new faces. "I've never seen them."

"You see, there are four Zives," Nicky explained. "In each dorm Zive, there are about a thousand students in each, six levels, six groups at each level."

"What?"

"You know our class?" Nicky tried to put it differently. "In our Zive alone, there are six groups total just like us, only in level two. That's why we don't see half the people in our own Zive every day."

"How come I didn't see these mission people during the final Tricky Trials?"

"Oh, the test after the Ambush game? We were split into groups, so Ms. Borthwick and Miss Yardley took care of the other people in our Zive."

"Yardley?"

"Yeah. There's a lot of teachers we don't know about. We only see the teachers for *our* Zive alone. But there are three more sets. I know, it's confusing. But once you get it, you realize how many students and teachers are living here. It's crazy."

Finally, there was a soft click and a loud drum sound. The lights, one by one, flickered on. The first set of lights by Pulie's heads turned on. Then the second set, a good six feet above the first, flashed on. Then, the third and the fourth. And the lights continued to beam brightly, all the way up. When Pulie looked up, she gasped.

Above them was a ceiling way above their heads. She didn't know the Miralmalma was this tall. High above her head, intricate obstacles of vines and metal bars and ropes dangled in different directions. It was a thick jungle up there that Pulie could barely even *see* the ceiling. However, what she could see was three open windows at the very top. *No wonder the room has so much fog.*

"First, class—" Mrs. Slendersan cleared her throat, "I will introduce my name. My name is Mrs. Slendersan. For many years, I have been delegated to train a special group of students chosen from the annual Tricky Trials. You will all be members of this year's mission. No mistake, this class will be extremely tough. Those who struggle will be assigned additional training. Those who *continue* to struggle will then be replaced. This is no game like the trials. This is real. We train hard. We are fighters. Ten hours of training a day is a minimum. *Every day—*"

    Nicky's jaw dropped.

    "—until the final day. Last year, my best students often slept here overnight, completely forgetting about their outside lives. You have been selected with careful precision to complete a highly tasked mission. If you fail, you put millions of others at stake. Until the mission, you will follow strict diet rules and behavior methods. Have I made myself clear?"

    Pulie swallowed hard. She could see the lumps in other student's throats swelling as well.

    "Every one of you has been assigned different jobs. Starting today, we will review and go through every procedure and every bit of action to take place on the final day. We will map out a plan of what the mission will look like from start to end and *also* train to accomplish the plan." Mrs. Slendersan enlarged a digital pad onto the screen.

    Mission T7OY9S. Tricky Mission. Conto Island.

    "On January Thirteenth, all fifteen of you will leave the palace by foot straight to the village of Occultatum. There is only one main obstacle up till there; the Mortem River. It is known for its ravaging and untamed waters and the mystery of what is lurking within. We will drill on the river situations later. Next, once you reach Occultatum, you will notice that their security is very advanced. An electric barricade surrounds this strange village, which can be disabled by finding the tower system and shutting it down. Our research program was not able to obtain enough information about this part of the mission. All I know is that it is not an ordinary village with regular procedures. Take, for example, the fact that they are surrounded by immense security. *That* section of this mission will have to depend on your skill and quick wit.

"Once you enter the village, you will find your food to eat and locate a hidden spot for the night's rest next to Harvey's Pizza House on Dover's drive. The Trickies foundation will cater *twenty* boxes of pizza along with other orders from other people that will be delivered by a truck. The truck will be heading to a different city." Mrs. Slendersan paused. "But, *your* job is to hijack the truck the moment it leaves the village borders."

"Like steal it? What about the driver?" Someone from the room asked.

"That is why we have this new class created for you and your group to discuss and plan. However you do it, you will take the truck. This truck is the only vehicle with a hidden GPS of Conto Island. This island is hidden so that no normal tracker could locate it, so we need *this* specific truck in our hands. Drive this truck into the Pontux city on the coast. You will have a sufficient supply of food inside the truck."

Mrs. Slendersan selected an image of a rusty old truck with a pizza logo on the side. "Okay, we will pause on the mission planning for now and jump to the jobs. Erik, you will be driving you and the entire crew in this vehicle labeled pizza delivery truck. License plate 4J23778H. Erik is the leader, and you will guide the mission crew. Celena, you are in charge of all the equipment, and you will put together equipment packages like these. You will give the rest of the class a vest like this—Dash, please pay attention—"

Dash spun his head as Mrs. Slendersan pulled out a thin black vest. Attached inside was a parachute, and equipped in the pockets were a flashlight, a pocket knife, and a small timer.

"There is a specific vest for every one of you. If you don't have the exact equipment, you won't be able to carry out the plan."

Nicky whispered, "I'm gonna ask Celena to pack lots of candy."

"*Oster*. I don't know you that well, but I have heard many things about you. Let's keep our mouths quiet for a little longer."

Nicky shrank a bit, although it was clear she was still thinking about candy.

"Next, *Nicky*, Alexia, Maya, and Piden are the Distractors. This is a dangerous job, I warn you. But let's quickly jump back to the mission because, in order to understand your jobs, you must know what is going on. We must waste no time and get the start at the get-go."

A map was displayed. The dome was located smack center of the island, surrounded by a strangely shaped forest. Pulie realized the forest was shaped like a spider. *What—*

"Once you arrive at the dock of Pontux City, you will load your truck onto boat number 139. This large boat is equipped with a smaller boat in the lower half. Why do we need this specific advantage? The CAOT has a tracking radar. Once we approach Conto Island, we will board the smaller boat and the truck and slip out the back of the larger boat. This is a small distraction. The larger boat will keep heading in the direction of the main dock, right here—" She pointed to the port at the front of the island. "While we slip around the island southwards outside its radar and sail to the back. Most definitely, the CAOT will notice the larger boat and shoot it down. This gives us time to go to the back where there is no place to dock, but it is unguarded. Before we land, our hackers will disable the east security system so that no cameras or sensors will detect our landing or entrance. The system can only be shut down for a maximum of an hour, so you must act very quickly when you land. The truck will be loaded onto the ground, and you will immediately head to the forest for safety.

"This is when things get tricky. You will stop the truck at twenty degrees northeast of the dome hole, and three main groups will begin their tasks. Distractors will head southwest to a point far from our location and create a distraction—"

"What kind of distraction?" Nicky asked.

Mrs. Slendersan answered, "That's up to you and your group to decide. Now, if we'll continue, once the distraction is created, the guards from the front side of the island will head there while the distractors escape back to the truck. There are no wanderers on duty that day, which is why we are attacking that *specific* day. The hackers—Dash! I am explaining your part right now. Stop trying to bury your foot. At least Nicky listened at her part."

"That's cause you yelled at her!"

Mrs. Slendersan said, crossly, "If you want to stay on the team, don't argue with me." She drew a deep breath. "Hackers, you will stay in the truck with all our devices and set up the system so that Pulie, the bomber, can enter the top of the hole. Now, the bombing helpers and the bomber. You will head north and to the upper forest. You will slip in through the back of the dome, which will be guarded with very heavy security. But most of the guards are away, and the hackers will shut off the electric gates. Daria, you are the bombing leader so you will lead the bombing crew and then report back to the truck because you will have other tasks too. The bombing assistants will use Inflexus gadgets to bend the bars back to create space to slip in. Pulie will *quickly* climb up the dome, and when the timing is right, she will drop the bombs and *get the hell out of there*. You are not to enter the building. Pulie and the bombing assistants will wear this." Mrs. Slendersan pulled out a backpack.

"Inside, is a parachute, the bomb holder, knife, flashlight, and walkie talkie. Any questions?"

It was silent. Pulie stopped shivering.

"Very well. I know this is *a lot* of information at once. I will repeat this daily so that you cannot forget the procedures. We will now move onto the CAOT. Many of you might be wondering why we are putting in so much effort to bomb this place? Well, here is the reason. This building is dome-shaped, just like the dome in the courtyard. It's a CAOT datacenter."

"What if—the leader is there?"

Mrs. Slendersan nodded. "Precisely why we are sending you to Conto Island. The leader will *not* be present there. Neither will most of her team. It is the least protected of all her centers and thus the least important. However, some of their identifications, computer bases, files, and map-outs are located here. However, the CAOT have built many other centers for their team, so why this dome? There, they have set up their plans for their next mission; to destroy the tiny city of Pecunia. It is known for its great economy and rich mines and the thousands of innocent, helpless citizens who live there. The CAOT's mission is to blackmail and murder all the powerful, wealthy citizens first and then attack and control the others. They have made this goal very secretive, and the problem is Pecunia doesn't know about *us* or the CAOT. And even if we inform the city of the event that will take place, arming themselves will not help. No, no. The CAOT have their own special way of invading. They invade from both inside and outside. They will weave a web around the city in complete silence. So by bombing the dome, we will also erase and destroy all their databases. Many people will be spared. But remember, by doing so, we will end the lives of some CAOT, but this is for the right cause." Mrs. Slendersan selected a hologram display from a tiny metal clip on the ground. She spun it around a full three hundred and sixty degrees so everyone could see from all sides of it.

It was a massive white dome with a hole at the top. It looked kind of like Mrs. Wapanog's dome below on the main floor. Mrs. Slendersan slid her finger to a clicking button, and suddenly the hologram displayed snow surrounding the building.

"The bomber will ascend to the top of the dome and climb in to drop the bomb." A tiny person in the hologram was shown red and bold as it climbed up the steep sides of the dome and plopped three minuscule objects into the dome.

"That's funny!" Alex shouted, scratching his head. "I question the reason behind such an easy get through. Why's there a hole at the top?"

He was right. Strangely enough, a building of such importance displayed an elementary and obvious entrance.

"Great question— you— ahh, I am afraid I don't know your name yet—"

"Alexander Walter, but preferably Alex. My mother's intent with the name was to give me a short name during my childhood and a more mature and longer name in my scouting years."

"Ah, yes, yes, Alex—brilliant question. I will answer the question now. Most of the connections made by the dome stay underground to avoid suspicion from the outside world. However, they figured *one* source of connection above the ground is needed, so they constructed a hole at the top of the dome. No intruders can enter because it is heavily fortified with lasers. But at a certain time for *ten seconds* every once in a while, the laser is disarmed to let the connection flow. Our Tricky foundation has cracked this crazy calculation pattern that changes every nanosecond of when the laser will be disarmed. Pulie will not enter the dome itself; she will simply drop the bombs through the hole, slide down the dome, and escape back to the trees."

For the rest of their training that day, everyone was split into rotational groups, mapping out specific details and preparations for their tasks.

The distractors devised multiple distraction ideas in case of Plan B. The hackers were sent to the computer lab to retrieve computer devices, and the bombing crew got together to plan their routes. Daria was the leader. She brought out a digital pad where she drew the island and their plans. Pulie could not help but stare at the forest outline that was shaped like a spider. Did no one else notice?

"Do you see the spider?" Pulie pointed to the green marks. Everyone peered at it and then nodded. "Why?"

"It's a spider," Pulie said. "Is there some kind of meaning behind that?"

Daria answered, "Spider is believed ta be their mascot. Nobody knows why, but so far, it ain't a big deal."

It was a mascot. Why hadn't she realized? So each time Señor Rodriguez and her parents freaked out about *spiders* was because it was the mascot of their enemy. So her parents really were scouts in the Trickies. *Spider. Spider.* Pulie was satisfied.

Soon, she was called over to Mrs. Slendersan's desk. The woman had pulled out a mini model of the dome and a tiny little plastic figure. "Let's see. Pulie Jark. Fifteen?"

"Yes."

"I expected an older age for this job, but I guess it will do. And you—" Mrs. Slendersan paused. "This your *first* year?"

Pulie nodded.

"Do you even know how to read?"

Pulie explained her situation to the teacher.

"Ahh. That makes sense. I am surprised that Mr. Wace would assign a student with less than a year of experience as a bomber. This is the most simple yet most difficult job of all. Do you know how to use a parachute?"

"No."

"Well, you'll need to know that skill. But that can wait. We'll begin with the climax of the mission. You will figure out how you will be able to ascend to the top of the dome—" Mrs. Slendersan pointed to the top of the miniature dome. "And then drop *three* bombs once the timer goes off and the laser is disabled after setting all three, parachute down the dome. Do not enter the hole at all and drop the first two bombs down the furthest and the third near the top. The dome will completely explode, so make sure you and the evacuators and the bombing helpers are in the truck before then. This is very important." Mrs. Slendersan dropped the toy bomb into the hole and made sound effects with her mouth.

"Can't I go through the floor entrance?"

"Our palace strictly forbids young and inexperienced trickies to come in full contact with the CAOT. This mission may be issued because there are not enough Tricksters to execute this plan, but remember, you are still children and this is to make you experienced with missions for when you are older. Heaven knows what might happen if you are caught! They might torture you, and you will end up spilling all the information about Trickies. Or they might use some kind of Truth Serum or whatever they have been cooking. You will go up the *top* so that you won't be involved in any of that."

"How will I get up there?" Pulie asked.

"I'm afraid that's what you have to think of." Then Mrs. Slendersan told Pulie to take her miniature models and digital pad somewhere else so she could call other students up to her desk.

Pulie sat on the floor with the mini electric pen squeezed between her fingers, draining the color from her hands. She switched on the screen of her device.

She decided to draw the plans that came up on a whim. Her first idea was a ladder. She sketched a ladder from the ground up to the top of the dome. *A ladder as tall as a mountain?* She deleted that one.

What about a plane... She sketched a mini plane flying up to the peak of the building. *Or maybe...* ropes to hook onto the top and climb! A long rope was drawn from the bottom to the top.

Vines. That was it. And she was sure this palace had a full supply of those plants. She returned back to Mrs. Slendersan's desk and explained her brilliant idea.

"You can't use vines because you need to go *up*."

"But what about those Vines we use to get up to Zives?"

"Those are turning by a rotation wheel."

The feedback languished Pulie immediately. She brought the miniature model back to her workspace. Suddenly, a notification sprang from the corner of the screen.

From an unknown sender.

Pulie silently and secretly clicked the notification.

GNAR perfect idea — Nos, A

"It looks like a code," Pulie murmured softly, "Is it a teacher?" She scrolled through all the messages sent through the device.

None. No messages had been sent. That meant it wasn't one of the teachers.

Then, what does Gnar mean?

Pulie's eyes widened. A Rang! A backward message. The sender was hinting at the Rangs! Of course. Those plants were long, sturdy, violent, and absolutely *perfect*.

She was overwhelmed with gratitude and typed a response: Thank you so much. I really appreciate it.

She waited and waited. There was no response. So, in the meantime, she informed Mrs. Slendersan of how she enhanced her idea.

Pulie was given the stamp of approval.

A new notification had sprung up by the time Pulie arrived back at her spot.

No problem. I hope this helps.

Pulie hesitated. Who are you?

There was no reply.

The next few weeks, orders whizzed in through the palace. Boxes of newly created Rangs were transported into the mission room, where Pulie learned how to grow, freeze, cut, and handle a Rang. So far, things were going fine. Just fine.

***

"P-u-l-i-e—"

The one voice Pulie dreaded to hear as she walked all alone to the eating room. Nicky was up in Señor Rodriguez's class for gear information and Ema was at the computer lab, learning the program software for their mission.

"Aren't *you* ready for this mission… "

Selma poked Pulie as she snorted. Bonnie was located on the other side of Selma. Pulie ignored them and continued walking. They weren't worth her while.

But Selma wouldn't stop. She poked, and she spit, and she flapped at Pulie's heels.

"I can't believe out of *all* people—you." Selma sighed, almost as if she pitied Pulie. "Glory from cheating in the Tricky Trials doesn't last long, you know."

Pulie continued to ignore her.

"Why aren't you listening to me?" Selma threw her hands up and blocked Pulie from walking.

"Listen, I really don't want any trouble today." Pulie eased away from her.

"*I don't want any trouble*," Selma mimicked, waggling her head side to side. "*I'm* not trouble. *You're* the trouble. Ever since you got here, bada bing bada boom. *You* took my spot on the trials."

"There's a reason why you're not on the mission team."

Selma stuck out her lip. "I don't know what it is." She glared at Pulie. "But I don't like you. You remind me of the CAOT. You're probably a spy. Anyway, I just can't wait till Halloween. I'm going to beat you up."

"Fine then."

Still, Selma and Bonnie did not leave her side.

"So— is *Dash* in your class?"

"Who?"

"Dash. Don't you know who that is?"

"*Oh*, him. Of course."

"You see him every day?"

"Yeah. Why?" Pulie replied, walking as fast as she could.

"Drop the mission."

Pulie halted. "What did you say?"

"Drop the mission—or I will tie Anne to a tree and hang her upside down. Or I'll steal Nicky's tar, or I'll poison Ema's food."

Pulie pointed the finger at the girl's face. "Don't even try."

"I *will*. Unless you drop the class, and we're even."

Pulie grew very angry. "Even? What do you mean, *even*?" Pulie pointed her finger again. "Leave me and my friends *alone*. You aren't the boss of anyone—"

Bonnie squealed. "Don't talk to Selma like that!"

Selma nodded with a mischievous expression. "I am giving you one last chance, you *ungrateful* child. Drop the mission. I leave."

Pulie glared sourly. "I don't listen to people like you."

Selma narrowed her eyes and reached behind her bag, but before Pulie could say another word, she saw a tiny blur flying at her hand.

Crack! Pulie let out a yelp as she fell on her knees, cringing in pain. Blood and pus oozed from the center of her palm, where there was a dart sinking into her skin.

"Bonnie, help." Selma grabbed the wounded hand, Bonnie the other, and Pulie was dragged to the Miralmalma door.

Pulie hollered and kicked. She tried to use the backflip trick, but the pain from her hand was too great. It burned and stung, and to compensate for it, Pulie bit her lips as hard as she could. She could not let Selma get away with this. Selma had literally thrown a dart at her hand.

Instead of the staircase or the ladder method, Selma rushed to the side next to the door and uncovered a tiny string with a golden bell attached to it. She slid her earring over the bell, and from above, a hammock was lowered down. Amazed and terrified, Pulie was tossed into the large cloth folding like a doll, and Selma and Bonnie plunged in afterward.

Pulie thought about purposely falling out of the hammock until she realized that going straight to the Miralmalma was the best option anyway. All the teachers were up there, and Mr. Wace could help her. Or they could help Selma to the insane asylum. That was a better place for her.

Pulie didn't resist nor retaliate until she was thrown out of the hammock and onto the main floor of the Miralmalma. The dart sat in her hand like a thorn protruding from a stem. Pulie needed medical attention. Fast.

Selma called out at the top of her lungs. "Don't worry, Pulie. *We'll* get you to the nurse right away!"

"No, she won't!" Pulie hollered even louder. "Mr. Wace! Mr. Wace! Help! Selma has gone crazier than crazy! Help—"

"Ms. Leapando! Quick!" Selma interrupted. It was a shouting battle now. Pulie stood up and began searching for teachers when she bumped into this nurse who stepped out of the hospital treatment unit room.

"What's all this fuss? Oh, dear!" The nurse gaped at the pointy object in her hand. "Come in, come in. What on Earth happened?"

Pulie drew a sigh of relief at last. *Finally*. Pulie stepped into the treatment unit. It was a vast room with hospital beds lined up against both walls at her sides all the way down. The windows at the end of the room had been closed, so it was dark far over there. Pulie waited for the nurse to help her. But the nurse remained outside. Pulie could hear Selma and the woman conversing.

"I don't know." Selma *sobbed*, "It's *so* unfortunate. She was playing with the darts in the courtyard. Perhaps to prepare for the mission. But she was not skilled enough and…"

Pulie didn't hear the rest because Ms. Leapando and Selma and Bonnie barged back into the room.

Ms. Leapando shook her head, sighing when she entered. She immediately set out a mattress for Pulie and helped her onto it. Selma and Bonnie waited by the door.

"Ms. Leapando," Pulie began, "Whatever you heard from Selma, is a *lie*. I did *not* accidentally stick a dart into my own palm. Selma threw it at me because I wouldn't drop the freaking mission—"

Ms. Leapando's face grew grave. "Miss, I cannot accept that. The first step you must take is to express gratitude to Selma and Bonnie, for they have assisted you to the treatment unit to help you. Do not accuse another person because of your mistakes. Selma is one of the sweetest girls I know, as well as Bonnie. I don't accept this accusation of yours." The nurse reached over and forcefully plucked the dart tip out of her palm and wrapped the bloody sweaty hand in bandages. Pulie winced, and the nurse continued. "If they had not been here for you, *what* would have happened? And besides, why would Selma throw a *dart* at you?"

"She was threatening me to drop the mission class." Pulie leaned back in her mattress and called out in a loud voice. "Because *I'm* in the mission class, and *she* isn't!"

Selma crossed her arms and stuck out her tongue. But Ms. Leapando didn't see this. Her back was turned as she pressed the alcohol pads against the wound.

"Girls. Pulie. The mission is a privilege, *not* a bragging right." Ms. Leapando stood up and wiped her hands on her apron. "Pulie, I think I must tell Mr. Wace about this, however—"

"No!"

"Yes." Pulie bobbed her head, earnestly. "Please do so."

Ms. Leapando squinted. "Don't give me that attitude. I will have the Twig check on your injury and report back to Mr. Wace. If you miss too much training due to it, you might be replaced. I will check with the leaders."

"Don't worry. I'll heal," Pulie rejoined.

Selma shrugged at the nurse. Bonny joined the shrugging.

"*I* don't think it will happen," Selma said. "Tell me at any time if substitution is needed, Ms. Leapando."

The three headed out the door, leaving Pulie alone, sitting against her hospital bed.

"*You* won't get away with it," Pulie muttered under her breath. "Mr. Wace will hear of your plan to get me out of the class, and he will punish you. You won't get away with it."

Thoughts flooded her brain. *Selma. Evil. Bonnie. Gullible Nurse.*

"Is her name *Selma*?" A scraggly and meek voice called out. Pulie perked up.

Then, suddenly, Pulie noticed that she hadn't been alone in the room all along. Another figure sat in the far bed with only her face sticking out of the sheets. Pulie could make out the outlines of her face. She had sunken eyes and pale skin. Her ebony hair streamed down and fell off the bed. Pulie held her breath. Who was that girl?

"Is her name *Selma*?" The stranger asked again.

Pulie nodded. "Yes. Do you know her?"

The girl stayed quiet, remaining hidden underneath her covers. Then she asked again, "Does your hand hurt?"

It did. The hand stung as if Pulie was clasping a burning fire in between her hands.

"Yes, it does. The nurse did nothing but let it bleed even more." Pulie slouched in her bed, questioning Selma's intelligence based on how she had just cut another student's hand with a dart.

I'm a Tricky, too. Pulie gritted. *I'm a Tricky too.*

"Don't worry," the strange girl whispered. "The Twig will help you."

"The Twig?" Pulie asked.

It was quiet after that, so Pulie let her mind stray elsewhere when she glanced around the aesthetic walls of the treatment unit. One wall was designated for the names of the students who had died during training at the palace long ago.

Another wall was a collection of art with paintings of the leaders and the founders of the palace, while the wall right in front of her was full of photographs of the most accomplished students.

One photograph caught her eye. Two twin girls were holding hands. They looked almost too identical if it had not been for the strange perceptive difference in their faces that Pulie caught. The girl on the right-hand side wore a friendly smile like a bright light shining on her face and face only. But the twin on the left seemed to have been cast in the shadows; no light lit up her face. There was just a mysterious snicker in her eyes, almost as if she was plotting something.

THE TWIG

A man stepped into the room with a digital pad in his left arm and a large briefcase in the other. Both objects seemed to be weighing down the man himself.

"Pulie Jark? Zive two?" The man asked and his eyes settled on Pulie. "I am The Twig. Is it your right or left hand?"

The man really *was* a twig— skinny, frail, and tall as if he had been stretched out. His blueberry jeans were tattered and his face was a long mourning painting with no color. He lacked hair as much as he lacked happiness.

Pulie shrank. She was in this strange room with two strange people. She didn't like this at all. What if the Twig didn't help her? Was he just like Ms. Leapando? Was everyone here?

The Twig seated himself on the edge of Pulie's bed and unlatched his briefcase. He placed his glasses on his nose and brought out his tools. Her bandage unraveled and fell onto the sheets. He inspected the gash carefully.

"Very interesting." He paused. "Unless you had been trying to commit suicide—or try to jab yourself on purpose, playing with a dart would not have resulted in this deep of a wound. Were you trying to hurt yourself?"

"No!"

"Then you were attacked." The Twig put away his tools.

"Finally, someone with *common* sense. Will it heal?"

"It will be healing in no time. If bones had been broken, surely, you would've been replaced and sent out of the mission crew. But it will probably heal within a month. I will discuss this with Mr. Wace and see what he thinks about this matter. I don't know if he wants the *bomber* to stay out of training for that long. Well, he might find an alternative. Either way, he's a smart man and he'll most likely make the right decision. That means in the meantime, no EP, no running, no push-ups, only mild training, and no using the hands. The fastest it'll heal is probably one month."

"That only leaves two months for real training, though."

The Twig shrugged. "It is what it is."

Pulie fell back on her mattress. "No, no, no. It was Selma, sir. Selma Dutchstill? Do you know her? She's got it for me, I swear. She wanted me out of the mission group and here I am. What am I to do?"

The Twig made a face. "If it really matters to you that much, I would report to Mr. Wace. But then again—" He paused. "If things do go your way, Miss Dutchstill's hatred towards you will only grow stronger. I'm quite experienced with the consequences around here."

He revealed a missing finger.

Pulie's face went pale.

"Hopefully you recover fast." Then the door shut and Pulie was alone again, except for that creepy silent girl who was just watching everything from the shadows.

Pulie let out a groan.

"Pulie?"

Pulie spun around, nearly falling off the bed. It was Ema, standing by the door. She looked at Pulie like a hallucination.

Ema's fist crumpled after Pulie told her what happened.

"All those Dutchstills are *sour grapes*. Sorry for my bad profanity." Ema shook her head. "Why *you*?"

"I don't know. But she made it pretty clear she wanted me *out* from the mission."

"Well, the only thing I've got in mind, is to keep you *in* this mission. Come on, let's go to lunch."

***

"That *tall* twit," Nicky hissed under her breath after Pulie explained the story to those who were sitting at her table.

"You have just created an alliteration," Alex added.

"A *what*?"

"An alliteration is a literary device in which all the words in a sentence begin with the same—"

"That's not the point, Alex," Nicky interrupted. "Selma has *got to go*."

Everyone nodded in agreement.

"Report her."

"Get her back."

"No! She should be locked up in Alcatraz in San Francisco, while tourists watch her suffer miserably between bars," Alex said, pointing his finger up. He looked pleased with himself when he sat down.

THE LITTLE TROUBLEMAKERS

They climbed out of the lunchroom and up to the courtyard.

"You all can go ahead. There's something I need to do," Pulie said.

Nicky spun around. "You sure? What is it? We can help." Nicky stared at Pulie's red bandaged hand and looked up. "*We* can help—"

Pulie hesitated. "I want revenge on Selma."

Nicky's face lit up, and she squeezed Pulie's healthy hand.

"My *child*— all grown up! Finally, learning how to deal with people here," Nicky squealed. "Are you kidding me! I *want* to help! So—what are we gonna do? Destroy her make-up cabinet? Or maybe, we can smack her in the *face* with a Launcher after we steal the cradle from her—"

"Nicky!" Ema exclaimed, "It's Pulie's time for revenge. She needs her space to create an idea."

Nicky breathed slowly and nodded. "Yeah, that's probably right. But keep those ideas in mind."

Minutes later, they were in their room.

"This is *awesome!*" Ema cried. "I mean, genius idea. It's quiet and sneaky. How are we going to get the message to her? We don't have any paper to write a letter."

"The school allows cardboard boxes," Nicky suggested. "But then again, that's too large."

"*I* have paper." Pulie brought out her old notebook from home.

Nicky shook her head. "Selma saw that notebook, remember? She's going to know it's you. How about we just keep it simple and send her a digital message."

"We can do that?" Pulie asked.

"Yeah, we have *Ema*. She's the computer lab queen. All we have to do is make the message pop up on Selma's device."

Later, Ema secretly brought them into the upper computer lab, the tech room for the staff, and accessed Selma's device system. She hacked into her computer chip. And then, they had Nicky do the typing.

"Dear Selma, your eyes shine like the moon. Your cheeks so full, and your lashes like dancing waves. You are so beautiful, and I can't explain the love I have for you. If you could just give me one chance, tonight… at midnight when the moonlight shines through the palace boundaries… will you meet me at the front of the Miralmalma?

Ever since I have been assigned the mission, your absence is killing me. See you tonight.

Love,
Dash—"

Ema and Pulie both cracked up when they heard Nicky read what she had written so far. Pulie's eyes were swollen from the constant laughing.

"Can Dash even write that well?"

"I mean, Selma will believe it."

"I hope so. You know, love hurts more than a bruise on your hand."

They all nodded in agreement.

The message was delivered.

"*Dash* also has access to the computer system, and Selma knows that," Ema added. "This is going to be great."

"Did you say, meet me at twelve? Or meet me at one?" Pulie asked.

Nicky shrugged. "I honestly forgot, but I don't think it really matters, right?"

"That's right. Either way, you sent an RSVP to Awolo."

It was payback time.

***

The courtyard was slowly transforming.

Giant stretched out cobwebs draped from every tree, and the walls splashed in bright red paint.

"It was Halloween?" Pulie joked.

"No!" Nicky answered in all seriousness. "It's *tomorrow*."

"Already?" Pulie asked, examining the dead rat decoration on the floor with awe.

"Hey, little boys," Nicky greeted Alex and Piden as they walked on over. Pulie was still crouched over the fake rat.

"Pulie?" Alex said, his voice starting to shake.

"Yes?"

"I don't think that's a decoration."

Pulie let out a yelp.

Nicky laughed. "*Halloween* is my favorite day of the entire year. It's the best! Someone out there, come out and defy me. There's no chance. An entire day of nonstop tricks and pranks. I am just so excited."

"Same," Piden said, "And if you watch carefully, the decorating workers are moving the decorations out of Larry's storage room into the courtyard."

"And?"

A grin on Nicky's face stretched as easy as rubber.

"Well, *some* first-level Tricky is getting creative in this palace." Nicky fist-pumped Piden.

***

The back door hinges squeaked, and then the door shut softly. The room was pitch dark.

"Where's the light? I should've brought a flashlight—"

Nicky couldn't finish her sentence when the boxes fell on top of her.

Then the door swung open. Bright lights shined in from the outside courtyard. And like a gun had gone off, the five geese buried their heads in the dirt, silenced, hoping the visitor wouldn't see any of them.

"Mike?" Hollered a man, "Start on the pumpkins. Move them to the south gates, okay? Mike?" His footsteps wandered back out to the courtyard.

Nicky blew a soft whistle, signaling the beginning of their mission.

Pulie slithered from underneath the shelf and snatched a pumpkin from the stack. She followed Piden and Alex out of the storage room and into the living room where Larry would usually sit, fiddling with a carving or two. Stacking the pumpkins, they soon created a pyramid of Halloween decorations. Larry wasn't in his workspace. As Pulie passed the desk, she saw a large box with a familiar glass bottle of liquid.

Back in the storage room, Ema found a box of caramel sweets and tarts.

"Jack Pot," Pulie whispered. Without hesitation, their pockets were overflowing with candy.

Then, the door slammed. The same man reentered the storage room. The five geese dove into their nests once more, hiding behind the closet and waiting for a reaction.

When the man came back, the five hid behind the closet, waiting for his reaction.

"Ummm, where are yar pumpkins?" Mike peered around the room. When he turned his head, Pulie saw the same blood-red tattoo on the back of his ear, although half of it was hidden under his curly black hair. "You were saying."

"What? I just saw them—they were *right here*—" The man grasped his hair, trying to explain it all to Mike.

"Let's get these gravestones outa here first, before yar little pumpkins. Come on!"

"But— but—"

"No butts! Get on with it! They can't magically disappear! And it's not like some of those Tricky rascals snuck in and messed with your head! Come on!" Mike hollered from outside. "We have an hour till the decorations need to be done. Mrs. Casteron arrives in like an hour. We need to help sort out the eating room, too. Get yar butt moving!"

Reluctantly, the door shut behind the man after he dragged the cart of gravestones outside. The five burst into laughter.

"Did you see his face?"

"Oh, I can't wait till he passes Larry's desk and finds a stack of pumpkins smiling up at him!"

***

"Ahh," Nicky said as she laid on the carpet floor, snug in her pajamas. "I cannot wait until tomorrow."

They had just got back from the shop. It had been a mess; the entire store swarmed with students slamming against the shelves scrummaging for the perfect costume. Blobs of face paint, streamers, and strings made a pillow for the customers. Even going through the door had been an obstacle. It was trying to fit an elephant inside a box. Impossible.

Nicky smoothed her bag over the floor. "Our costumes our picked, our candy was bought, our traps were created—Oh, right. Pulie?"

"Yeah?" Pulie seated herself right next to Nicky.

"Remember that *tomorrow* is a day when you are allowed to —"

"Trick and treat."

Nicky was flabbergasted. "You meant, trick *or* treat, right?"

"Does it matter?"

"Yes!" Nicky squealed.

"Sorry, I've never gone trick and, I mean, or treating before."

"Really? Not even in your punke years? Oh, right. Your parents homeschooled you."

"Yeah. I rarely left my house."

"Well, tonight, we're going to down to the eating tables to submit a survey. Your answer, *Trick* or *Treat*. Simple. But this determines your actions the next day entirely. Tomorrow, you can *only* do what you chose. Of course, everyone chooses *Trick*. Who's stupid enough to hand out candy to everyone the entire day? Well, everyone has to set a bowl of candy outside their door. But the people who choose *Treat* can't trick *anyone*. And besides, *Trick* is especially nerve-wracking and exciting because all your nightmares come to haunt you. Trust me. One student left the school after what people did to her. But on the bright side, tomorrow is the real payback day. Everyone goes *all-out*. No other day is as special as Halloween."

"That means I can trick Selma? And Erik?"

"Anyone. That is if you choose *Trick* tonight. *If* you end up choosing Treat, you can't trick people, and you can only hand out candy and treat other people nicely. It's really pretty self-explanatory. I mean, that's why it's called *Trick* or *Treat!*"

Pulie realized she would have to be extremely careful around Selma and Erik.

When the dinner bell rang, everyone gathered in the lively, crowded eating room. A large colorful metal box had been planted in the center of all the excitement and chaos. Nicky stepped up to the box and punched in her name after she scanned her earring. Then, she slapped the glowing green button with the letters *Trick*. Beside it, another purple button with dust piling on top had *Treat* engraved in it.

Pulie slapped the green one as well.

Tomorrow was No School. Tomorrow was a new day. Tomorrow was *Halloween*.

MISS IDADOSI

Her eyes opened in a flash as the echoing morning bell rang. *Halloween.* The day everyone was crazy about.

Following shortly, a waterfall from the ceiling gushed onto her face. The icy cold water was drowning all her senses, the senses she would need to be keen for the day ahead. Pulie wiped her eyes with her furry sleeves, listening to the clanking of the bucket lid. Thankfully, her injured hand was not wet, although the rest of her hammock was drenched with water dripping from the bottom and forming a puddle in the carpet below. Nicky was balancing on Pulie's hammock, gripping tightly to a vine and an empty bucket, with a grin extending from one side of the earth to the other. She looked content and proud. Pulie knew that would abate in a matter of seconds.

Well played, Miss Oster.

From underneath her soaking pillow that seemed to be juicy from the impact, Pulie snatched a tin can and sprayed a cream filling all over Nicky's face. Nicky was soon clinging to a Vine, licking the delicious whip cream off her lips.

Pulie giggled and laughed in her swampy hammock. The water had run all the way down to her socks.

Both Nicky and Pulie battled again once they landed on the floor, spraying water and whipped cream all over each other. But where was Ema?

Suddenly, a tiny metal sphere rolled to where Nicky and Pulie were standing.

"Bomb!" Nicky shouted. They dove for the ground as the tiny object exploded. Instead of smoke and fire, it released a nasty stench—a stink bomb.

Pulie heard Ema laughing from the sink. She had a mask on, but it was clear there was a grin too big for her face.

Pulie pinched her nose tightly. The smell seemed to be everywhere in the room.

"Gross!" Nicky shouted, trying not to breathe it in. She grabbed her bottle of water and sprayed it at Ema, who slammed into Pulie, and her mask flew off. Nicky dumped an entire bucket of ice water over Ema's head. Ema wore the bucket on her head, and the two tripped over each other's legs. Pulie whip creamed Ema's back and then tossed the whipped cream can to Nicky, who at once began to indulge herself with the treat.

Then, they heard the doorbell ring at their front door.

At their door was a plump woman wearing a tight velvet dress with bright cherry lips and large red glasses. Her hair was all curled with shines, and her nails were painted with fresh coatings of red. Miss Idadosi.

"I have come to check your—I see this Halloween plague has already erupted all over Zive number two—" She cleared her throat as if she were already annoyed. "What is this smell? Ugh!" She squeezed her nostrils together with her hand and continued, "I *have come to check* that you have signed the agreement here. It states you shall not inflict severe damage to anyone on Halloween day and that you must follow your decision you submitted yesterday. Any disobeyers will be sent to the moat for cleaning and laundry duty. Sign here." She handed them the device, with the rules and statements typed in the form. They each took turns signing the screen with the bright red device pen.

"Oster, I see. We'll see how long you last today. Miss Rafferty, quite the student I've heard. And you— Miss *Jark*?" Ms. Idadosi reread the last name. And then she eyed Pulie with queer suspicion. Miss Idadosi was like that neighbor, suspecting you of stealing the blueberry pie off her porch when she set it out for cooling. She was the cat that *slithered* around your backyard whenever she got the chance.

She was—

"Strange," Miss Idadosi whispered, "I've heard this last name before. Wait a minute!" She slammed her hand on her device screen. "This the very last name—the last time I saw it was when a crook murdered my aunt in her own house! You little terminators ain't got no business here! I know a Jark when I see one. You're a CAOT! I know you! I must report you immediately! A Jark looks *exactly*—like you—tan... black hair..." She shook her fists but then mumbled. "You better watch out. I know this last name."

"What do you mean, you know my last name?"

Nicky added in, "Yeah! So what? Does that bother you? I mean, Ms. Idadosi ain't that nice of a name either!"

"Watch your mouth, Miss Oster. I don't want none of your sass today," the lady hissed, her spit slicing through her bright red lips like blades and daggers.

Nicky was hushed in a snap.

"*Jark.*" Ms. Idadosi gave Pulie one last glance and then turned for the next room down the hall. Ema slammed the door and locked it shut.

"She knows me?" Pulie asked, in a whisper so faint she could hardly hear what she had said herself.

"She's just getting in your head. She does that to *everyone*. Just ignore her. You ain't a murderer or whatever she was blabbering about. She's a little crazy sometimes, and you got to ignore it. She's never even seen you in your entire life. Just a *coincidence*. Okay?" Nicky explained.

"Yeah," Pulie replied, even softer. So far, Ms. Idadosi was the only one who showed signs of knowing her parents, besides Mr. Wace. Not in the most pleasant way. She knew that calling someone a CAOT was very offensive around here. And her parents were Trickies. They were on a scout mission at the moment, for heaven's sake. But Ms. Idadosi knew Pulie from her last name.

This couldn't be a coincidence.

HALLOWEEN

Pulie, Nicky, and Ema jumped into their costumes. Nicky and Ema had assisted Pulie with the makeup and extra costume parts because Pulie had to rest her other arm. All three of them were dressed up as zombies in nightgowns.

Even the mission classes had been canceled for this festive day. Students went door to door grabbing candy from the bowls every dorm had left out for the passer-byes on the way. Ema had bought their own room a bag of candy for the treaters. Pulie's bag was overflowing and she had never been happier.

They bumped into Anne, Lulu, and Livia and they all immediately formed a truce to prevent any attacking between them for the rest of the day. Truces were extremely important, especially to make this day last.

Santiago and Colin planted a huge stink bomb on the fourth floor of their zive and the smell pervaded the entire area. Everyone fled for their lives. And then, Dan released a small stink bomb of his own—one that wasn't artificially made.

Halloween wasn't always about candy apples and sweets.

The courtyard had transformed completely. A dark shade was pulled over the top of the palace to make the courtyard darker.

Red oozing and bubbling paint had been dumped onto every inch of the floor. Jack-o-lanterns sprinkled the campus, witch figures and ogres stood at every corner. Lights had been dimmed, walls painted black, to give the sense of a real night on Halloween. From the corner of the floor, she saw people running and laughing and falling and crying. It was a festival of emotions. It was the survival of the fittest.

Pulie heard a student bellowing nearby with heavy paint and a mask on his face. He was dressed as a clown with long lips and cuts and bruises everywhere. Pulie recognized the low deep voice. *Erik Pontz*. The one person who she had been waiting for.

"Pulie, I know what you're thinking. I was too," Nicky muttered, "Don't do it. Not now. Do you see all his friends? They are completely ripped and they won't hesitate to *rip* you apart. *Dexter,* the one with no costume and funny trousers? He has no mercy for some level two girls. They will tie us to a tree, upside down—or drown us in the moat. Last Halloween, they almost drowned a total of four kids—no mercy at all. This isn't the best place. We'll figure out another plan. Like the letter we sent Selma or something. But not here... no, not here."

But it was too late.

"Oh look!" Erik hollered, "It's the little Junior Tricky troop. Aha! I recognized their stupid faces disguised under that makeup. Dexter, the one on the right is a hacking geek, the one in the middle, she's an Oster. Her brother..."

Pulie couldn't hear the rest because they both started to laugh.

"Oh, and the one on the left—" Erik snarled, "She's a new kid. *Pulie Jark.*" It was as if her name was poisonous and the letters spliced through his tongue each time he said it.

"Hey, Oster!" Dexter called, "Where'd all your money go? How'd you lose it?" He had a British accent, so thick, Pulie could boil it to make soup.

Erik's group burst into laughter.

"Come on, Nicky—" Pulie tugged on Nicky's arm, "That's a joke. Not a funny one, either. Let's get *outta* here."

"Oster! Where's Theo? Is that his grave?" Erik pointed to a nearby tombstone decoration. There was a bunch of knee-slapping and barking from the group of boys.

Nicky was as still as a stone wall, her eyes fixed upon Dexter and Erik like a hawk. Pulie could see the water was filling her eyes— but she wasn't letting it show.

Theo would bring tears to a girl who rarely cried.

"Laugh all you want," Ema said. "You'll be lying in the grave right next to Theo by the end of the day."

The way Ema hissed at them, Pulie was even startled. Halloween really was no joke.

"What do you mean, shortie?" Dexter retorted.

Ema answered, furiously. "I mean *get lost*. If you're gonna laugh at someone, go take a look in the mirror."

Erik chuckled, "Aha! Good one. So, *Dexter*, now we are supposed to be crying." They burst into laughter. "We ain't little *girls*. And it's *trick* day after all and this crackhead couldn't keep her own family alive. So, we're just going with the rules."

Pulie tugged on both Ema and Nicky's arms. "Let's go."

"Oh look, Dexter." Erik pointed straight at Pulie. It was clear that the Halloween makeup on her face did not disguise her. "Pulie's trying to run away. She's *scared*. Did you know she accidentally stabbed her hand with a dart? What kind of moron is that?"

"Shall we tie her up?"

The rest of Erik's group cackled with laughter.

"Pulie, start running," Nicky whispered from the corner of her mouth.

Pulie couldn't move.

"Pulie, run." Ema was nudging her.

The next moment, all three of them started sprinting.

"Hey! They're getting away!"

"I wanna drown them in the moat."

Pulie heard that from all the way across the courtyard.

***

The door slammed shut with a heave.

"Not good, not good, not good," Nicky muttered. "It's only been a couple of hours since Halloween started and Erik has already got his eye on us. I don't want to spend the entire day running from his friends."

"No time to complain," Pulie said. "We need to go up to the Miralmalma."

"We aren't allowed in the Miralmalma today unless it's an emergency," Ema reprimanded.

"This is an emergency," Pulie said, panting. "I'll go find the ladder. Ema, make sure no one can get in here as long as we're safe."

"I can hear heavy footsteps." Ema's head was on the large door. "They're coming very fast."

"Pulie? Hurry!"

"I'm trying!"

Finally, Pulie's fingers found the button, her earring slid across the panel, and a ladder was lowered.

"Go! Go! Ema, let go of the door now and let's get it going!" Nicky cried. "Oh shoot! Pulie! How are you supposed to climb the ladder with only one hand?"

"I can do it!"

"Okay, Ema let go of the door!" And then Nicky frantically followed Pulie up the ladder. Ema joined in.

Pulie reached up with her good hand and used her other elbow to climb up. It was slower, but it was better than the long staircase.

There was banging on the door when the three were halfway up the ladder.

"We know you're in there," snickered a voice, "And we also know you aren't fast on the stairs."

The two clowns burst into the first floor of the Miralmalma.

"Are they already on the stairs?"

"Is that a ladder?" Derek pointed.

"Crap. Pulie, keep going. Don't look down," Nicky muttered, climbing her way up. "Why do they have to be wearing clown suits?"

Suddenly, the ladder sagged, still staying in position attached to the top of the Miralmalma. Erik and Derek had started to climb as well.

"Go! Go!" Ema cried, behind Nicky.

"I'm trying!" Pulie shouted. Finally, her fingers could touch the second floor of the Miralmalma and she heaved herself up. Nicky and Ema came out of the tube as well.

"We have to close it!"

"No, we can't!"

"I did it last time," Pulie said, running to a lever at the edge of the hole. "Help me."

In no time, the opening of the ladder was closed.

"We're safe—" Ema said, "Until they climb back down to the bottom and run up the stairs. We've all seen how fast Erik can run up the stairs."

"Let's hide in one of the rooms."

"Last time, this room was locked." Nicky pushed the door and entered a room that smelled of spoiled water. It was full of computers and chairs and giant screens.

"The Spectra tech room—" Ema said with a gasp. "They've opened up the tech room!"

"You mean the computer lab? Or—" Pulie asked.

"This tech room is where Spectra opens up the way to the Palace for us."

"Spectra?"

"When you're entering the palace," Nicky explained, "You hold your earring to the sensor. Spectra is the person who lets you in."

"No time! You'll understand later—" Ema said, "But let's first lock the door."

***

The girls huddled in the back of the room, dreading the moment Erik and his friend arrived at the Miralmalma.

"It will take them longer because they have to climb back down her ladder," Ema assured them.

"Please, fall down the stairs." Nicky held her hands up to the ceiling.

"Please, forget to tie your shoes."

"Please—"

A scream.

They froze.

"What was that?" Ema asked, scanning the room.

"I don't want to know."

They waited for a few minutes.

There was another scream and then silence.

"It's a girl," Nicky finally said. "I think it's from Awolo's room. She must be using that taser tool."

Pulie shivered at the thought of being punished by Awolo.

Footsteps were heard coming straight at their room.
"It's Awolo!"
"She's in the other room."
"Then, it's Erik?"
"Go through the back door."
They quietly crept to the back door and down the cramped tunnel that led to the nearby room.
It was dark. But then, it as bright.
"Well, well. Who do we have here?"
Ema, Pulie, and Nicky froze like manikins. Their eyes were large and quivering.
"You don't understand—" Nicky began.
"I understand it all." Ms. Awolo grabbed them by the ear and commanded the other girl to come with her outside of the room. Pulie couldn't see who the other girl was.
"All four of you, stand straight up. No slouching."
Backs straightened.
"We'll begin with you, girl, and go down the line." Awolo pointed one nasty long finger at Pulie. "Answer. Why are you being punished right now?"
"What do you mean?"
"Shut up!" Awolo screeched. "Do you know anything? Recite the introduction."
"What's the introduction?"
"I said shut up!" Awolo was nearly tearing the hair out of her scalp. "Let's begin with you, Rafferty."
Ema shifted uncomfortably in her position. "I recite this to Mistress Awolo, the great leader of this perfect palace. I have done terribly wrong and I deserve with all my heart to be punished severely."
Awolo nodded and said, "Now, *you* girl. Do exactly as she did."

Pulie recited the sentence after Ema, but she missed a word.

"You forgot to say I!" Awolo screamed. "—terribly wrong and *I* deserve with all my heart to be punished severely. Get down on the ground, lay flat on your back, and stay there."

A second later, Pulie was a starfish on the carpet of the Miralmalma.

"Nicky Oster! Your turn."

It was then, Pulie realized how quiet Nicky had stayed the entire time.

Nicky recited the sentence with perfect fluency, and it was clear she had the experience.

"Now, you. Dutchstill, begin."

Selma?

Ema, Pulie, and Nicky spun around to look at the other girl.

Selma stood, shivering behind them, scars on her arms, her eyes puffy and her face swollen. Her hair was a complete mess and she was dressed in a large jumpsuit of orange.

"I recite this to Mistress Awolo, the great leader of this perfect palace. I have done terribly wrong and I deserve with all my heart to be punished severely." Her voice was shaky.

"Very well. Get up now, you. And all four of you."

A lady in the back scurried to the stairs. She let off a sewage stench from her coat.

"Who are you? No staff is allowed in the Miralmalma today. Everyone should be in the eating rooms preparing for Casteron's speech," Awolo snapped. She was a raven, pecking at all the worms she found on the ground.

"Mr. Wace sent me, Mistress." The chubby lady was holding a large cardboard box.

"Very well, go away then." Awolo turned back to the girls.

A while later, Erik and Dexter burst into the room, panting. They stopped dead when they saw Awolo.

"Does no one know that the Miralmalma is closed today?" Ms. Awolo screeched. "Who are you? Take off your masks."

Erik changed his voice, and grunted, "My name is Dunkin. I can't take off my mask."

"Come right here because I know that is a lie!"

When Erik was arm's length away from the woman, she reached out and yanked off the wig and attachments. The makeup was now smeared, revealing his face.

"Erik Pontz. I suppose that is the Dexter kid." She said. "All of you will spend the entire day until Halloween dinner today in my room."

***

When the dinner bell rang, all six students bowed down to Awolo and started sprinting, far far away from the Miralmalma. Erik and Dexter had already disappeared once they hit the courtyard. Selma walked with the rest, silently. Out of all of them, Nicky had endured the taser pain the best—because she was the most experienced.

"That was the worst Halloween ever." Ema sighed. "We didn't even get to do the prank with Colin and Dan."

"Well, Selma," Nicky blurted out, putting her hands on her hips. "What did *you* do?"

Selma remained silent, rubbing her arms.

"Nicky—" Ema tried to stop the ongoing feud.

"What did you do, Selma?"

Selma was trembling now.

"Come on, Nicky, chill. We can find out later." Pulie joined Ema.

"What'd you do?"

"I was caught in the Miralmalma at midnight." They were the first words from Selma in a long time.

Nicky froze, wide-eyed. Pulie knew it. It was their message. Their message had gotten her in trouble.

"Oh shoot," Nicky muttered.

"What?" Selma snapped, suspicious.

"Nicky, here," Ema answered, "did the *same* thing, last year. Right, Nicky?"

Nicky nodded, uneasily. "I'm sorry, that must've been terrible."

Selma rolled her eyes. "You don't know how bad it was." Then she stormed off.

Nicky smiled. "That's my Selma."

For dinner, there were pumpkins, pumpkin soup, chicken, steak, apple cinnamon bread, apple spiced meatloaf, wheat bread, freshly-made-from-the-oven corn, carrots, mashed potatoes, gravy, turkey meat, macaroni and cheese, and the chef's specials. The chef's specials were made on special occasions. Today, it was lemon spiced bread with ham and egg, with a side dish of grilled potatoes and vegetables.

All their friends ran up to them, questioning the scars and marks on their faces. But mostly, it blended in with the Halloween theme.

When Pulie ordered the chef's special, she found it… very unappetizing.

Chef Susie.

"Why did they have her cook Halloween dinner?" Dan asked, poking at his bread. "Wait—guys—I think my bread is alive."

"You bread cannot be alive, Dan," Alex said. "Not unless you insert a living organism inside of the bread, you cannot call it alive. And even then, the bread is not alive. The organism is."

Dan chortled. "You're right. This bread isn't alive. It just came back from the dead."

"Honestly—" Nicky tried to speak with her mouth stuffed full, "I rould prepper airy emonay—"

"*Chew,*" Ema ordered. Nicky obediently swallowed her full and drank a bit of her lemonade and winced.

"Honestly, I would prefer Larry's lemonade. I wonder why he hasn't been out on the Lollipop stand these days. He used to do it *every day*. I mean, that's where I got most of my candy," Nicky said.

"That *is* odd," Ema added. "But then again, he's always in his shell—"

"*Hiding from humanity. Resting without insanity,*" Nicky and Ema repeated in unison.

"What?" Pulie asked.

Dan snorted. "It's what Larry said all last year."

Shortly after people started eating their foods, Mr. Wace stepped up onto the stage with a black metal piece hanging on his lip, connecting to his ear.

"Everyone… it is wonderful to see that you are all here and to see that you all… have had fun today," he said. The crowd cheered and whistled.

"I want to give special thanks to the chefs inside who have prepared us a wonderful meal."

Nicky spat out her potatoes with disgust.

"*Today*, I just want to make a short announcement that the mission will be starting in precisely ninety-six days. Our mission group has been working awfully hard…"

Selma sneered. She wouldn't have if she knew that ten feet away from Pulie's table was a good distance to fling a potato up her pointy nose.

"And as a leader, I have found it most necessary to share with the rest of the academy about what *exactly* is going on. What the mission process is—what is for—and the purpose of sending off a group of students on a bombing mission. Correct?"

The audience nodded.

"So, I shall explain—everyone, for heaven's sake! Settle down! Do *not* put that fork in your ear, or you'll be sent to the treatment unit. Dash, put *that* fist down. Do not punch him." Mr. Wace hollered from his speaker. His face was very red, almost fuming in heat.

Selma was at the edge of her seat, scanning for the comical event that Dash was a part of. Fortunately, the crowded space left no room for her affairs.

"Silence!" Mr. Wace boomed.

Dash and the other boy let go of each other's shirts and settled back into their seats.

"I have my eyes on you both—finally, a time for me to speak. Today, we have Mrs. Casteron speaking to us. We will give her our greatest respect and honor. As you all perfectly know, the bombing is to take place at a hidden communication center on an island. This place is crucial to the CAOT and in order to sustain—"

Blood-curdling screams rang from the courtyard above.

Mr. Wace tilted his head back with his eyes closed and muttered, "When do I *ever* get to speak?" Then, he clicked his earpiece and listened for instructions from outside. "Wandering student, I suppose?" He asked through his connection device.

But it was clear that the answer was not what he had been expecting. Mr. Wace's face paled as white as the table cloth, and he leaped over the tables full of food to get to the other side of the eating room and disappeared after leaving specific instructions for the teachers.

Immediately, all the teachers dispersed to their positions, four of the staff escorted each Zive in order, safely out of the eating room and into another lower basement. And of course, Zive two was left under the hands of— Ms. Idadosi.

"Great. Just great," Nicky muttered under her breath. Almost every student gritted their teeth.

Ms. Idadosi lifted her head up and down. "Settle—*down*." Her voice got lower at the end of the command. "Zive two. Follow me. Stay strictly with your group. Come along."

They squeezed through the crowd, Pulie made sure that her hands were still holding Nicky's and Ema's. Pushing and tripping over people. There was no light. Just the whites of one's eyes offering brightness to the sight of any object in their way.

Everyone's walking pace slowed down to a complete stop. The air was sweaty and damp, with the body heat toasting the area to crisp. Pulie lifted her head up to stop nearly suffocating from the lack of air.

Finally, there was the shut of a door, and Ms. Idadosi flicked on the lights.

"We're in the escape room two right now. This is Zive two's underground hide-out. We are to remain here until given orders."

Murmurs arose.

"*No*. I am not exactly aware of what happened. But what I *do* know is that there was a murder up in the courtyard. A woman was killed."

Everyone gasped.

"Killed? Like actually *dead* or pretending to be dead?" A boy shouted.

Ms. Idadosi did not answer that question. "This woman comes from an *awfully* rich family. She was our guest speaker for tonight, but she needed to get something from the Miralmalma, and the next minute, she was found dead. This is just *awful*."

It was interesting to listen to how much Ms. Idadosi emphasized the word *awful*. It was the perfect word to describe herself.

"Is the criminal a teacher?" Another student asked.

Ms. Idadosi raised her eyebrow. "And *why* do you think that? Is this some kind of accusation? Is that it?"

"No."

"Exactly, office at four-thirty tomorrow evening. No question."

"Excuse me, we won't be having *anyone* up there tomorrow morning," boomed a deep familiar voice. Ms. Idadosi spun around. Señor Rodriguez had entered the secret room.

"We found *Larry* holding the weapon and lying right next to her dead body."

Pulie's eyes opened wide. *Larry?*

"He will be having... no office time. He was merely stating an opinion."

Ms. Idadosi nodded her head, her lower lip trembling. "Children, Señor Rodriguez is your guard now. I need to run to the restroom." And with that, Ms. Idadosi trudged out of the room. Pulie could even see steam evaporating from her head from the amount of anger that was fuming in her soul. Thankfully now, Señor Rodriguez was in charge.

"Everyone, heed closely to my instructions. You will find your bunking mates and return to your rooms *right* now. Teachers will handle this completely. And nobody is to go out of the Zives. Anyone caught will meet Ms. Awolo afterward, privately in her room. Do I make myself clear? Now! Hurry up, move your gears!"

And then there was chaos. The buzzing of students whispering and chittering under their breaths as each and every one of them frantically scrambled to get to their rooms. No one wanted to be left behind with a murderer on the campus. Pulie, Nicky, and Ema were squeezing each other's hands as they passed the scenery.

Blood was splattered here and there on the floor where lay the body of Larry, with a bloodstained knife in his motionless hands.

It was too hard to believe why Larry would've wanted to do such a thing.

The dead victim had already been evacuated, but Larry lay there, still and quiet. Around him, all the teachers gasped at his face in horror.

"I knew from the start, there was something strange about his brain."

"What punishment awaits him?"

"Execution, perhaps."

"The factory would be appropriate for the time being."

Mr. Wace walked and raised his hands. "He will not be punished nor executed… yet. He will go to court, and we will decide there, that he is either guilty or innocent. The trial will be held on the first of February."

"But, sir! You think there's a chance it is *not* him?"

"Why is he unconscious? There are many possibilities. After all, this is the academy with one of the brightest people. Fooling a crime scene is quite simple. It's only fair to give him the trial he deserves."

"Where will he stay during the time period? Certainly not in the palace with all the children. Maybe a prison."

"He will be in a house, not a prison."

"Are you insane? Wace, I am deeply sorry to argue against you but the young lady has *died* as far as we know. Larry is still living, and since he is the only suspect, he could pose a threat to anyone around him."

"Most of the evidence is pointed in his direction. But not all. One is innocent until proven guilty."

"Wace. That is a rule for the normal people down below. The Trickies have thrived under different rules and different methods. Our system for persecution is very different."

"Mr. Wace," Señor Rodriguez appeared at the crowd. "The clips of the security cameras have been sent to the department. But so far, they have detected no evidence at all." He placed his hand on his heart. "Perhaps, it was too dark to record any movement."

"Very well then, the fastest trial will begin on the first of February. Let us see how it goes."

The teachers dispersed, leaving Larry's unconscious body on the floor, as the specially trained Tricky detectives scanned the scene and the entire campus with their devices, clicking and typing all the information they could obtain.

"Yikes," Nicky whispered once they had reached their Zive lobby. "Well, I did think he was crazy."

"Yes," Ema whispered, "Now, let's get our rear's moving before we're suspected of taking so long!"

They were walking down the hall of their Zive with everyone else when Pulie whispered, "But why?"

"What do you mean?" Nicky asked with a clueless expression.

"Why did *he* kill someone?" Ema answered, rolling her eyes.

Nicky pointed out, "You know, you are allowed to say his name. You don't have to say *he*."

"Oh, whatever, Nicky! You don't get the point! Why would Larry try to kill someone on Halloween!" Ema huffed. They all shook their heads in disbelief.

***

"This *has* to be a setup," Pulie said, she crept underneath the cold blanket. "He did it when everyone was down in the eating rooms. I don't think this is a coincidence."

"I don't know." Nicky sighed. "Maybe it was Larry. Maybe it wasn't. But that's not *our* business, right? Now, let's go to sleep already."

The entire palace had gone silent. No staying up. No laughing from the room next door. No stomping from the upstairs dorms. Just silent. Like Halloween was supposed to be.

But the silence was too loud for her. Why would he want to murder? Why on Halloween?

Larry was a rude man of plain ignorance and a lack of sympathy. But he was not a killer.

Gracefully, Pulie slipped out of her hammock, quieting the creak in her step. Her mind swarmed with ideas and conspiracies. She couldn't sleep anyway. Her fingers wrapped around the smooth surface of the camera Colin had given her, and then her palms reached for the doorknob.

Never before had the courtyard been so empty of students. The teachers were all huddled up in the Miralmalma with the lights on. A lot was probably going on inside their brains.

The entire courtyard had been blocked off with tape. Several men in shiny security armor stood surrounding Larry's pale motionless body like a brick wall. But where Pulie wanted to get to, wasn't the crime scene but instead, Larry's House. It was shadowed in the corner with the lights off and the Halloween decors collecting dust.

But one mistake and she would be in big trouble. Maybe even framed. Pulie shuddered. Worse than that, she would have to spend an entire day in Ms. Awolo's room all alone, again.

But still, she wanted to try.

She weaved through the tree lines and the west side of the courtyard where it was pitch dark and slipped under the tape. Soon, she was poking at the back door until it opened softly, allowing her to slip inside the darkness. The smell of soggy cardboard and musky oils drifted through her nostrils—also, the smell of spilling water.

Turning on the lights would only attract attention, so Pulie had to swerve through the Labyrinth of boxes and shelves in the unlit room where there was only one color; black. Everything was pitch black without a light to guide her. She tripped on an empty box and skidded into the shelf. There was a large *thump*. There were voices outside, and Pulie held her breath as if she were trying to explode her stomach. Then, the voices outside died. She felt the sides of the shelves and made her way around the mess she created. She remembered the shelf she had fallen through—the trap door, which had led straight to the sewers. She shuddered, imagining the darkness beneath her.

Finally, her cold trembling fingers grabbed the stiff familiar metal knob of the entrance into Larry's living room. Her eyes finally began to see color. Light bloomed from all corners. And although the only light lit inside the room was the old lavender desk lamp in the corner near the heater, the room seemed to luminous and electrifying.

Pulie first crawled and then slowly stood up and examined the desk of the criminal. There was an infinite amount of old scrapings of wood and carving tools. In addition, was a cracked coffee mug, a dumbbell, a rusty thimble, a golden necklace with a heart charm, a fork with a missing tine, a leather pocket watch with no hands, and an eraser.

The golden heart charm sparkled in the dusky air, and Pulie felt the urge to stroke it. She knew if her fingerprint was found on any of his belongings, she might've been accused of assisting Larry in the crime. She rubbed the heart in her hands. Then there was a click. So soft, she thought she heard things, but the charm opened! Revealing a small key.

She had no idea what to do with the key but she found it prudent to try finding the host of it. The very last drawer was the only one locked. It sprang out with ease when the key was inserted. Inside was a stack of digital pads. Pulie stared at the top pad, with the words *Open with caution. From, unknown,* typed into the top box.

Her camera went clicking endlessly away at every little thing she could find. Some of it had nothing to do with the incident, but she wanted to know where Larry got all his hot cocoa ingredients.

Soon, her eyes weighed her thoughts down, and she swiftly returned to her cozy room. No longer was her mind thinking about *anything.*

HAIRY QUESTIONS

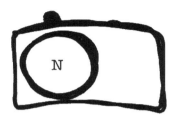

The next morning was another school day, but Pulie had not slept an inch. She woke her friends up at three to discuss her discovery.

"Nicky! Ema!"

Nicky's face was pale when Pulie shook her hammock. Ema rubbed her eyes, "Oh! Are we late?"

"No."

"Then, why this early?"

"I have something to tell you guys! Hurry!"

They climbed out, and they all sat on the carpet floor in a circle.

"Pulie, you have dark circles around your eyes—" Nicky said, peering through her own swollen, tired eyes.

"And you don't? Now, listen!" Pulie squirmed in her spot, excited. "Okay! So, yesterday night, I crept out—"

"You what?" Ema and Nicky shouted in unison.

"I crept out. And I went to Larry's House—"

"You what?" they shouted, once more.

"I said, I crept out to—"

Ema smacked her forehead. "We know! Pulie, when we meant to break the rules and stuff, we didn't mean, enter a crime scene alone and—"

"Wait, let her talk! I want to hear what happened!" Nicky settled down.

"Yes, let me talk!" Pulie shouted, waving her hands in the air. She quieted her voice. "I know, I know. It wasn't safe. But I am alive right now. So can you please listen? I went outside and into Larry's house to find any more clues.

"I found in a secret drawer using this key—" she held up the necklace, "— a little metal computer block with odd writing— Here, let me find the camera—" Pulie got up and searched for the camera. She had left it on the table next to the door.

"Found it?"

There was silence for a long time.

"Have you two taken my camera during the night? Please, can you tell me? *It's* not *funny*."

Nicky and Ema shook their heads.

"The only reason we're up this early is because of you! No one in their right mind would've woken up—"

"Where is the camera?" Ema interrupted Nicky's sleep rant.

Pulie swallowed hard.

"I can't find it."

Ema and Nicky both raised their eyebrows.

"Pulie. Come on. We know you have it!"

"I don't. I mean it, guys. *Someone* must have taken it during the night."

Ema looked at Nicky. "Pulie, I think you need some rest. I think you're tired. Or it could be a side effect of your hand from losing blood," Ema said, as she patted Pulie's hammock, motioning her to sleep once more as if she were a baby.

"Then, where's my camera? The one Colin gave me! You have to believe me. I *did* go down there and take pictures of Larry's house. Believe me! Let's go down to Larry's House and see for yourself!"

Pulie slipped on some shorts and a shirt in a split second, and soon she was out of the room, with Ema and Nicky, worriedly following her.

"You should have watched her," Ema whispered to Nicky.

The crime scene was left untouched, but the bodyguards at the center were gone, Larry's body as well, and light returned to the courtyard. A caution tape still wrapped around Larry's house and the floor where the blood was spilled, but they could open the back door to the entrance.

"They do not do a good job with this *crime* scene stuff. I'm a bit disappointed in Señor and Mr. Wace. They're in charge of this whole commotion," Nicky said. "Where are the guards? The detectives? The news reporters? More security?"

"Quiet, Nicky."

Larry's desk was vacant as usual, and it was still messy and unorganized. Pulie unlocked the drawer, confident that there was going to be the evidence. To her surprise, it was the opposite.

"What, Pulie? There are no metal computer blocks inside the drawer." Ema muttered.

Pulie's heart thudded. She was muddled. She had clearly seen *everything* so clearly last night. And just like that, within five hours, the evidence had disappeared.

"There—this is *impossible*. I clearly saw—" Pulie shook her hands, "This isn't just some random person. The person must've *cleared it!* I clearly came down here last night." Pulie started panting, her forehead wrinkling in frustration.

"They must've cleared everything for evidence," Nicky suggested.

"*Only* I have the key. And everything else is the same. Just that metal block disappeared. That's it."

"It's okay—" Ema assured her, "The investigators will probably figure it out."

"But this means someone else was in the same room at the same time I was looking through his desk. And this also means—" Pulie paused, "—that person didn't want what I found to be discovered—"

"Which is why they also took the camera after they saw you go into your room—" Nicky added, her eyes slowly widening, her lower eyelids sagging a little less. "They didn't want someone else to see the picture you took!"

"But that's just so strange. Why didn't they like *kill* you too then? Your memory is still in your head. You could be a potential danger to their plan… if we're right about this conspiracy." Ema interrupted, "We're probably just thinking about something else—"

"No," the answer came as solid as gold from both Nicky and Pulie.

"This can't be right. I'm sure Larry wasn't the only one in this crime scene," Nicky corrected, blowing the hair out of her face. She helped Pulie clip the necklace around her neck. Now Pulie wore two chains.

"Or maybe not even the criminal—" Ema slowly began to catch up. Pulie swallowed a lump in her throat.

The fact that someone had been watching her every move last night and had come up to her room to steal the camera made her shiver, the chill crawling through her veins and all around her.

There was a feeling she dreaded: the palace wasn't as safe as she thought.

ROBOTIC ARACHNID

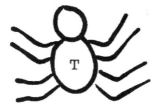

The Miralmalma's lights flickered on.

"We better hurry. I don't want to be found lurking around her at three in the morning."

Pulie and Mrs. Slendersan had just managed to sort out a way to train for the mission without increasing the damage to her hand. She would build and strengthen her legs first, up to her abs, and then, soon, her upper body.

But the mission class today had been cut short due to a staff meeting that Mr. Wace had called to order. Most likely, the discussion consisted of the incident that occurred the night before. Pulie and the mission just managed to sort out a way to train without increasing the damage to her hand.

"Do you think Larry did it?" Nicky asked Colin and Dan. They both tilted their heads and shrugged.

Celena bit her lip, thinking thoroughly. "Yes. All the evidence points to him," Celena responded, "Although he needs a fair trial, I guess."

"I don't think it was only Larry in on this—" Nicky shared her idea. "Did you know that the only thing he used to say to me was, *You look like my daughter*. It got to the point where I'd just let him call me his daughter—"

"Spider!" Pulie screamed. Everyone in the Miralmalma froze like marble stones. Their actions halted in midair.

"Where?" Nicky cried.

In the corner of Pulie's eye, she saw the large spider. It was too large for a regular spider, however. It scampered away, the legs moving in such a robotic manner, one foot ahead of the other at the exact same tempo. And oddly enough, there was a button on the back of the spider. *A button on a spider meant—*

"It's not a spider!" Pulie hollered.

Everyone by now was looking at Pulie weirdly.

"Pulie! What spider?"

"There! It's escaping! Run and catch it!" Pulie jumped up and down. Her fingers pointed to the large robot disguised as an arachnid crawling around the carpet floors, searching for juicy insects to feast on.

"Run!" Tilda hollered.

"No! Don't go around screaming like that—" Nicky cried, but it was too late. Everyone dispersed, shouting and crying, the staircase was overflowing with students who tried to reach the floor as fast as possible.

When the crowd had left, the only ones left were Celena, Nicky, Ema, Colin, and Dan, who stood alongside Pulie. But Pulie didn't know why she hadn't run off as well.

Celena spotted the spider and dove for it. Her head nearly crashed into a flower vase, and the spider slipped between her hands, like jello squeezing through the cracks.

"Eww! Don't touch it!" Ema squeaked.

Colin tried scooping it between his legs, but it crawled right past him. Dan ran around until he hit his head on the wall, and Colin had to help him.

"It's not a spider!" Pulie hollered, flapping her arms. She had no idea what was going on, either.

Ema tried trapping it with a cup. Nicky tried to step on it. Tilda tried to— run away, but Celena didn't let her.

Soon, the spider was twirling in circles with no possible route of escape.

"Pulie! Catch!" Celena threw Pulie a small metal circle piece. Pulie caught the metal device which she realized was a dart. She was the closest to the rampaging spider.

She aimed steadily at the scrambling robot arachnid and shot the dart.

There was a puff of smoke and a nasty smell from the acid in the needle. Fumes of electric sparks created a dense layer of air near Pulie's head.

The spider jerked to a stop, and the dart was implanted in the head. Celena took a step forward and scooped up the spider.

"Pulie, you were right. It's a spider robot. But, spiders are not a good sign, you know—the CAOT. Thank god we caught it. We should take this to the leaders."

"If you go to Awolo and Borthwick, count me out!" Nicky made a face. "Ever since Awolo caught us snooping yesterday on Halloween and ever since I put tar on Borthwick's hairbrush, they watch me like an owl."

"Okay then, let's go find Mr. Wace." Celena zipped the bag with the spider inside. Unfortunately, he was not present in his room. So they took their catch down to the courtyard in hopes of finding the man.

"Mr. Wace!" Nicky let out a sigh when she finally spotted the man exiting the eating room.

"What is it?" Mr. Wace said, sensing irregularity. "*Celena?* What may I ask is happening?"

"Pulie should explain. She found it." Celena handed the bag to Pulie.

"Mr. Wace. We caught a spider up in the Miralmalma. It's a robot, actually."

"May I take a look?" Mr. Wace inspected the object inside the bag.

"Ah." Mr. Wace announced, "That was a close one. Dangerous. Definitely not a robot of ours. It's a spy."

"What?"

"A spy from a different association, most well known as the CAOT. As long as it didn't go inside the mission room, we may destroy this. We get a couple of these arachnid robots once in a while. However, none of them have ever gotten so close to the Miralmalma. I mean, the spider would've had to crawl up hundreds of stairs without anyone noticing—"

"Why would they send a spider?" Ema asked.

Mr. Wace shrugged, "I don't know. I didn't send it."

DAN AND THE LETTER

"Are you alright, Dan?" Ema worriedly wobbled around the room.

Dan lay in a bed in the treatment unit, pressing an ice pack on his head. "I think I'm alright." He scratched his head. "Am I still handsome?"

Nicky rolled her eyes. "You never were."

Colin sighed. "This better not be a concussion or anything. Why does it seem like *everyone* is getting hurt before the mission?"

"Colin?"

They all turned around.

"Zanes? What are you doing here?" Colin asked.

A young man had stepped into the room, accompanied by a woman. The man had the same ruffled blond hair as Colin and the same bright blue eyes. He was a lanky figure, but very tall, *almost* as skinny as the Twig, but not quite. The other woman was quite peculiar; her eyes were the color of light cream, so pale in contrast to her smooth tanned skin. Perched upon her head was a cloth folded in such a manner; it looked like she was wearing a pair of pants on her head. Engraved on her forehead, the most intricate designs, dark shapes and lines, and waves with odd symbols, flowing in beauty above her brows.

"Why do you keep calling me Zanes?" The man threw his hands up. "I'm *Leot*."

"Right," Dan said. "Because you changed your name."

"What are you doing here?" Colin asked again.

"To come and check on my little brother. Come here—" The man grabbed Colin's flappy hair and wrestled him to the ground.

When they were done with their family greetings, Leot introduced the quiet woman in the back.

"That's Miss Lora, everyone. She is a recruiter for the Scouts."

"Good day, little ones," Miss Lora said. Her voice was low but clear. "Nice to meet you."

"*Leot* is a professionally trained Tricker," Nicky told Pulie. "He graduated from AT Tricksters. He is also—a headache."

"What'd you say, Nucky Ducky?"

"Nothing."

"What happened? Is Mr. Zipmore going to be alright?" Miss Lora asked, approaching the bed.

"I'm alright," Dan said. "It just feels like the world is spinning." He cracked a smile. "I'm the sun right now. I always knew I was a bright one."

Everyone let out a groan. *He's alright.* They seemed to say without words.

"He hit his head against the wall," Nicky explained.

"But Leot—" Ema turned to the man. "What *are* you doing here?"

"The Trickies Foundation sent me to check on the whole Larry incident. Mr. Diablo told me to investigate the staff. But Miss Lora is here to talk to Mr. Wace about the mission."

"Yes," Miss Lora said. "I was told that *all* of you are a part of the mission this year."

"Yeah."

"I wish you the best of luck. I will be staying here for a while to help with the staff mission. See you around."

Miss Lora left first.

"Well, Colin," Leot said, holding his hand out. "Goodbye from a Strussmore. And Dan, I hope you get better. Bye, everyone."

When he left, it was just Dan in the bed, Ema, Pulie, Nicky, and Colin.

"Mrs. Slendersan is *not* going to be a happy lady today," Nicky said, tapping her feet. "How did you even hit your head?"

Dan shrugged. "I don't know. But what I do remember is that I saw stars."

They all sighed.

"I'll stay here," Colin said. "You all can go."

"We have nothing else to do either," Nicky assured him. "We'll just each lay in one of these beds and rest. The dinner bell doesn't ring until like—like—what time is it?"

"Three forty."

All of them froze. The voice had come from the dark corner of the treatment unit. It was the girl again.

"Thanks," Nicky answered, without hesitating. "Wait, but the dinner bell rings at what—"

"Six fifteen." The voice said again.

"Exactly."

Colin peered into the shadow. "Hello. What's your name?"

The girl fell silent. So they resumed their conversations.

Pulie lolled on the hospital bed, yawning and stretching. It felt nice to just do—*nothing*.

"Hey, guys. Look."

Colin pulled out a piece of paper from beneath the bed he sat in. "What's this?"

"Oh, you better not touch that, Colin. If a teacher walks in right now, he or she's going to think you're hiding paper."

"If a teacher walks in, he or she's going to be angry that all of you are lying on a bed with your shoes on." Dan grinned obnoxiously.

Ema crinkled her nose. "Can I see?"

They all got up and huddled around the parched, crinkled paper with thin and flaky edges. And it was blank.

Nicky shrugged. "There's nothing on here."

"Use a flashlight."

The light was shone onto the paper, but nothing changed.

"It *could* just be a regular paper," Ema suggested.

Dan bent over from his position with his eyes wide. "What if—it's a message?"

"What kind?"

"The kind that tells you—" Dan paused. "That it's just a piece of paper."

Ema shook her head, smiling. "I think you rest. We'll figure it out. Sounds good?"

"Nope."

Pulie shook her head. "Wait, what was that oil that Mrs. Wapanog taught us about?"

"What? Tinker oil?" Colin asked.

"Yes. Do any of you have some?"

Ema grinned. "Nicky does. She pilfered that teacher's closet all last year. But it's in our room."

"Use your saliva," Dan suggested. "It will work. Here let me try."

Before anyone could stop him, he snatched the paper out of Pulie's hand and rubbed his spit all over the blank paper.

Nicky let out a sigh. "The sad thing is, I can't say that his head injury made him any different."

Colin had gotten out of his bed and went to the cupboard at the treatment unit's front. He brought back a glass bottle.

"Bingo. Tinker oil."

They rubbed it onto the paper, and fortunately, some words popped up.

"*Oh*." Pulie sighed. It was just a letter a student had written a few years ago.

"Where'd the writer get paper, though?"

"I'm sure there was some way around it."

Pulie studied the writing.

Dear Friend,

I have been asking the leaders if I could stay home for the summer. I don't dare go back—not this summer. You know why.

But for the project. Here are the clues. "It's blue like the sea, but green like the grass. It's smooth; it's small, it's no bigger than my eye." That's all I got so far, but I promise there will be more.

Cheers. Pray for me, so I don't have to go back.

"There's no name," Nicky noted. "It's a funny letter. No wonder the letter didn't get anywhere. This person doesn't understand the fact that communication outside of the palace is not allowed."

"Why doesn't she want to go home?"

"Evil stepmother?" Nicky shrugged. "But what are the clues even for?"

They didn't have an answer to that either.

The dinner bell rang, and they all rushed to smooth the blankets and fluff the pillow. Colin restored the Tinker oil to its original spot, and they all departed the treatment unit for dinner, leaving Dan alone with a burning headache.

THE SCHEME

One day, after their mission class had dismissed them, Nicky and Pulie both collapsed onto the carpet while Ema took the hammock above them.

"Look at this *beauty*." Nicky held up her new gadget and breathed on it so she could shine it more. A few members in the mission class had received them after winning the game. Pulie, Nicky, Noel, and Daria. The gadget was the shape of a yin and yang. Each half was detachable, and both were connected. It was basically a hearing gadget. Leave the black piece on the table, clip the white side to your ear, and you could hear everything said back at the table. Of course, there were limits in the distance.

Soon, Pulie and Nicky read over their Mission notes for the day while performing their daily stretching. Ema was up in her hammock, rolling around.

"Harvey's Pizza House on Dover's Drive. Catering twenty pizza boxes, three chicken rolls, four boxes of wings, one order of marinated pork, and plates plus the beverages. That is our supply of food until we arrive on the island."

"Find boat 139, space gray, Atlanta. In this boat, there will be a miniature boat stored on the second floor, level to the sea."

Ema coughed and hiccuped, on and on, moaning on her hammock. She huddled in her hammock, pulling the thin blankets over her. Pulie and Nicky looked at each other. Pulie swung up to the hammock and hopped into hers and leaned over to where Ema lay.

"Ema, are you okay?"

There was no response.

"Ema?" Pulie reached over and felt Ema's forehead. Like a blazing fire burning her palm with a thousand prickly needles.

"She's got a fever!"

"Calm down, Pulie! Let me see." Nicky hopped up and felt Ema's forehead. "Jiminy Crickets! First Dan, now Ema? Pulie, can you run down and get the nurse?"

"Run? Is there no other way?"

"Nope, you better hurry."

Pulie's legs ran with a mind of their own, speeding down through the courtyard. Ms. Cherry's hill sprints came into action at this very moment. The courtyard was a swarm of busy students who were trying to get to their next class.

At last, she arrived at the Miralmalma. She sped up the dark spiral stairs and lunged and grasped at every next step.

At the top, she leaped out and burst through the treatment unit entrance and bumped into—

Selma.

Pulie scrunched her face; only the mission group was not in class at this time period. Selma was supposed to be in class. But instead, she was conversing with Miss Leapando.

"Nurse, sorry to interrupt—" Pulie glanced at Selma. "—this strange conversation. But I need your help. My friend's forehead is heating up right now, and I need you to help me transport her to the treatment unit. We need to hurry because there's no time. We need medicine—"

Miss Leapando looked quite sordid over the situation and replied, "I'm quite busy with my own matters at the moment. As you can see, I was discussing a very important matter with Miss Dutchstill. Your situation will have to wait."

"But my friend is sick—"

"I believe she already said that she's busy, Jark," snickered Selma.

What was this girl even doing here?

"You're a *nurse*, right?" Pulie asked Miss Leapando, then holding her bandaged hand up. "Not a very good one either, but you have a job. It's to treat sick people. Not listening to mentally-unstable people who like throwing darts at other people's hands just to get out of the mission group they didn't qualify for.." Pulie glared at Selma.

"That's enough," Miss Leapando snapped. "If a nurse demands time with another girl, she should get it. Now—"

"Is there no other nurse?" Pulie searched the room. "Hello? Nurses? Mr. *Twig*? Mr. Wace!" Pulie hollered.

"Everyone's in the eating room, stupid. She's the only one on duty right now," Selma said with a smile.

"*Thank you*, Selma. She *is* on *duty*. Miss Leapando, I demand your help."

There was an odd pause, until the nurse snapped, "I believe there are more important matters to discuss right now!" She stomped her feet.

"This is an emergency! If you don't go down there and help my friend, I'll tell Mr. Wace about this!"

The nurse shook her head. "I didn't do anything wrong. And *you* wouldn't *dare*."

Selma leaned against the wall, observing the conversation as if it were all some sort of amusement to her. Her lips spread from ear to ear, smiling like the Joker. There was still a long scar on the side of her cheek from the day at Awolo's.

The nurse reprimanded, "Well, little girl, I've wasted enough time listening to your silly pleas and requests, but I'm done with that. Run to your room and see what you can do there. I'll come in an hour or so."

Pulie didn't move.

"I *said* you can go now."

Pulie didn't budge until she remembered that in her back pocket was the yin yang gadget.

"It's time for you to *go*, now, young woman. I'll throw you down if I have to," the nurse hollered.

Pulie stayed silent but put her hands behind her back and gently snapped the circle gadget into the two parts. She felt the black chip and the button.

"Go." Miss Leapando pointed to the stairs. Pulie gripped the black chip in her hand.

Miss Leapando groaned. "Here, take a thermometer!" She threw the instrument at Pulie. "Check her temperature. *Then* tell me your story. Sound, alright?"

Pulie pressed the connection button. "No," Pulie answered.

"She wasn't asking for your opinion." Selma snorted, twisting her shiny brown hair, tapping her feet on the carpet.

"Hurry up!" Selma hollered. "Go away. You aren't wanted *here*." Selma then shoved Pulie away from the treatment unit while Pulie stretched out her arm and slipped the black chip down Selma's back pocket.

Then, Pulie was left with no choice to return to her room.

***

"One hundred and four degrees!" Nicky yelped, "Pulie, why didn't you just bring the nurse?"

"I already told you. She wouldn't come! She was too busy conversing with Selma."

Pulie didn't have time to listen to the white hearing piece, but everything Selma and the nurse discussed would be saved in the gadget.

Moans continued to leave the lips of the pale victim's lips with red cheeks who lay tumbling about in her hammock.

Nicky furrowed her brows. "Now, what do we do?" She ran back to the sink to dip the towel in cold water. Nicky wrung the towels tightly in the sink. Her fingers were getting awfully cold now. She ran over to Ema and placed the towel on her forehead. Ema burped really loudly and continued to cough. Her face was fading into a darker shade of red. As the cool towel touched her forehead, she shivered and then subsided into her blankets, absorbing the iciness.

The next moment, Pulie was running to the exit of the Zive.

"Mr. Wace? Mr. Wace?"

Mr. Wace had just entered her Zive, holding a load of boxes. "Pulie? How may I help you today?"

"Ema—she has a fever!"

Mr. Wace raised his eyebrows, still not setting the pile down. "At what degree, may I ask you?"

"One hundred four degrees."

Mr. Wace set the load down in an instant. "Well, what are we waiting for! Let's get going! One hundred and four degrees? A mission member with a fever is not good, not good!"

He spat into his communication device, ordering for a stretcher and crew members to take Ema up the Miralmalma.

In the blink of an eye, the Twig and the two other workers were drawn out of the eating room and sent up with a stretcher. Ema was sent in a treatment bed up to the Miralmalma.

***

Pulie flicked a little piece of cloth off her chair and sighed. She and Nicky had been waiting in the Miralmalma for hours for news of Ema.

Nicky drummed her fingers on the armchair. "It's been hours since Ema was transported inside that room and the nurses haven't come out yet? I mean, I remember the one time *I* had a fever. All they did was give me a shot or two and send me off to sleep. If that's all they're doing, maybe the shots are ginormous, and it takes six people to lift it. When I think about it, that might be what is happening. A colossal shot inserting a large needle into Ema? That—"

"Nicky, I don't think that's the case."

Nicky slumped. "I know."

Minutes later, Mr. Wace left the nurse's room with an angry face. "Miss Jark, Miss Oster, I think I'd like to talk to you about something."

Pulie and Nicky immediately stood up. This didn't sound good.

"Is she okay?"

"She is fine. She will stay in the treatment unit for four days." Mr. Wace's face was still irritated. "What I am about to ask you is entirely about you two."

Pulie swallowed hard.

Mr. Wace sighed and covered his hands with his face. "The Trickies foundation has assigned a *very very* important job for me. Do you know what it is?"

"Uh–"

"To get you all trained for the scouts!" He hollered, and everyone in the Miralmalma turned to stare. "If I don't get you all on this mission… if this mission isn't executed properly, this palace might shut down. My job might be replaced. This entire palace depends on each and every one of our mission participants helping each other. First you, Pulie, then Dan with the concussion whatever, and now Ema? We chose you because you are capable of this mission, and if even one of you cannot fulfill the requirement, this is terrible news for *all of us*. It throws us off our plan. And your hand, Pulie, I don't know what happened, but accidents like that cannot happen again. I mean, if Ema wasn't part of the mission crew, I definitely wouldn't have ordered a stretcher!"

"You wouldn't have?"

"Nope. Certainly not."

"Now, that's just sad," Nicky whispered.

"But my question is unless you were not beside her, why didn't you help her?"

"We tried."

"Trying is useless unless successful."

"It wasn't our fault—" Pulie added, "I had no idea what to do!"

Mr. Wace shook his head. "It's a very simple and systematic process. I clearly remember Awolo explaining that if any of you are ill, send another to the nurse immediately. There is no emergency call, but you must report to the Miralmalma as soon as possible. All you needed to do was go to the nurse! Nicky! You've been at this palace for more than a year! You should've known."

Pulie jumped in. "The nurse, Miss Leapando—she refused to help us."

"Leapando? Leapando!" Mr. Wace snapped up like a spring when he heard the name. It was like he had been waiting for this moment. His voice bounced off every object in the Miralmalma and hit Pulie's ear like a drum.

"Yes?" called a sweet distant voice. The nurse came out of the back door.

Mr. Wace turned back to Pulie. "May I ask, what was she doing instead of helping?"

Pulie brought out her white chip. "I don't know, sir. She was talking to Selma—"

"She was?"

"Yes. I don't know what it was about. But everything they discussed after I left is all in here.

Mr. Wace's eyes grew wide. "And the other half?"

"In Selma's back left pocket."

"Very clever. I'm going to read this file on my computer. Miss Leapando! Wait in the mission room."

"Of course."

Mr. Wace disappeared into his room, with the chip in his hand.

Soon after, he came out again but marched straight over the mission room. The door remained shut for a long time. When Mr. Wace finally exited, he commanded Miss Idadosi and Mrs. Lora to enter.

He then came over to Pulie and Nicky. He looked... relieved in some way. The wrinkles on his forehead had loosened, and he sighed.

"What happened?"

"I fired her."

Nicky had her jaw open. "What?"

"Not only because she failed to assist you. It was after I listened to the chip. Miss Leapando and Miss Dutchstill were devising a plan. Selma would've paid the nurse a large sum of credits if Miss Leapando chose Selma to win the spot in the council for next year. I knew it for a long time that Miss Leapando had been breaking the rules. I didn't have any evidence."

"How can Miss Leapando help with that, though? She's only the nurse."

"She's not *only* the nurse." Mr. Wace grimaced. "Ms. Borthwick hired her to be both nurse and administrator of the competition."

"That's terrible." Nicky shook her head. "It's a pity that some people are so desperate because they aren't capable enough. Well, I guess it was the best Selma could do. She *never* would've gotten the spot on her own."

"Don't you cry. We'll fix it. There's *nothing* to be ashamed of, Aela." Pulie heard Ms. Idadosi behind the door, soothing Miss Leapando.

"For what reason did *I… I…* get fired?" sobbed the nurse.

"There's nothing sane about that man, but we can negotiate with Awolo somehow and perhaps get rid of that… whatever her name is."

"You know perfectly well of what her name is, Miss Idadosi," Mrs. Lora said from the room. "She's quite intelligent if you ask me. Using yin yang chips." Pulie heard a chuckle. "On the other hand—let's clean her up and send her away."

Pulie heard the nurse break into more sobs. Pulie grinned. She was beginning to really like Mrs. Lora.

"Well, if it isn't Professor Snitch." A voice snarled behind her. Selma. Again.

Pulie returned to her position to eavesdrop on the teachers.

"I see you got rid of Miss Leapando," Selma said. "Who's next? Are you going to get rid of everyone here?"

"Correct. You better watch out. *You're* next."

Selma fumed, her body shaking and trembling in anger. "You'll never get away with this. I'll have my father know about this."

"Hey, hey, hey," Pulie said in a loud voice. "Don't throw another dart at me, okay? There are other ways."

"You're lucky we're in the Miralmalma," Selma retorted. "I would've torn every limb off your body by now if we were in the courtyard. All because of you, Mr. Wace disqualified me from any chances of obtaining the spot at the student council next year. All because of you."

"You're welcome."

Selma shook her fist. "I'll get you back. I will get you back. Just watch me." She then dug into her back pocket and brought out the black half of the yin yang. She dropped it on the floor and used her shoe to shatter the device to pieces.

"Stop!"

The wires and the button cracked. There was a small lump of broken shards on the ground now.

"*That's* for ruining my life. Now, I can never be the president and help guide the world like my father did."

"I *really* care." Pulie popped a gum into her mouth and started to chew it furiously.

Selma huffed. "You're just lucky Mr. Wace likes you. When I get rid of him, you'll be as helpless as a baby bird. Flap all you want, but I'll have my father shoot you the moment you get out of your nest." She crossed her arms and disappeared back into the dark halls.

Pulie scooped up the broken half of the device and winced. Mrs. Slendersan said she would not give out extras. *Just great.*

Miss Idadosi escorted Miss Leapando out of the mission room, patting and embracing her. The nurse's apron was wet with tears, her mascara dribbling down her cheeks like black blood.

"*Jark*," Miss Idadosi spat, as they paused in front of Pulie.

Pulie looked up at Ms. Leapando's dreary eyes. "I'm not afraid. But you thought I was afraid to tell Mr. Wace. You were wrong."

More sobs. Pulie looked at the tears like delightful puddles and smiled.

HEIGHTS

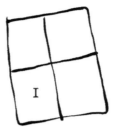

The next morning, Ema was already wide awake when Pulie and Nicky came to check on her. Dan was in the next bed, fast asleep.

"Hello," Ema said, smiling.

"You'll never guess what happened," Nicky said as she barged into the room. Pulie followed her in, with much more tranquility.

"Quiet. Dan's still sleeping. But what?" Ema asked.

Nicky collapsed on the bed next to Ema's with her shoes on. "You know how you were here yesterday. Mr. Wace came out and talked to us, blah blah blah. Then he went bam bam pew at Ms. Leapando and got her fired. And then I went back to the Zives after Mr. Wace told us we could go. Pulie stayed here. I don't know why. And then, while I was walking back, I decided to go to the gym to work out. It was like almost empty. I went to the weight lifting room because I haven't been there in a long time because of the mission class. The weight lifting room was empty and then all of a sudden, the door slammed shut behind me." Nicky's eyes grew wide. "And then I jumped up because the slam was pretty loud. And I turned around, and no one was there. So I tried to open the door, but it wouldn't budge. It was just locked. And I tried the other exit to the bathrooms, which was all the way across the room and then—" Nicky paused. "I saw this shadow behind me in the long mirrors. It was like—I don't know!" Nicky buried her head into her arms and began to sob. Well, it was a fake sob. Nicky glanced up back at Pulie and Ema to see if they were paying attention.

"You sure that isn't a dream?" Ema asked. "How'd you get out?"

Nicky began again, "I saw the shadow behind me, and it was holding like some kind of weird long stick. And I sprinted to the entrance door, but it was locked, and I wasn't looking at the mirror. I banged and banged and banged until finally, the door somehow opened, and then I sprinted to the main room where everyone else was. I survived."

Ema raised an eyebrow. "You are quite the storyteller."

"It happened! I ain't lying! I saw the shadow with my own eyes."

"She's told me this story four times since I left the Miralmalma yesterday," Pulie told Ema. "I'm beginning to worry about Nicky too."

Nicky shook her head. "If I didn't see the shadow, then why did the door slam shut?"

"Air conditioning. Wind. Fan blower. Coincidence. Should I go on?"

"No."

Ema sighed. "That's strange. If it's true, then I don't know who or what that shadow was. Or what it was holding. I mean, why didn't it just kill you if they locked you in on purpose. Not to scare you."

Nicky shivered. "I'm gonna die before the mission. I'm gonna die! Someone's out to get me."

"You'll be alright. Just don't go to places alone. It could've been Selma," Pulie interrupted.

"Even my water bottle is missing!" Nicky threw her hands up. "It disappeared yesterday!"

"I think I accidentally drank yours, Nicky. It was on the table in our room and I thought it was ours," Ema said. "I left it in the bathrooms yesterday because I had a stomach ache. Sorry, I'll get you a new one."

"Nah, I was planning on buying that new water bottle from Señor anyway. How are you feeling though?"

"Alright. I guess I'm missing training for a week. At least I get to miss one week of painful gymnastics."

"Don't worry—" Pulie assured her, "We'll take your notes and everything. You'll just need to adjust when you get back." Pulie glanced at the far corner bed, watching for any movement in the shadows. Was the girl still there?

"What zar zou ladies doing here?" Mr. Lizarstrang asked as he walked into the room, carrying a bandaged arm. His face was puffed up, a left black eye, and his shoes were muddied.

"What happened to you, sir?" Dan asked, just getting up, rubbing his eyes.

"Nothing." Mr. Lizarstrang cleared his throat. "I was asking zou a question."

"Well, they're both sick right now. *She* had a fever yesterday," Nicky continued, "104 degrees. It was very high. She spent the night in the treatment unit here, and now we're checking on her in the morning. And *he* hit his head somehow and ended up with some kind of injury."

"Zour not allowed to be zup zis early. I'll be sending this note to zour teachers to announce naughty behavior. What are zour names?"

"We were in your class!" they cried in unison.

"What?"

Nicky huffed, "My name is Fiona, her name is Selma, and her name is Bonnie. Please, we were just fooling around," Nicky answered confidently.

"And the boy?"

"Dash."

"Thank zou. Zou may now go to zour rooms. Why are zou zup so early anyway? Class starts at *seven*."

After their teacher left the room, they cracked up.

"I guess he *does* have a thousand kids to remember," Ema said, tapping her nails on the book.

"That is a lot."

"Well," Ema said, counting her fingers, "We only see one-fourth of the kids right now because we only see the students from our Zive. Each Zive has about one thousand students. The other Zive groups go to the other Zives."

"I just can not wait until we move up to the Third Level—if I pass. We get to tease the little kids and it's like Middle School in regular schools. But next year, the Leader Board is *for real*. Competition gets really tough to prepare for scouting."

"Scouting?"

"Yes, well, in a scout, you are basically a mission group. You work with those people to execute missions from real Tricksters. Once you're in scout league, you're a fully trained Trickster."

"I would like to be scouted but then work at SkyClouds. My father said the jobs are so much better there." Ema's eyes shined.

"I think I want to go to AT Tricksters," Nicky said promptly. "Sky Clouds are different than Tricksters. Sky Clouds work—" Nicky glanced up at the sky. "Up there! Even if they have all these cool glass operators, I want to be a fully trained Trickster."

"That's very cool. What time is it?"

"Shoot. We're late."

***

Pulie slid the door handle and pulled on the knob, gently, to peek inside.

"The proceedings of this will lead to the pizza delivery picking us up…"

"Oh *Lord*," Nicky whispered.

The class had already started, and they were once *again* late.

"Pulie and Nicky, come up to me when I call Practice Time."

"It's not that hard, *girls*," Erik sneered.

Mrs. Slendersan snapped, "Erik, why don't you start with typing your own notes in your device before minding other people's business. And you two. Hurry up! Start writing this down. You're lucky we finished our warm-ups before note-taking."

Pulie pulled out her sketch pad and began to enter all the information as Mrs. Slendersan proceeded.

"I will have to start over again, but listening twice is nothing but good than listening once."

Erik let out a groan, although his note screen was completely blank.

"Please type. Group one: Nicky, Alexia, Piden, Maya. Group two: Dash, Ema, Tilda, Alex. Group three: Daria, Dan, Noel, Colin, and Pulie. We are going into Phase Fourteen of in-depth procedures."

The screen was displayed. A video of what their mission execution would look like if all went well.

"Step one, Erik will make sure to steer the boat at exactly 180 degrees from the east perimeter. This way, we are collinear with both the dock and the navigation system. Step two, once you reach twenty feet from the radar, everyone should already be seated in the small boat on the second level. The only three people should be inside the main boat by now: Erik, who will switch settings to hands-free, and Celena and Daria, who will scan the boat for nor missing people or luggage. By ten feet, everyone is *inside* the small boat. And by five feet, open up level two, and the small boat will slide out the back and into the water. The large boat will keep moving in the same direction, straight to Conto Island. Meanwhile, Erik will steer the boat in a different direction. Follow the radar with about forty feet from the signals and go around to the east side of the island."

Alex raised his hand.

"Yes?"

"You said we would be inside the boat. Does this also mean inside the truck which would be located *inside* the boat?"

"No. You will enter the truck once you enter the east perimeter. Okay, now, we will go into Phase Fifteen. Thirty-five feet from the signals at the east perimeter, group two will gather inside the *truck*. Only group two. Everyone else will be on the lookout. Group two will shut down security numbers 34C through 45 C. You will have less than ten minutes to do so."

"Will we use Inter-22?" Alex asked. "Or Inter-23? In my opinion, both are very great options. It depends on the preference of how the screen detaches, you know."

Mrs. Slendersan smiled weakly. "Yes. Now. Where was I? Right. You will have less than ten minutes. After they are shut down, you can enter the east side safely until you reach land. You will have another ten minutes to shut down the land security. Use programs Fortis and Rotix 33. By now, everyone is inside the truck. Erik, you will drive the truck out onto the land. The leader of the CAOT will not be present at the island, so the guards will be reduced to a minimum. We have now entered phase sixteen."

The lecture notes were over for today. The teacher called both Nicky and Pulie up to her desk after everyone else's dismissal.

"Late again. The reason?"

"We visited Ema in the morning in the treatment unit," Nicky answered. "I've been sick before, and it's quite dreary when you have no company except that strange girl in the back who's like a ghost. She usually doesn't talk. We just paid Ema a visit to see how things were holding up."

Mrs. Slendersan sighed. "Well, don't be late again. This is your what... tenth? Seventh? Fifth time?"

"Second."

"Very well. You are dismissed to your training."

Today was Solo training. That meant that Pulie was on her own the entire time. She was climbing up the walls with her sticky shoes as she lunged up and grasped the vines and poles. She leaped onto the high swinging board, the tallest point, and then grabbed onto the window ledge, huddling for the head of the sun. Mrs. Slendersan had insisted they lower the temperature of the room during training since Conto Island was blanketed in snow.

It was a long way down, but the long drop to the floor didn't scare her anymore. She had fallen too many times already. She gazed outside the window, admiring the back view of the palace.

And then all of a sudden, she saw something in the back of the palace. It was long, and it was dark. Not in color, but the way it was always covered in the shadows, no matter where it went. Pulie could barely see the figure, even when she squinted. She pressed her face against the window and peered. And then, she saw it.

***

"It was a revolting face. It was down there, in the back of the palace. I was up on the top window. I saw it."

"So, that is why you screamed?" Mrs. Slendersan asked. "You scared the lights out of everyone with that high pitch scream of yours."

"It was real! It was horrible! If you saw it, you would've screamed, too." Pulie tried to explain.

Soon, the mission class was dismissed, and only a couple of people waited beside her to listen to the story.

"Black outlined eyes—large large eyes with grey shaded all around it. And the shading dripped down to the cheeks! And it—"

"So, you just saw this creepy stranger down there?" Nicky asked.

"Yes, now listen. It had a face as white as paper, and its hair was straight black. Its lips were the color of blood gushing out…"

"Okay, okay. So it's a human?" Nicky asked, heading down the stairs.

"Not exactly… no… well, I'm not all that sure… I only saw the face."

"Continue…" Alex said, his eyes bulging in interest.

"I was at the top window, right? I look down, and there's this dark person-like thing just wandering around and its face was just so… creepy." Pulie shuddered.

"Why are you calling *it* and *it*?" Piden asked. "*It* could be a human."

"And I first saw reaching into the shadows—" Pulie tried to ignore Piden's comment and Alex's big eyes enlarging every time she spoke. Interesting conversations really made him into a dead human.

"And then what happened?"

"Well, it looked up at me, and then, I guess I screamed."

"You *guess* you screamed?" Piden and Nicky asked in unison.

"You literally screamed the heck out of the room," Nicky added. "Erik's spread the word of your anxiety attacks all over the palace."

"That witch!"

"Wizard," Alex corrected.

"But there really was that person there! I swear! And I don't have anxiety!"

"We know!" Everyone shouted.

"We *do*?" Alex asked, confused.

Today was the twenty-third of December. Pulie's birthday had already passed. Tomorrow was Christmas Eve.

She had hidden the presents in her cabinet while everyone was at the shop, which was everyone's new favorite location. They were either buying a Christmas tree, finding food, choosing presents, or stealing decorations. Pulie had twenty credits in her bag. Nicky had twenty as well, and Ema had thirty. The mini Christmas Tree cost forty credits, so they were able to buy decorations for their room. The small Christmas tree sat by their window, sparkling with lights, and streamers dangled on every corner of their room. And if you unscrewed an ornament, a piece of candy would be waiting for you behind its shell. It was a delightful tree.

Christmas wasn't as big of a day as Halloween. Classes and training still continued, although everyone was just mostly excited that the school year was almost over. In addition, Christmas was also the only time food fights were allowed in the eating room.

Everyone skipped breakfast to eat big meals for the rest of the day. During dinner, a plethora of food sat on the tables such as steaks, drumsticks, mashed potatoes, vegetables, fries, soups, juices, and drinks were served.

Dan *and* Ema were both better. They were out of the treatment unit and frolicking happier than ever.

After buying the tree, the girls grew broke, so Piden suggested they steal boxes of candy from Larry's abandoned workshop below next to the eating room. They sold the candies after taking over the lollipop stand. Almost everyone ran for the caramels and chocolates. Pulie opened up the bags of the pepperRaffertys, spearRaffertys, and the Frosts. The people with more credits, like Selma, *scooped* up bags of candies, paying for the huge amount, while people with little credits savored each lick of a Butterscotch Winkle.

By the end of the day, they each had themselves a stack of fifty credits.

MISSION GETTING CLOSER

Christmas jolly was over, and soon, *serious* was getting serious.

No more smiles, a lot more sweat. Day after day, lectures, lectures, and more lectures. And then many hours of training. Pulie felt the muscles growing and toning down on the sides of her arms and her legs.

Mrs. Slendersan took the mission crew often over to Señor Rodriguez's room to distribute equipment, gadgets, and weapons. They selected the vest sizes, parachute lengths, and clothing for the mission in the safety room.

The palace's colors are violet and black, so the year's designs followed the same color rules as well. The girl's outfits included a black sleeveless top, cotton pullover sweaters, smooth black leggings, long waterproof socks, and two pairs of shoes. The boy's outfits included a tight black shirt, cotton pullover sweaters, black and grey camo sweats, long waterproof socks, and also two pairs of shoes. On everyone's top, in purple and gold, the letter T was printed in the center, the special design of the Trickies.

The slender backpack Pulie was to wear could hold a small pocket knife, a flashlight, an attached parachute, and the bombs.

The real bombs for the actual time of the mission weren't in her hands just yet.

"Our squad of teachers on the separate mission is leaving the day just before you do, so be sure to check and adjust your gadgets with Señor Rodriguez before he leaves."

***

One day, during Pulie's training at six in the morning, Mrs. Slendersan led Pulie outside of the Palace, far past the moat. Mrs. Slendersan gave her five *real* bombs, not cheese bombs or prototypes.

"It's about time you learn how to deal with the real ones," Mrs. Slendersan said, "I hate them with all my heart, but I know that this is the best option to defeat the CAOT."

Pulie's fingers slid across the indented Trickies golden symbol. She clutched one in between her fingers, and with the other hand, she would press the bright red gleaming button on the side. Then, sitting at the top of the ladder, she would lance the bomb at the target on the floor. The timer would tick away, and in ten seconds, the bomb would explode. Mrs. Slendersan dove as far away as possible. Smoke like clouds filled the air.

Mrs. Slendersan watched Pulie toss all five of them and then left an entire box of bombs for Pulie to practice. Now, Pulie was alone outside the palace.

Her target grew more accurate every toss. Her nose acquainted with the thick smell of smoke and metal. And her fingers memorized the patterns on the bomb. On the side was a little clip to attach the bomb to either her belt or to the ground. The bomb was now a part of her.

***

"We'll be in the southwest area after group two shuts down camera systems 14 and 25," Nicky pointed to the map. "And last-minute change, Mrs. Slendersan said that alarms wouldn't work. It would be obvious and suspicious. We need to think of a new distraction quickly. Mrs. Slendersan gave my group only a day to figure it out. So we're a bit behind."

Pulie sprang up to her hammock and watched Nicky, Ema, Alex, and Piden discuss the matter from above.

"I don't know what to do," Nicky muttered.

Piden thought for awhile. "Well, I mean, we only need something to draw the guards off their posts and have them focus on something else for a while."

"Yes, exactly. What can we do?"

"Something very dangerous—that always gets people nervous and afraid," Piden added. "Do you know what I'm thinking?"

"Hurricane?"

"Water gunfight?"

"Bacterial meningitis?"

"Fire?"

"Yes! Fire!" Piden said, "It always sparks people. If we can get a fire starting—"

"The island is literally a snowball!" Nicky argued. "You can't start—"

"Oak, Hickory, Ash, or Cedar. All are incredible at starting fires. Dry wood will be collected, and we'll create bedding of tinder to start the large fire," Alex informed them.

"That *could* work. And we could light up the whole patch!"

"Wait," Piden paused, "What if the dome catches on fire?"

"Then, at least we all die *extra* hot," Nicky said.

Everyone burst out laughing.

TWO DAYS TILL THE MISSION

Time flew by. The fire was their *go* for distraction.

It was already the Thirteenth of January, and everyone was terrified. The last two days were set for essential exercising, adequate sleep, healthy eating, and making sure no one got injured or sick.

"Good luck, Jark!" Selma screeched. The scratchy voice clearly satisfied Pulie's ear at five in the morning.

"Thanks."

Selma rolled her eyes. "It was sarcasm."

Pulie started walking faster. "Have fun at the palace without me. I know you'll miss me."

"No one will miss you. I hope you die."

Pulie sighed, hoping that was not going to happen. "What are you even doing this early? Your class starts at seven." Then, Pulie sped walked even faster.

Selma caught up to her as Pulie heaved open the door of the Miralmalma.

"Try it." A little piece of candy sat in Selma's palm.

Pulie grabbed the candy. "Thanks."

Selma watched Pulie even more closely with sharp pointy eyes. "You leave for the mission tomorrow."

"I know that."

"You scared? Do you feel like you don't want to do it? Do you have mission phobia?"

"No, I'm quite ready and elated, thank you very much." Selma scowled.

From the corner of her eyes, Pulie saw Nicky heading right towards them and sighed with relief.

Pulie popped a candy in her mouth, swishing the delicious ball around with her tongue. Selma snickered when she saw this.

"Well, Selma, see you around. I have to go to Mission class."

Selma bit her lip, but Pulie and Nicky closed the door. Selma yanked the door back open. Handling Selma was like handling a piece of gum in your hair. You need to cut it off— with a knife the size of the moon.

"Do you mind? We have to go to class!" Pulie said, yanking the door back.

"I got to go too!"

"Since when were you part of the Mission, Selma?" Nicky interrupted.

"Hmmfff, very funny, Nicky."

Nicky shrugged as Selma followed them up the staircase. When they entered room T4, instead of Mrs. Slendersan, Mr. Wace sat at the desk.

"Good morning, Miss Oster, Miss Jark—Miss *Dutchstill?*"

"Correct. Good morning, Mr. Wace," Selma merrily chirped. And her face blushed so hard when she spotted Dash, Pulie thought it might as well blow up.

Mr. Wace lifted his head from his monitor. "What are you doing here?"

"I am filling in for Anne."

"Since when did somebody say there would be substitution?"

"But she's sick!"

Mr. Wace sighed and ordered them to sit in their assigned seats anyway. Ema waved Nicky and Pulie over as they copied off of the guidelines for a parachute.

Selma shifted in her position against the wall.

Celena came in, then Erik, then Colin, then Piden and Alex. Slowly, everyone filled in their seats. Selma smiled, liking her chances of Anne never entering the room.

However, at about 5:30, Little Miss Truo walked into the room. Selma scowled. But, her eyes told Pulie that she wouldn't leave any time soon.

"Miss Dutchstill, you may leave now. Thank you for the brief substitution."

"But she was sick! Anne, aren't you sick?"

"You mean, I *was* sick." Anne threw Selma a nasty look.

Mr. Wace furrowed his eyebrows. "Miss Dutchstill, please leave the room. The class will be starting."

"Mrs. Slendersan said there would be substitution when needed."

"But we do not need it right now! Nor would we need it ever! And if we did, we would certainly not pick you!" Mr. Wace slammed his hand onto the desk.

Tears slithered down Selma's face. "You horrible man!" Selma wailed, forgetting Dash was in the same room. Selma looked like a volcano about to erupt. Lava was going to be oozing everywhere.

"You are the oldest, meanest cruelest man ever!" Selma screamed, pointing her finger at Mr. Wace. "I will tell my father, and—and— he will banish you forever!"

"Then go ahead! But please, get out."

Miss Dutchstill stormed out of the room, slamming the door behind her.

Peace was restored to the mission group, and soon, they were all on their backs, lifting weights and grabbing bars. Pulie's sweat slid down her shirt as they did their sit-ups.

Nicky nudged Pulie in the shoulder.

"Didn't you eat some kind of candy in the morning? Did Selma give it to you?"

Pulie shook her head. "Nope. I ate the candy *you* gave me on Christmas."

"*Clever girl.*" Nicky imitated Mr. Wace. They both laughed.

"Oster, Jark. Thirty more for talking!"

***

"So, we wake up at two tomorrow?" Pulie asked, setting her toothbrush and shower towels by the door. She needed to be prepared so she could quickly wash up before the long trip tomorrow.

"Yes. Even worse than five, I guess," Nicky answered.

"I'm so nervous," Ema added. She shuddered. "I'm scared."

"Me too."

"Got to admit it. I am too." Nicky sighed. "But if we die during the mission, we will be remembered and honored. It's better than dying from cancer or something."

"Nicky!"

"What?" Nicky shrugged. "Anyways, I can't wait until I get to use these—" Nicky pulled out her bag full of firelighters. "Twenty-two? I think. Señor Rodriguez said that all you have to do is pour a little of this package on the edge and throw it on the dry wood. He says my face would burn off if I get close to it!"

"Which is perfect because your face will become double hotter!" Pulie noted.

"Hey, that's my line!" Nicky shouted.

They all cracked up.

"Today is *the* most stressful and the least stressful day, all in one." Ema pointed to her head. "All we have to do is avoid Selma, don't play on the vines, eat a minimum amount of food, and then get a good night's sleep before the long day ahead! But the problem is that we have a mission ahead of us."

"At least Celena and Mr. Wace pack our equipment and send us our clothes tonight."

"Very true."

THE STARTS OF A LONG DAY

Pulie was the first to awake when the alarm by the desk began squealing at one in the morning. She gently nudged Nicky and Ema, who awoke in seconds. Their suits had been waiting for this time on the shelf, neatly arranged and folded.

They grabbed their clothes and headed straight to the bathroom. There, the water was turned on, the air becoming toasty and humid. Each of them stepped into the boiling shower, knowing they wouldn't have one for days.

In the lobby, before they headed down the vines, they checked to see if they had brought all the required items for the mission. Pulie smoothed down her clothes, the leggings snug tight on her legs, her tank top revealing her bare shoulders. She couldn't tell her tremulous body was shaking because of the cold weather or because the mission was starting in about thirty minutes. She pulled on the warm fluffy sweater and clipped her backpack onto her waist. Nicky and Piden clipped on steel helmets to their bags, and Ema and Alex secured their bags of devices. The complete darkness outside was spotted with bright small stars shimmering like gems in a sea of nothing. The Palace was completely silent.

Everyone in the mission group gathered in the courtyard, where Mr. Wace and Celena would check off and approve of every clothing piece, gadget, and source of information. Dash brought the wrong shoes and was sent back for the new pair.

Besides that, Miss Slendersan was sobbing in approval, explaining how diligent and hard-working everyone was through her heavy tears.

"Hush, Miss Slendersan, we mustn't let emotions overcome us."

"Ye-e-es sirr-r," Miss Slendersan croaked, as she blew her nose. Mr. Wace gestured Celena to begin her duty.

She trembled as she grabbed the list. Even the once so brave Celena was shaking at this point.

"Everyone here agrees to go forth and execute this mission as a loyal Tricky?"

"Aye." The unanimous answer was said.

"If you do not have any of the following items on the checklist, please step forward. Last call for bathroom and extra water. Is everyone here set?" Her voice was louder.

"Aye."

"Does everyone have explicit knowledge of *all* procedures and the jobs assigned to them?

"Aye."

"Does everyone *understand* that death or fatal injuries can occur during the execution of the mission? And that although you die in honor, the risk of bringing back your body to the palace *will* be difficult? And that the mission must go on, no matter what?"

"Aye." This question got everyone on their nerves. Pulie shivered. She wanted her body back to her house *if* she died. But she was determined not to die either way.

"Does everyone understand the importance of this mission and each individual's task to the palace and the Trickies as a whole? One mistake could lead to disasters such as the leakage of footage, secret passcodes, and information to the CAOT?"

"Aye…"

"And lastly, during the execution of the mission, remember these few words of the wiser. Be prepared for the worst. Do not trust *anyone*. Do not overestimate or underestimate *anyone*. Do not follow *anyone*. And do not *ever* allow your emotions or your curiosity to get the better of you. All lives at this palace are at stake. Do you understand?"

"Aye."

Celena turned to Mr. Wace. "I think we're ready."

***

They crossed the moat, then the large space in between the palace and the borders. They ascended up the staircase and into the SkyClouds world of glass and transparency. They boarded the Tubus and got off at Stop 43.

At one of the doors at this stop, they descended and made their way down to the normal dirt land Pulie had always known and did a full check-up one last time. Hiking shoes were pulled on, shoelaces were triple knotted, and then Miss Slendersan and Mr. Wace departed them from there.

The cold misty air at two-thirty in the morning, her grumbling stomach, the howling wind, the air slipping up her sweater, and her nose was freezing into a triangular block. Nicky, Ema, and Pulie huddled together, trying to contain body heat. Nine more hours of this until they reached the village. Pulie was too cold to hop around the patches of cow manure and rocks that stood in her way. She let them paint her shoes in silence. The food sat in the back of her small bag. It would have to wait for a long time.

Unfortunately, the fact that they were on an actual dangerous and serious mission had no effect on Erik, who had been assigned as the pre-bombing leader. And being the leader meant that he could do whatever he wanted. And he abused this right to the extreme.

The ground was soon sandy and muddy, and the air was no warmer than before. They trudged across the Black Mud as Alex called it. It was basically mud, but much heavier. At the top of this *mud* was a thin layer of water that swarmed with little shrimp looking creatures that occasionally nipped at Pulie's hand when she reached to clean her boot.

Finally, after hours and hours in the darkness, they could see a tree lit by the dawning light of the sun. This was their resting spot. Pulie collapsed onto one of the roots and immediately unwrapped the foods she packed. Pulie bit into her sandwich and chugged her water while Piden climbed up a tree and took a bite of his pizza, dropping all of his napkins on Pulie's head.

After everything was put away, Erik began his rather usual routine.

"Listen up, everyone! If your boots are a big old mess, start cleaning them until they look like mine. They'll start hardening in the sun and stick to the grass itself," Erik smirked, as he showed his boots by clicking his heels on the ground.

"But there isn't any sunlight!" Tilda groaned, pulling on her boots. The usual Tilda.

"Ohhh, there will be. If I were you, I'd enjoy this lovely cold we are having right now. You all are moaning and shivering, but soon it's gonna be as hot as the Zive bathrooms. So, chop-chop, everyone! We gotta get a move on!"

There were murmurs, and soon, the mission crew was back in business. Pulie wiped her boots with the bark of the tree, flicking the red ants as they crawled up and down her back.

"My boots look like a clump of mud." Nicky groaned. Her boot was a lumpy mold of watery dirt.

"Hey, rub them on the grass!" Ema said as she grabbed her boot and started wiping it across the frosted green grass. Pulie tossed the strip of bark away and did the same. She could soon see the laces of her shoes.

After a few more minutes of rest, the hike began once more. Erik constantly tapped his wrist gadget, and a map appeared in the air. There was still a long way to go.

Going up one hill was tough. Going up a dozen peaks was enslavement. Her sweater still felt useless, and she rubbed her icy fingers together. Pulie panted as her breath turned into a cloud of fog, blowing away in the wind.

Finally, the sun revealed its warming sunbeams from behind the clouds as Erik had said, and the leftover spots of mud on her boots hardened to stone. The warmth heated up their cold goosebumps and the ice flakes in their hair. After a long treacherous tiring hike, at their next stopping point, they lunched for a bit to re-energize.

Nicky had her tuna sandwich, while Pulie poured the hot water she had saved from before and poured a little into her frozen tomato soup bowl. It sizzled and melted, and Piden and Pulie split the bowl, fighting over every single droplet. Ema was chewing the free pasta plates from Chef Susie with disgust. It was Orange Pasta, the taste of oranges. Pulie let Ema sip some of her soup until Ema couldn't stop begging for more.

The sun was a chunk of glimmering gold in the blue sky, and the blades of emerald grass thawed and fluttered at every breeze. Nicky's thumb was suffocated in a bandage after an insect bite. Her thumb was swelling faster than she could talk—and Nicky could talk *fast*.

A couple of times along their journey, they were interrupted by strangers once in a while. Usually picnickers or hikers. When this happened, the group split into multiple groups and spread out to avoid suspicion.

    Finally, after a long journey, they halted at a river. Mortem River, everyone recalled from their lecture notes. Along drifted an old fisherman sitting in his boat in the ravaging waters, and it was quite obvious he had never caught any fish in his whole life. However, when his squinchy eyeballs saw their uniforms, he immediately steered his boat to a stop and got off. The boat constantly battled to be freed from the ropes, and the anchor with the unpredictable plundering waters assisted it.

    "They at it again, ain't they?" The old man spit out a lump of green and yellow onto the lush green, healthy grass. "Ya fools! Do ya think that you a gonna get what ya want? The corporation's as corrupt as the underlying enemy in front of ya!"

    "What?" Erik asked.

    "There are never two sides!" The man threw his hands up. "What don't ya understand? Two? No! One! We all are one! But the filthy corporation can't wrap their hands around that!" The old man started cussing loudly in his scraggly voice, hollering, and poking the mission group with his cane. His flappy skin wiggled across his face sending ripples of jiggles. His itchy voice made Pulie shrink. Nails on a chalkboard.

    "His voice." Nicky cringed. "Where can I get the tickets for his singing show?"

    "He hosts a singing show?" Alex said, biting on his nails.

    "*Yes, Alex.* He hosts a singing show." Nicky rolled her eyes.

    "Then why would you want to buy his tickets?" Alex asked, getting more serious.

    "Alex, I think Piden's over there—" Pulie interrupted the conversation. They all turned their focus—back to the old man.

    He was still shouting and spatting at Erik, who, at this point, was at his boiling rage. Erik wasn't used to getting spat at.

"Just get you and your stupid boat out of here already!" Erik bellowed, pointing to the boat, and then he clamped his hands over his ears. "You sound like a dying—something! Go away."

Everyone sighed. The volcano had finally erupted.

"I said get your—"

"Stop!" Daria shouted, shaking her head. She walked to the man and made a gesture of peace. It was the box formed by the thumb and the index finger and then twisted into the infinity sign. He sighed, still shaking his head, placing his dusty wrinkled fishing hat on his bald self. He then climbed into the boat and paddled away.

"Well, mate, that… was *easy*," Daria muttered, dusting her hands.

Erik's face grew bright red, and he grunted, pulling his backpack straps up higher. His voice rattled Pulie's ears as he called for line formation.

"Listen up! We have to get across the river. People who don't do as I say will be washed down the river. Understood?" Erik boomed, raising his finger in the air.

Pulie swallowed hard when she glanced at the wide thrashing river. The waters seemed to be fighting each other, leaping up into the air and devouring everything in its way. It seemed like a mile from the edge of one side to the other.

"Very well then, let us begin. At the bottom of the river, there is sticky sand. Not something you want to step in. But that's our only way there." Erik pointed to the other side of the river.

"When we get in, lift your legs up and down as you walk across. Leave your foot in the sticky sand for more than thirty seconds, and they will stick to the sand—good luck getting out of this kind of sand." He chuckled, looking up into the sky, facing the sun. His sunburnt skin crinkled, and his pupils dilated.

"The sun is setting soon. We gotta hurry before it's too dark to make it to the village. Levels One through Three! Or Young Trickies, Junior Trickies, Trickers, get in first. The rest wait for my command!"

Pulie saw her brother go into the water with Alex. All shoes were zipped up in their bags, and slowly, people trudged in through the murky waters. Trying to withstand the heavy water was tiresome and impossible. Piden looked like a paper boat, trying to go upstream.

When Pulie's toe dipped into the water, *cold* shuttered up her spine. Her feet pushed through the sand, and then she heaved her foot out of the gushy thickness. She looked around, hoping she wasn't the only one struggling. She spotted Dan, frozen in the middle of the river. What was he doing?

"Dan, getta move on!" Daria commanded as she helped Anne into the water.

He didn't respond. He stood still.

He has ten more seconds until he's potentially stuck in the sand. Why isn't he moving?

Suddenly from behind her, a voice screamed.

"Alligator!" Alex was swinging his arms around, his mouth opened in panic.

Alligator? Pulie glanced at Celena, whose eyes were as wide as silver platters, as she spotted the creature, lurking unwelcome in the water. The rushing water was an invisible cloak to the beast, for its scales mimicked the turbulent water. Pulie was almost carried down the river when she slipped on a rock. Getting across the river was hard enough. Now, they had an alligator to manage.

"Don't move a muscle," Celena said. Everyone came to a halt.

Dan was still frozen, his eyes following the scaly back of the alligator. It was like watching a snake slinking across the sand.

Pulie saw Piden, ripping a chunk of his leftover meatloaf and tossing it downstream. Curiosity and the smell of meat overwhelmed the creature and it slithered away, giving a chance for everyone to paddle closer to the other side.

But meatloaf was a mere appetizer. In a *flash*, the meat was gone. Then, the gator was back again, gliding up the stream and snarling a gnarly snout. Pulie was trying to move her foot another step closer to her destination when Celena shouted. In the water, she saw scales shimmering in the light. Slick and devilish eyes, the slimy outer layer of the eye continuously flapped up and down, the medallion iris, turning, the green iris, turning—clicking—watching.

Her eyes shut, tears filling in the edges of her eyes, her eyelashes wet. *Stay calm… stay extra calm…* She was trembling furiously that her fingers were a blur. She felt a tail brushing against her left leg. *Stay calm… stay still…*

When she opened her eyes, the gator was nowhere in sight. Instead, bubbles broiled at the surface around her. *Where had it gone?*

Suddenly, there was a scream. She turned her head, and to her horror, the gator had bitten someone. Dan.

Everyone screamed all at once.

Celena cried, "Everyone! Retreat! Swim for your lives! Run past the river!"

Then it was chaos. Everyone was screaming, scrambling to get to the shore, grasping at the inch-long grass blades, hoping to survive. Pulie swam quickly to the dirt. Then she looked back.

The gator dragged Dan down into the water, using its tail to keep his head underneath the surface. Dan kicked and thrashed, but the alligator was too massive and too powerful. Watching the fight was a mere simulation of ant battling a human. All Dan could do was nip at the thick skin. The alligator's body was long enough to use it as a bridge to walk across the vast river. Well, almost.

The gator lifted his jaw up and plunged his teeth into Dan's foot, sinking in deep as the water glowed red. Pulie's voice box rattled as she screamed, her eyes submerging in tears.

"Help!" Dan's voice was muffled, "Help! Help!" He screamed over and over again, but his head was pushed under the water. Celena escorted everyone onto the other side of the river. Then, they got their weapons ready.

"Gadget Three, everyone!"

There was a domino of clicks as the row of people flipped open the wristband, loaded with venomous launcher arrows only the size of toothpicks. Yet in the right spot, it was sure to be fatal. The tiny arrows whizzed over the waters, hitting the scaly beast.

Erik was back in the water again with a knife tightly gripped in his calloused hands. Pulie squinted through the aiming hole, pointing her arrow at the gator's eyes. She closed her eyes when Erik plunged the dagger into the back of the beast.

Blood oozed out of the scaly back when Pulie's eyes fluttered open. The monster let go of Dan and eyed Erik as he climbed ashore. He was scrambling back up the rocks to where everyone else was waiting.

"Erik!" Piden hollered, shaking his hands in the air. "Alligators can run up to eleven miles per hour. Run for your lives! It can go on land too!"

Pulie screamed along with everyone else. She couldn't believe that for once, she was on the same side as Erik. And soon, the bloody gator slithered up the rocks, effortlessly and onto the grass, inches away from Erik.

"Run!" Celena screamed, and everyone launched their darts at the alligator and started to sprint as fast as they could while Daria stayed behind, pulling Dan out of the water. The gator didn't chase off after the rest with only its gleaming jolly eyes on the limping Dan, licking his teeth.

Erik hauled Dan over his shoulder, and with Daria, their legs began to sprint faster than they ever did.

From afar with the rest of the group, Pulie squinted and saw the three people running towards her. The rest of the mission crew reunited with Dan for a while and began to run once again, to a distance far away from any source of water. Finally, they found a large oak tree as a stopping point.

Erik was in the middle of panting and crying, a hysteric mess. If she were at the palace, she would be enjoying this moment, feeling so superior. But that was not possible right now.

"There was that old man with the boat again," Erik said in between breaths, " the creature lost interest in us. Let's just hope the boat can move fast— "

Dan was spread out under the oak tree, and everyone grimaced at his leg. His limb was hanging onto his hip nearly with a thread of a muscle. His face scarred with bruises, his eyes closed, his uniform completely ripped apart. The grass flowed dark red. Celena pulled out her medicine kit to stop the bleeding with bandages. Daria and Noel accompanied her, aiding Celena with the medicines. Everyone else was behind the oak tree. There was a deafening silence.

Later, Celena and Erik wobbled over to the circle of the mission people. Both of their heads hung low—lower than the ground itself. When Celena looked up to wipe a tear, Pulie met her eyes. *It was over.* Celena looked down in an instant; her tears showering over her lap like rain.

"It's not over till it's over—" Erik stumbled over his words. "I don't know—if he's—alive. We—we—have-e-e currently—" He paused, his bold tone fading, "Dan Zipmore," was all he said in a whisper. Nicky gasped, and Ema turned pale. Pulie could not believe it.

Everyone knew that it was the end; it was written in the air.

A few minutes later, Daria spoke quietly, "We gotta ta continue—according to Mr. Wace—we all have ta complete our mission—and do what we came here for—we gotta leave Dan behind—"

"We're just going to leave him here?" Colin asked gritting.

"I'm so sorry, we have ta," Daria answered. "All we can do is hope for the best. Celena stopped tha bleeding and cleaned up the wound—gave him an oxygen max so he can breathe until about tomorrow. We called for a plane ta pick him up and send him ta the hospital. We don't know when it's going to come—"

"It has to come quickly," Noel said.

"We can't go on without him!" Colin cried.

Celena said, "Planes are going to attract attention while we are in CAOT territory. This is the reason we're walking in the first place."

"Who cares about the frickin' CAOT?" Nicky hollered. "Dan's abouta die!"

Then, there was chaos. Everyone was shouting at once. Pointing fingers. Screaming. But they all knew one thing—only miracles could keep Dan alive.

"No!" Colin wept, "You can go on— You all can!" Colin glared at everyone, "But I am not leaving Dan. I'm waiting until a plane comes—"

"Colin!"

"He's alive. He's gonna be alive—he's gonna be alright—"

"Colin—"

"And we're still going to—"

"Colin!" Celena shouted.

Colin's lower lip quivered. Celena walked over to him and put her arm over his shoulder like an umbrella to push away the rainwater tears. Colin erupted into sobs and sobs in her arms.

Pulie could not bear to look back at the tightly bandaged body that lay still on the grass.

Who knew? Who knew that someone would die? Who knew Dan would die—a real death…

The mission crew had not experienced witnessing death so vivid and so full of melancholy; it threw them off track—mentally and emotionally. There was no adult to take control. Even Daria, Celena, and Erik were absorbed in their thoughts. After all, they were still teens too. Everyone was on their knees, their face buried in their mission shirts—crying.

"It's okay, Colin," Celena whispered, her voice quavering, "We still have hope."

Hope.

The word was a false promise of life.

Pulie could already sense that everyone knew; there was no *hope*. There was no hope at all.

BARRIERS

In the center of the dusty, sandy plain, there was a small village, protected by intense security. Inside the village lay the pizza shop.

Everyone walked in silence until they reached their destination. No one could believe what had happened.

"Everyone," Daria said. "Listen up. Y'all, I know—" She paused. "We need ta just push through this mission. We gotta just be able ta go with the flow, alright? We mustn't let our emotions overcome us. I know, I know, y'all." She paused again. "*I* can't believe—that just happened. But we have a mission ta complete. We'll make sure Mr. Wace retrieves Dan's body—if he dies—but for now, we need to focus. We're at a very tricky point right now. And if we're not energized and ready, we might all meet the same futures as Dan. Understood?"

Everyone nodded and began to prepare. Colin was still in the back of the group with his shirt pulled over his face.

"Yes, this *is* going to be *tricky*—" Celena sighed, squinting through the hot, dusty view at the village in the distance. "And especially because the CAOT colonized this village. There's gonna be technology so advanced in this old town; it will be scary. Take, for instance, how do you think we can get *inside* the village?"

Around the circumference of the town was a thick wall of electric and pointed wires.

Pulie whispered aloud, "Mrs. Slendersan said we need to find out how to shut the wires off."

"Exactly—" Celena said, "And she instructed us to look for a main power source building. Somewhere around—" Celena pulled out a digital map. Everyone leaned towards her.

"Shoot! This is the map of the pizza delivery shop. There's gotta be a map of the city!" Celena rummaged through her bag for the other tablet until she found her leftover sandwich.

"If the system is outside of the town, we could try looking around us—" Pulie suggested.

"If my calculations are correct, may I ask—what is that?" Alex said, pointing to a tall thin tower, standing not far away from the village.

"That must be the main system power thingy!" Nicky cried.

"Great usage of words, Nicky. The correct way to say it is —" Alex began.

"No—no. I know what it is," Nicky interrupted.

"We'll send four people into the tower. Who are the four people that are supposed to go into the dome?" Celena asked.

"Great," Pulie muttered under her breath. She was hoping Celena would hear it.

"There's only three," Colin answered, "Me, Noel, and Pulie."

"The file says, Colin, Noel, Pulie and—" Celena shut her tablet screen. "Anyone want to volunteer for the fourth spot?"

Tilda raised her hand. "I will."

"Thank you, Tilda. Now, everyone has their gadgets, and does everyone have their ConnecT?"

Everyone nodded. The ConnecT was the small square device clipped to the ear.

"Remember, don't speak at the same time! I don't want a jumble of voices all at once," Celena reminded them as Pulie clicked her pocket knife onto her side pocket. Before, Pulie's dream was to be assigned on the mission, but now, she was deeply regretting it.

"Pulie, Colin, Noel, and Tilda, please head to the tower. The rest will remain here, watching for any outsiders."

"Souls live forever, even if our body walks away!" They recited.

"Our spirit will stand tall if we fight and save the day!" everyone cried in unison as they raised their hands. "Trickies!"

Pulie was astonished to find not a single guard blocking the entrance of the building. She had expected something more challenging, but she assumed the CAOT hadn't done an excellent job of protecting the village. *After all, what could be so great about that old village?*

"Suspecting that there are traps in the inside?" Noel said, peering around.

"Probably why. Let's go in unless you want to climb the walls. It looks like the outer wall is covered in this paste." Tilda slid her fingers across the brick walls. She sniffed her fingers and immediately wiped her hands on the sand. "Tar. Go inside."

One by one, they opened the frail wooden door and crept inside the mysterious building. Torches illuminated the darkness of the stone tower. Sweat dripped from Pulie's forehead; the room's tightness and dampness created a bit of claustrophobia.

"Staircase." Noel pointed at the first handle that appeared. It wasn't really a staircase but a slanted ladder.

"I don't think I can do this." Colin suddenly stepped back.

Tilda, Noel, and Pulie all bit their lips, not knowing what to say.

"Colin, as much as it hurts to say—we need you to move on."

"Yeah. I know."

"We're so sorry—we just—"

"I get it. Let's *just* go."

Colin started up the ladder first. Then Tilda. Then Pulie. Then Noel.

They climbed and climbed until Colin arrived at a stone step past the ladder. It must've meant that the ladder had come to an end.

"Wait, Colin—" Noel shouted as Colin moved his foot up, "Don't go yet! CAOT are specialized in leaving their colonies full of booby traps. Señor Rodriguez taught us about the most intricate and deadliest traps of all. If this is one of them, we will all die. When a ladder leads to a single stone step, we must jump onto the stone step at the very same time. The ones who don't match the timing will fall off and—die. I forgot the name of this ancient trap. When I get to three—" Noel said. "One— two— three— Jump!"

The four jumped onto the step simultaneously, Tilda's foot nearly halfway on the step, until the ladder snapped off completely, and the long way they had come up vanished. It was a dead drop to the first floor.

"Ladder Breaking Trap! That's what it was called."

"Thanks, Noel, could've died without that—" Pulie looked down the dark drop. The torches had been blown out.

"No problem. Now let's continue."

"Where—where do we go exactly?" Pulie asked. The stone step was blocked on three sides with stone walls, besides the deadly drop side. The space was so cramped, Pulie couldn't breathe.

"Look for any signs on the walls or any messages," Noel hinted, "When I was little, my mum made me take coding classes. If you spot an upside-down W or an M, it most likely means that there are other messages carved into the wall that normal people will take as decoration."

"Is *SSERP* supposed to mean anything? I mean, it's in fancy letters. Very very small font."

"That's it," Noel said. "*Press* the letters."

Colin pressed the *letters*, and the walls slid open. They stepped into the mysterious room, and the walls closed behind them. The floor was carpeted in furs and clothes of all kinds—paintings of royalty hung from the golden walls. And in the center of the room lay an hourglass draining golden sand.

"Is it counting for a minute?" Tilda asked.

"I don't know. But it's draining fast." Noel backed away, "We better hurry. We have to cut a red wire. The blue one strengthens security, so never cut a blue wire—just the red ones. Let's go now! Everyone, go look for the system controls."

Colin ripped a piece of paper off the wall,

"You guys—we have a clue—" He read the small font. The four gathered into a huddle to see.

Six-sided; counts the universe.

Fits inside a very small purse.

"Well, we better look for something like that—I have no idea what it means, though," Tilda said, taking one look at the paper in disgust.

Pulie started searching in the pictures and behind the pictures when she came across a little dice. Gold and embroidered with dots of silver. Small and deliberately made by the hand of a true artisan. The dice was so tiny it slipped through her fingers. She managed to shove it down her pocket.

"Pulie! We gotta hurry. We don't have any time," Noel called out. Pulie began searching right away, looking through the back of the bookshelf.

"*Noel*, this is impossible," Tilda groaned, "There are like ten seconds left of this hourglass."

Tilda was complaining—again.

"Just keep searching."

"No, let's just go back down. We're all going to die—"

"We can do it, okay?"

"No, this is impossible. But I have an idea."

"No time for ideas."

"But it just might work—"

"Just—"

Without anyone's consent, Tilda flipped open her pocket knife and cracked the hourglass through the top. There was a large spiky hole at the top with jagged glass edges and pieces everywhere while the golden sand spilled onto the floor.

There was a pause in the room. Pulie glanced at Colin, whose eyes were wide open.

"Guys?"

"See Noel, nothing happened. Now we have unlimited time to—"

Then, a nearby lamp began to shake, and the top of the ceiling cracked open. The roof caved in while the floor trembled.

"Earthquake?"

"No! The building is collapsing!" Noel hollered, "The frick? Quick, break a window! Jump for your lives!"

Everyone charged for the window, attempting to breakthrough. There was no chance of surviving unless they jumped the building. Chair legs were thrown at the window, banging and screaming. The air began to thicken, and warm heat rolled in. Pulie's sweat sprayed across the floor and she grabbed a lamp and smacked it against the broad window. The window was too thick for anything dull to breakthrough. *What was going on? We weren't prepared for this at all.*

Finally, Tilda's knife cracked through.

Crack… Crack! CRACK!

"Piden. You there?" Pulie called through the ConnecT as Colin yanked out their parachutes.

"No!" Noel cried. "Don't use emergency parachutes until the actual mission!"

"Would you rather die?" Colin hollered, avoiding falling chunks of the ceiling.

"No! Colin! We'll set up blanket landing!" Pulie screamed at the top of her lungs. Then, her ConnecT buzzed. It was Piden.

"Uh, Pulie—the building looks like it's going to collapse."

"Exactly. We are going to jump out."

"What—"

"I know, but we need a safe landing. Over and out."

"But…"

Pulie could hear Piden's voice flickering as she turned her ConnecT off.

Noel had expanded the crack Tilda had created. It was now a ginormous hole in the window as stones began to shower.

"Grab anything you can!" Tilda shouted, stuffing a clock into her pocket.

"Why?"

"Because Señor said—Ahhhh!" Tilda dove away from the mirror that had fallen. "Señor said that sometimes to disable a mechanism, you need to take it out of its area and signal. Like out of the building!"

"We don't have that much time!" Noel was still creating a large enough exit route. His fist slammed against the shattering glass as Tilda's knife jabbed at the window again and again.

"Just do it!" Tilda hollered. Obediently, Pulie shoved a tiny piggy bank, a jar of marbles, a pillow, and a lamp bulb into her bag.

"Come on!" Colin cried. "The hole is ready!"

"When I say three, jump!" Noel breathed in. All four of them stood at the ledge, the wind howling, and the long way down right before them.

"One... Two... Three!"

Pulie lunged out of the cracked window just as the building came crashing down. Her hair had gone up completely, and could barely open her eyes. Debris and ashes packed her nose. Air went up to her shirt and out the top, blowing into her face. Everything was all a blur, the clouds, the sky, the ground. She was bungee jumping without a cord. She was flying without wings. She was thinking without a brain.

At full speed, she hit the open blanket that had been prepared for her below, and she bounced onto the floor. Tilda, Noel, and Colin came tumbling after.

"Run!" Colin screamed, and the whole crew sprinted past the village borders as debris and cement snowed the area. The control building was soon nowhere to be seen.

Everyone was coughing and stumbling to get up. The air was so rough and dry; it cut Pulie's face each time a slight breeze passed her. Pulie was sprawled on the floor with her face covered in dirt.

"Well, I'm *never* doing *that*—again." Pulie spit into the ground.

"Did you do it?" Celena asked, squinting at the village far away. The fences still glowed with power.

"No... we failed... because of me." Tilda sobbed.

Everyone sighed while Tilda cried her heart out.

"Tilda, it's not a big deal. There's always another way," Colin said.

"No, there isn't. It will be all my fault when we die of hunger and depression now," Tilda sobbed.

"We could originally go with the old-school way by sawing through the wires—" Celena ignored the crying girl. "You were all brave enough to try and test it out. It failed—no big deal—" She patted Tilda on the back.

"But we could've had a slight chance if anybody brought something from up there," Tilda continued to groan.

"I have a tiny piggy bank, some marbles, a small pillow, and a lamp bulb, but the piggy bank flew out while I was diving, and the lamp bulb is burnt. My marbles are all gone, and the pillow is still here." Pulie tugged the pillow out of her bag.

"But, it's most likely not in a pillow." Celena grabbed the pillow and ripped it apart, feathers sprinkling all around her. Colin took out a small sphere from his bag and smashed the glass with his hand. There was nothing but water.

"Wait!" Pulie raised her hand and started to dig her pockets. "I have *this*." She pulled out the dice.

"Did you get that from the room up there?" Noel pointed to where the building once was, only now, it was a pile of rocks.

"Of course! Until it got *destroyed*." Pulie said, glaring at Tilda. Tilda began to sniffle.

"Pulie, do you mind if I borrow that dice for a minute?" Celena asked.

"Yes?"

Celena snatched the dice out of Pulie's sweaty palms regardlessly and took out her pocket knife. Celena split open the dice gently, revealing a delicate thin red wire coiled inside the cube.

She sliced the wire, and lights flickered, and a beep echoed through the plain.

Everyone erupted into revelry.

Pulie's jaw dropped, her hands midair.

"This was the missing piece we needed all along!" Tilda cried. "Six-sided and counts the universe with numbers, and is small! Way to go, Pulie!" She punched Pulie playfully on the shoulder.

"The missing piece was in our hands all along!" Alex slowly caught on, an exuberant grin appearing on his face.

Everyone got up and pranced around the little dice as the electric fence around the village dozed off.

"Great job, y'all!" Daria glowed with happiness. "Teamwork at its finest."

"Who even built this building?" Pulie asked. "Why do we need to go through—*that* to get into a village? How do people even go on vacation without dying?"

"CAOT built this village. And I'm pretty sure them villagers can just show their ID card and get in through security," Daria said.

Pulie's jaw dropped. "Then next time—I'm faking an ID! Who in their right mind would go through—that?"

"Who cares? We're back on track."

"Okay! Finally! Stop this nonsense. I'm pretty sure the village heard the building crumble. There are going to be cops or security guards searching for the culprit. It's not every day their great old building falls. Let's get inside the town and look for Harvey's Pizza House an' Delivery!" Erik called out.

The mission group squeezed in between the shutdown metal wires. This was why Dunkin Boar wasn't on the mission team.

Piden was rummaging through the trashcan by the time Pulie was inside the village borders.

"Dude, what in the world are you doing? It stinks!" Pulie whispered as she pinched her nose.

"I am *starving*. This is the only free food here." Piden eyed a half-empty coke bottle.

"Free? Who said it had to be free?" Noel said from behind them, popping open a bag of chips.

The shop was old, with a vintage theme floating around every corner. Most of the walls of every house were wooden, some brick, but mostly wood. The windows were bug splattered, the doorknobs were the circle bulbs that broke every time you touched it, and the streets were still sandy.

"Pulie!" Called a voice. Nicky and Ema were across the street, waving her over. They stood in front of a closed deli shop with a lock pick in their teeth.

Pulie sprinted in just before they shut and locked the door.

"Pull the shades down," Ema whispered, clicking the radio on. "Oh, good job with the dice, by the way."

Pulie reached for the string dangling by the window and pulled down the cloth.

"I hate this stupid mission," Nicky muttered. "I hate it."

"I—"

"No teacher warned us about alligators! We never prepared for it! What are we going to do? I mean, can you believe Dan—just died? What are we going to do? What is poor Colin going to do? How is this happening? Dan was—"

"Nicky, focus."

"This is so stupid—"

"Nicky, you have to focus. Everyone here signed up to sacrifice all they have for the mission. We can't go out on a Tricky mission with a mindset like this. You know who we are, Nicky. The

Trickies? I mean, my goodness—the largest corporation training the best of all international and global spies ever to be made? This isn't for nothing. Dan wasn't for nothin. We have to focus now."

There was silence for a long time.

"Ema, do you mind if you turn on the lights." Pulie shifted nervously on the wooden floor below her. "Where are you guys?"

"Right here."

"Where's here?"

There was a loud crunch sound.

"I think I found food!"

"That was my foot you just stepped on," Ema grumbled.

"No, not that, *that*!" Nicky pointed to the meat in the fridge.

All three lips opened, and fat drools slithered out of the corners. Pulie hadn't eaten anything for hours. And she was hungry. Nicky clicked on the light switch.

"It's too bright—I can't see!" Ema cried, "Everything is blotchy blue and green!" Ema moaned, squinting.

"Quit complaining; we hit the jackpot," Nicky whispered. She found fresh sourdough bread laid on the counter, wrapped up for pick up. There were thin slices of Spanish ham, salami, olives, and buttery cheese on the side. But Pulie's eyes were on the meat, stacked up in the fridge. Her hands reached out and yanked open the doors to the cold box. Then, an alarm went off.

Jesus, so much for security.

"Quick! Stuff your pockets and go!" Pulie cried, loading her bag with bread and salami.

"They're coming through the front. They're so fast! They look like old fashioned sheriffs!" Ema hollered as she peered through the crack in the door. "They must've started the search!"

"We can't go through the front!" Nicky whispered, flickering the lights off. Pulie crawled around, searching for an escape route, when she found a small back door. *Dog door.*

"Pssst. Who wants to go pee?"

***

The cops busted open the door with their axes. Many had many scars slashed across their faces. Their belts clipped with guns of all kinds. The leader took out his gun and his flashlight, as his men flipped over chairs and tables.

"Sir! I think there's something over there!" one of the cops called, looking behind the fridge. The sheriff moved the refrigerator, and his eyes went wide.

"Aha! Found you!"

FOUND YOU!

Pulie, Nicky, and Ema had crawled out the doggy door safely, while before they left, they fed the back door guard cat a slice of their meat.

"Celena, we just busted a shop. The best part is—we escaped. Where were we supposed to meet?" Pulie said, speaking into her ConnecT.

"Kind of busy. Some beggar thinks we were some kind of prophet, and he's chasing us like crazy. Man, this guy is fast. Colin, go back around! No, not there. Um… sorry, let's meet at the deli shop down the street, gotta go." And the device flickered off.

Ema slapped her forehead.

"She's going to go right to the cops. We have to find out where she is."

"Who is with her?"

"Probably Erik. They *are* cousins. Oh, and Colin. I heard his name when you were calling Celena," Ema said.

"Nicky, try Colin. Maybe he can do it."

"Colin, this is Nicky. Can you tell Celena not to go to the deli shop? Or tell everyone."

"Sorry, Nicky. But this man is chasing us and it started out with—"

"Just tell everyone to *not* go back to the deli shop."

"But, I can't—I can't talk into this thing anymore. People are staring at me. Bye—"

"No—" Nicky groaned, but Colin had shut down his ConnecT.

"Guess we have to go and warn people *ourselves*?"

"Can't this thingy do everyone's ConnecT at once?" Pulie asked, pressing the button on the side.

"Hello?"

"Hello?"

"I'm busy!"

"Shh."

"Hey."

There was a cluster of voices at once.

"This is Pulie. I just wanted to remind you not to meet at the deli shop."

"Where do we meet then?" said a high voice. Probably Alexia.

"Meet at the bathrooms," said a gruff voice.

"What?"

"The main town bathrooms. It's near the border of the village. The cops won't go that far. It's safest."

"Okay? Is everyone listening?"

"Yes."

"How do you know if everyone's listening or not?"

"Dunno."

"Just meet at the bathrooms."

The device disconnected.

Nicky clutched her stomach. "Let's first find a table so we can eat."

After they had found a table, they made sure to cover their faces and act like villagers when the cops went circling the town for any problems.

"I'm sorry but this is D-E Licious." Ema devoured her bread.

"I've never tasted food this good," Pulie said, "What are they putting in here?"

"Perhaps a bit of magic cheese. Magic salami. Magic bread."

***

"I want pizza. Even though I *just* ate two sandwiches," Nicky moaned as they passed a pizza shop filled with villagers. The smell of melting cheese and freshly boiled tomato sauce drifted through the streets.

"Wait a minute." Ema pointed to the sign. "Isn't that *Harvey's Pizza House*?"

Nicky's eyes grew wide, even if they were already huge.

"But first, to the bathrooms."

When they arrived at the bathrooms, the smell of luxurious pizza had disappeared, and instead, the smell of rotting foods and urine boiled into the air.

"Since the bathrooms are on the same street as the pizza house, that means this is Dover Drive," Ema said, uncovering the sign covered in sand. The letters of the street name were painted in red but had gradually graded into yellow.

From the clearing, Celena and the rest of the people tiptoed next to Pulie and Nicky while Ema led them to a little meeting spot in between the bathroom walls and the bushes.

"Where's Piden?" Pulie asked, not seeing any sign of her brother.

"In the bathroom." Alex said, "And there's no soap or water!" he exclaimed, dusting his hands. Everyone scooted away from him.

"Perfect spot," Celena said, standing up and wiping the sweat from her neck. "Right on the same street as Harvey's. Okay, if the cops find us, we disperse. Group one will go into the pizza house—group two to the bathrooms. Group three, scatter around the paths. But for now, everyone's here, safe, and not starving. We wait here until the truck starts its engine and leaves the restaurant garage at two in the morning tomorrow. Then, when it waits for crosswalks and all that stuff, we slip onto the truck until we leave the town. After we are clear from the village, we chase the driver out and take over the truck to continue our journey to the coast. It's not too far from here."

Everyone squirmed in their spots.

"But for now, let's have our last sit-down meal together. Tomorrow morning, our mission begins, so fatten up, and stay healthy," Erik declared. Everyone brought out what they had stolen. Meat, bread, milk, cheese, water, salad bowls, forks, chocolates, puddings, pastries, and melted caramels. The sky was getting darker, and the streets were becoming vacant. The bushes became a barrier, and so far, no one had noticed them. When night came, they crept farther into the trees to rest. Daria would stay up since she was the oldest and watch the truck throughout the entire night.

The rest fell into a deep sleep.

REAL MISSION BEGINS

"Wake up."

Those two words were enough to remind everyone.

The sky was pitch dark. The sounds of backpacks clicking and the faint rustling behind the bushes blended with the rough vibration of the truck's engine.

"Not a problem! I get two hundred bucks today for the catering. I'm driving all the way to Conner's city. Yeah, it's far. Of course not! Why do you think I'm up at two? Yes, it's two here. Anyway, my wife was so happy when I finally got the job, she said she'd stop stealing. Yes. That's what she said. The happiest man is a working man. I don't know." The delivery man chuckled behind the door on the phone. "Tell your family I send ma greetings. Uh-huh, no problem."

Keys jingled, and the truck was steered onto the dusty streets. Gravel and sand blew up into the air. The truck traveled slowly on the village streets but fast enough to keep the mission group running hard. When the truck halted for the security check just before the gates, the crew had enough time to slip onto the vehicle's back ledge. They passed the surveillance in utter silence.

Once the village was a speck in the heated sandy plain, far from the secured heavy wired borders, phase seven began. One by one, they boosted themselves on top of the roof of the truck, Erik and Daria going first. Once everyone was balanced on the top of the truck, hugging and gripping the slippery sides as hard as possible, Erik crawled over to the front of the truck. Then, he smacked his hand onto the large front window.

The driver shouted from inside the vehicle, honked, and then steered his truck in circles until it skidded to a stop.

The mission crew almost fell off the roof. The driver kicked the door and stumbled out and bellowed, "Who was that? Come out!"

From above, Pulie could hear the soft unbuckle of a gun from a belt.

"We just need the truck, sir," Erik called out, still not revealing himself.

"Where are you? Come out, right now!"

Pulie heard his boots pace around on the sand.

"We just need the truck, sir," Erik repeated. "Please step away and drop your gun."

"Hands up then, you fundernuggets! This baby's mine!" The driver stepped into the clearing, his pistol firmly adjusted and gripped in his calloused hands.

"Fundernuggets?" Nicky whispered. Pulie shrugged but kept a firm eye on the butt of the pistol from the side view.

"Let's not take this the wrong way, sir. Step away and drop your gun, and we'll be on our way."

"Get out of my car!" The man hollered. "Get out. Come on! What do you think I am? A fool? No, no. I am no fool. So if you think, I'm afraid of you, whoever you are, come out and let's see! Ha! Don't be shy!" The man shouted in his broad accent. "Or on the count of three, this baby's going to blow your little guts into —"

Pulie clamped her ears on that part.

Daria gave the signal, and Alexia lowered herself to the back of the truck. And then she rolled through the bottom of the vehicle, a small metal ball. It landed a few feet behind the man's feet.

In a few seconds, *Bam!* The metal ball exploded into smoke.

The man with the gun let out a shriek, and although he was nowhere near the bomb, he began to panic.

"Release!" Erik hollered.

Piden and Noel leaped off the truck, holding a long rope in one hand each, landing right beside the man with the gun loaded. But in a flash, they knotted the man up into a yarn ball, so he could not move.

"Argh!" He cried. "Get me out!"

"Sir, we asked you to *please* move out, and we warned you," Celena said, now standing at the top of the truck, hands on her hips.

Now, the aggravating man was on his back, tied to the floor, trying to wrestle himself out of the rope. Piden picked up the abandoned gun.

"You're a bunch of children? What are you going to do to me? Who are you?" Screamed the man, "Listen, kid. Please, spare my life. I'll give you the keys. Don't shoot me. *Please*. I'll give you everything I have. I'll give you this golden watch, or this ring. Or my—"

Piden was turning the gun.

"Please."

Piden set it into place.

"Lord, save me."

Piden ran his fingers up and down the back of the gun. Then, he placed his finger on the trigger.

"Bamm!"

"Ahhhh, the world is turning black!" screamed the man; he hurled himself around on the floor, prostrate.

"Got you." Piden slipped the gun into his pocket. "Why would a man like you carry a foolish thing like this."

"Coyotes. Gators. Snakes. *Black snow.*"

"The heck snow?" Piden said, scrunching his brows.

"*Black snow,*" the man said, shaking his head. "Legend has it that every year it comes around, killing what it *needs* to kill." He paused, darting his eyes to scan the area. "We believe it's a spirit. A deadly one, though."

"You can't shoot a spirit… you know that, *right?*" Nicky said.

"Oh, yes, ma'am, I know perfectly well that I cannot."

"Then, why?"

"Five years ago, Black Snow came to our village. And there was Benny, the good o' shop worker." The man's eyes began to tear up. "He disappeared for a day. He came back. And he had become a *monster*. His skin was as pale as Death himself. Only ya could feel the boy rotting inside of himself own body! He was like transparent really! His lips blood red, and his eyes sunken. The first day he appeared, he wandered around, murdering person after person. All the cops were scared too. Ha! They were 'fraid to their pits that the spirit gon gets them too like it got Benny. Benny went on killing until Benny's own mother finally decided that it was enough, came out of her house, and shot him dead with her brother's rifle. If she hadn't a gun, heaven knows what would've happened."

Pulie shuddered.

"I think we'll go now," Celena said, pushing the rest away. Tilda looked as if she were about to throw up.

"So yar goin' ta leave me like this?" the man hollered, shaking his fists. Everyone climbed into the truck.

"No, but you can tug on the little string right over there," Celena said as she closed the door. The man pinched on the string piece, and the rope unraveled completely.

"Oh, here's your little gun. Might need it, eh?" Erik said, tossing the gun at the blank-faced man. He took a few steps back and started sprinting back to the village.

"That village is downright crazy. Even their people," Nicky exclaimed.

"They aren't the only ones crazy," Colin muttered.

"C'mon, now! Everyone, take yar places!" Daria commanded, taking her position at the front inside. "He's going to report us, sooner or later. Let's leave before those cops come."

"*Seatbelts!*" Erik hollered from the driver's seat, clicking on his own seat belt.

"We don't *have* seat belts," Nicky informed him. "Or seats."

It was true. Their section of the truck was simply the large crates of food stacked in the back and a bunch of empty spaces.

"Then, sit down," Erik said, waving his hand to swat a fly. "Let's get a move on. I fly at a fast pace, and I don't like being slowed down. The first step, *check!*"

The engines roared, and the tiny rickety truck sped through the dry land and far off into the distance.

***

"Arane, Make Myself At Home location guide," Erik said to his silver laptop; its golden keyboard had been crafted by the Tricky Foundation Spy Gear unit, just for the mission. The truck had stopped in the middle of nowhere to navigate the island's point.

"Please scan your face."

Erik leaned forward, and the computer shot out a ray to capture his face.

"Hello, Susan. Guidance starting. Follow the instructions that will appear on my screen. Connect the system to car controls by pressing button three. Then, set the car navigation system to incognito. The last step is to slide the fill-in button to the right and remove the normal status code. And if you'd like, press A for comfort zone."

"My *name* is not Susan," Erik barked angrily. But the computer was silent.

"Arane?" Erik asked, jabbing his stubby finger at the monitor.

"Hello, Susan. I am so sorry. I must've fallen into deep sleep mode. Continue process or cancel?"

"*Process*. I'm not Susan, Arane. I'm Erik," Erik grumbled, working the system.

"System now connected. Are you sure you want File 359 uploaded to your computer? This is an unknown file, not in my database. Are you sure?"

"Yes."

"Files uploaded."

A bright green map appeared on his screen. There was a route leading through the port of the coast and through the waters.

"Thanks, Arane. Shut Down Mode."

"I am done with my service. Press A for comfort zone. Press B for more details about the system. Press C to continue sleep mode."

Erik pressed A on the keyboard.

"Thank you. Chair adjusting, Susan?"

"Yes," responded Erik, tucking his arms behind his head and sitting back lazily. Instantly, the chair moved backward and tucked into a bed-form, and the craggy snores from his nose began.

"Erik," Celena shouted, "—we need to get out of this place. Your pace is slow for me, too. We need to reach the coast in time."

"Just let me sleep."

"Well, Sleepin' Beauty," Daria interrupted, "We have a mission to complete. Arane quit Comfort Mode. Open up the navigation system."

Erik's seat folded back, and he grumbled. "Arane, hands-free mode."

"Hands-Free mode. Following guidance on map 3."

They continued their long journey on some very bumpy roads for the next couple of hours.

***

"Get your equipment ready. We're near the bay," Daria ordered. Everyone rustled around the truck as it swerved onto a street. Celena began listing procedures.

"Erik, remember, your name is Dunny Bonders. The one who owns the truck. While we pass through security, everyone else inside the truck will remain quiet. We need to make it seem like Erik is the only human on the vehicle. If they hear a sound, they'll search the truck. Understood?"

Everyone nodded, taking deep nods.

Celena slid Erik's information, ID card, and driver's license to him underneath the seat, in addition to a summary about Dunny's life.

The truck approached the entrance.

THE SEA TRIP

Backpacks were tightly zipped up, snacks assorted, gears tested, simply preparing for the moment Erik stepped out of the truck, revealing his fake identity.

"Good morning. Name?" An officer stopped the truck midway in the gates, writing away at his clipboard.

"Dunny Bonders—and I have to deliver pizza. Nobody's in the truck—and I am heading to Conner City."

We're a goner. Pulie thought, smacking her damp forehead.

"I believe I know that." The officer peered through the window with clear suspicion. "I have the information here. ID card, please." The officer extended an arm towards Erik's sweating face in the front seat.

"I— *do* have the card—in my pocket!" Erik said, searching his pockets. "And here it is." Erik pulled out the card from Dunny's wallet.

Ema whispered to Pulie, "You can see how he failed Imitations."

"Your face looks *very* different from when I last saw you, Dunny." The officer grabbed the card from Erik's trembling hands, inspecting suspiciously.

"Yes. They do, don't they? I've gotten a lot older."

"Officer Stans? Can we have you in the lobby? It's urgent." The officer's walkie-talkie buzzed.

"*I'm* busy."

"No, you aren't. Miss Elizabeth Rolan is here to talk with you," crackled his speaker.

The officer grew pale and tossed Erik's stolen identity card back.

"What's this all about?" The officer asked.

"There's been a bombing in Area 23. And a bunch of sitings of mysterious individuals lurking around with strange technology."

Officer's face grew pale and he turned back to Erik. "Very sorry, Dunny. I have an urgent request. My assistant will replace me."

"Stans, I don't have time," Erik muttered, leaning against the window.

The officer sighed but immediately opened up the entrance to the truck. "Very well, head to the spot over there. Thomas will come."

Erik parked his truck at the spot, anxiously waiting for this assistant. Everyone was nervous. What if the assistant decided to check the truck?

Minutes later, a man waddled over to the quietly parked truck with a bucket on his head. A woman assisted him.

"Nice to meet you, Miss Thomas?" Erik asked after getting out of the truck and shaking the woman's hand.

"Oh, no. I am Miss Silver." She pushed the blank-faced man forwards. "*This* is Thomas."

Thomas was a skinny guy, his eyes staring up at the sky, his pail tumbling around on his head. He looked at Erik sadly as he patted his head and whispered, "Sorry for your loss."

"What the—"

"He has a kind of *mental* problem," the woman said quickly, rubbing her hands together, her bright red purse hanging from her left arm. "Alright, Thomas, you be a good boy. I will be here at about four to check on your blood pressure. *Okay?*" she added, walking to her car.

"Bye, Miranda. See you later in the war!" peeped Thomas, jumping up and down.

"Bye, Thomas. Have a good time, and don't bite anyone else!" She hollered, speeding away.

Erik stepped back. "You bite me, and you eat my first, you piece of crap! Understand?" Erik held up his fist. Thomas wasn't paying attention. He was looking up at the blue sky, cawing at the crows that sat perched on the trees.

"Thomas?"

"Cooooo coooo, ahweoo!" Thomas flapped his wings.

"This guy's an officer?" Erik's voice cracked through the ConnecT.

"Stop getting distracted. Thomas is supposed to tell you where the boats are."

Erik rolled his eyes. "I'm trying! Hey Thomas, which way are the boats?"

Thomas lifted one foot and continued cawing.

"What's with the foot, I mean seriously." Erik's voice sizzled in the speaker.

"Follow the direction his foot is pointing, idiot," Celena said. Pulie had noticed it too. With his raised foot, Thomas was pointing towards the arrow sign with the letters, *Dock*.

Erik scrambled to the truck and started the engine. "Thanks."

Thomas bobbed his head.

"Let's get out of here," Erik mumbled, stepping on the gas pedal.

Boat 139 was at the tip of the dock. The stolen truck was now hidden inside the large stinky smelling seawater boat. Water sprayed from the back, propelling them forwards.

Soon, they shot out to sea.

Nicky stuck her head out of the lower window, like a dog on a road trip. In amazement, she cried, "The skies are like stones of blue! And oh! The sun is a shiny dandelion!"

"Since when did you become so poetic," Ema said, "But stop screaming in my ear!"

"Miss Slendersan said there'd be lots of fog. Why is it so clear, today?" Nicky asked, settling back down in her seat.

"We're nowhere near the island yet. The island we are headed at is hidden in layers of fog," Noel answered, peering out at sea. "I would enjoy this weather. In a few minutes, all we're going to see is snow."

It was going to be a thirty-two-hour ride. Not because the island was far—but because of the lack of clear direction provided to the location. The man-made artificial island was not in the satellite, and only the truck itself had the destination on a map.

Daria allowed them to take naps if needed, although she encouraged everyone to stay awake. In the end, about half of the group ended up sleeping on the floors using their jackets as pillows. Erik was maneuvering at the top of the boat with Celena. They all survived on the pizza, and for the rest of the ride, there was nothing left to do but sit and wait—in complete nervosity.

Suddenly, after what seemed like hours, the speaker on the ceilings, activated, "Approaching. 180 from the east perimeter. We are set. Everyone inside the boat. Daria and Celena, begin safety checks."

The rest grabbed their bags and scrambled to get back inside the truck. The truck was inside the smaller boat, which was inside the larger boat on the second floor. It was very stuffy. Everyone was piled into dark grey space.

Soon, Erik, Celena, and Daria appeared inside the truck too.

"We have about twenty minutes. Erik and Celena are gonna exit the truck ta steer the small boat. We all know the steps. If we're not careful, the CAOT might shoot the entire boat down along with us, and we might not be able to survive," Daria explained. "Stay quiet until then, and review yar tasks."

A minute later, Celena marched back in with her hands behind her back.

"We're here." She exhaled slowly. "Everyone take a deep breath. Close your eyes."

Pulie closed one eye and caught Celena trembling again. The room wasn't cold.

"I know," Celena continued, "you're scared—I'm scared—this is absolutely terrifying." She swallowed hard after every fragment. "But we are the Trickies and we fight the injustice to help the people on this planet. If we die, we die in honor. And we will fight until our bodies turn red!"

"Why red?" Alex asked.

"From our blood," Celena said.

"Yeah, but—"

Celena interrupted. "We came this far, and we worked this hard—I mean—this is it. The moment we've all been dreaming and dreading for." She raised her fist and shouted, "Let's do this. Do this for Dan. Do this for yourselves. Take your seats, everyone."

The truck began to tilt backward. Everyone inside the truck automatically slid to the back. Then it lurched and rocked forward, and then there was a loud *splash*. The small boat hit the water.

Everyone was staring at their shoes as if something was interesting about them as they felt the boat turn and curve and speed across the waters.

Erik spoke through his speaker again. "Boat 139 down. The CAOT has already shot it down."

It was silent for a long time.

Erik spoke again, "I am switching off all air conditioning and lighting for about ten minutes. Just in case they realize that the boat they shot down isn't the only one."

Then a minute later, in the darkroom, the speaker rang again. "CAOT has sent a crew to monitor the sunken group. We are clear from the security at the front of the island."

Soon, Erik's voice appeared again, "Phase fifteen. We are forty feet from the perimeter. Groups one and three, please exit the truck. Group one began to shut down security numbers 34C through 45C. Ten minutes on the clock."

Groups one and three hurried out while group two rearranged the space to set up their computers and opened up the files on the monitors.

Pulie, along with the rest, was now outside in the small truck.

"Group one. Please prepare for distractions."

Piden and Nicky hurried to get the firelighters while Maya and Alexia brought their equipment out.

"Good job, Group two. You have successfully shut down security 1. Only nine more to go. Round two beginning now! The rest of you, we are entering the east side."

The rest of the nine rounds of security were successfully hacked and shut down.

"In two minutes, group two will begin to shut down the mainland security round 1. Everyone else, go back inside the truck. I will be there in a moment."

The devices were pushed to the left corner of the truck so that the rest of the crew could fit inside the other half. Pulie saw how furiously Ema and Alex were typing away at the keyboard.

"Good job, again, Group two. Land security has been shut down for an hour. In a minute, we will hit the land."

The boat stopped bobbing up and down after a big thud.

Erik appeared in the truck and began to maneuver it. The truck slid down the back ramp of the boat and onto the land. *Bump. Bump. Bump.* The wheels sank into the paths of snow.

"Phase sixteen," Daria announced. "You know the procedures."

The truck drove through the icy snow and to the layer of frosted hoar trees.

"The dome lies behind the long fence," Daria said, "Erik will give the command word ta begin our positions."

"Yes." The voices echoed softly.

"Erik, drive us through a little more," Celena said, patting the front seat. There were cracks of crushing gravels from the tires.

They waited a few seconds to adjust. They were parked in between two giant ice frosted trees. Groups one and three were lined up by the door. Group two were to remain in the truck with their computers. Erik and Celena also were to stay by the truck to give orders. Daria would go with the bomber and the bombing assistants to the dome.

Pulie stood by the truck's exit door with the rest, waiting for the single most important word. Everyone held their breath. For once, even Nicky was silent.

"*Go*," Erik whispered.

The back doors slid open with a *clink* and the Trickies raced to their positions. Group one made their way southwest to light the fire. Group three and Daria headed up north, trudging through the thick layers of snow.

Daria led Pulie's group. Pulie marched through the deep seeping ice, her boots slowly building up with frost. They were now deep in the forest, surrounded in this wood of darkness. However, Daria was following the sides of the walls, so Pulie was reassured the girl knew what she was doing. After all, Daria was graduating next year—to enter a Scout team. She must have a lot of experience.

Daria reached out and touched the frozen wall. "This is it. Around the corner is the Dome. We will wait here until Group one tells us the fire is ready."

A few seconds later, there was a loud explosion in the distance. From far away, Pulie could feel the heat on her face.

Daria's ConnecT activated.

"This is Alexia. The fire is burning. You better go now."

"Got it. Thanks."

The bombing crew peeked around the corner and saw many of the guards running to the fire. Pulie could see the blaze now and also hear what the CAOTs were saying.

"Sending six groups to the—" A guard stopped as he watched more fire spread across the snowy hills.

"Every single guard to that fire! *Run!*" The leader of the guards screamed as he too started scrambling. The guards opened up the gates and poured out, scuttling towards the flame. Then, it was silent. The only sounds were far, far away on the hills where a burning fire toasted the ice and a million soldier men tackled the mysterious burst.

Not all the soldiers had left, however. But the back of the dome was left unguarded.

Daria whispered, "Follow me. Let's go."

They crept out of the shadows and into the open. The dome stood shiny with its reflection gleaming in the dim sunlight. It was constructed entirely of thick translucent glass that stretched across the walls of the beautiful structure. Pulie, herself was in awe at the incredibly built glassy dome that she was about to destroy.

A layer of bars surrounded the dome, but the spacing between the poles were too thin to slip through. Also, anyone who touched the barricade would be electrocuted. Noel pulled out a small pole with plier looking object at the end. Noel squeezed it between the bars and pressed the button. This would deactivate the electricity passing through the metal. Then, Colin put a large bar between the same poles and bent the bars. It was just wide enough for Pulie to slip through.

"Coast clear," Daria said. "Let's getcha in."

"Piden? Nicky? The guards are getting really close to you," Pulie informed them through her ConnecT.

"We see them," Nicky answered, "but we've headed back to the truck. All clear, Pulie. Go on."

"Yeah, have fun," Piden joined. "You *got* this."

"That sounded a tiny bit sarcastic. But thanks, I hope I see you if I make it."

"Stop being silly," Nicky answered.

Piden retorted, "I'll bring your body back."

Pulie grinned as she clicked the ConnecT off. She slipped through the gates and looked outside at her bombing assistants.

"Good luck, Pulie," Daria said. "We'll be watchin' from back there."

Pulie nodded and turned around to face the dome. She could see her breath blow into the air every time she exhaled, a cloud of puffy cold air dancing into the windy sky. She held the rang in one gloved hand, and the pocket knife in the other. After taking a deep breath, she threw the Rang up with all her might onto the walls of the dome, just like she had practiced in the Miralmalma.

Rangs want to go up. But you need support, Pulie recalled.

The other edge of the rang was snaking up the dome without her, while the other side was trying to do the same. The special glove she had velcroed to her left hand was made of extremely thick material, making her hands very sweaty. She pressed the other side of the dangling squirming rang into the glove. The scaly vines dug deeper and deeper.

"Rang, don't fail me now," Pulie gritted. The vine was spreading all over her hand, suffocating her fingers. This would create a firm grip so she wouldn't fall on her journey up. Then Pulie started to climb up the curved wall. She had to hurry.

"Don't look down—don't look down," Pulie whispered to herself.

She was now high up from the snowy floor and she heaved herself up the glass wall until the very top. She was finally at the top of the dome. The air was denser and she swallowed her spit to stop the popping and crackling in her ears. The wind whipped at her face like a leather belt, slapping her across the face for everything she had done wrong.

Was this right? To burn an entire dome full of people? Was Mr. Wace, right? Did they deserve it?

Suddenly, her ConnecT vibrated.

"Run!" Someone shouted.

"Head back to the truck! Hurry up!" Another cried.

Pulie gasped. "What's going on?"

"Ahhh! Run! Keep running! Go!"

Daria's voice popped up, "Pulie, *keep* going. The crew back at the truck has found trouble. But you need ta complete the mission. Hurry up."

Pulie trembled. Was everything okay? Where was Celena? Or group two? They needed to give her the right time.

"Pulie, Daria, again."

"And this is Celena."

"This is Alex."

"Ema, here."

"Dash."

"And Tilda."

Pulie sighed with relief and then buzzed in. "Pulie, here. I'm at the top, waiting for instructions."

"Good, according to the computer, it says you have approximately ten seconds and forty-three milliseconds until the hole at the top opens up."

Pulie stared at the red flickering closed-hole, waiting for its time to open up for the machines to absorb information and signals from distant machines. Pulie yanked the rang out of her glove. A breeze almost pushed her off the top. The hole was a perfect round curve with a metal slate blocking the entrance.

"Pulie?"

"Yes?"

"Approximately seven seconds and twenty-one milliseconds. Celena will begin a count down at five seconds."

"Yes, I will," Celena joined the conversation. "And remember, all you have to do is turn the bombs on and drop them in—no need to enter the dome. The hole will be opened for about ten minutes. This is the one time it opens up in an entire day, so you have to use your time carefully," Celena advised.

Pulie sighed. She knew the instructions. Reminding her would only make it worse. Here she was… finally… the moment she had been waiting for. Now all she had to do was drop the bomb from the opening, one after another, and she could safely parachute off.

"Five," Celena began her countdown.

"Four."

"Three."

"Two."

"One."

"Bomber, the dome is now opened to information, ready for duty."

The ConnecT was shut down.

The metal slate slid out and then the red laser, revealing the inside of the building. Down there, it was only darkness. Now all she had to do, was to drop the bombs in, and she was done. It was a simple job.

Pulie hesitated, however. There was an itch. A terribly annoying itch.

In the Dome. In the Dome…

She wasn't supposed to go inside. She knew this wasn't the plan. But she could only think about what waited for her inside.

I have ten minutes after all. I'll just take a look around.

She prepared to jump but caught herself. *No. No. No. You're crazy.* She turned back around. She bit her icy lip.

"I'm doing it."

Her backpack flopped against her back and she fell into darkness.

Her landing made a big screech, the surroundings getting darker than outside. The floor was made of thin metal and easily shook, for it hadn't been screwed down together. It was all quiet and cold. Not a single sound echoed through the walls. She felt something odd. *Was she cold? She felt a bit of coldness inside of her, not in her skin but in her heart.* She shook the feeling off. *In the Dome.* She had done it. It was her feet. Her stupid feet were freely choosing what to do. Now, she was in a mess. *Now*, she had to hurry. If she wanted to take a look around, she might as well do it quickly.

In the glimpse of her eye, she saw the top of a ladder and descended down to a new area. Everything was dark, but on the far side, she saw another room, bright and loud.

A meeting room.

She slipped her pocket knife into her bag and took out the first bomb. She gripped it in her torn glove tightly as she snuck around the boxes and shelves, motionless and quiet. She was a mouse at night, pilfering a farmer's produce in complete utter silence. She crept towards the ajar door, barely opened, letting as much light possible through for Pulie to read and set the time limit on the bomb.

"Three minutes. Just enough time for me to get out of here," she muttered. Her finger pressed the button. *Click*.

Pulie pulled out the other two bombs and headed back out.

In the Dome... In the Dome. Pulie was torn apart inside. Confusion flooded her head.

She leaned over and climbed the second ladder next to the door of the meeting room. *I came this far. I have to see more...*

When Pulie reached the top, she crawled on the creaky wooden boards as she constantly blew the dust out of her mouth. Then she gasped. Her gasp was almost too loud. Her vision was almost too clear.

Below her, she saw the CAOT.

There was a woman in a sleek black shirt, and long pants sat in a chair, embroidered in emeralds. Her face was pale, and her lips as red as blood. Her face was skinny, her eyes sharp like a hawk. She placed her thin fingers on the long glass table. Her nails were painted black, and they tapped slowly on the glossy table, making Pulie shiver. She clearly *reminded* Pulie of someone.

"Next," she said, softly, yet in a sharp tone.

Two people with familiar faces brought out a trembling man, his hands held behind his back by the two servants. Almost as if a rock had hit her head, she realized who those faces were. It was the *same* creepy face she had seen the day of the mission class when she had screamed. The face had been so unreal and fake, but now it was clear. Their face, whiter than the strange woman, black shaded around their eyes, their lips the color of Idadosi's dress.

I saw a CAOT face! At the Palace! Pulie held her breath, knowing the bomb would soon explode. She had to watch just a little more— She hesitated with each move she made. The man they were holding was led to the woman who had started sipping her glass. After she had finished a long sip, a plump maid rushed to wipe the woman's mouth with the greatest care not to ruin the lipstick.

"*Name*," the wealthy looking woman said.

"Colet Ronald, Master," the two scary looking servants said.

Master? Pulie wondered, Is that who she is? But Mrs. Slendersan said the leader was not going to be here.

The master snorted, dipping her golden fork into a single piece of chocolate filled with cherry filling, placed on a wide elegant plate.

"Information," Master said again, pushing the chocolate away in disgust. The plump lady quickly whisked the plate away and headed out the back door.

How can she just reject a perfectly fine piece of chocolate? Pulie thought, a drool leaking out of her mouth. Scared that drool would slip through the wide cracks and onto the CAOT table, Pulie quickly wiped her mouth. Unfortunately, her hand smacked the metal boards below her.

"*What*—was that?" The master asked abruptly, sitting taller in her chair. Pulie held her breath, eyelids pressing hard against each other.

"I'm pretty sure it was just the house cat or a mouse, Master," one of the servants answered in such a bold and cool manner.

Their voices weren't as bad as they look.

The Master looked relieved, sinking back into her chair. "Continue."

"Lived in Canada. Athletic. Rated A-16. Twenty-one years old," the two servants said in unison. It was all a very slow process.

"Let me see," the woman said, pushing her chair out, and standing up. The servants pushed the man towards her. She was a skyscraper compared to the trembling man. She reached with her arms and placed them on his cheek. She slid her nails across his rosy cheeks, leaving marks trailing after.

"*Handsome… Athletic… Accepted…*" she whispered, waving her hand in the air. The two servants pushed him into a room next to another room with green lights flashing all over.

"Thank you, *Master*," Pulie heard Colet saying, honorably.

"Next."

The plump lady came again, this time, holding a plate of cream cakes. She pushed it to the Master and left in an instant. Another two servants came out of the same room Ronald had first come out of, and this time, they had another man. The room was all so quiet.

"Name."

"Ludovik Tumbler."

"Information," the Master muttered, pushing her elegant silver fork into the cake. She placed the piece on her tongue. Then, the two servants spoke again.

"Lived in Australia. Intelligent. A-10. Sixteen years old."

Master rolled her eyes. "A-10? Mhmm. Let me see." She stood up and went to the man. His mustache cloaked a round chubby face, his merry eyes dancing in the green lights on the ceiling.

"You applied for a *wanderer?*" Master sneered, patting the stout man. He nodded eagerly. His eyes followed her movement as she inspected him.

"*Corrector,*" she whispered.

The happy smile vanished, replaced with a frown and a red face. Ludovik bowed down to her feet.

"Oh please, Master, I will serve you well. I am pretty good with mechanics. Please."

"We don't need a mechanic!" She snickered. The wicked woman stepped on his portly finger with her polished black heels, and the plump little man cried and howled in pain.

"I said Corrector!" she hollered a blood-curdling scream. Pulie was shaking so hard; she couldn't control herself. She clamped her fingers over her ears. But the sounds were too loud.

Ludovik screamed and kicked as the two servants led him into the flickering red room, next to the room where Colet had entered, contently.

Corrector?

One servant gripped the poor man as the other heaved open the heavy metal door. It was labeled in bold red letters; *Corrector*. He was pushed into the room while the two servants slammed the doors. All was quiet, then a dim green light flashed inside, and the man's horrifying scream echoed throughout the room. Then, it was quiet again. The two creepy looking hippies went back inside and exited, dragging the lifeless body of a man.

Ludovik. Dead.

Pulie grimaced, heart thumping so hard she was afraid the Master would hear.

She had to get out of here.

"I think it's time the guests come in. You've locked Luella up in the aircraft outside, haven't you?" Master said.

"Yes. Master, we are getting slightly suspicious data from the southwest side of the island. An uncontrollable fire has erupted. The guards have stopped it from spreading, but it was very sudden."

"Does it have anything do to with that boat?"

"The general says it doesn't, but he doesn't know for sure."

The master shrugged. "He's a stupid man. I should have him punished for his lack of concern and skill. Send a group of wanderers to the fire right now."

"But, Master—" One of the wanderers said, "We were supposed to have a meeting. All of us."

"Then send Arco. He's a smart boy."

The two servants nodded marched out the back door. Pulie knew it was *time*. She crawled carefully on the crumbly metal boards and clipped the first bomb. Then, she pressed the start button and leaped down the ladder.

"Meow."

A black cat. Green eyes shimmering, almost ghostly. Another meow. Its back arching and hunching into a frown. *The house cat*. Pulie knew she had to ignore it, crawling on her hands past the creature, but every step closer to the exit, the cat took a step forwards.

And all of a sudden, on two feet, Pulie sprinted to the ladder she had entered with, hearing the cat chasing after. She gripped the solid metal bar and heaved herself up.

Then, there was a sharp scratch across her leg. Water bubbled in her eyes as she looked down. Hanging from her leg, the claws of the creature digging deeper into her flesh was the cat. She tried to shake the cat off, but she was afraid the claws would rip down her whole leg and through the earth's core.

"Shew. Meow. Go away," Pulie whimpered, the claws digging farther in. She wanted to scream with all her might, the excruciating pain stinging like a blade in her heart.

Then, the first bomb erupted. She was only twenty feet away when it happened. Metal fragments, shelves, dust, wood, flew everywhere, and the cat was tossed away from Pulie and scampered away. Pulie fell to the ground, her vision blurry with the ash. She could see shadows rustling around inside the meeting room. Trying to forget the pain, she managed to grin. And that was only the weakest bomb. What had she done? If she had stayed up there, everything would've been fine.

She clipped the second bomb onto the floor beside her. Her fingers pressed the start button again. Then, she stood up only to meet her worst enemy.

BATTLE

Pain. When she lifted herself up, a thin slice of metal from the wall cut into her leg. She couldn't stand it anymore. But there were only two and a half minutes till the second bomb would explode, and it was much more powerful than the first. Pulie choked on the dust in her lungs as she pushed herself up from the ground and up and up the ladder. She scampered onto the next floor, where the light from outside shone from the dull cracked ceiling. Blood gushed out. Pulie tried to cup her hands around her leg to block the blood from leaving a trail, but it overflowed. She couldn't stand it anymore, and she screamed. Her voice echoed, but it was muffled by the sounds of crashing tables and glass. *Why did I go inside?* The sheet of metals had sunk right through the four claw marks.

"Stupid cat," Pulie gritted. Pulling a piece of cloth from her bag, she wrapped it around her wound. It was soon soaked, but it was better than nothing.

From below, she heard the Master.

"You betrayers! It took *two and a half* years to build this dome! And one of you completely ruined it all! I will kill you! I will kill you with my own hands! I will slit your throats and have you drowned in your blood!" the high pitched voice of the master screamed. Pulie heard howling and screams in the meeting room.

She had to get out of this place—and fast. She pressed the start button on her last bomb and chucked it as far as she could, watching the shape tumble down the narrow dark passages. Clunk. Clunk. Clunk.

Immediately after, Pulie started running up to the top of the hole of the dome. She had spent too much time in the dome, and if the exit closed, she would be trapped until both the second and the last bomb exploded.

You have to run! How could you be so stupid! Why did you even want to come down here?

Pulie leaped up the bars, her sweat piercing her skin like nails. She was on the floor beneath the top of the dome.

Faster.

"Samuel?"

Pulie froze. A woman in the clearing screamed for the man.

Keep going, Pulie reminded herself, but her eyes drifted to the stranger. Something was odd.

"Mom?" Pulie stuttered.

"Who are you?" The woman screamed.

No, no, this is a hallucination. That woman is not my mother.

But the word leaked out of Pulie's bleeding lips and called the name of the person who made everything confusing.

"Mom?" Her voice was slightly muffled by the crashing of glass and boxes tumbling down the structure.

"Pulie?" The woman cried. And as fast as her broken feet could take her, Pulie ran and ran to her mother. They collapsed in each other's arms, both hearts heavy and weakened.

"What are you doing here?" Pulie's mother grasped Pulie's face and sobbed. "Do you have your necklace? What are you doing here?"

"I was going to ask you the same question." Then Pulie gasped. "No!" Pulie took a step backward. "No! You're a prisoner?"

"Pulie—"

"They took you! That day when you left—they took you here! For two years! I knew it. I knew it! I knew it from the beginning! I knew something was weird! I told Piden—I tried to tell him—honest to God, I knew there was something weird. I searched the databases at school and everything." Pulie's eyes grew wide. "But it's alright, Mother! I can help you! I'll rescue you! Everyone else is below—in the forest. We can help you and Father escape."

"Pulie—"

"I thought you were on a Scout mission at some point. I believed all the lies. But you were here! Of course. The CAOT. They took you. I knew something was weird. Why didn't you just tell us?"

"Pulie!" The mother cried. "What are you talking about?"

"I need to rescue you from this horrible place," Pulie said.

The mother hesitated to speak. "Pulie, I work here."

Pulie froze. "What?" Her ears plugged out every sound and left the world in silence. "You're a CAOT?"

"Who are you with?" The mother asked. "Who brought you here?"

"You're a CAOT—"

"Yes. Who are you with?"

"My parents are CAOT…"

"I thought you received it."

"Received *what*?"

"The surprise. A mail was supposed to come to you and your brother that it was the time you knew we work at the CAOT and time you'd join us."

"But I thought—"

"Thought what?"

"But—but—Mr. Wace—from the Palace of the Trickies…"

"Palace of what?"

"The Trickies, Mom."

The mother stumbled backward. "Trickies—oh no—"

"That wasn't the surprise?"

"I—"

"Natalie?" A weak and brittle voice moaned from below. The mother leaped around, still holding Pulie's shaking hands, "Is that you, Samuel?"

No reply.

"Dad?" Pulie screamed. "Mom? That wasn't the surprise?"

Soon, the second bomb exploded, and ripples of fire erupted everywhere. The halls flooded in flames.

"Tell me!"

"No. It wasn't the surprise."

"Why didn't the relative that was supposed to come—tell you then? That we were gone?"

"Pulie, none of your relatives were going to come. Me and your father—we left all the clues possible back home. You were supposed to find your way to your campsite. There, you would meet your instructor but I believe another group blasted the connection portal and now it is in ruins. Oh, Pulie, I'm sorry I let this happen." Her mother collapsed to the ground, crying.

Nearby, a desk caught on fire and the heat blurred the air.

"You have to go, Pulie. I have to go…" mom said, their hands departing.

"No, we can find him together— we can—"

"No! It's bad enough if we lose your father. This place will soon explode. Go save yourself."

"What? Are you crazy! *I* was the one who did this— I joined the Trickies and bombed this place, it's *my fault* everything happened, I have to—"

"No, you won't." Tears glittered in Mother's eyes. "Do you want to be a CAOT?"

"What?"

"Do you want to? Be one of us?"

Pulie paused. "I don't care! Just let me get you out of here."

"Do you want to be a CAOT?" The mother hollered at the top of her voice.

"No!" Pulie blinked her tears away.

Pulie's mother nodded slowly. "Never—let Master see you. Never let her find you. Do you understand? You do not know her. You do not know what she will do to you if she finds out. Understand? Listen to me, Pulie! Blink! Blink, honey! Use the webbed stone that lies in your hands—"

"No! No!" Pulie screamed, stomping the crackling floor. "You can't just do this to me!"

Her mom shook her head.

"We can fix this! And after! And after, all four of us can live the life we had before! At home! All together! Remember!" Pulie screamed, although her mother was right in front of her. "There's no option. Just let me fix this together!"

"*I love you,*" The mother whispered, hugging Pulie one last time. Then, she rushed down the steps. Pulie screamed, sprinting after her mother, grasping for her torn loose shirt but a metal door sizzling from the fire crashed and blocked the path between the two.

"You're just going to get yourself killed!" Pulie screamed her lungs out. "It's suicide! I hope you stay there forever! Die, you fool!" Pulie stomped on the floor some more with her bleeding leg. "Die! I hope you die—I hope—I hope—"

Pulie fell to the floor.

Her lungs began to shake, but her brain took control.

I need to get out of here.

You have to save your parents.

Mom said to save myself.

Pulie was the cause of this. She couldn't just let her parents die. But her mother said to save herself. Pulie gritted her teeth as sprinkles of glass hailed from above.

Her mind was not yet made up, but she had to escape to an area where it was not consumed by fire. She grabbed her rang and swung it onto the top of the wall. She put on her Stick Shoes, which she had kept in her bag, and started climbing the wall.

Glass showered heavily as the fire started spreading faster and faster. Pulie tried to hold onto the Rang but found it nearly impossible. Each time she squeezed her fingers, blood ripped out, pain squelching Pulie's head. And her leg had not yet gotten rid of its pain either. She tore the bottom of her shirt and wrapped the cloth around her fingers as more shards of glass poured down.

She looked at her timer for the bombs clipped onto her belt. There were thirteen seconds left until the final bomb exploded. This bomb would destroy everything inside, including her parents.

She swung herself onto the Rang.

Finally, she pulled herself up the final bit. She was at the top of the dome, out of the hole in time to escape. She squeezed her necklace, coated in her thick sweat and fresh blood.

She glanced back down through the hole.
Flames
Destruction
Darkness
The truck was waiting on the other side of the world, thousands of feet below—everyone on the mission, waiting for her parachute to open.

Four seconds remaining.
My parents are in there. They are hurt and defenseless.
Three seconds remaining.
Should I go back? I have to save them...
Two seconds remaining.
They're in there...
One second remaining.
I have to save them.

DECISION

She leaped back down the hole, seconds before the exit at the top closed, but the final bomb exploded, and the tremendous heat blasted her back out and off the top of the dome. Right off the top. Like the ocean waves.

Pulie woke up just in time from the shock to open her parachute. Her body quickly soared down to the ground, her body feeling faint. When she hit the floor, she unbuckled her parachute and threw her backpack off, and sprinted to the truck with the assistants following at her heels.

"New location," Celena hollered from her ConnecT. "Pulie, Daria, new location. Follow the tracker."

The truck had been relocated. They needed to get there fast. The heat of the explosion would be so great; they would perish. Escape was their number one goal. Piden was at the door, and he pulled Pulie, the last one, into the truck, and the doors slammed. The tires squealed and Pulie pressed her face on the back window of the truck, watching the dome ablaze, the glass melting in the fire like ice in the sun. The truck sped off through the glazed forest and straight for the windy harbor. Her heart was feeling the explosion the building had just experienced. Her eyes grew heavy. But she would not let a single tear fall. The dome was now a sunken smoking structure collapsing minute by minute as if a meteorite had crashed straight down the top.

It grew smaller and smaller and the world became darker and darker.

**

Everything was dark. Then, everything was bright.

Pulie glanced at her leg. Celena had sanitized it and scraped out the ashes and the infected skin on her leg, and wrapped it in clean bandages and towels. The pain was still screaming inside her leg, but at least she could breathe now.

Pulie's ears would not hear a sound, and her eyes would not see. But Pulie sat at the edge of the bus, tears falling as if they were magnetic to the ground. A lump as large as a rock, clumped in her throat, refused to slide down as her tears were precious gems splattering into a deep sea of water. The loudest screams were mere whispers, and the brightest light was a mere glimmer.

How could you have been so stupid, Pulie? There is no way they could've survived—You've killed your own parents—

Pulie clamped her hands on her face, sighed, and then curled up into a ball at the back of a bus, like a turtle when fear is in the air.

Please, wake up! Tell me this never happened. Tell me, I am dreaming.

She wanted to scream but instead pinched her arm. She opened her eyes.

It was real. It was real, alright.

She buried herself in her arms again.

"Hello," Piden's voice spoke, staring at his sister sobbing. "Good job, by the way. I don't think anybody—*said* that yet. But they mean it. We all know you are really brave—" Piden said.

She scooted away from him. She felt like the little sibling. She wasn't the older sister her parents wanted her to be. Letting herself and Piden get taken away by Mr. Wace wasn't protecting him. And now, she could never protect him.

"Is everything okay?" he asked. "Like after you walked in the truck, you kind of passed out right away, so we cleaned up your leg. And all the glass stuff. Yikes, I feel bad, it must've really hurt and now you're sad and grumpy. Celena said that the only way you would've gotten a cut like that is if you went inside. Is that true?"

"Leave me *alone*, Piden."

"But what's going on? As a little brother, I have to know." He put on a serious face.

"You *don't* want to know."

"Yes, I do!"

"No, later, I'll tell you."

"No, you will tell me now!"

"Leave me—"

"You're so—"

"Stop calling me that!"

"I didn't say anything."

"Just—"

"This isn't the—"

"I said, stop!" She barked, slamming her hand onto the seat.

Piden wilted. Like a flower in the snow. His eyes were like glistening bowls of water. She had hurt him. She had hurt him badly.

"Just, please—" Pulie cried, "Please go away." And then she buried herself again.

Why did we go with Mr. Wace?

If we had waited, we would've received the— actual surprise from our parents? We would've known that our parents were CAOT.

354

Pulie glanced around the truck. Across from her, on a pile of pizza boxes, Maya, Alexia and Dash lay, wrapped in layers of bandages.

What happened?

They lay, eyes closed, breathing slowly. Did the CAOT do that to them?

Suddenly, a realization sparked her brain. She was still in the truck. But something was strange. Was *nobody* watching them escape? CAOT guards were scattered all around the island. And the CAOT were quite intelligent. She felt uneasy about the effortless escape. It was almost as if someone knew about it. The CAOT weren't this stupid. Her parents weren't this stupid. She pressed her cheeks against the window to get a better look outside. And on the side of the window, Pulie squinted. There was a sphere. It was hanging on tight. It was red. And it was ticking.

"Bomb!" Pulie hollered, spitting in the air. Everyone froze, midway in unclipping all the gears and extra clothing.

"What?" Celena asked.

Pulie ordered them to observe the tiny sphere clinging to their window. And she was right. It was a bomb. And it was going to explode.

"Alright, everyone, don't panic." Daria hushed.

"What do you mean don't panic, this truck's going to explode!" Tilda shrieked, who was now tearing the hair out of her own scalp.

"Please, everyone." Celena put her finger to her lips. "Gather your belongings. Bring all the computers, group two. We can't risk it. Dash—wait no—Ema and Alex, can you check how long it will take for the bomb to explode. The rest of you, we will exit this truck the instant we arrive and board the boat and sail away from this island just in time. Don't leave your belongings—" Celena made her hands rattle to create an explosion.

Everyone nodded.

"We're almost there!" Erik shouted from the driver's seat.

The vehicle sped towards the waters, the heavy chained wheels almost dipping into the water. The truck came to a halt.

"We're here. Everyone off!" Celena commanded.

Everyone hurried to get out of the truck.

"Wait! We forgot these devices!" Pulie shouted when she found a drawer full of computer chips.

"Pulie! We don't have time!" Daria shouted from outside.

"They're important!" Pulie placed the last piece of the device into her bag.

"Pulie—"

Pulie threw her bag outside after everyone had exited and stuffed her pockets with the forgotten wires and gadgets. Then, she slammed the door, still inside.

"Pulie? What are you doing?" Piden shouted.

But there was no answer.

"*Get* away from that truck," ordered Erik, "Go to the boat. Celena and I will take care of this. Run."

Daria led the rest to the boat; everyone piling in.

Then, the bomb exploded. It was as if Pulie had *enough* of bombs.

Celena gasped. Everyone inside the boat was scrambling to see what had happened.

The van blew into pieces, a pile of ashes huddled on the ground, the air around it smelling like debris.

"*No…*" Celena whimpered.

Everything was silent—even Erik.

FUNNY ENDS OF SURPRISES

Everything was silent—even Erik.

The ashes settled to the ground, Celena's head hung low. There was silence.

"Look!" Daria shouted.

Celena lifted her head, only to see—Pulie?

"Hello, everyone." Pulie waved.

"What the—"

"Is she immortal?" Pulie could hear Alex say behind the glass window of the boat.

Celena's face erupted into a smile, but she snatched Pulie's hand and dragged her into the boat. Any CAOT survivors or guards would easily find them; they hadn't covered their tracks at all.

The boat propeller spit out water and the boat sped through the waters, cutting through walls and walls of mist and fog.

Everyone was all over Pulie, asking her questions. She dumped the devices she had saved onto a table.

"Are you immortal?" Alex asked, poking Pulie's hand to see if it was real.

"Of course not. But I *did use* a special trick," Pulie said. Celena bent over into the circle to listen as well.

"So, what is it?" Alex asked, pulling out his notebook.

Pulie sighed but managed to give him a sly grin. Piden felt something suspicious. He knew her sister better than any of them.

"Drum roll, please—" Pulie said.

Everyone drummed their fingers on their laps, anxiously.

"I used the back door."

No one blinked.

"You freaked us out when you slammed the door!" Nicky cried.

"I thought you were immortal. I was going to sample your DNA and blood type." Alex said, disappointed, closing his notebook.

Everyone cracked up.

"Just went out the back door." Pulie shrugged, slipping her hands in her pockets.

The ride back to the dock was faster since there were clear directions to the site. Everyone was exhausted and lay sprawled on the seats or the floor, staring up at the ceiling in shock.

"Everyone!" Erik's voice boomed in the speaker, "Dock in range!" Erik shouted in the speaker in the final hour of the ride.

Daria spoke, "I think he means ta get our bags ready *again*. We are finally done with the mission. Now, let's get on that jet and relax until we get ta the palace."

"When does this school end?" Piden asked, zipping his bag uptight and placing it next to Alex's.

"Mid February. You're almost there. Now, since we're done with this mission, we get an award ceremony, *and* we continue our school days like anybody else."

"Oh, come on! No free days off?"

"No, especially not for ya! Now, everyone, stay on the ship; our only goal is not ta be seen. Celena will lead you out the boat and behind the police station while I contact Mr. Wace."

Dash, Alexia, and Maya had been attacked by wolves.

Although mostly everyone had been attacked, only three had been bitten and severely wounded. But they would not die. Erik and Celena carried them on their backs.

The mission crew waited cramped behind a canoe and one small raft, the salty smell of the sea wafted through her nose. The dock rocked along with the waves occasionally, but Pulie made sure she kept her mouth shut.

"How are we going to go to the airport?" Alex asked.

"It's not *at* an airport, nitwit. Mr. Wace just ended his mission and is coming to get us and take us back. So, it's a private jet, and it's *not* supposed to be seen. If we're caught, we're kind of in trouble," Erik said as if it wasn't obvious enough.

"But then, where is it going to land?"

"Right here." Erik pointed to the ground by his feet.

"You said we can't be seen—"

"I know," Erik interrupted, walking quickly away to Noel.

"I am very confused," Alex said, with a worried expression. "If the plane lands here—"

Nicky held up her hand. "Does anyone have duck tape?"

"Plane incoming!" Colin squinted into the sky. He was right; a tiny jet was angled to land literally in the parking lot like Erik had said.

"Come out from behind the boats, everyone, get onto the plane," Celena hollered. Pulie couldn't believe that a plane was actually landing on the parking lot without permission. Air blasted into Pulie's face, her hair flapping at her mouth.

"Hey!" Called a voice. "You aren't authorized to land here! Nobody's authorized to land in the middle of a parking lot!" shouted a man from behind. It was Officer Stans and he had his pistol gripped tightly in his hands, ready to shoot. "I *said,* get down from there!" he yelled, taking a step forward. Other policemen surrounded the parking lot.

"Actually, you never *said* that before," Alex mumbled, but loud enough for the officers to hear.

"Well, now, I did. You're surrounded, kiddos. What are you even doing here, all alone?" Officer Stans shouted. Pulie helped Anne get on the last of the steps. Celena placed everyone's bags into the luggage room. Erik was facing the officers alone. He leaned on the walls of the door.

"We work for a company, jerk. Read the sign." Erik said, pointing to the logo on the side of the plane. The officers wrote the name down for evidence.

"Don't care what company you are. This is *illegal.* I never knew *anyone* crazy enough to land a little plane—in the middle of a parking lot!" Officer Stans bellowed, his men taking out more guns.

"Well, I *am* that crazy person," said a voice. It was Mr. Wace. Pulie felt a rush of relief when she saw him. Someone who knew what he was doing was finally in charge.

"Who are you?" the officer questioned.

"Me? My name is Mr. Wacarend," Mr. Wace said, promptly liking his new name. "And we got to get going, so excuse me, will you excuse us please?" he swatted Erik inside the plane. Everyone but Mr. Wace was now inside.

"Oh, you aren't going anywhere. And isn't that Dunny Bonders?" Officer Stans pointed to Erik, who slipped inside the aircraft.

"Who?" Mr. Wace asked, with a confused look.

"Dunny!"

"I really don't have time for this, Officer. Good day," Mr. Wace said, walking in.

"Whoa, gentlemen." Miss Rolan stepped into the conversation. Eyes turned, and the stiff lady walked to the blasting air of the jet.

All of the men took a bow with respect towards her, and she stared straight at Mr. Wace.

"I'm not sure what is going on right now. Another strange incident in less than three days. This isn't right. And I *know* how to fix this," she said, rubbing her hands together. She was draped with velvet cloth, and her jewelry was made entirely of diamonds. "Mr. Wacarend, I have a deal. You give me a payment, and we will resolve this," she continued.

"What do you mean?" Mr. Wace paused from closing the door.

"Give me what I need, and I will let you go," she said promptly.

"How much?"

"Twenty thousand."

"You are funny, ma'am."

Miss Rolan was taken back in horror. Nobody ever called her ma'am or spoke to her in such a manner.

"This is no joke," she retorted, building her confidence again.

"Twenty thousand?" Mr. Wace continued. "Ridiculous. I'm sorry, my students and I are extremely busy. Excuse us for this quick landing." And then the door slammed shut.

They were all huddled in a very small room, smaller than a bathroom stall. Pulie could see out the small window. Ms. Rolan, with an irregular frown, screaming orders at the men to aim at the plane. Ms. Rolan's thin, perfected eyebrows lowered. Her snippy chin curved almost magically.

"Ready... " Ms. Rolan commanded. Pulie's heart thumped furiously, palms sweaty.

I don't want to die in a parking lot. Please.

"Aim... "

"Liftoff!" roared Mr. Wace. His jet sped forwards in the vast vacant lot and shot up into the air. Gunshots sounded, but the air from the propeller blasted the officers back. The police station was now only a speck next to the large blue sea as they soared higher and higher.

The mission crew screamed with joy.

"Good job, everyone. But you surely aren't going to just be here and celebrating, right?" Mr. Wace squeezed his way through to the left of the compartment.

"Isn't this the only room?" Tilda asked.

"I put a lot of money on this plane. Go and greet your teachers. We've just come back from our separate mission. They are in the room next to you."

Mr. Wace lifted a flab on the wall, revealing a hidden doorknob.

Ema was the first to enter the secret room.

"Oh, this is wonderful!" she cried. And it was.

The floor was carpet, there were rows of seats on each side of the room, and the large middle space was set to display an array of foods and drinks. The teachers were already seated in their chairs, looking very tired and exhausted from their mission.

Pulie spotted Mr. Rodriguez and a couple of other teachers that taught her Zive. The rest of the teachers probably taught the other Zives. But she politely greeted all of them and sat with the mission crew in the back.

Pulie sank into her chair, groaning, and pulled the blankets over her head.

"I'm going to get some nachos. Anyone want to join me?" Nicky said.

"Maybe later." Ema adjusted the chair until she was lying down completely. And then, she was quiet, except for the mild snoring coming from underneath the blankets.

Pulie couldn't blame her. The mission crew hadn't gotten good sleep since what seemed like forever.

Pulie turned on some music and drifted off to sleep as well.

There was a voice. A voice was calling her name. Over and over again. Pulie. Pulie. Pulie. Help. Help.

Pulie was on a bridge as thin as a tightrope. She was balancing so well, though. The voice was coming from the other side. Then, Pulie fell into the water below her, her necklace breaking into shards as she hit the surface.

Pulie gasped and lurched forward in her seat. She panted for a few moments, holding the armrests tightly. She had fallen asleep so quickly that the dream had seemed real.

Pulie scratched her head and looked around. Everyone else was either sleeping, talking, or eating. Some were just staring off into space.

When I wake up from this dream, Pulie thought, *I'll find myself at home. This is just another dream. Mother and Father will be having coffee in the family room, and Piden will be searching for food in the refrigerator. We will all play chess together or drink lemonade in the summer haze. We'll have our benches out and our soccer ball near the grass.*

Pulie winced. She didn't even get to say goodbye to her father. This *had* to be a dream. This *couldn't* be real.

Was it real? Pulie began to hate herself. Would it had been better if she didn't go inside the dome? Would she not be feeling this guilt? Would this be—no, if she had not entered the dome, she never would've known her parents were CAOT. And she deserved to know what her parents are doing. There were so many different CAOT locations. But, Thoyos was the building the Trickies happened to bomb and the same building her parents were inside?

Had she not seen the CAOT sign before, *somewhere* in her house? No, she had never seen it. Why?

Then, it struck her. Maybe the reason behind all the concealment in her family was because they didn't want Pulie and her brother to know about the CAOT—yet. In addition, her mom had told her never to be caught by the Master. But why? It struck her again. Was it to give her a choice? To not be a CAOT? Or what?

She didn't know yet, but she vowed to herself she would never join the CAOT.

"Pulie, do you want some?"

Pulie opened her eyes and took off her headset. Ema was holding a plate of nachos and fruits.

"Umm—sure. Thank, Ema," Pulie said, uneasily. She placed a chip in her mouth and the cheese melted.

"Pulie, your eyes are *red*. Are you okay?"

"Yes, I'm fine." Pulie looked away.

Ema sat down. "Are you okay, for sure?"

Pulie looked right into Ema's eyes. Ema had always been there for her. She was trustworthy.

Pulie bit her lip and sighed. "Allergies."

Ema nodded, "Same. In the spring, they're always terrible. Anyways, if you ask Señor Rodriguez nicely, he'll even give you the ice cream stored up in the fridge!" Ema excitedly chewed really hard on her banana.

She has no idea.

"Do you know if I can speak to Mr. Wace right now?"

Ema shook her head. "I believe he has to manage the jet right now. But when we reach the palace, you can."

"Hey, girls." Nicky hopped into the seat next to them. "Erik really got them at the beginning, which *does* surprise me."

"What?" Pulie asked, raising her brows. This was the first time Nicky complemented Erik.

"Remember. Erik told the police officers to look at the logo on the side of the plane. It said the Pet Food Industry of Antarctica."

Ema cracked up. Pulie managed a weak smile.

Spotting Piden by Alex's side, blabbering away, Pulie could only help thinking. *Piden has no idea either.* He doesn't know he'll never get to see them again.

She was going to walk to him and explain to him why she had been so grumpy, but she realized it wasn't time. She didn't want anyone to know. Maybe with the exception of Mr. Wace. She felt there was something odd about him.

Oh, how Piden didn't know that when he walked into his home after school ended for the break, it would be empty. And that it would stay empty forever.

Pulie stayed in her chair for the rest of the flight, despite the fact that a nurse came to her and fed her a pill that would get rid of the pain in her leg. She couldn't wait till she finally got to the palace, and got a good day's sleep, all at once.

LANDING

T

The plane landed.

The teachers led the mission group to a hill. It was not the same hill Pulie and Piden had hiked up that day Mr. Wace took them to the land of blue and glass. It was a different hill. But the same procedures were taken.

Seventeen steps up. Scan the earring into a busy world.

"SkyCloud," Alex said, rubbing his dirty shoes on the glass. "They're famous for their technology up here."

"So, we're actually in the clouds?" Piden asked.

"Precisely."

"How come I can't see this place from down there? Without an earring?"

"The earring is a sensor. It notifies the SkyClouds that a Tricky wants to enter. This place is invisible so that it can stay concealed—from the CAOT and the rest of the world."

"How is it invisible?"

"Well, it's not *actually* invisible," Alex smirked. "The glass around it seems transparent, but on the outside, it reflects what is seen on the outside. It's an illusion to create the quote invisible catch."

"Don't planes fly into this area, though?"

"No, apparently, SkyClouds can monitor the plane field as well. The Sky clouds is a thin panel that stretches across the globe in a spider web network. They can also effectively steer the planes off course and move them to where they want to be. Just so they don't crash into this place. The panels are also retractable. If something is hardcore falling from space, the floor will reshape and move away from the falling object."

"What about birds? You can't move birds, can you?"

"Nope. That's why we're the number one bird killing machine." Alex *blessed* himself. "Amen for the dead ones."

"My house is on the North Cutway," Nicky told Pulie.

"You live up here, too?"

"Yeah? You don't?"

"I would love to," Pulie said. "Does everyone live up here?"

"Yes, to avoid contact and the exchange of information and ideas with beings down there. Also, to isolate ourselves so our conflicts will not directly impact their lives," Alex explained. "My house is on South Cutway. Thank god we're not neighbors."

The mission crew entered the tube buses and sped across the air in their little world until they reached the Trickies Palace stop.

"The Palace is a hidden bubble down below as well," Alex explained. "The palace is located in a jungle, to be exact. But no one can see the palace because it uses the same invisible method the SkyClouds use."

"What if, someone wants to walk through the jungle?" Piden asked. "Or what if animals want to."

"Well, the palace itself is surrounded by that large area of space where we did all the Tricky Trials, you know. And around that large area is another wall that is—invisible. It wraps around the entire area. When an animal goes near it, we don't care. But one time, a human approached the wall and found out about the palace. The Trickies had to—end his life."

"What?"

"If the man found out about the Trickies, that means danger for *us*."

The group descended the staircase and returned to the entrance, and ahead of them in the distance was the great mystic building with the beehive Zives and the Miralmalma tree trunk shooting out from behind.

She was finally at the palace.

EMA'S CURIOSITY

Mr. Wace had sent Señor Rodriguez and Mr. Lizarstrang back out to retrieve Dan's body from the tree.

At the treatment unit, Pulie received a couple of painful stitches from the new nurse. Fortunately, only muscles were damaged and her bones were spared. With only one healthy leg and a thick brace on the other thigh, her walking skills had deteriorated, and she felt like a wooden block, clunking around the courtyard.

However, everything else was back to normal. *Everything* except the memories and visions that swirled in her head, capped tightly with a cork.

When Pulie returned to her room, she collapsed on her hammock and took into her head all the things she had missed. The vines hanging from her ceiling, the sweet scent of Ema's raspberry hand lotion, and the hammocks.

Their room door didn't open for an entire day. The rest of the mission group did the same. They were given the time to relax and slowly recover from the events that had occurred in the past days. Dash, Alexia, and Maya stayed in the hospital due to extreme blood loss.

***

She was running. Then she was swimming. Then she was flying. Then she was falling. She saw her mother and her father screaming for her. She screamed back, but her voice was swallowed by fire and a loud thundering unknown voice. Fingers reached out to grab her. Then she saw the dome, but instead of burning into flames, it was dripping in blood. She looked down and saw the bloody knife in her hands. She dropped it and started running. There was a lake before her, and she jumped in but something below her grabbed her by the feet and dragged her down. She flapped her arms, letting the water pour over her head.

Nightmare. At the dead of night, Pulie awoke to the sound of splashing and swashing of water. From her hammock, she saw a fuzzy beam of light down below from the sink. It was Ema. She was rinsing her hands thoroughly, sloshing them around in a bowl of soap water.

Pulie felt her shirt. It was drenched from sweat. It really had been a nightmare.

Pulie glanced back at Ema. "It's midnight. What are you doing?" Pulie glanced out the huge window. But the Tricky room lights were still on— like usual.

"I touched... *that*," Ema said, pointing with her eyes because her hands were full.

Pulie followed her gaze. It was a package ripped open on the sides.

"The container inside— it cracked on the way here. It's all over my hands."

"Why'd you wake up so early?" Pulie slid out of her hammock, scratching her socks.

The gooey substance was even on the ground.

"I was trying to clean the packaging so it wouldn't spill over the carpet. The room maid knocked on our door and it was

just there—outside our door. I should've just left it outside…"
Ema continued to scrub her hands. "I hope it isn't mercury or anything."

"Ema? Your hand look kind of… well… green?"

Her hands were emerald clovers, shifting to a darker green.

"Oh no—I just hope it's not liquid—" Ema said, dumping all of the soap onto her skin. Bubbles erupted into smaller ones like a shower of snow.

"Ema, no! I don't think that's helping."

"No, I am fine. Just a little more soap—"

"It's *very* green," Pulie remarked.

"I know that."

"Come, let's go to the nurse." She tugged on Ema's dripping arms.

"I'm fine. Just… need… a… little… more… soap." Ema shook the entire bottle onto her fingers.

"You are not okay, Ema. You don't need more soap, either. It wasn't this green when I first saw you. Come on. If it gets worse, you might not be able to go to the ceremony either."

A small gasp left Ema's lips. Pulie knew that the ceremony was what she had been waiting for the entire year *if* she survived the mission. And she did survive.

"Okay, let's go. But don't tell Nicky."

"Why not?"

"The package had her name on it."

MYSTERY HATCHING

"This is a perfect storm—and when it rains, it pours." The Twig shook his head. It was him again, the same old man who had treated Pulie during the mission.

"Strange indeed," Señor Rodriguez said, walking into the room, boots clicking against the shiny floor.

"Señor Rodriguez?" Ema and Pulie cried. "Back already? Did you get Dan back to the palace?"

Señor took off his humongous *sombrero* and placed it on his chest. "Yes, Estudiantes, and it was horrible to see him with his eyes closed like that. The leaders and the staff members will go through the reasons for his death and make sure everything was justified." He paused, "But back to Ema—"

Ema frowned. "What am I to do? Will my hands be green forever?"

The Twig shrugged. "I don't know yet. Knowing comes after knowledge. I will take a look at the liquid once my assistant brings it here."

"What did happen?" Señor asked, intrigued by the situation.

"I found a package outside our door..." Ema mumbled. "I shouldn't have opened it, but the maid was awfully loud, and I had lost all interest in sleeping, so I decided to check on it."

"And then?" Señor Rodriguez questioned.

"Well, I opened it. But, the sides of the paper were all so gooey, so I decided to clean it first. I think it was cracked when she delivered it because when I opened it, the liquid just poured all over my hands..." she continued. "I started washing my hands afterward."

"I found the jar, Twig." A woman in a purple lab coat with the embroidering of the Trickies symbol burst into the room, holding a clear bag with the cracked jar in it. "The lab man tested it. Here are the results."

"Let me see," Señor Rodriguez said, reaching for the results. "Unknown chemical. Can I see the jar for a second?"

The woman hesitated, then handed him the bag.

"The description says this was supposed to be a juice. A power drink. *The Ultimate Power Drink*. UltraDelicious," He read the tag on the side of the broken bottle with his gloves on. "Doesn't sound familiar."

"I think I've heard of it before," the woman interrupted. She had floppy brown hair and was very chubby, especially around the chin. Pulie made a face. She had seen this woman somewhere. She had definitely seen her.

"Really? It is not verified by the association however and therefore must not be drunken," Señor declared, eyeing the woman oddly. "*You* may be dismissed."

She lowered her head and left, but Pulie thought she saw her mumbling a few words underneath her breath.

"Whoever sent it," Señor said after the lady had left, "was trying to hurt you three."

"Actually, not really…" Ema said softly. Everyone turned to look at her.

"What do you mean?" Señor Rodriguez asked, a sincere suspicious look on his face.

"The package said *for* Nicky, and Nicky only. The sender was unknown," she said.

"Well, there *is* a lab worker named Nick, down there," The Twig added. "Perhaps, the maid sent the package to the wrong address or got confused about where it was supposed to go. Maybe it was a miscommunication. All I can say is you are very lucky you didn't drink it. That might've been fatal."

"Ema, you'll be ready just in time for you to go to the mission ceremony. But unfortunately, you'll have to stay in this room for the rest of the night," Señor added.

"That's okay. I'll stay here with her," Pulie said.

"Well, then," Señor Rodriguez said, nearing the door, "Goodnight and see you tomorrow at the ceremony."

The door shut.

The Twig brought out a paste mixed in a plastic wrapping from his bag. Then he started spreading the teal mixture onto Ema's greenish hands. It was very silent.

"Twig?" Pulie asked. He looked up. His eyes looked very faded, and his skin was saggy, like fresh sap dropping from a tree. He really looked like a twig.

"Do you like your name? *Twig*?"

The old man shrugged, continuing to smooth the paste back and forth with the instrument. "It's not my given name, of course."

"Well, what *is* your real name anyway?" Ema grew kind of interested.

"Rory Hanson."

"Does anybody call you by that?"

"No." The Twig's eyes began to soften, the coldness and stone-like features of his face seemed to melt.

"Everyone's been calling me the Twig ever since my punke years. I didn't like it, but I don't care much anymore. I mean, now that I think of it—being a twig is a fine thing to be."

"Even your parents call you the Twig?"

"My father started the name."

Pulie raised her eyebrows.

"But my mother never said such a thing. I was her *Little Rory of Glory*." He gazed up at the ceiling and pointed one long wrinkly finger upwards. "That's my mother up there." Above their heads, a painting of a woman looked back down. She had the same long faces as Hanson, a nose that peaked like a mountain, and wrinkled skin like a baked raisin. But her lively eyes were too unlike the faded, dull light blue of her son's eyes.

"My mother had always been the light in our family. She brought brightness and comfort to all my troubled days. You see, my father was always crabby and waspish, and I called him the snappy small parrot, only in my head, though. My mother was the head nurse like I am when I was your age. Everything was just fine until she died in a mission."

"Where was your dad?"

"He was the head chief at his place." Twig's melancholy eyes drifted elsewhere and added, "Richard Hanson—my father was a CAOT. He deserted my family when I was little."

Ema gasped and put her hand over her mouth. Pulie just stared. This man's father was a CAOT. How could this be? Could he tell her something her parents didn't tell her? But she knew she had to keep it to herself. She let the Twig continue.

"I've always wondered where I would go when I died. To this day, I still plead for an answer. Perhaps, I might reunite with my mother. I only got to see her for a couple of years. Death is a very difficult question. You see, it is not an answer. Death is full of question marks themselves. When, where, why, how, to where… and there is no *answer* to this. But is there really a heaven? A hell? Or an underworld?"

"Of course, there's a heaven!" Ema said, "Well, that's what I learned."

The Twig shrugged, his thin frame wobbled. "My father left on my ninth birthday during the spring break. He left before dinner. He said he'd be out for a while. He said he forgot to buy me my present, the soldier toy I wanted. So he'd be right back. He said he was very sorry." The Twig narrowed his eyes. "Did he bring back a present? No. Did he bring back anything? No. Did he come back? No—never again. He left my mother alone to take care of me. He left me fatherless on my ninth birthday." The Twig had stopped applying the medicine on Ema's hand. He shook with anger. "My mother waited and waited. We cried and cried. My mother was heartbroken, believing that he was dead and gone for good. Although, that day, my foolish head was simply crying over my present, leaving my mother to panic. She searched and searched, reported to the Trickies, SkyCloud, all our relatives, friends, neighbors, just to make sure he was okay. She barely slept, in fact, or ate. She was worried. Afraid that he was hurt.

"For years, we were left with an empty box. No answers. No calls. No mails. But four years later, my mother's assistant located him at the CAOT, kneeling at the heal of their leader, deserting us like we never mattered. He looked quite happy under that changed face of his. They always do the same surgery process for all their people. The long thin, withered nose, enlarged cold eyes, paled skin, painted blood-red lips, and straightened black hair. He became a wanderer, an honored status of the CAOT."

Pulie trembled and closed her eyes. The faces from the mission reappeared in her head. Rory's descriptions only made it worse. But she listened attentively.

"My mother was sent on a mission to rescue Trickies near my father's location, but she died. My father probably killed her with his own hands."

Finally, someone who understood Pulie without her having to say a word. Her parents, too, were gone unless they had survived the bombing. Rory's father might be alive, but it was his mother that mattered. Hope was lost.

"We are all the same," Rory finally said. "Trickies, CAOT, SkyClouds. We are the same chunk of human. The same people and the same foolish brains. It doesn't matter. We are humans. Just like people below us. It's what my mother always said to me." He zipped the bag of paste and put away his tools into a kit.

"My apologies for filling your joyous night with my sorrows. Tomorrow is your celebration. Congratulations on the mission. I am also sorry about Dan; he was always a good boy. Get a good night's sleep. Ema, your hands should be fine before tomorrow."

His long bony hands flicked off the lights.

"Thank you, sir," Ema said.

Pulie nodded. "Thank you—Mr. Hanson."

Rory beamed, and the door clicked shut.

"Thanks for staying here with me," Ema whispered, she flipped over in her bed. Pulie was in the next bed down the aisle.

"No problem. I don't want to go back to sleep. I had a nightmare. But anyway, you should be proud of yourself."

Ema gave her a *look* through the darkness.

"In a way, you saved Nicky's life. Nicky is not cautious; she would eat or drink anything she found. And if she had found that bottle, she would've died. You heard, Twig—I mean Hanson. If you hadn't—"

"Sloshed the poison all over my hands, Nicky could've been in danger." Ema continued Pulie's sentence. "Yeah, I guess."

There was a long pause.

"But I still don't get why Nicky's name was on the package and I *don't* think it was an accident."

"Me neither." Pulie shrugged. "That package was sent for Nicky for a reason."

"She does have a lot of enemies—Selma is the most likely suspect," Ema said. "But trying to kill her is quite past the boundary lines."

A few odd silent minutes passed.

"Pulie, did you really go inside the dome? This is just what I heard. I thought it might be a rumor. Is that what happened to your leg?"

"Yes," Pulie whispered. Her eyes were starting to water up. She longed to tell Ema *everything* that had happened: inside the dome, the CAOT, her parents, her family, and everything about herself and the reason she came here.

"Ever since the mission, I feel like there's nothing left for me to do." Pulie waited for Ema to respond.

"You sound like Rory. But, it's alright, Pulie. I understand."

No, she didn't. She would never understand.

Pulie pulled the covers over her head and rubbed her eyes, still scared to go back to sleep. Her parents' faces kept appearing in her head. They were screaming and screaming and screaming her name. Pulie bit her lip furiously, trying to distract herself. Her lips began to bleed, just a little.

How long am I going to keep this secret about Mother and Father? How long before I erupt? How long am I capable of doing this? But what if…

No… The dome burned to the ground. Everything in there had to have perished. I'm going to ask Mr. Wace tomorrow—about everything.

CELEBRATION

"Pulie, Ema, wake up!" Nicky dragged Pulie and Ema down the Miralmalma until they awoke.

"Finally, now that you're awake," Nicky said, "I have a question. How did I wake up in a room with no one? Why were you up there?"

"*I* fell off the hammock at night— on my hands—they *really* hurt." Ema winced. "Pulie helped me to the nurse. And we fell asleep there."

"I've known you for too long that whenever you tap your feet in a three-beat, you're *lying*. I don't care this time. But we need to hurry. The celebration is today! Come on!"

The bathrooms were crowded. Pulie's ears were overwhelmed with the sounds: the blasting of the blow dryers, the tapping of the cotton wipes, the shutting and opening of doors, the throwing of clothes, and the squeaky splashes of water from the showers.

Cold water poured onto her dry sandy hair. Not showering for days made her smell like Mrs. Wapanog's damp, smelly, and putrid room. Her hair dripped with a glob of fresh strawberry and peach shampoo and she squeezed it all over her head, feeling the dirt wash down and the hard strands of her hair softening. She yanked the towel off her head when she came out of the showers and let her wet hair down onto her shoulders. She was wearing her mission top, blue jeans, and polished sneakers. Pulie, Ema, and Nicky dressed as triplets.

Then, Pulie spotted her old adversary standing at the far sink, throwing confetti and glitter over her face. Pulie's sweet time without Selma had gone by too fast.

"Looks like you got a little something on your face there, Selma," Nicky shouted from across the room. "If I were you, I'd wipe it off before Mr. Dash sees you."

There were laughing and shoving and kicking after that. Pulie, Nicky, and Ema quickly retreated to their own room.

Piden had thrown on his regular clothes. The only special adjustment was that he had finally combed his hair instead of the mushy salad hairstyle. Alex was by his side, dressed in flannel. Both had temporarily tattooed the Trickies symbol to their foreheads.

"I cannot wait until the ceremony!" Alex cried. "Every year, we have a dance party. I was chosen for split dance DJ last year," he boasted. "And I always choose the best music. The students threw paper cups at me when I turned on my favorite song last year. One time, they even led me out of the dance area for the rest of the ceremony."

"That's the spirit."

After getting ready, Pulie rushed to the Miralmalma to talk to Mr. Wace. Everything was a shock that she couldn't absorb. *This is not real. This is ridiculous. This is definitely just another nightmare. Nothing happened. I'll wake up in my bed at home and my parents will be there with me.*

Unfortunately, the breakfast bell rang, and she couldn't miss breakfast. Everyone had to go. In addition, Mr. Wace had his kitchen duty today. Pulie had forgotten. She made up her mind to go to the Miralmalma after the party.

"Fiona, it's the cripple." Pulie heard a sharp voice say behind her. Pulie spun around. It was Selma… again.

Pulie smiled. "Why, thank you. Dash has one just like this on his arms. You like my brace, don't you?"

"No, it just makes you look even more hideous. Wait till I show the place how much I shine!" Selma twirled around in her long yellow dress. "My dad bought this for me. It was three hundred credits. What have your parents ever given you?"

"A life."

Bonnie cracked up. "Man, that was a good come back, Pulie. I would—"

Selma slapped Bonnie in the stomach, then turned to Pulie. "You're just lucky you didn't end up like Dan. I bet the whole school wished it was you who died. I certainly prayed to the Lord every night." Then, she stormed off.

Nicky appeared behind Pulie and whispered, "Just ignore those two dung bombs."

And when they were out of sight, Nicky added, "I *actually* put dung bombs in their bags. They'll be smelling like urine at the ceremony."

Pulie heard a scream from the other side of the courtyard. It was Selma and Bonnie.

"The dung bombs worked!" Nicky chortled.

The door to the eating room was opened. They walked down the stairs, and inside, the eating room was filled with food and music. It was so loud, Pulie couldn't hear her own voice.

The lines for food flooded the room. The entire palace in the same room was quite enough to handle. On the menu today was steak with mashed potatoes, olives, spiced peppers, baguettes dipped in olive oil and melted butter, caesar salad sprinkled in parmesan, roasted rosemary chicken with garlic dressing powdering, fresh lemonade, orange squeeze, lemon water, sodas. For dessert, there was fudge ice cream with cherry sprinkles, fresh whip cream, red velvet dipping cookies, hot chocolate, and a slice of cheesecake stuffed with organic fresh strawberries dipped in chocolate. There were also cherry puddings, creme brûlée, milk chocolate shaped into the Trickies Symbol, and strawberry ice cream. Pulie's plate was a mountain and at the peak was her fork. She balanced the stack of food up and out of the tumultuous eating room and into the courtyard. Everyone was scattered so Pulie sat with Nicky, Ema and her brother, and Alex. Then, more people joined. First Anne, then Colin, then Santiago, then Antono. Soon, it was all just a big jumble of people.

"I can't wait for the ceremony!" Anne exclaimed.

Pulie nodded. "This year's been *crazy*. Do you know if Mr. Wace is out of the Miralmalma yet? I have to ask him a question."

"No, sorry. Is it about the mission? I heard you did great! I'm so proud of you!"

Proud, Pulie scoffed in her head. *Proud? Was that the word my parents think of me as?* Even if they had survived, they would never be proud of her. They would be—disappointed. Their own children turning against them, a family then and rivals now.

Pulie bit into her bread. The warm bread melted into her mouth and she dipped another bit into her soup. She remembered when her family would all be together, maybe by the warming fireplace, maybe in their lawn playing soccer, or in the pool, or at the table eating dinner. It wasn't a big deal, but they were still memories. Happy ones. Where she could replay them in her head over and over, whenever she wanted. A tear slid down her cheek, with the joy of remembering this happiness. There would be no more of that until she was with her parents again. *If they were still out there... no, that was impossible... the bomb destroyed everything... but what if...* she remembered what Rory had said about death. If she went there, she could find her parents. But no, what if they were still alive. Each side of her brain was tied to two long palm trees, being torn apart—again and again, and again.

She wanted to scream. But she was ashamed. There were thousands out there with no parents. Was she the only one like this? Was she the only fool crying in the inside for herself? Was she the only one who kept quiet? She was a murderer. She had to be strong. She had to be the girl her parents wanted her to be. But who was that? Who did her parents want her to be?

"Pulie?" Nicky waved her hand in Pulie's face, and she instantly snapped to attention.

"Pulie?" Ema asked. "Are you okay? Are you—"

"Crying?" Nicky cried. "On ceremony day?"

Pulie rubbed her tears. "No! I am not crying! I yawned."

She could tell Nicky and Ema weren't buying it.

Thankfully, Mr. Wace began the ceremony by saying into the speaker, "Everyone, sorry for interrupting your meal, but we have the ceremony. Pick up *all* of your trash and come sit over here."

The courtyard transformed into a mess of busy and impatient people. Pulie saw Piden in the far distance.

"Piden!" Pulie called out, walking towards him. "Come with me to talk to Mr. Wace. After the ceremony and the party. I have to ask him something, and I think you better come too."

"Okay." He stared cautiously at her. "About what?"

"I'll explain later. Let's enjoy it right now."

How can I enjoy anything?

Piden nodded. "At the Miralmalma?"

"Yes, I'll just walk with you when the party is over."

How can I party either?

Pulie was helplessly confusing herself.

Don't cry. Stay strong. You are a Tricky. The exact opposite thing your parents wanted you to be.

Everyone seated themselves.

Mr. Wace appeared on stage as the crowd hushed.

The man began, "As you know, we have already survived throughout almost a whole year."

The crowd uneasily chuckled. All the teachers sat at the back of the stage in their little chairs, even the janitors, the lab man, and the teachers, but not Rory, which was strange. He had said he was going to attend it as well.

Pulie leaned over to Ema. "Where's Rory?" Ema squinted but couldn't see the skinny shriveled man they had befriended the day before.

"Maybe a sick child?" Ema shrugged, holding up her wrapped hand.

Mr. Wace continued, "Since my generation and back further, we, the Trickies, have always been a target. Of course, this is what we get for trying to stop the *bad*. Surviving this year was a miracle for each and every one of you. Who knows when we'll be attacked or annihilated."

Pulie shivered.

"This year," Mr. Wace put his hand on his heart. "Two people have not made it with us. One has died of a respiratory disease that we failed to treat. The other fought on the mission and died in bravery. They are both Trickies and will remain Trickies until the end. Both have died while in training and so they were loyal and brave. The *rest* of us—we were just lucky. Fortunately, compared to the last few years, deaths have decreased dramatically. But remember, our goal is not to survive but to destroy our enemies. We aren't trying to protect our lives and we are willing to risk it all. No matter what it takes. Our goal is to end demolition brought upon by the CAOT and further organizations of tyrannical criminals. And we still have a long way ahead of us.

"This year's mission was extremely tough. There have been many complaints regarding the several injuries that have occurred during the mission. Many are relating the cause of not having *enough* older members and too many young ones. But to those who were concerned about the people selected, well here we are. They did just fine. Besides our young fellow Dan, they all made it. He died in honor, and we shall not lose to that."

Pulie heard many people in the crowd yelling his name. She also heard a boy ask how it happened.

Mr. Wace raised his eyebrows. "How did he die? Well, I guess I can say why. He died after an alligator attacked him."

The memory of his limbless body and the blood draining from his hips brought visions from the dome back, and then her parents. All over again. Pulie closed her eyes. She wished it would all be erased. She caught sight of Colin wilting in his chair, covering his face with the collar of his shirt.

"Anyways, to those in the mission group, will you please come up?"

The crowd clapped. Pulie had no will to get up. None of the members did. Everyone was so tired—tired of the things they had seen and witnessed. Yet their feet carried them away and up onto the stage.

They were each given a medal—a medal for surviving. If the alligator had attacked Pulie instead of Dan, things would have been different. If there was no alligator, things would've been different. If her parents hadn't been inside the dome, things would've been different.

Pulie shuddered at the thought of holding the golden medallion in her hands. *A prize for what? For killing my own parents? For shredding my entire life? Holding the medal in honor of murder?*

"To, Erik Pontz. Our leader of the pre-mission and all transportation." Mr. Wace handed him a medal. Everyone cheered furiously for him as he raised his arms in victory.

"To Celena Drone. Our medic and our leader of safety. She was responsible for healing the damages done to the health of our members and was responsible for the equipment." Celena received her medal and received loud cheers. So many cheering for her. So many proud of what she did.

Nobody would be proud of Pulie if they knew the real truth. They would punch and swat at her like a pesky fly and tell her to leave.

Mr. Wace continued announcing the mission people and handing out the glimmering golden medals.

"Daria Chwala. Mission leader of the bombing. Lead the bombing unit and executed plans alongside Erik." Daria received his medal, and the crowd cheered loudly again.

"Lastly, our bomber—Pulie Jark. She was the bomber, of course. Everyone give them a round of applause!" Mr. Wace shouted as he handed Pulie the medal. It gleamed in the sunlight next to her other two necklaces. The crowd cheered wildly. Pulie stepped back.

"Trickies… Trickies… Trickies… Trickies… Trickies… Trickies!" the crowd screamed. Pulie could feel her heart racing and on the verge of explosion. She felt faint and hurried back to her seat. She could still hear the Leaders speaking.

"Thank you, everyone," Mr. Wace said, the audience settling down. "The success of this mission has killed an estimated thirty of those ferocious CAOT workers. And we have done the right thing."

Right thing? What was he talking about? He doesn't even know who he killed and he assumes it was the right thing?

"And now, let us have the party. Lights!" he shouted, raising his arms. The whole palace grew dark. Then, little colorful lights sprouted like saplings of rainbows everywhere around the palace. On the walls of the gates. On Zives, on trash cans. The whole place started to glow. In the center, a gleaming light lit up the symbol of the Trickies. Everyone cheered. The music started. Everyone was jumping up and down. The mission people hopped off the stage and joined their friends. The music got louder. Nicky was dancing and shaking her head off. Ema was too, jumping up and down. Everyone was.

Yet Pulie was dizzy, her head full of vertigo. She was tremulous, her hands were shaking uncontrollably but matched the beat of the loud noises from the speaker. Pulie screamed but her voice was drowned by the music. She kicked and punched at the air yet it was taken as a form of dancing. She cried but it was understood as singing. She was done. She was done hiding her anger and her heavy heart. How could Mr. Wace say such a thing?

But her tantrum halted. Her emotions stopped. The red blinking light from the top of the Miralmalma caught her eye. That only happened when…

Ema spun around meeting Pulie face to face. "Rory!" They both shouted. And they ran out of the squished crowd and to the Miralmalma.

A RING OF DEATH

"Where is he?" Ema asked, glancing around. Now, the room was silent. They had arrived at the Miralmalma's top floor.

"Check the treatment unit!" Pulie pointed to the room. They peeped through the crack in the door. A man was lying on the bed, being pushed out of the treatment room and out some private back door.

"Hurry, follow me," Ema whispered, sneaking in and slipping between the beds.

But Pulie couldn't resist it anymore. "Rory!" she screamed. The nurses all froze and looked around the room. Pulie darted towards the bed. It was from Rory. His face was weak and sad. But his eyes were still alive.

"Pulie?" he said in a hoarse voice. "And Ema?"

Ema had just followed Pulie out of their hiding spot.

"What happened?" Ema sobbed.

"I-I—"

"He jumped down the tunnel of the Miralmalma," the new nurse explained.

"Oh, no! You must be careful," Ema reprimanded.

"It wasn't an accident," The new nurse said sharply. "108-foot drop. It was suicide. A bit of a failure. Still worked."

Rory grinned slightly. "My time is up. I want to see my mother."

"And ladies, you aren't allowed in here," the nurse said, clicking Rory's bed to a stop.

"Let them be," Rory croaked. The bedsheets around him were stained in red.

"What? Don't be serious. You don't have to do this."

"I am old," Rory huffed, "I am satisfied."

"Ladies, please give him some rest."

"Miranda—let them be. I want to be alone with them before I go. Please leave."

The door shut quietly.

"Pulie? Ema?" Rory's breathing was choppy now.

"Yes, Rory?"

"Have this—" He unfolded his palms and revealed a ring. It was a beautiful diamond on a golden band. "My mother used to say the ring is lost forever. That it is in the wrong place, please, please, keep it safe. I stole it from my father when I was on a mission. It was his wedding ring."

"Don't talk so much, sir! You're wasting energy!" Ema cried.

"Then, I will talk more. Now listen. There is one thing I want both of you to do for me. Just for me. Are you listening?"

They nodded.

"Nobody knows that this was my father's ring. But it is lost and needs to be found. I don't know what my mother meant by this. But figure it out. And that is all. Do it for me. Do it for my dead mother." He folded the ring into Ema's hand.

Ema handed it to Pulie, but Pulie shook her head. "You keep it. I might lose it."

Rory smiled. "Now, I am going to have my final moments of peace, if that's alright."

"Of course."

His raspy breathing was all Pulie could hear. *Inhale. Exhale. Inhale. Exhale.*

"What was your mother's first name?" Pulie asked, her tongue and teeth moving without her command. In an instant, she regretted it. She had to obey a dying man's wish.

"Luella," Rory responded gladly. Then there was a silence. He breathed no more.

He was gone.

Pulie turned the doorknob and shut the door, not believing anything she had just witnessed. She was out of the treatment unit.

"Doesn't Luella sound really familiar to you too, Ema?" Pulie asked, staring at the door handle still.

Ema shook her head. "Why?"

It was a name that had been said. Before Rory had said it. But—

Pulie's eyes grew wide. "No! No! No!" She tried to get back into the treatment unit. "We need to go back, Ema!"

You've locked Luella up in the aircraft outside, haven't you? Master's cold voice replaying in her head.

"Pulie! Stop!" Ema yanked Pulie's arm back. "What is wrong with you? He's gone! He's gone! Okay? Now, wake up from this useless imagination and get back into reality. He wants to see his mother and that was his goal. Now let him alone." Ema shoved her back.

"That's the point. His mother's *alive*. He isn't going to see her, no matter what."

"How do *you* know?"

"She was inside the prison in a jet at the CAOT dome. I heard them talking!"

Ema froze. "Oh, no."

Pulie slipped to her feet and sat at the door of the hospital, crying. It was her routine now. Her tears so familiar to her face, it was like using her eyes to see. But this time, she was accompanied by Ema's tears as well. They both wept at the door of the hospital room.

"Pulie, so you really did go inside the dome?" Ema broke the long period of silence after checking to make sure no one was listening.

"I already told you," Pulie whispered back, wiping her tears.

"Yeah, I know." Ema shrugged. "I still don't believe you did though. CAOT are dangerous, Pulie."

Flashbacks of the man forced into the Corrector entered her mind again. She shook it away.

"I know." Was her dry reply.

"You're probably one of the few kids in this entire school who has seen one now. The actual CAOT group."

My parents were CAOT. Of course, I am!

"We should get back to the dance party… it's getting really late."

They reunited with Nicky down in the large party area. It wasn't looking pretty.

"Where were you guys?" Nicky said. "I was looking everywhere for you!"

Ema sighed. "We had to watch Rory pass away."

"Who is Rory?" Nicky said, with an odd look on her face.

"The Twig or preferably Rory Hanson."

Nicky shook her head but chugged a glass of fruit punch. Drinks and candies were selling by the palace walls. Mrs. Wapanog was handing out frosting puddings.

Night grew. People started to head back to their rooms, the music quieted and the colored lights grew dimmer. Most of the teachers had gone up to the Miralmalma, including Mr. Wace.

"Pulie, aren't you coming?" Nicky said, waving her over as the party men started to clean up. Pulie shook her head. "I have to go talk to Mr. Wace. See you later."

She found Piden waiting for her by the door.

"*So*, we're going to—*talk?*"

"Yes. Let's go."

***

"Who is it?" said a voice after Pulie knocked on Mr. Wace's room. Mr. Wace opened the door. He spotted the siblings, waiting nervously at his door-step.

"Ahh, I suppose I know… come in… I tidied it up yesterday." Mr. Wace said, opening the door wider. The two followed inside.

"You know what we came for?" Pulie asked, confused.

"Yes, Miss Jark. Sit down. I'll get you two a cup of tea. I know this talk will be a *long* one." Mr. Wace started pouring a hot liquid out of the kettle into the three little glass cups.

"Now… where shall we start?" he said, leaning on his rocking chair. "Ahh, I suppose the mission, right? The—" he paused. "Pulie, do you want to start?"

"Yes, sir," Pulie said, firmly.

"Start on what?" Piden asked.

Pulie plainly ignored him and said, "My first question. Did you know that my parents were in the CAOT job?"

"What?" Piden jerked his head up.

Mr. Wace ignored Piden as well. He sipped his cup of tea for a long time and seemed to ponder. "As a matter of fact, yes, I did."

Pulie's eyes opened wide. It was an unexpected answer. "But—"

"Now, now, I have reasons for everything." Mr. Wace held up his hand. "As you know, your parents are on the CAOT team. So have your grandparents before… and before them as well… your entire ancestry has been full of not necessarily CAOT, but of criminal blood." He paused. "Your parents did not tell you about the CAOT beforehand, knowing that if they did, one way or another, Master would find that your parents had children and would take both you and you to train. I am guessing your parents wanted you to decide and let you choose your own paths before that happened. But before the long trip, they both agreed that they'd tell you about it for the first time. And they decided that they'd let you know what their job is while they were gone. After a long time, they finally agreed that either way, you'd become a CAOT."

"So, I saved you. You are now not a part of the CAOT," he added.

Pulie glared at her hands. They were the only things that she could stare at instead of Mr. Wace's face.

Mr. Wace chortled. "Now, I must say, I had *no* idea they were in that dome. And no one knew that your parents were criminals… except me."

Piden opened his mouth to speak but was cut off.

"The Master still lives…" Mr. Wace said softly.

"What?" Pulie cried.

"Master? Who are we talking about?" Piden asked.

"Hold on, Piden."

"As I was saying. The Master still lives. She was escorted by her wanderers right before the third bomb exploded. But, all the secret memories and passwords were destroyed. All the secret plans and data were disabled. Thanks to us, the Trickies. And you may disagree, but I am not guilty of bringing you both here.

"Our foundation has the list of almost all of the CAOT members working for the association. We are trying to track them down, one by one. My search team detected a CAOT family, Natalie and Samuel Jark, living in an ordinary house in the middle of a remote and deserted area. When I discovered that there were children in this house, I was surprised. Your parents' files were clearly listed as childless. So, I stayed at the village hotel, which is not too far away from your estate. My team was preparing to invade your home but then I saw you two, sneaking around the village." Mr. Wace peered at the two. "I knew things had to be done. So they *were* done." He sat back in his chair. "That was a lengthy talk of mine if that was what you were here for. In addition, my apologies for saying that the CAOT *deserved* to die in the speech. It is a sensitive topic for you and I didn't realize it. But, what needs to be done, is done. They were not in the happiest nor righteous occupation. And Piden, let me explain." His face darkened.

Piden cringed into his seat, overwhelmed with ideas. "What is this about?"

"Pulie, do you wish to tell him?"

Pulie nodded, pursing her lips. She then took a deep breath.

"Our parents are CAOT—"

"What?"

"And they were inside the dome we bombed."

Piden's mouth hung open and his entire body froze until he clamped his hands over his ears. He glanced at Mr. Wace and Pulie. Then, he began to laugh.

"You got to be kidding me. I know what this is. It's another *prank*. Stop trying to trick me." He continued to chuckle. Pulie and Mr. Wace remained doleful and sordid, respectfully.

Piden stopped laughing. "What? It's real."

Mr. Wace spoke up, "Your sister, didn't follow the procedure do stay outside of the dome and entered the—"

"Pulie?"

"She saw her parents inside while she started the bombs. The place completely exploded after she escaped. But to add a bit of hope, they might still be alive."

"Wait a minute," Pulie interrupted, "How do *you* know all this? I never told anyone about what I saw inside."

"Your ConnecT accidentally connected to mine while talking to Daria and Celena. I hear muffled talking somewhere in my bag, and I realized it was my ConnecT. I thought you were calling for help, but when I listened, it was a conversation. I'm surprised the ConnecT even connected overseas."

"My parents?" Piden asked. He was beginning to tremble. "Ha! No, that's impossible. My parents are not CAOT. They are good people! You don't know this. Pulie, tell me he's lying."

Pulie stayed quiet.

"No!" Piden screamed, "This is a lie!"

Mr. Wace sat patiently, the steam of his coffee was fading.

"Pulie! You're a liar!" Piden hollered, pointing at her like a mad man. "You all are. And I'm dreaming!" He pinched himself.

"Please, Piden," Mr. Wace said softly.

"No!" Pulie glared, "You leave my brother alone! He can cry when he wants. He just lost his parents! You do not have the right—"

"Pulie—"

"It's a coincidence? I don't think so! Mr. Wace are you sure you didn't know my parents were in there? Answer honestly sir!" She shook her finger at him.

Mr. Wace closed his eyes and shook his head. "Pulie, I had no idea. And it's getting late. Tomorrow is a regular day, you shall remember—"

Pulie furrowed her brows. Anger was boiling inside her, searing her stomach and her throat. The boiling kettle was overflowing with steaming water.

"That's it? Of all this mission where I killed my own parents, and I am still stuck here? Did you think I'd actually stay here *right after* my parents just died? Well—"

"Please settle down—" Mr. Wace said.

"You lied to me! At the beginning of the year, you clearly said, that you had sorted everything out with my parents!"

Mr. Wace raised his hand, but Pulie went on, flickering her tongue.

"How would *you* feel if your parents died because some stranger was looking at your life and *decided* it was right and took you away so that you could kill your own parents without knowing? And that we didn't have a single clue what our parents were doing? How would you feel?" Pulie paused. "You clearly *said* in the beginning that you'd *take care* of it, but you didn't! But I bet you haven't noticed how down I am because nothing like this has ever happened in your own stupid life!"

Piden sat astonished, his eyes still glistening with tears, wide open.

"This one mission, this one tiny honor, this one stupid medal, and this one freaking ceremony, not even remembering my parents' death that no one cares about it? My parent's bodies are ashes in that dome I was told to blow up. And no one will ever know about their death, no one will ever make a funeral, or pray or whatever they do… they'll just sit in those ashes, forgotten, forever…" The more she talked, the more anger stacked up in her chest. "My parents were CAOT. But they were my parents. And now they're gone because of your *stupid* mission and your *stupid* thought process!" she roared. "Why was Master even in that palace? Mrs. Slendersan told us she wouldn't be there! She told us that it wouldn't be protected! Well, there's a nasty woman in that dome I nearly blew up whose out to slit my throat now! It wouldn't have mattered if I had stayed outside! This so-called intelligent palace and you and your stupid leader group can go start something real—that won't end up making an alligator eat a boy or have my parents blown up in a dome!"

"Pulie, please." Mr. Wace pleaded.

Pulie shook her head. "No. Please? What do you have to say? About the ceremony? My parents dying? I don't want to hear…" Pulie buried her face into her hands.

"Actually—" Mr. Wace took a deep breath. "Yes, it is about parents dying. In fact, all three of us *have* experienced this tragedy."

"I don't care." Pulie refused to listen.

Piden had not spoken in a long time. "What do you mean?" He asked Mr. Wace.

"I haven't told many kids, but—" the man paused. "My parents built this palace and they were the original owners of this palace. The original place was somewhere out there." Mr. Wace spread his fingers to picture a place beyond this palace. "But it was blown up… by the CAOT, of course. And so, we constructed another palace— here." Mr. Wace slid his hands down the walls of the room. "I was so happy as a young boy. I had everyone I needed. Until the Great Death… "

"What?" Piden perked up.

"It was a catastrophic event."

"Sounds like a fairy tale."

Mr. Wace ignored Pulie's comment and continued. "The Great Death was the period when each time someone left this palace, they would suddenly disappear or be found dead on the sidewalks of where ever they were headed at. No evidence was found. The leaders of the Tricky foundation assigned my parents to be the leaders of a mission to go and find evidence." Mr. Wace crumpled his fist. "Oh, and the council *knew* that there was no possibility of living— my parents were found dead near a lake. The council said they died of honor, but *oh,* I knew better than that."

Pulie had never seen Mr. Wace so angry.

"The council knew that each time they sent a scouting group *out* of these doors, they wouldn't return, ever. But they went on sending more and more, and my parents were chosen. Why? Because the rascals wanted to take the palace themselves! But I wasn't going to let that happen! I rose up and took my parents' spots. But along the way, we got Ms. Borthwick and Ms. Awolo. Both of them were the head council man's daughter and friend. The council continued… by the end of two years; over three hundred Trickies were dead. And fourteen of them were my family members."

"I'm sorry."

Mr. Wace waved his hands away. "No need. What I need you to understand is *that,* was the past. *Now,*" he pointed to his feet. "*Now,* is now. Now is when things are different than before. This school is to bring the beast out of you. And if I was wrong about bringing you two here, then please, don't hesitate to leave this palace at any moment. Normally, children aren't allowed to leave because they've seen too much. But this…" He drew a breath. "This was a mistake by me. You deserve better. So leaving at any point is completely normal. Just come and talk to me and we'll sort it out."

"So you didn't know my parents were in the dome?" Pulie asked, peering at him still.

"No."

"Well, I think it's time we go back to our rooms," Piden said, getting back up again. Everyone was standing up now.

"And Jarks?" Mr. Wace shifted uncomfortably in his spot. "Can we all promise one thing?"

"What?"

"Do not talk about this to *anyone*. We will figure this out soon. If you choose to leave, we will have you escorted back to your home and leave you there in peace. If you choose to stay, we will sort a couple of things out. But let's keep this a confidential meeting. We will all promise to not let a word of this talk slip from our lips."

They reached the doorstep of Mr. Wace's room.

"Wait a minute," Piden said. He rushed back in.

"Am I allowed to take these cookies?" Piden asked.

Mr. Wace grinned. "Please, take as many as you want."

And Piden took it *seriously*.

Pulie and Piden walked up together to their dorms. It was just like home, in a completely different place with completely different people.

"I guess you won the bet," Piden whispered.

Pulie shook her head. "No. I didn't win. You didn't win. Nobody won this time. I hate Mr. Wace and everyone here." She kicked a piece of stone as hard as she could. "They're all idiots. They all are. Mr. Wace doesn't understand anything. All he thinks about is—"

"Pulie?" Piden looked up at her with his large watering eyes. "What are we going to do now?"

"I don't know. Do you want to stay here?"

Piden shrugged. "Where else do we go?"

"Home." Pulie bit her lip. It sounded so unfamiliar.

"But we don't have anyone else there."

"Then, let's stay here until the school's over. We'll pack up after that."

"What will happen to us?" His face didn't show the fear he had in his voice. It quaked like a wave and drifted off.

"Everything. Everything is going to be alright."

Nothing was going to be alright…

But… something was strange. If the Master survived the incident, surely more than one person did as well? What if her parents weren't dead? After all, they were professional criminals. What if they weren't dead?

But false hope was worse than giving any hope at all.

"I don't believe it, Pulie. I don't believe any of this. Why didn't you tell me before?"

"I didn't believe it either."

NEW DAY

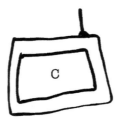

It was a normal day besides the fact that they were in a very abnormal place full of very abnormal people. The showers were crammed like always. Pulie found a fake cobweb in her shower stall, but she didn't succumb to her humor nor her dread. And instead, she left the web in the exact place, untouched for the next person, believing it too laborious to switch it up. She was just too disconcerted.

After they consumed their breakfast, they headed on over to Mrs. Wapanog's class. Each time Pulie examined the glass dome from a range, she fidgeted and remembered the glass dome ablaze in the snow, burning and collapsing. She shook away the vision, although it proved formidable.

"I heard about your leg, Pulie. What happened?" Mrs. Wapanog asked.

"It was cut during the mission."

"I trust you're feeling alright. Roll call!" She barked. Everyone scooted into a line.

"Welcome, we are switching seats," she said and expected some loud groaning from her pupils.

"Santiago Gomez, right here. Then, Ema Rafferty, Eleanor Gray, and Olivia Powell. Behind them will sit Pulie Jark, then Colin Strussmore, Livia Gulgorin, Nicky Oster, Dunkin Boar. Next row, Everly Green, right here! Then Hugo Hastings, Albert Leonardo, Travis Willa, Orla Agatha Margery, Tom Clay, Dash Dupupboir, Bonnie Johns, Fiona March, Lane Remington, Anne Truo, Terrance Kadi, Lulu Wong, Selma Dutchstill, Adrian Bonita, Oliver McCarson, Orson Logan, and Daniel—" Mrs. Wapanog halted. "Twenty-six here today…"

"Attention, students." Mrs. Wapanog whacked her ruler onto her desk and looked at them. Pulie was still very tired from the conversation the night before.

"The leaders have issued the need for the learning of Rangs. It was very useful and helped execute the mission successfully. We all now think it is important for even Junior Trickies to learn it at this age. Come get your gloves. Thirty seconds. After that, pair up with the person to your right."

Everyone left their seats and prepared for the task. There were murmurs. No second-level students were ever taught how to use Rangs. Pairs pushed their desks together and placed a lab mat on top of their table.

"There are many types of Rangs. Terrance, stop staring at Everly. Turn around. Okay, now let us begin. There are many types of Rangs. Two main groups have evolved from the original Rang that was biologically engineered from a Pipus Vine: terrestrial and aquatic. In the terrestrial group, there is the Common Green, Veneciti's Blue, and the Albino Green Rang. Remember, the Albino Green Rang has a false name. Its original color is white but it is not an albino. Our bomber used the Common Green Rang during the mission and it is the species we will be using today. We won't go over the Aquatics today. So let's begin our activity."

Mrs. Wapanog brought out a ginormous jar of black seeds. She screwed open the lid, and a repugnant smell floated out the top. Everyone groaned.

"I know this smell isn't *pleasant*," Mrs. Wapanog stated.

"It smells terrible!" Dunkin croaked, then smacking his face onto the floor. Mrs. Wapanog rolled her eyes.

"Anyone know why these smell so horrifying?"

Everyone shook their heads.

"It is the formula in the jar," Mrs. Wapanog answered right away as if she knew nobody would know.

"The Formula is the chemical compound that is mixed in with the vines when they are young. It keeps the plant alive with no soil or water."

"So they aren't creatures themselves?" Orla asked.

Mrs. Wapanog shook her head. "As I said, they were biologically engineered. But they are living organisms. Anyways, these are the baby Rangs about to sprout. *But,* they require *your* help to do it. Everyone, please remain patient. Will somebody come up and distribute the seeds?" she asked.

Everyone was silent, still pinching their noses.

"Fine then," Mrs. Wapanog yapped, "I will do it *myself.*" She slipped on thick gloves and placed a seed on each of their mats.

"Gross." Pulie heard much say. The tiny black seed made such a putrid smell enough to fog the whole dome. When Pulie received hers, she clamped her palm about her nose, squinting at the miniature seed.

"Enough with the complaining!" Mrs. Wapanog shouted, slapping her ruler onto her desk. It was silent.

"Please take excellent care of what you're doing. The first step, *never* spit onto a Rang seed."

A few moments after, Pulie heard a loud scream from across the room. It was Dunkin. Spit was dribbling from his chin. Ivy-like vines sprouting from the tiny seed weaved through his arms and twisted his throat. His legs were intertwined with the thick emerald plants.

"Help me!" he shrieked, trying to run, but the vines held him still.

Mrs. Wapanog rushed to him, bringing a knife, and she chopped the seed in half. The vines' growth ceased, but the ends of the Rangs still squeezed onto Dunkin's body as hard as they could.

"Help," he gasped. Mrs. Wapanog then yanked the vines out one by one. Finally, she freed him from the grasp of the plant.

"Those monsters..." he croaked, "Those wretched monsters..."

"They are plants. You're the monster," Mrs. Wapanog castigated. "Bring him to the treatment unit." Mrs. Wapanog pointed to Santiago, who obediently hauled the Boar boy out of the room.

Everyone froze in their spots while Mrs. Wapanog dusted her hands.

"*That* was lesson Number One. Never spit on a Rang. Common Greens were biologically engineered and created for almost instantaneous growth when touched with a liquid." she said calmly. "Everyone back to your seats, Hugo, stop pretending to throw up now. Everyone, study your seed with the person next to you."

Pulie did not want to end up like Dunkin.

"Mrs. Wapanog?" Someone asked. "Are we allowed to touch the seed?"

"That is an absolutely good question. This vine is not to be watered. A single drop of moisture will make it grow. Spit is one of the most effective of liquids. Therefore, the Rang starts to think like it has a mind of its own. Everyone who wants to touch it *must* make sure their hands are dry. Understood?"

Everyone nodded.

Pulie and Colin were partners.

"We *can* touch it," Pulie said.

Colin just stared at the seed with a very sordid expression.

"Colin." Pulie waved her hand in front of him.

"Yeah?"

"Are you okay?"

Colin sighed and shook his head. He looked so exhausted. His lower lip trembled.

"Colin?"

"I'm okay. I'm okay."

Pulie rubbed her forehead. What could she do? He looked so miserable. He needed some rest.

"Go get some rest, Colin." Pulie pushed the tray with the seed to her side. "Go tell Mrs. Wapanog you're going to get some rest."

"It doesn't work that way, Pulie. I can't lose credit."

"Then, I'll just do the work," Pulie said. "Go up to her and tell her you're going to take a break today."

Colin flinched but did not budge from his seat.

"Colin. Go."

Still, Colin remained seated.

"Colin. If you do not go, I will spit on this rang and throw the tray at you. You don't want to end up like Dunkin, do you?"

Colin gave her a weak smile. "You know that's not how it works. The Rang could attack you too."

"Don't argue with me. I spent all my mission training with these vines. Now go."

Colin stared down at the floor and sighed. He got up and slung his bag over his shoulder.

"Thank you."

After he talked to Mrs. Wapanog, the room door shut behind him.

"Pulie? You will be demonstrating today to fulfill your partner's credit as well." Mrs. Wapanog beckoned Pulie to come up to the front. Pulie set her tray up on the desk.

"Touch the Rang seed."

Everyone in the class watched her.

Pulie had already touched a Rang so it wasn't a big deal. *Well, with a glove—and it wasn't a seed. It was a grown Rang...* Pulie thought.

She made sure her hands were dry and reached forwards. The seed felt cool against her finger. But, it also felt slimy. It had looked shiny yet the feeling was grimy and gooey. It was as if it was coated in a fine layer of liquid paste. It was so small, however, but the feeling was strangely satisfying.

"How did it feel?" Mrs. Wapanog asked. Pulie answered it.

"It was slimy and cold, and—" Pulie shuddered. "It felt weird."

Mrs. Wapanog nodded. "Now, our next project is growing a live Rang, starting with your seeds. You will use the seed and create a Rang. The points for today and tomorrow will be based on how well your Rang grows and acts. Then you will start to train with one. *Tomorrow*, we will start the experiment. But, for now, one person from each partnership, come here and place the seed gently in these jars. Make sure to write your name on your jar. Let's go, let's go! We don't have much time! Hurry up."

***

"Today, we are going to learn about a little more ambush!" Señor Rodriguez said at the front of the room. "I am going to bring out my boxes of weaponry. I warn you not to *touch* or *use* unless I give you permission." He raised his eyebrows. "If I see anyone touching anything, they will immediately be suspended from classes for two weeks."

The door creaked open. Santiago and Dunkin appeared. Santiago helped Dunkin into his seat. Dunkin's face was puffy and red, his arms wrapped in band-aids. He stared at his desk quietly.

"I will explain the lesson for today to you too, but first, let's pull these weapons out!" Señor Rodriguez said, he stepped onto his desk and jumped onto the ladder near his desk, and he went skidding on his ladder on his box shelf until he stopped at a certain point. Wobbling on one foot, twenty feet in the air on a flimsy ladder, he balanced on his arms a stack of cardboard boxes.

"Someone, catch this box if I drop it." He pulled out two more. They were regular cardboard boxes, ones embedded with many letters and scribbles of a deep inky sharpie—the ones with many ragged edges and torn tape poking out on all sides. But what mattered were the wonders lay inside.

When Señor Rodriguez climbed down from his ladder, he pulled out his glasses and examined the boxes on his desk. He blew a heap of dust into the air as he smoothed the top of the box.

"This is the box of gadgets. While many may use guns or swords, we like our technology to help us. Our society has been developing faster than we ever expected." He slid open the lid of the box and brought out a strange-looking object with many loops and rings around the top of the gadget and a digital pad in the center.

"The Travegator, or the heat sensor. It is powerful enough to detect heat through heavy material and even walls."

"Why would we need to detect heat?" Bonnie asked.

"To find hidden people hiding in certain places. It's quite useful when you're surrounded by spies." Señor Rodriguez answered, "But, other than that, it's more of an antique than a tool."

He pulled out another object.

"This, my friends, is the ConnecT tool. Very useful for missions; lightweight; and easy connection with other ConnecT. It is very advanced and is also equipped with a timer and thermometer. I know the mission group stopped by here before the mission to borrow these. That's how important they are. Some of you might receive one."

He continued, pulling out stranger and stranger objects that Pulie had never seen.

"Most of these gadgets are not given to students because they should not be handled without care. But danger can be useful to us sometimes."

He pulled out the Googles, highly advanced glasses that could zoom in and out from a distance, allowing the bearer to see far away. There were gloves that would imitate another person's hands once you put them on; every fingerprint and wrinkle. There were also these inflatable wrist pads that the pads would blow up and break whatever was around your wrist if you were handcuffed. There were blow darts shooters, hairbands with arrows, boots that locked on the ground, and so on. Pulie had never had that much fun, and it was a sad time when Señor Rodriguez had to put them all away.

"Let's give our brains a break with some television. But, *pay attention*," he said sternly.

The television buzzed black and white. It was a little movie about a cartoon. It wasn't interesting, but Pulie obeyed and watched closely. Then, the screen flickered, and the screen turned blank for a split second. Pulie rolled her eyes. It was an old TV, after all. But, something caught her eye. In the center of the flickering screen, she squinted hard enough that she could see a tiny letter. An *M*. Pulie pondered why a tiny letter would be in the center of the screen. In a split second, the letter was gone. She looked around. Most of the people weren't paying attention. She sat up in her seat and continued to observe for a glitch. Then, she saw another letter again. This time, there were two, however. Two *E's*. Pulie grabbed a pen out of her bag and scribbled it onto her hand. The ink seeped into her skin. She looked up, then again, there was a letter. It was a *T*, this time. It happened again and again. Finally, after the movie was done, Pulie had letters all over her palm. She looked at them.

MEETMEAFTERCLASSQUIETLY.

She made a face but spelled the words out until she created sentences.

Meet me after class quietly.

That's why Señor Rodriguez had told them to pay attention with such emphasis before the movie—there was a hidden message in the video itself. Pulie wondered if anyone else could see the mysterious letters.

The bell rang again. Most of the class bolted out. Three people remained sitting in their seats, besides Nicky and Ema, who were waiting by the door for Pulie to come. The three people were Santiago, Lulu, and Pulie. They all glanced at each other with *you-knew-too?* expressions on their faces.

"The rest of you, please come to me." Señor Rodriguez said, beckoning them to his desk. He handed them each a bag.

"But we didn't know about this," Ema said, pointing to both her and Nicky.

Señor Rodriguez shrugged. "Thank you for your honesty; therefore, each of you gets a prize bag. They each have a free ConnecT in them. Thank you for *paying* attention," he said.

"Oh, thank you!" Nicky exclaimed. "Mrs. Slendersan didn't let us keep ours from the mission, but I really wanted them!"

"Don't ConnecT's cost *a lot*?" Santiago asked.

Señor Rodriguez tugged on his mustache, "Do you think anything in here doesn't cost a lot?" Señor grinned. "Now go on, to whatever class you're going to, the bell's ringing in like a minute. Thank you for participating!"

Everyone started sprinting. They didn't want to be late.

When Pulie, Nicky, and Ema reached Ms. Cherry's Zive, they went to the locker rooms and changed into their EP clothes. Then, they hurried into the gym.

"Welcome class," Miss Cherry exclaimed. "I haven't seen *many of you* in a while, but we'll start anyway. I'll start checking for miserableness." She began to check off the names of people in the class.

Today, she wore baby blue leggings, a loose top shirt, and flip flops. Her hair was still wet from a recent shower.

"Ahh, okay, anyone with health problems, sprained knees, swollen hands…"

Pulie and Ms. Cherry met eyes for a split second that seemed too long. Inside of her, Pulie gasped. Ms. Cherry looked startled when she turned back to the class, as well.

Perhaps it was the look on my face. Pulie shivered. There something so familiar about Miss Cherry's face. Pulie grasped at her memory, trying to remember who it was.

That's it. Miss Cherry looked exactly like Master—with less makeup and happier.

That's strange.

Was Miss Cherry a CAOT, too? Pulie began to think. She looks just like one. Much prettier. But she could be disguised.

Pulie narrowed her eyes at the woman. If Miss Cherry was a spy, then her position was perfect. Surrounded by information every day, surrounded by Trickies every day.

"Today is a fun day. Nothing hard." Ms. Cherry's voice cut through the loud drumming of the seats and the yelling across the room.

"Everyone here knows by now the Leaping Bar practice that I have shown you on the first day of school. Today, there will be no running and no jumping around. We'll simply play a very common sport down at schools, called soccer. Everyone, get into groups of fourteen and line up on this line!" she hollered. "Oh, and Pulie?" Ms. Cherry said, "If you feel that this isn't going to work with your leg, just tell me, okay?" she asked. Pulie nodded, politely although it was difficult not to lower her brow.

She was CAOT for sure. She was athletic, beautiful, and what was the other one? Oh, accepted. She was definitely one of them.

"Okay, people with the red jerseys, you are the guest team. The ones without jerseys, you guys are the home team. Let's go, you boys, against this group. This will be the first round. Come on! Ready, the game begins, Now!" Ms. Cherry blew the whistle.

The two groups stumbled as they tried kicking the ball across the court.

"Next team!" Ms. Cherry blew the whistle again.

The next two teams went on against each other, kicking as hard as they could. The goalies tried catching the drifting ball, but it hit their faces instead. Ms. Cherry did *not* look impressed.

"Next team!" Ms. Cherry cried again, the whistleblowing in everyone's ears.

Pulie stumbled out onto the field, limping on her lame leg. She was in the offense. She remembered soccer with her family. As Nicky passed the ball to her, Pulie dribbled the ball forwards, carefully swerving past the other team players, her wounded leg dragged behind the other. Then, she passed the ball to Nicky again, who tried shooting through the goal. The goalie kicked the ball high into the air. Pulie sprinted back, trying to get her head aligned with the ball. Then, a loud crack sound echoed through her head. The ball landed square on her head. She had stopped the ball. She continued dribbling. The pain in her limbs throbbed. All she could hear were the loud cheering and booing of the rest of the crowd. She leaped forwards, making sure the ball was in the middle of her foot, and she kicked with all her might.

The ball went fizzling towards the goalie's face and it knocked her over. The ball didn't make the goal. Then, Nicky came running over and tapped the ball and sent it rolling into the goal. The crowd cheered wildly. Ema came to high five them both as they headed to their seats. That was the final goal until lunch started. They had won. Five to Four.

Next was Mr. Eerie, the Imitation teacher. She had forgotten how his class rolled because of the mission preparation, and she was quite glad she was going back to normal, except that she was sitting right next to Selma.

"Welcome, class, and classes, and so forth," he shouted, as everyone got into their seats. "Welcome to Imitations again and again and again and again and—"

"*We* get it, alright!" Selma said, slamming her hand onto her seat. Mr. Eerie looked hurt.

"Very well then," he continued. "Today, we will practice voice imitations. We've all done it before, so it won't be too difficult."

Today, he was dressed as a doctor, with a vest, a headband with the red cross, a clipboard, baggy pants, nice trimmed shoes, and a kit of medical instruments.

"What's with the clothes?" Fiona asked.

Mr. Eerie smiled. "These? These are my grandmother's medical clothes! Anyways, everyone line up here. Choose a character from this chart. You will have to imitate it. Anyone joking around will lose points on their grade."

Mr. Eerie went around to everyone in line, letting them choose a character.

These voice imitations had to be good. Your voice had to in the same wave and the same scratchy or smooth accent as your character.

Santiago was SpongeBob, but his voice went too low at the end when he tried to say, "Hey Patrick!"

"Minus two points, Santiago. Please try harder."

Others did worse or did better, but no one got a perfect score but Bonnie. She was known to have a varied voice, and she had the most points in Imitations.

When Pulie was up, she tried to imitate Hermione Granger from her favorite book.

Mr. Eerie shook his head disappointedly. Her points on the LeaderBoard had just dropped by ten points.

"This is my worst class," Pulie muttered to Ema as they walked back to their desks.

"Same. Just can't wait till my parents see how far down I am in the LeaderBoard." Ema rolled her eyes.

"It's no big deal this year, Ema. It's just practice."

"Yeah, but if I do this bad in practice, how bad am I going to do when I'm a Tricker next year?" Ema blew into the air with a huff, her brows slimming into a V.

Mr. Eerie saluted and took a bow, then sashaying out the back door while the familiar ticking sound ringed in the student's ears. The walls were changing.

The ceiling allowed slight cracks on all four sides of the perfect square for the shelves to slip through and replaced the room with new decors. The process was fast, rickety, and a miracle.

A man walked in with a rush and erupted into a ginormous sneeze.

"Welcome, zerverywan, I vas having a cold over zis time, and I am ztill very sick. Please excuze me soft voice." He coughed. "Let'z begin the lesson. Today, ve will practice voga. Help me move tese desks to ze side of ze room. Hurry Zeveryone!" Mr. Lizarstrang clapped his hands. The ailment had caused his voice to go even lower.

Everyone got up and pushed the little desks to the side of the room. Mr. Lizarstrang placed mats everywhere on the floor.

"Zu may sit whereever zu vants, however, be a good ztudent," he said. Pulie, Ema, and Nicky moved closer to each other like magnets.

"A one, a two, a three. Lay down quietly zon your mats, as I turn soft music zon. Lie down calmly and softly, breath zin and zout. For vevery movement, I vill deduct ten class points. This is the healthy art of practicing breathing and playing dead."

Pulie took a deep breath and exhaled. It felt so relaxing. The classroom lights were off, and it was silent besides the faint music that played in the back. Pulie's eyes drifted to sleep.

Memories.

Screaming. CAOT faces. Their bloody lips and large eyes. Suddenly, her parents' faces took place in one of the faces. *It was your daughter who burned down my building. Both you and your child will pay the price...* Master would hiss. *Do you have another child? Is there another secret you keep to yourself? Say it or I will kill you...* Her mother screamed, *No, I do not! You will never find my daughter. She is safe from you...*

"Pulie, vake up," A voice whispered. Someone was shaking her. It was Mr. Lizarstrang.

Pulie opened her eyes and continued to tremble.

Mr. Lizarstrang pulled her out of the classroom into the halls of the Zive.

"Pulie, vou just screamed the heck vout of the classroom. And vou nearly got vourself a hundred points deducted. Vou cracked my lamp. And vou sleep valked around zhe classroom. I'm very surprised vou didn't step on a student's face. Vhat is going on?"

"I—" Pulie stuttered, "I sleepwalk on a daily basis."

Which was true back home. But ever since she moved into high hammocks, she trained herself not to move so much.

Mr. Lizarstrang raised his eyebrows.

"I'm sending vou to zhe Miralmalma. Go see Mr. Wace. I have a slip for vou."

**

"Pulie, what in the world are you doing here in the middle of class?" Mr. Wace asked.

Pulie shrugged.

"Nicky must be a bad influence." Mr. Wace scratched his head. "What happened?"

Pulie told him about her nightmare.

"I fear this is just a symptom of death." Mr. Wace sighed.

"I'm going to die?"

Mr. Wace rolled his eyes. "No. I know you are going through abstruse times. When a loved one passes away, this is what happens. It happened to me, only I didn't sleepwalk, nor scream, nor crack my teacher's lamp."

"So, we're not compatible," Pulie added.

Mr. Wace set out a chair for two, as he stroked his long mustache of silver intertwined with brown.

"I wasn't going to ask you this so soon, Pulie. However, are you capable of telling me what you really saw in the dome?"

Pulie reluctantly explained everything.

"The Corrector?" Mr. Wace looked very confused, "This is far much more different than what I had imagined. I can tell it was quite shocking for you as well. I couldn't believe it either when I was notified that Master herself was at the location. It was a very bold decision from the Tricky Foundation to send young students directly to her. Well, I guess, they too did not know."

"Yes. And those bloody faces… they're masks… right?"

Mr. Wace shook his head, "Not all of them. The lower CAOT get masks. The more trained CAOT change their faces."

"So my parents were—"

"No, they are different. Very high status. They were too trained and skilled, they got an option. Just like everything else. Living away from the rest. Keeping their children away from the rest. Hiding all their secrets from everyone else."

Pulie hesitated to ask about Ms. Cherry. It would be rude to accuse her if she wasn't, but at this point, she was very sure.

"Mr. Wace? I also saw one of those faces once when I was training." Pulie squinted her eyes. *Why did you say that?* Her mouth refused to listen. "I was in the mission room near the window and I saw the same face on a body walking around behind the Miralmalma."

Mr. Wace made a face. "I'm sure it was a hallucination—"

"No, Mr. Wace! It wasn't! I saw it with my own eyes."

"It was a CAOT face?" Mr. Wace questioned.

"Yes."

"Interesting— I will go through our staff. But on the other side, maybe you should get more sleep."

"No! I swear it wasn't —"

Mr. Wace smiled, standing up. "I'll have a research teamwork on that. Good day, Pulie Jark."

***

Lights flickered on and everyone moaned.

"That felt so relaxing," Ema said, stretching and yawning. The bright light all of a sudden made it worse.

"Thank zou, the bell zis zabout to ring. Have za good day!" Mr. Lizarstrang said as he waved. Pulie was sitting on the high stool because she couldn't participate.

"Pulie, what are you doing there?" Ema asked, skipping around.

"I was sleepwalking and lost points." Pulie groaned.

Nicky laughed, pointing at Pulie, but then quickly stopped. "It's alright. Remember, he told us there'd be another try on this next week."

"Yes, it's just that, my name went down the LeaderBoard by seven."

"Did you count Mission points? It's an automatic forty plus! Even if it went down by seven, add forty to your points and that boosts you up to another eight. I believe so? If that wasn't there, I'd say I would be in the low hundreds. What were you dreaming about?"

Pulie paused. *I can't tell them about my dream.*

"Scary demons chasing me around the school," was the answer instead.

"I hate those chasing dreams," Nicky said as she shivered. "There's always so many other people but they always chase me!"

They were the last ones out of the classrooms. Pulie saw Larry's house standing in the far corner of the courtyard, deserted.

"What happened to Larry?"

Nicky frowned. "What do you mean?"

"Remember? We believed it wasn't him."

"Oh yeah," Nicky said suddenly. It was like an electric zap trickled up to her brain. "It was a bit suspicious. I'm kind of surprised that none of the teachers thought that too. They're so skilled and everything. How would they not know?"

"Yeah." Ema scratched her chin. "That's weird. What should we do?"

"No, no." Pulie said, "Where should we start?"

THE DETECTIVES

They were lying on their carpet back in their room.

"Larry's crime wasn't the only strange thing that happened, though," Ema said. "There was the poisoning."

"What poisoning?" Nicky asked.

Ema paused. "Remember that day, both Pulie and I were up in the Miralmalma and you woke up in the morning alone?"

"Yeah?"

"I didn't fall off the hammock. I opened a jar delivered to our room when it cracked. The liquid spread all over my hands and they turned green. I didn't tell you because the package had your name on it."

"What?"

Ema explained the package directed to Nicky.

"Probably my aunt," Nicky muttered.

"Your aunt?"

Nicky shook her head. "Just a joke! But there *was* a rumor that my aunt came into my room once when I was a baby in a crib. She tried to kill me with a knife. *Well*, she was discovered in my bedroom with a knife, so they assumed an assault, had her sent away completely. My family is overprotective."

"But that means it can't be your aunt because she's far away. And you live right here."

"It was just a joke."

"Could be Selma, though. She's always trying to kill us."

"I don't know. Larry seems to pull me from all edges. It was strange in every way you look at it. Larry is the main suspect of the crime so far. But Mr. Wace requested a trial because he believed that if it truly was Larry, he wasn't alone. So, Larry isn't in the factory yet, right?" Ema asked.

"Not yet."

"But if Larry was in a temporary prison, guarded and supervised, who stole my evidence and my camera?"

"You're right. Either he hand an accomplice or another person framed him."

"We need to know whether Larry did it and if he did— why? Where should we investigate first?"

"The shop," Pulie said.

"The what?" Ema and Nicky said in unison.

Pulie retold the story of her touching the picture frame and setting off an alarm while trying to steal the key.

"But what does that have to do with Larry?" Ema asked.

Pulie shrugged. "We don't have a place to start. And it was the first thing that happened."

***

Cling! The tiny golden shop bells clanged against each other when the door opened. The shop was still buzzing with students.

"We just need to get inside there." Pulie pointed down the dark hall.

"All clear," Nicky mumbled in her breath. They slipped behind the back shelf and crept down the halls, trying to be as light as possible with their squeaky shoes.

"We should use our *new* ConnecT," Ema suggested as she slapped the gadget on her wrist.

"Look! That's the room." Pulie pointed to the room on their left.

Ema nodded. "We *need* a plan," she said softly.

Nicky shook her head. "Who needs plans? We have our *instincts*!" She karate-chopped the air. "And besides, this lady isn't dangerous or anything. If she catches us, we'll just be like, '*We got lost.*'"

"In the hallway?" Ema raised her eyebrow. "Yeah, right. Now, what's the plan?"

Pulie pondered for a moment. "Two people can slip in and look around while the other stays on guard."

"Good plan, now let's get moving," Nicky said, pushing forward.

"But we need an executive plan like the mission—" Ema stopped.

There were clunking and sounds of keys jangling down in the far doorway.

"Come on! Someone might find us." Pulie said. "Slip inside. No one's in the office."

One by one, like mice in a cupboard, squeezing through the doorway, they slipped inside the office and shut the door in utter silence. However, the floor seemed to be a piano keyboard, ringing on every step on the tile floor.

"She likes country music… she likes to dance… her favorite animal is a trombone…" Nicky read off the walls.

"That's not even an animal." Ema pointed out as she shuffled through the papers on the desk. "What are we even doing here?" she asked.

"Because of this," Pulie said, pointing to the painting with the picture frame.

"What is it? Is it because it's so dusty in here?" Nicky coughed as she spit out a cobweb she had found flying in the air.

"Looks like she's *not* on a diet." Nicky pointed to the desk. Dozens of wrappers from burgers and chips lay scattered everywhere. On her desk was the security computer.

"Ema, do your hacking magic," Nicky commanded.

Ema sat by the desk and began to type on the computer. She was finally able to log in.

"Look!" Ema said. "If you click this icon, it takes you to this security camera area."

"We're getting distracted," Pulie said. "This painting is an alarm. I touched it—I merely brushed my finger against it—and it started beeping. What kind of painting beeps when you touch it?"

"The Mona Lisa," Nicky said. "Pulie, come over here! When was the day of the crime?" Nicky asked, clicking on some videos.

"There!" Ema pointed to the screen of a row of clips.

Pulie finally came over to look.

It was there—the row of clips from the whole day of the incident.

"Start from the morning. Four in the morning."

Ema stared hard at the screen. There was nobody but the paint workers working on the wall murals outside.

"Next clip," Nicky said. Ema clicked to the next time frame. It was six in the morning.

Teachers were starting to walk to their classrooms. But nothing suspicious.

They went through all the morning and the afternoon clips. Nothing strange. But it was hard to catch anybody doing anything strange because it was always packed with people.

"Look! We're right there!" Ema pressed the screen. "We're running to the Miralmalma. That was so scary!" she exclaimed, zooming in. It was a funny sight, seeing the three fleeing for their lives. They continued swiping through videos until the page would no longer load any more files. It was the end.

"Wait—" Ema fell back into the rolly chair. "That's it, that was the last clip of the day."

They stood there, confused.

"Oh yeah, they moved the field for evidence. For the investigation."

"Oh, I forgot about the investigation. We aren't the only ones interested in what happened."

"Remember, Señor Rodriguez said that even the videos were too dark to detect any movement."

A female voice hollered outside the door. "You got a loose running animal? Got it, I'll check it right now."

"Oh no!" Ema squeaked, "Quick, where do we go?"

"Run?" Nicky suggested. Pulie's sweat dripped on the tiles and she saw her reflection and the ceiling behind her.

Pulie shook her head. "She'll catch us, our best option is to hide somewhere and *make* sure we don't get caught."

The door opened with the sound of a key jingle.

"Honey Guacamole, I must've forgotten to lock the door," the woman said, collapsing on the spinny chair.

She scrolled through the security camera. "And I forgot to shut off the computer! Silly me," she said to herself, pulling up a clip. She spoke into her walkie talkie.

"Yes, it looks like a bloodhound. What in the world would that dog be doing here?" she said. She listened and nodded. "Alright, I'll try."

Then, the door slammed shut.

"Whew, close call, thanks for the shoes", Nicky said, sliding onto the floor. Ema had found pairs of odd shoes called Mucilage Shoes with suction cups on the bottoms. Using the ladder on the shelf, they climbed up, and stuck to the ceiling, hoping the lady would not turn around and look up.

"No problem. *And* I stole these," Ema said, pulling out three digital notepads.

"What's for?" Nicky asked, taking one.

"We need to write everything we know about Larry. We're getting to the bottom of this."

"Okay, okay, so let's write down the weird things that happened," Nicky said, plopping onto the floor, and starting to type on her device. "Well, there was the poisoning, Larry incident, Pulie's painting alarm, and what else?"

"My missing *camera*," Pulie said, writing the events down as well onto her notes.

Ema nodded, "Yes, *her camera*."

"It just disappeared that night. Someone must've crept into our room."

Ema gasped.

"What is it?" Nicky asked. Ema pointed to a yellow sticky note on the wall. It was a little sticky note, with the phrase: Love is Aways the Right way to go when You are having Rough times.

"What's wrong?" Nicky asked again, "It's a beautiful sentence."

Pulie figured out the clue before her other companion. "Look at the capital letters."

Nicky squinted. "Laryr? Doesn't make any sense—" Nicky paused. "Oh. So it might be the woman who was working here, the woman who just came in here! *She* probably has something to do with Larry!!"

"I saw her nameplate, it was Ania Delgado, I think…" Ema's voice trailed off.

Pulie shook her head. "She isn't the only woman who works here. Last time, the woman I saw was much more—" Pulie pulled her hands out to the sides, "Much larger… How do we know which one is which?"

"Well, she could've gone on a diet," Ema said. "Or, maybe you're right. Multiple people just work here, but *I* think it's this woman, Ania Delgado." Ema wrote the name down onto her tablet. "Hey, this is getting kind of interesting," she said, smiling. Then, they heard a loud rip sound.

"Nicky!"

Nicky froze as she ripped the yellow sticky note off the wall. "Sorry, I need evidence!" she said, taking a picture of the small piece of evidence on her device and setting it back on the wall. "And detectives *need* evidence."

"Good, okay, now, what do we do?" Pulie asked.

"We should tell Mr. Wace."

"About what? That someone framed Larry? Most of the evidence is already pointing *to* Larry."

"But then why would they take away my camera *and* the note that I found on Larry's desk when Larry was being taken care of?" Pulie asked, her mind getting heavy.

Ema hesitated. 'Well, that *is* a point, but couldn't it just be the janitor who *happened* to sweep Pulie's—"

"Camera into the trash? No way. Someone probably framed Larry!" Nicky shouted.

"Shhhhh!" Ema and Pulie said at once.

"Sorry."

"Everyone, back to the painting. It's an alarm." Pulie pointed to the painting.

"Are you sure, Pulie? It seems like an ordinary painting," Ema said.

Pulie shook her head, "Not when you touch it. Last time you guys sent me in here for the key, I tapped the frame, and a whole siren went off."

"Maybe it's just to keep children like us out. But I also think we should go to Mr. Wace." Nicky said, peering out the door.

"Why?"

"Just follow me." Nicky shushed them. By now, Pulie knew Nicky wouldn't explain anything about her plan when she was excited.

***

"Mr. Wace!" Nicky greeted the leader, who was scrubbing the dishes in the backroom of the cafeteria. The smell of grapefruit bubble dish soap clouded her nostrils.

"We just wanted to ask a question," Nicky told Mr. Wace who was still focused on washing the dishes.

"*We* did?" Pulie nudged Ema and whispered.

Mr. Wace wiped his hands on the towels and placed his apron on the counter. "Go ahead."

"When is the trial for Larry?"

Mr. Wace made a face. "Are you guys *up* to something?" he asked.

"No, we just wanted to know what has happened to him. Nicky's family knows Larry very well," Ema said, quickly.

"I thought I did too. Very well then, the trial is on the first of February. Only a couple of days from now. Did I answer your question?"

"Yes."

Then Nicky dragged her two friends out of the eating room and straight to the Miralmalma.

"Here, again? Are we going to prank Selma again?"

They were in the computer lab. Ema sank into the chair.

"Nicky, why are we here?"

"Ema, I need you to do something that might get us in trouble."

"What?" Ema peered at Nicky.

"The Trial is on the first of February. That means we have four days to prepare."

"For what?"

"We need to watch what happens during the trials."

Pulie tilted her head. "I thought the trials happened in some other place."

"They do. That's why we have Ema."

"So—what do you want me to do?" Ema asked.

Nicky bit her lip. "I need you to hack into surveillance. We need to be able to see from here what goes on at the other place through a camera. No doubt there are security cameras at every angle in the room where it happens. We just need to hack into one. Can you do this?"

Ema drummed her fingers against the table, calculating something in the air.

"I don't know. But we got to try. But first, *can* we please eat dinner, I'm starving!" Ema groaned, clutching her stomach as if she were going to faint.

"Fine, let's get this dying cat out of here," Nicky said, pushing Ema in her chair as if she were a suitcase.

"Hey!" Ema retorted, trying to tackle Nicky. All three of them began chasing each other.

"The last one to get to the eating room is a *Selma!*"

The three ran as fast as they could.

UNSETTLE

Pulie awoke in an empty room. Ema had gone up to the computer lab alone while Nicky was talking to cameras with Señor Rodriguez.

She decided to go to her brother's room and see what they were up to. She rapped her knuckles against the door. Two sleepy boys peeked through the crack in the door.

"Who? Oh, come in," the yawning voices answered.

Inside was a landfill of putrid-smelling things. Piles of trash overflowing from the trash bags, their clothes like a red velvet carpet leading wherever they went. It was a junkyard with a smelly stench.

"What happened?" Pulie pointed to the mess.

Alex shook his head, "What? The messy room part? Oh, it's called BLS."

"Being Lazy Sometimes," Piden added.

Pulie rolled her eyes. "You can't just leave your rooms this messy! What happens if—"

"A hippopotamus barges into the room and destroys everything here?" Alex said. "Oh, don't worry, that will not happen.

Hippopotamuses cannot climb the entrance vines, nor be able to track our room successfully."

"Well, I know that. But aren't you bothered by the stenches and the way you have to tiptoe across the room because there's so much—" She stared at the object. A molding sock.

Alex and Piden shook their heads and gawked at her like she had asked the stupidest question. Soon after, they disappeared under their blankets.

"Hello?" Pulie was beginning to feel sick. "It's almost breakfast!"

At the same time, the two boys opened their eyes and leaped out of their beds. Scrambling for the little sink at the edge of the room, fighting for space, they tossed a bit of water on themselves, scrubbed their teeth, and waddled to their bags.

"Aren't you guys going to do that stuff in the bathrooms? Or have you never heard of such a thing?"

The two stared at each other and shook their head.

"Nope."

Pulie sighed. "Well, I'll be on my way." Pulie tried to close the door, but a piece of cloth under the door was stopping it.

"What's—wrong—ugh—with—your door?" Pulie yanked and yanked, but it wouldn't budge.

She looked around the door and found a bag. It wasn't a school bag; it was a— bag.

"What's this?" Pulie asked, holding it up.

Both Alex and Piden's eyes grew wide. They dove for the object in her hand and tried to get her out of the room.

"What? What is it?" Pulie cried, still holding it.

"It's a—bag," Piden answered. "A lovely one, too."

"Why yes," Alex said. "It's my mother's bag. But she hated it and she gave it to me."

"No, blockheads," Pulie shook the bag. "What's inside?"

Alex and Piden both fell to their knees and cried.

"Don't tell anyone, Pulie! *Please* don't tell!" Piden sobbed.

"Don't *dare* tell?" Alex hollered. "Ms. Awolo will *kill* us if she finds out that we were snooping around Larry's house."

Pulie stopped shaking the bag. "Larry?" She dropped the bag to the floor and knelt down to open it. It was padlocked.

"She can't open it," Piden whispered quietly to Alex. "Not without the key."

"I heard that." Pulie used the bobby pin in her hair to shake through the lock until she unlocked it.

"Shoot. Junior Trickies learn how to do that," Alex said.

Piden and Alex took a step closer to Pulie.

"You're not going to tell, right?"

Pulie didn't answer and searched inside the bag. It was full of dozens of papers and also a little bottle. It was the same bottle she had seen many times before.

Strange items that made no sense—*made sense.*

Underneath the bottle, she saw Larry's name printed on a small piece of paper. That was when she knew that Piden and Alex were sticking their noses around too.

"You don't think Larry did it either, right?" Pulie asked, plopping herself down.

Alex and Piden shrugged. "*Maybe.*"

"I don't think it's him either. And I won't tell."

The boys both sighed with relief.

"Under one condition—" Pulie raised a finger. "From now on, you are going to help us, too, with this *investigation.*"

"Who's *us?*"

"Nicky, Ema, and me. You're going to help us."

Piden and Alex turned to each other. "Okay."

***

Starting from that day, all five would gather in the girl's room and sort things out.

"Before we begin the hacking into the camera system, we need to know what happens. Like the basic picture."

"Well, all we got is a needle, a bottle, and we know there's a knife," Ema answered. "I don't know how any of those correlate."

"They might not." Pulie scratched her head. "They might be objects that were just in the wrong place at the wrong time. Like the needle. Why would there be a needle?"

Piden raised his hand, "It was shattered underneath the cabinet. It was right next to the bottle. The bottle is the main factor because we found labels everywhere."

"Well, there's only one way to find out!" Alex grinned. "Fingerprinting."

"But he was wearing gloves," Nicky said.

"Who's he?" Pulie asked.

Nicky made a face. "Well, obviously, it's the person who framed Larry!"

"No, what she means is what if the *person* is not a he." Piden pointed out. "What if it was a *she*?"

"Well, that makes it harder!" Nicky groaned.

Piden brought out the fingerprinting kit from underneath the shoe rack.

"We need to test the needle tip to see what it came in contact with." Pulie pushed the plastic bag of the needle to Nicky.

"I don't know how to use that. Does anyone else know?" Nicky asked.

"No." Everyone answered in unison.

Nicky bit her lip. "There is *one* person. But he's not going to want to help us."

***

"Wow, wow, wow. So, you found this in Larry's House? How did you even get in there?" Colin asked, with a confused expression on his face. "I'm surprised that you were able to get all of this." Colin sniffed the bottle. "I thought I saw the crew taking everything out and Señor Rodriguez clearly said that all the evidence had been moved out."

"Well, we snuck in on the day of Halloween, right before they examined the house," Piden answered. "Most of the evidence was cleared out in the morning after, so when we came back, we only found the old notes and papers in his waste bin. Everything else was gone."

"You do know, if *anyone* finds out, you might all be sent to the Factory?" Colin asked.

"Why is that?" Pulie asked.

"You are meddling with serious crime evidence," Colin exclaimed.

Nicky sighed. "Colin, we know you're not in the mood. But can you do it or not?"

He bit his lip. "If I get caught, I'm blaming this on you. You guys kidnapped me and ordered me to do this for you all."

"Whatever."

"Well, then." Colin heaved a sigh. "Let's get started."

The test was completed.

"So, the needle did go into Larry… through his back," Ema whispered.

"How do we know it wasn't at the nurse?"

Colin shook his head, "It was on that day and this was *through* his shirt."

"So—" Pulie began, "Someone stabbed him from *behind* with a needle."

"What substance was in the needle?"

Colin applied a solution to the bottle again.

"Strange. I believe it's a substance that triggers the brain."

"So he or she stabbed Larry with the needle and got him to follow their orders!" Piden said.

"If only it were that easy. We don't know for sure. And, we still don't know who the culprit is," Colin muttered.

"We have eliminated most people. We have a couple of suspects, actually, Colin."

Colin snapped the case back. "Who?"

"We found a note that spells Larry—kind of in the security office and the clips were deleted in the computer there."

Pulie blurted out, "And, I saw the exact same bottle and another syringe in the closet of the office."

"You did?" Nicky cried, "Why didn't you tell us before? That means it *has* to be one of the people that work there!"

"This is a *lot* of information, guys," Colin said, standing up.

"You're leaving? Already?" Nicky asked. "We have so much to do! And we need to get—"

Colin shook his head. "I need to get some rest." And with that, he left the room.

"It's four-thirty." Alex raised an eyebrow.

"He's probably just upset."

Pulie responded, "That too. But we have to keep an eye on him. We gave him too much information and he just left."

"Colin's our friend. I've known him for a long time. Don't worry!" Nicky assured Pulie.

But death symptoms are unpredictable. Nobody would be in their right mind after a loved one passes away.

"We got to keep going, with or without Colin." Nicky sorted all the evidence into Piden's bag.

Everyone was quiet.

Nicky shook her head in dismay. "Look on the bright side, if we catch the culprit, we'll get the—"

"Youth Trickster Most honored Prize of Blue Bell!" Alex chimed. He gazed wonderingly at the ceiling.

"Exactly!" Nicky said excitedly.

It was the first time Pulie had ever heard Nicky and Alex agree on something.

"Few students ever receive that prize!" Ema said, starting to feel amused. "We will be known in our lives for helping the Tricky Society! We receive a medal and *lots* of credits!"

"We *have* to get this job done," Nicky said firmly, smacking her palm on her thigh. "Who are the suspects?"

"Larry."

"Larry."

"Larry."

"Larry."

Nicky shook her head in frustration. "It's not Larry! It has to be someone else!"

Ema made a face. "Well, it could be one of the ladies that work at the security desk, but then again, that's too obvious."

"We have to put the security ladies as one of them!" Pulie said. "Besides, what if that's their plan!"

"Okay, then, who else has access to the cameras?" Piden asked. "Mr. Wace, Señor Rodriguez—"

Alex gasped. "You *are* right! It could be Señor Rodriguez!"

"How?"

"He has access to the desk first of all, second, he has alcohol and chemicals stored up in his closet."

"He's right." Nicky agreed. "I hate to say this, but he might be one of our main suspects."

They all nodded, reluctantly.

"*But* what about the security woman?" Pulie asked. "She has access, it's the most unwillingly obvious position, that none of you believe it's her, and she has the weird alarm in the room, *and* I think I saw my camera in one of the drawers.

TRIAL

"So, it has to be *her*. That's too obvious. But why would she do that?" Nicky questioned.

"For the same reason, you don't think it's her right now. She's intelligent and she knows how to play mind tricks."

"But, that's impossible. What did she want from that?"

Pulie shrugged.

Nicky said. "The trial for Larry is tomorrow. So let's get to work."

Ema and Alex worked for hours after classes in the computer lab. It was usually empty anyway.

Once they were able to connect the camera, Señor Rodriguez told Nicky that in order to see through a camera from another place, she would need a specific computer monitor. Fortunately, he wasn't the type to nose around another's business and he just gave the group what they wanted.

"Everything good?" Ema asked, holding up her thumbs. All five were present at the meeting spot behind the lollipop stand. They all nodded.

"Do you have my camera?" Pulie whined. Nicky was supposed to retrieve her camera from the desk of the security lady's office.

"Later!" Nicky snapped, "We have to do this. The trial is starting after class. We need to use this chance carefully and search for any clues or evidence that the teachers know. And also look at Larry's face. I think I can tell when he's guilty or not."

***

The last bell rang, and soon the five were back in Pulie's room, huddled next to the computer.

Click. Click.

"Password," Alex said, clicking swiftly onto the keyboard. "Next, we activate Camera and display for Full View."

The screen enlarged displaying a dim room, with a sea of wooden chairs and a vast elegant lectern in the middle of all of it.

"I thought this was the front camera."

"Then, we can't see Larry's face."

"But this camera is in the corner of the room. There are like a million people blocking our view. How are we supposed to hear anything?"

"Just wait, Nicky! You are so impatient," Ema scolded. "We don't know yet."

Soon, the view cleared and they could see many other adults in a semi-circle facing the judge and Larry, who was in a transparent cube, sitting in a chair in the center.

The judge was a woman, her hair like pure gold and curled. She wore a long velvet dress with puffs around the edges.

She began to talk for a long time until she pointed to the man on the left side of her. "Mr. Diablo?"

A man with a bouncy long mustache and buck teeth cleared his throat profoundly and began to speak.

"Bernardo Larry. The murderer of Trisha Casterton. Murder weapon: a knife." Mr. Diablo read on about the crime scene. But they could not hear what he said because people in the back started rustling around, searching for something in their bags.

"We chose the wrong camera," Nicky said.

"Shh, quiet."

"—no further evidence found on why or how it happened." Mr. Diablo's voice was clear again. "Camera clips have been scanned with the help of Señor Rodriguez, Mr. Wace, and the chief secretary, Ania Delgado and Elizabeth Chandler. Señor Rodriguez has actively researched the case and it is clear that—"

Pulie leaned towards the computer to hear better.

"Therefore," The judge announced, "Bernardo Larry is now a member of the Factory. February 1st." Then she continued about a bunch of other things.

"It is clear that the majority always wins. Cloak him, now gentlemen." The judge rang the little bell on her desk and a uniform was pulled over Larry's face. Larry was blurry but Pulie could tell he wasn't awake. He looked like a drunken man, saliva dribbling down his cheek, with a forehead as red as the sun. His new uniform was long trousers, a shirt, and a sweater coated in purple spots. The sign of the Trickies.

This is not at all like a regular court. This is not a fair trial! Pulie thought, *Where's the witness?*

"Factory?" Pulie asked.

"People like Larry or other criminals are put as laborers until their years are over. They sleep in like a regular prison room at night, but they work at this huge factory that makes equipment, clothes, weapons, and other tools. The Trickies wants to make *use* of everyone they have. But the whole factory is said to be haunted." Nicky shuddered. "They say that the air is so thick with coal and ashes that you cannot even see your own hands. Many die while working because of too much debris in their lungs."

"But also, I heard that when their factory time is over, they actually change into a better person though! Like Welk Baur was put in the factory for three years and now he hosts charity for the poor people!" Alex said. Everyone shushed them and continued staring at the screen.

"Lifetime sentence to the factory. During this period, he will repent his actions and pay the fines and debt of the damage he has created," the judge said.

Larry's cube was lowered into the ground.

Before the room grew dark, Pulie saw Mr. Diablo's eyes twinkling, a long grin spreading across his face. Then, it was pitch dark and there were screeching sounds of chairs.

Nicky shut the camera off and closed the computer.

"That's *it*." Pulie breathed. "If we're right, he was framed, and now he's going to work at the factory for nothing. That wasn't even a fair trial. Why didn't Larry say anything?"

"I think the substance from the needle gave him amnesia. The substance must've triggered all parts of the brain," Ema said softly. "They say he doesn't even know his name yet."

"This isn't fair," Piden said. "If Larry isn't the criminal, he'll work there for nothing. How could they be so sure?"

"I know Judge Josie," Ema whispered. "She is practically in love with Mr. Diablo—"

"Anyways—" Nicky interrupted. "Don't worry. *We* are the ones who will fix that. We'll get Larry out of the factory is if it's the last thing I can do. And even if none of us like his presence nor his character nor his rude manner—although he is *really rude* when it comes to—I'm getting off-topic again." Nicky cleared her throat. "Even if none of us like him, he will not die there like the thousands who have *if* he is innocent. Now, we just have to test the suspects. Working ladies, Mr. Wace, Señor Rodriguez, Larry, of course, and Ms. Idadosi."

"Why Ms. Idadosi?"

"There's always something odd about her red clothing," Nicky said, "That's about it. But it's almost dinner time, so let's go to the eating room."

Pulie folded up the computer and glanced at Nicky's notepad. Writing filled the monitor. She had typed a lot. Pulie wondered why Nicky was even into this project. She was never into *any* project.

***

"My camera!" Pulie squeezed her camera until she thought she heard a crack.

"Don't touch it with your bare hands. We need the fingerprints on the camera."

"Do we need Colin again?" Ema asked. "I don't think he'll come."

"Hello."

Everyone turned around.

"Colin? What are you doing here?"

He grinned. "You won't go far without me."

"Oh, thank you. Thank you very much." Nicky cried, a rattling box about to explode.

"Come on, cousin. He's trying to focus," Alex whispered.

"These are the fingerprints." Colin played out pieces of paper with indents of fingerprints in them. "All of you take one. We need to find the one who has the exact same fingerprint in the security lady's room."

Suddenly, a loudspeaker boomed, "Hello, this is Mr. Wace. Due to technical issues, the shop will be closed the entire week until summer break. Thanks! And for those who are climbing on the lollipop stand, come to the Miralmalma at eight."

All of the kids rushed to the large window in Pulie's room, pressing their hands against the glass to get a glimpse of who was called out. Piden brought out a long tube.

"The Vision. Señor gave it to me because I did extra work after lunch. It's like a telescope. Oh! Wait, is that—no... no..." Then Piden burst out into laughter. "It's Selma and Bonnie! They look like birds!"

Everyone cracked up. When the laughter died, Pulie realized something.

"The office—it's in the shop— we can't get any more evidence!"

"Holy Scuddle Butt! I completely forgot." Nicky smacked her sweaty forehead. "No evidence, no proof, noo Bluueee Belllll!" She cried.

"Right after the year ends, we meet up," Ema ordered.

Pulie clicked through the camera. All the photos were gone of the blond people. And of the evidence. It had to be the Security Lady.

Thud, thud.

Pulie spun around, glancing back at their door. The room was silent; Colin's face went pale. It was clear this was not the place he wanted to get caught in.

Nicky stood up and unlocked the door.

"Well, look who it is—" Nicky said, immediately beginning to close the door.

"Stop!" shouted the visitor. "I want to talk to you."

"I'm sorry, we're busy. And we are having a very confidential meeting right now."

"Nicky! Oh, come on!"

Crack.

"Moto!" Nicky cried, "You broke our emergency lock!" Nicky continued to slam the door shut, but Moto fought furiously.

"What—is so important—that you can't listen to me!" Moto squealed, jabbing at the door.

The rest of the room assisted at the door until it slammed shut. Pulie heaved a sigh.

"The lock! Our lock is broken!" Nicky cried. "You stay here and I will clean up the Then, there was another *thud* and the door was back open again.

"Moto!"

"Don't let her see it—"

"See what—Oh my!"

Everyone dove to hide all the evidence they had been meddling with.

Moto was all eyes, stiff as a tin soldier, straight as a spoon.

"You—I know what this is!" Moto said, "This is illegal fingerprinting! And you have paper—"

"Moto, don't you dare tell anyone. Please—"

"Oh, don't worry!" Moto snarked, "I will tell the most important person."

And swiftly, she sprinted out of the room, her ponderous feet like thunder against the hallway floors.

"Quick—someone stop her!" Colin said, scrambling to hide all the evidence underneath the desk. "We need to find who she's going to tell."

"A teacher! She wants to snitch on us. We'll split up. Nicky, Ema, Pulie, you go find her because you all have ConnecT," Alex commanded.

The ConnecT were slapped on thin wrists, and the girls began sprinting. Piden and Colin followed a few minutes later.

"You take left, I go right. Pulie, go straight to Señor Rodriguez," Ema ordered.

"Why?" Nicky asked, still running, her feet a blur.

"He controls all the issues with gadgets or any sort of technology. We could be framed at this point or maybe sentenced. He's the one who can really danger us. Pulie, go straight to him, okay?"

Only Pulie's legs understood and soon, she was up in a Zive. She darted for the large door and opened it. Señor sat at his chair, clicking at a timer.

"Pulie? You don't have class." Señor sat up and stroked his beard.

Either I beat Moto or she's not going to Señor because she's stupid.

"Did Moto, by any chance, stop by here?"

Señor bobbed his head. "She spoke to me about a Leaderboard subject. Nothing else. Have any questions?"

"No, Señor, thank you. That is all."

***

"We've asked every single teacher here and Moto hasn't snitched on us."

"Maybe a student?"

"No, she's not that stupid."

"Then, she was lying?"

Everyone was confused and worried about what Moto would say about them.

"Let's stop with the fingerprint kit for now. Hide it under the shelf over there. We need to be more careful."

***

The last five days of school were packed with secrets and excitement. First, their door was fixed. On the fourth to the last day, posters were created in the shape of the T and hung around the campus. Lemonade was sold to raise credits and the moat was opened up for a cleaning day.

Everyone's eyes opened once the morning bell chimed on the last day as easily as Christmas presents are torn open by the anxious hands of children. The three girls decided to wear the same thing again for the celebration.

The day was going to be a long hot and sunny day. The chairs spread across the entire courtyard. Pulie took her seat beside Nicky and Ema. She spotted Selma in a tight blue dress, her curled hair dyed in tints of blue, and her face splashed with makeup. She smirked when she saw the patched outfits of the three and smacked Nicky in the shin. Nicky scowled but told Pulie that she had dropped white oil on Selma's shoes. Hopefully, vandalism wasn't a big issue on the ceremony day.

When the students were snug and settled in their seats, from behind a chime rang and the entrance swung open. The palace flooded with exhilarated and nervous parents who washed through the golden wall barriers and into the students' backseats. A man in an emerald suit and curly blond hair seated himself in the tall chairs at the front of the back seats.

"Daddy!" Selma called out. The man winked at her. Next to him, a woman in a red flowy dress fluttered her eyelashes around as her cameras began clicking.

"Those are the Dutchstills. Somehow every one of them is spoiled and demented. Mrs. Dutchstill has maids carrying cameras to take footage of her when she is looking at her best," Nicky muttered.

Ema waved at a friendly-looking couple and Nicky waved to her own parents as well. Pulie was starting to feel nauseous.

No, not here. Not today. Don't let them see you cry.

"Pulie, where are your parents? I'm not good at matching faces," Nicky said, scanning the audience.

Pulie swallowed hard. "They're busy today." Pulie pretended to look for her parents. "My mother said she's sorry that she couldn't make it."

"I'm so sorry, Pulie. We can share my family today." Nicky patted her on the back.

"And mine. You get a total of four parents today, Pulie!" Ema chirped.

"Attention!" boomed the loudspeakers. Eyes swiveled to Mr. Wace.

"Thank you all for coming here and watching your students and children graduate up a level and become closer to the world as a Trickster," he said staring down at the audience of colorful spots.

"The Tricky Society has been doing a great deal for this world. We have been fighting against the dark spread of the CAOT, and trying to stop the rapidly spreading number of people joining the dark organization."

"But each and every one of us, young and old, strong and weak, can make a change to this plague. We can treat the world. So as long as you are promoted to a new level, challenged to a new skill, you will add a brick to the world's barrier. Now, let us begin the ceremony of the New Tricksters! Can I have the great Mister Yanon Dutchstill come up to the stage?"

Selma cheered loudly for her father.

"Thank you, thank you, everyone," Mr. Dutchstill said, flicking his hair back. "As many of you know, I have put in a tremendous amount of money and time into this place. And now look at us. Because of my great efforts, this palace has become a powerful academy to support these young kids."

Nicky let out an intentional loud groan.

"Thank you for your support, ladies, and gentlemen," Mr. Dutchstill continued, "—for placing your student into this palace and all because of me, this palace will produce the most skilled and advanced people who will help overcome the CAOT!" Then, Mr.

Dutchstill rambled about how much money he had put into the palace and how wealthy he was.

    Near the end of his *glorious* speech, Mr. Wace smiled weakly then snatched the microphone away and announced that it was time for the ceremony to begin. He thanked Mr. Dutchstill again for all his contributions. The audience glowed with cheers. Pulie was surprised how so many people were amused by his arrogance and his selfishness.

    Ms. Ellie now possessed the microphone and called out the names of the Tricksters who would soon be out in the world and choosing the Scout team.

    When the Tricksters sat back into their seats, the punkes got up and were officially announced and classified a part of the palace. They would have to attend *real* classes the following year and Nicky squealed when she saw the tiny toddlers, waddling around with their small certificates.

    "And to all the grades that will be advancing up, we will be giving them our honors, especially to the Junior Trickies, who will now ascend into the Middle Madness of our Palace. Their work will be graded, their behavior will be inspected, and all these will be logged up in your applications for whatever Scout you choose to go to. Some may not even choose to go to but we log them in anyways. The Leaderboard will be official as well so be prepared for intense competition. Next year, two different Zives will combine and you'll meet and see people you've never seen before. Our Middle Age for you to see and learn about life before you enter Junior Years before Scouts in your fifth year. This next year's lives at school will be harder, friends now will no longer be your friends, and sometimes all you can see in this palace is hatred and injustice. I hope you Junior Trickies had a great time enjoying your Elementary Era and I hope that next year treats you well.

"And to the parents, this year, we created a junior LeaderBoard for practice. Scores for the second level are in Mrs. Wapanog's room if you would like to see them. Now the LeaderBoard for the rest of our students—"

Soon, it was lunchtime. Kitchen maids danced around, rushing to set up tables, fill it with delicacies, and attend to people's needs. The palace was in revelry.

Pulie headed over to help herself with some of the Hors d'oeuvres.

Later, all the parents toured the classrooms, examining and studying what their children were doing and how they were improving. Pulie and Piden walked beside Nicky, Ema, and Alex's families, just so they wouldn't look like they were alone.

Mr. Wace announced there were a couple of games spread out in the eating room. There was this zone called Laser Tag and Avoid the Laser. Some were obstacles, and some were board games.

All three of the families hung out by the Laser games, laughing and tripping over lasers. Pulie felt happy. It was an unfamiliar sensation she hadn't felt in months.

Ema's parents pulled Ema aside for a while to talk in private. Pulie guessed it was probably about the mission. However, when the conversation ended, Ema came back with a consternation look on her face.

"Ema, what is it?" Pulie asked.

Ema took a deep breath. "I—" she stuttered. "I'm not coming back next year."

DEPARTURE

"What?" Nicky spat. "You've only been in training for two years and you're already Scouting—"

Ema shook her head, "No, my parents wanted me to go to a school closer to our home. It's called Academy of the Trickies or something? It's where most of my family members went. My dad's job was moved farther away, and they want it closer to our new home—"

Pulie still could not understand. "Surely we can find a way to bring you back here?"

"They've already bought the rooms and classes for me to stay in… all hope is lost."

Nicky looked dumbfounded. "But that means it'll only be us two then?"

Ema nodded. "Until I come back, it's not like I'm staying there forever, I hope…" Her voice drifted off uneasily.

"One year? Two years?"

Ema shook her head, "I don't know; it's as long as my dad works there."

"But we'll meet often, right?" Pulie asked.

Ema shrugged but pulled out three flat screened devices.

"This is my username for Facing," Ema added, clicking a profile.

Nicky made a face. "What's Facing?"

"It's like what people down there use, like FaceTime, we can do it whenever. Catch me up on this and it'll be fine."

"We just need the app," Pulie added. Ema nodded, handing each of them one of the tiny looking computers.

"Which is why my dad bought each of you this! It has the Facing app already inside!"

Pulie studied it. She clicked on the low bottom button and a 3D model of a regular computer came up. Ema started working hers.

"Now press the bottom button and type Facing App," Ema commanded, her screen showing a little red dot. "Press the red dot in the middle. Type my username and—" Ema's screen started flickering until Pulie typed Ema's username up and sent it.

Suddenly, on the green 3D model of Ema's face, clearer than ever! Pulie ran around, Nicky almost dropped the expensive electronic. Ema waved and Pulie could see the hologram Ema waving the exact same way.

"Thank you so much!" Nicky cried.

"Tell your parents we're really grateful," Pulie said.

Ema grinned. "Now, we can see each other whenever! But these are prohibited because of that slipping of information rule. Just don't tell anyone about these." Ema slipped the tablet inside her jacket.

The entrance doors of the palace buzzed and the moat bridge was lowered. Pulie saw the river of the rubber crocodiles and the odd stone steps.

Finally, she was going *home*. She was going back to where she was before. But with no one waiting.

Colin and Ema's families left the palace first.

It was hard to see the only *real* friends Pulie had ever met in all her life just *go*.

Nicky sighed. "We should've finished Larry's case. We have to before it's too late. I guess we'll have to do it over spring. We'll meet up."

"Yeah."

Then, it was Nicky and Alex's turn to leave the palace, side by side.

A lot had happened since Pulie first met Nicky. She couldn't believe how much she hated Nicky then.

When everyone had disappeared past the moat and past the far entrance, the palace became a fishbowl with no water and no fish. Now, it was just gravel.

Pulie and Piden hung around the palace till the very end, along with some other students who needed a ride home or those who stayed at the palace until the summer.

Mr. Wace finally lead the remaining students to the SkyClouds Tubus station and dropped them off at their stops.

When Pulie and Piden reached the hill near their house, they hopped off and descended the staircase down to the ground.

Pulie opened the front gates of their house with her keys. She walked through the muddy grass and the untrimmed weeds.

But the memories that flew inside her head were not of the glass table where her family would all gather to eat, nor the TV sofa on Saturday nights, nor the fireplace on Christmas.

Instead, she could only think about her parents—and how they were CAOT—and how they had kept that secret within the walls of this house for all fifteen years of her life.

Her parents were CAOT.

HOME

Their home was empty. They had nobody now. No embracing, no scolding, no crying, no welcoming. Nobody was at the doorstep to make sure they were okay.

Impossible.

With a *click* of a switch, the lights flickered and twitched, sighing in their bulbs above Pulie's head. The stairs creaked and moaned, sobbing every step Pulie took. The picture frames glumly peered down at her. And the table had quieted, despite the amount of dust that had collected upon the top.

The kitchen that lay untouched, the windows gray and cold. But it still felt like home.

"What are you bringing, Pulie? Mr. Wace will be here to pick us up at any moment." Piden's voice was so soft Pulie heard it in murmurs. He shoved and crammed all the toys and old photos and memories into his bag.

Pulie filled her backpack with earbuds, trinkets, and a photo book. The book was a collage of her family, pictures sticking out on the sides. She inserted the book into her bag carefully—with not a single rip or crinkle. Her feet carried her up the glass stairs, her fingers sliding across the railings, trailing the mountain of dust.

Creak. The floorboards groaned.

Screech. The doorknob squealed.

She was in her room again, the smell of home. Her lonely bed, her boxes of crayons, and jewelry. And near her desk, her old notebooks and pencils. It had been a long time since she had seen so much paper since the Palace regarded paper as inane and a waste of time. But the rough yet smooth thin sheets felt good against her fingers when she rubbed them softly.

What she wanted to fit inside her little bag seemed countless, and everywhere she looked, she would find yet another important object. She crept up to her father's old workspace and slipped into his closet. She had seen him do this many times. He would enter the closet, go to the left-hand corner, behind his cloaks and coats, and open a tiny box hidden behind the array of clothing. There, waited his computer.

Her fingers hesitated before they touched the silicon device. She bit her lip.

He wouldn't care now. He's gone.

Into her bag, it went.

Time raced across the clock, flashing before Pulie's eyes, and soon, they departed from their beloved home for a final time. The keys clinked snug in the lock and then rotated. She shoved the keys into her pocket and clutched as much as she could hold in her arms.

"Need a hand?" Mr. Wace stepped out of the plane and assisted them with their luggage. They were the only ones on the plane now. Everyone had gone *home*.

However, they weren't the only students back at the palace who were staying over the spring. Many parents had paid for their child to be there all break. However, Mr. Wace bent the rules for the Jarks, allowing their stay—free of charge. After all, they had no choice.

***

On the first day of break, in the middle of spring, Pulie arrived into her room again and she unfolded all the clothes she had brought. Piden did as well. They shared rooms while Piden's old room was going through a cleaning process for next year. She spread all her garments and hoodies across the floor, tucked them into neat squares, and placed them inside the shelf. She took out her notebooks and photos along with her special book on the desk and emptied her bag on the floor. Her computer slid out with a thud onto the floor.

"Pulie—" Piden gasped. "You did not just take Father's computer. He told us to never look at it."

"They kept a lot of secrets," Pulie muttered under her breath, ignoring her brother's words.

He stormed out of the room, slamming the door. His mood escalated and dropped like a rollercoaster these days. She couldn't blame him though, after everything that happened.

For a few minutes, she tried every passcode she could think of that her father had used until she was blocked out of the system completely. A face scanner was activated.

And to her surprise, her face worked. The green button lit up and she was logged into the computer!

She pulled up the screen and clicked through the files, searching for a game or two. Or maybe even perhaps a video of her family. A photo book could not tell stories as rich as that.

A tab popped up titled; RED-IPS Code Line. Pulie glanced around. Piden was not watching to snitch on anyone although he didn't have anyone to tattle to anyways. She clicked on the tab, opening a file and at that second, she knew she shouldn't have pressed the button. But the video caught her eye. Her eyeballs were magnetic to the screen.

Father?

She dragged the video to full-screen mode and observed with intensity. Her heart pounded and reverberated through the walls of her room. *Thump. Thump.*

Is that him? Pulie squinted. The film was blurry like fogged-up glass on a misty morning. Soon, she could see that he was running. And he was running fast.

"Father?" she asked aloud, knowing it was a video, but she refused to acknowledge it. *When was this?*

The video trembled and shook as he ran, his hand not capable of steadying at a fast pace. The view jiggled and waggled.

Finally, her father spoke.

"This message is to someone. I am not able to say who in case this falls into the wrong hands." He paused, swerving left past a hauntingly tall metal wall. "The dome has just fallen and we escaped."

Her eyes grew large and she didn't realize how hard she was shaking, like the tail of an angry snake.

What! And—he escaped? He escaped!

"Not all of us did, however," he added as if actually conversing. "Contact NO-S45. Please. And hurry. Master escaped as well and she is reporting safe in the Far Under Glacier Atmosphere. Please contact help! SOS."

The video blurred and ended. Pulie shut the computer.

He escaped. He escaped. He escaped.

"He's alive!" Pulie screamed. She ran around the room knocking down chairs and punching the air with her fists. She screamed some more.

She leaped onto her hammock and began to sing.

One of her *parents* was alive.

JOYOUS

Pulie shut the computer as Piden burst into tears. His sobs were heartbreaking and full of joy all at once.

Piden sniffled, "H-e-e's-s al-iv-ve?

Pulie nodded, still too shocked. "I mean, if he survived after that scene when he filmed the video, then *yes*," Pulie added.

There was silence.

"But Master—" Pulie realized. "Master— is alive."

Piden grimaced, "Are you talking about the CAOT lady?

"Master, to be correct."

"I know! Mr. Wace already told us."

Pulie shook her head, "He doesn't know where. She's in the *Far Under Glacier Atmosphere*. I have no idea what that means. I think I should ask Mr. Wace about that."

Piden frowned, "I don't think telling him is a good idea, though."

"Who said I was?" Pulie asked, folding her arms. "I'm simply asking where it is. Maybe my parents are there, or she knows where. I don't trust that man any more than I trust my own parents. And I really don't trust any of them now. It's just you and me now. We have to stick together, no matter what. Okay? And don't tell a soul about this."

"What are you going to do now?" Piden motioned to the computer and the paused video.

Pulie breathed heavily, "Now? I forget about it. I forget about everything and pretend nothing ever happened. Mr. Wace is gone. There's no one else for me to ask for help."

"What do you want to do?" Piden asked.

Pulie eyed her backpack. "We have a mystery to finish."

ENCOUNTERS

"Can you step any louder?" Pulie whispered. At Piden's every step, the floorboards creaked.

"Nope," he retorted. "I think I found it."

The hallways were dark as if night had decided to spread its wings over us inside the shop.

"The security lady's room is right there."

The two siblings unlocked the door with the stolen key and the doorknob squeaked.

"Close the door behind you and pull out the lights."

The door shut softly and Piden pulled out a small tube flashlight.

"Piden, my gut feeling is on here. The security lady has to be the culprit. She knows the campus all around. She wasn't there on Halloween—"

"Okay, I get it. Why'd we come here?"

"To investigate and get fingerprints. Slide the tape onto the handles of every drawer possible. Oh, and on the name tags. Over there."

The quiet sounds tap sticking and unsticking and the sounds of drawers closing and the opening made a silent harmony in the dark atmosphere.

"Done."

"Good, now let's get out of here. Put the evidence in your left inside pocket. Open the door."

The hallways were as quiet as they were before. Only the sound of the clocks up on the ceilings was heard; *tick, tick, tick, tick...*

With their soft dark socks, they stepped out of the room, locking the room, and crept down the store. The workers were all on vacation, including the security lady.

The once so busy bright store was dim-lit, empty, and desolate. The items moaned for the company and the trade of currency. Pulie crept towards the door and reached out for the handle with her black gloves. Yet, that moment, the familiar jingle of the back door sounded, the two golden bells at the top of the store door clanking against each other.

"*Hide,*" Pulie whispered. She dove under the cosmetic shelf. Piden slipped under the cashier table. It was silent again. *Did anyone even enter the store?*

Just then, there was a voice.

"Ahh, only if I could've torn out Benjamin Stutter's ears with *these* pliers, it would've been satisfying." The woman sighed, her heels clicking on the marble floor. There were only *three* people in the palace with the mind to do such a thing. Pulie shuddered. She held her breath, hoping she was wrong.

"That idiot."

Pulie heard the crashing of metal as the stranger kicked a box on the shelf. Glass shattered.

Stay calm... Don't scream... Stay calm...

Pulie eyed the shadow from under the shelves as it lurked towards the cashier's slot.

Oh no! Piden! And the evidence!

"And now Ms. Borthwick is lecturing me about the unity of the Trickies. Well, she's damn right we're united. Web—stone—ring. Whatever. If there's actually something that might destroy them, I might as well do my damned job right. If my boss finds out the mess I am in, I'll be in hot water."

It sounded like Ms. Awolo. But who was her boss? Mr. Wace? The head of all Trickies foundations?

"What the hell? Did all the workers leave? Why are there damn cobwebs on my coffee machine?" There was a snap and then a crack. The sounds of shards of glass crashing on the ground sounded. "Serves those twits right. They gotta do their job."

Ms. Awolo stepped away from the counter and her face came into clear view. The angry skinny face of the devil who happened to lead the palace. Just a few steps away from Pulie.

Ms. Awolo exited the shop, slamming the door shut.

There was a silent pause for a few seconds until Piden whispered,

"Pulie, you still there?"

Pulie stepped out of the clearing, the shelves still moaning and creaking. Most of the shop had been destroyed ever since Ms. Awolo had walked through its doors. All the glass jars and collections of different liquids and substances splattered in every corner.

"Piden?"

"Yeah?"

"If we don't get ourselves outta here, *we're* gonna be the ones in *hot water.*"

***

"That was too close," Piden whispered as they entered their room.

Pulie spread out the evidence and all the tools.

"She must be pretty upset. She destroyed a lot inside the shop."

Pulie nodded and said, "I wonder who her boss is. Mr. Wace is her coworker. They work together. Isn't Selma's father one of the leaders who control this palace?"

Piden shrugged but responded, "In that case, I would destroy an entire shopping mall."

It was nice having her brother back.

The fingerprint device clicked and beeped. The light beamed green and the process began. The device began to clear its memory. There was silence except for the squealing of the machine.

"Pulie?"

"Huh?"

"Are they really out there?"

"Who?"

Piden moved his head around uncomfortably, "You know, our parents?"

"Yeah, why?"

Piden shrank in his position, "I can't believe it." He wriggled around some more.

"Neither can I."

Piden breathed deeply. "If they are *really* out there, we're gonna find them, right? Before that Master lady does anything, in case she knows that *we* bombed that place and—"

Pulie responded, "If they're alive, we're gonna find them. If they're alive, I will not let anything stop us from getting the life we had before. We're gonna find them, and be safe from all of this.

We just got to blend in until we find out *how* and we're going to sneak out of here."

Piden looked more relieved, he stopped panting.

"And, we're gonna live at home? Like we always did?"

Pulie nodded.

"And every Christmas, we're going to eat blueberry pie? With maple syrup?"

"Yes. I miss Father's blueberry pie."

"Me too. It's too good to forget. And every evening, we have our dinner all together? On the glass table? With the heater on in the winter?"

Pulie smiled. That was one of the things she missed most. The glass table. Pulie reached over and took Piden's hands, "Everything will be the same. I promise. We're going to find our parents, get ourselves *out* of this mess. And then, we're going to have the life we had before."

Piden's lips quivered, "Promise?"

Pulie nodded and said, "I promise."

"Then, I'm helping. I want my family back."

"Yes, that's the spirit. And that is our new mission. No old betting system. This time, we are going to complete it."

Just then, the fingerprint scanner glowed red, signaling the end.

"Piden, pull out that list of all the secretaries."

From his tablet, he pulled out three different names.

Mia Smith

Ania Delgado

Elizabeth Chandler

"These are the only ones, correct?"

"Correct."

"And Colin showed us the fingerprint with the cameras."

"Yes."

"Did you get any fingerprints from Mia Smith's name tag?"

"Yes. This is it." He handed her a flat blue tape with fingerprint indents in which she slid in the glowing gadget and began to scan it.

The fingerprints were different.

"So not Mia Smith. Sorry if we ever judged you, ma'am," Piden whispered. "The next one is this one," he added, handing her a red piece of tape.

The scan showed the fingerprints were not identical.

"Not Ania either." Pulie sighed, staring at the results in disbelief.

Piden spoke, "We still have one more. Fingers crossed."

Pulie slid the green piece of tape into the device.

And when the results came out, she could not believe what she had received.

A world you cannot imagine—imagined.

Made in the USA
Middletown, DE
09 September 2022